Tale of an African Woman

Thomas Jing

Langaa Research & Publishing CIG
Mankon, Bamenda

Publisher:
Langaa Research & Publishing Common Initiative Group
P.O. Box 902 Mankon
Bamenda
North West Province
Cameroon
Langaagrp@gmail.com
www.langaapublisher.com

ISBN: 9956-558-09-5

1

"**H**ave a seat," I declared politely after my visitor from Ireland was ushered into my office and I shook hands with her. "I was actually expecting someone much older," I confessed to her when we began our discussion.

Slim, young and tall, with penetrating blue eyes, she was a far cry from the elderly and motherly figure I had in mind. I was probably too used to Irish women as nuns that I might have cast her in that mold. Whatever the case, she turned out to be more than what I had bargained for when we started to talk about the main object of her visit. I was still not really convinced about what she wanted me to do as we went into our conversation.

"Excellency," she then began formally after we seemed to have become used to each other and had actually started sharing some jokes and pleasantries, "I've come as I suggested in my letter to investigate and report on your life for our newspaper."

"*The Dubliner*," I declared, a bit nervous, still not sure the way I wanted her to address me as I cited the name of the paper for which she reported to let her know that I had taken her request very seriously. "I would like to apologize that I've been unable to be with you ever since you arrived here because of numerous pressing national commitments but I hope you're beginning to get used to our environment and discovering lots of new things."

"I can't ask for more," she replied. "The company you sent to assist me has been very useful and friendly and I would like to express my appreciation for that."

I nodded and smiled.

"Coming to the object of your mission, as much as I would love to help I still don't believe I have to recount my own story personally," I stated, taking her completely unaware. This declaration set the tone of the rest of our opening discussion.

"What do you mean?" she asked, visibly shaken by what I had said. I could see disappointment on her face, but she seemed determined to sell her point. I had an idea of the strength of her logic in the brief correspondence we had before she set out for Africa. Now, I sensed for sure she wouldn't go down without putting up a fight.

"You see, I belong to a tradition which preaches humility," I resumed, attempting to explain the circumstances which might have led me to such a decision.

"Me too," she cut in quickly and then instantly apologized for the interruption. She seemed to have read my mind and probably wanted to preempt any argument I had to advance. "Irish Catholicism also preaches humility," she continued.

"Of course," I responded, aware that she had raised a valid point which formed a major component of the argument I wanted to present. However, I was determined to let her see what I was getting at. "I don't believe that it's fair for me to recount my own story myself, especially when there are many friends and relatives still alive who've known me since I was a child and who I'm quite convinced are in a better position to make a fairer assessment of my life. I…"

"I don't doubt that," she conceded with another interruption and then excused herself as though she felt she was overstepping certain bounds. It made me feel bad because I did not want her to be intimidated by my position. I wanted us to build not on sentimental but solid intellectual and rational grounds and this could only happen if our discussions were conducted in a free and fair atmosphere.

"Shannon," I addressed her by her name and smiled to let know I meant well. "I really want to be convinced before I go ahead with this narration. You see, generally, most people, depending on how they've been raised, tend to exaggerate or downplay their own accomplishments, so when given the opportunity to talk about themselves, they often end up painting a poor or even inaccurate picture. I don't think that I'll be any different. To this, also add the fact that my African tradition puts a lot of emphasis on humility. Finally, as you already know, being as much an Irish as I am an African product, I also adhere to Roman Catholic values."

2

"I can fully understand why a person of your background would feel reluctant to go ahead with the narration of her own story, at least from the scanty knowledge I've gathered about you," she admitted with a warm smile. "But still it's only you who can recount your own story since nobody knows you better than yourself."

"You may be right in that sense but how can I be my own judge and you expect me not to be partial?"

"I know," she said calmly. "But coming from you, your story becomes more credible, don't you think?" she asked. "In the light of your position, how credible is an account of you given by relatives or friends, since to curry favor with you they may likely inflate some accounts? This is a practice very common among court attendants, so I'm not telling you anything new."

"Shannon, tell me, just how important is this story?" I asked, seriously jolted by the strength of the last argument she had launched. And, without even giving her room to answer, I took up a new line of argument. "For centuries, the story of my life has already been told in different ways by different women in different parts of the world. In other words, I don't think that the challenges I've faced are peculiar to me and so need to be recounted; nor am I even convinced that by recounting them, that'll make any great difference since the cries of women echo throughout the generations and seem all through to have always fallen only on deaf ears."

"For sure your account will make a tremendous difference!" she exclaimed reassuringly.

"How so?" I asked, still disturbed by this feeling that the world might take my action as an attempt at self-promotion. "Yes, I would like to know," I insisted and then continued, "Set more female hearts bleeding with grief or make tears roll down some already miserable cheeks? No, we've been through that before and I don't think I'm prepared to back up that same road again."

I think deep down I was looking for some form of vindication to go ahead with the narration.

"I won't blame you if you don't," she concurred, a strategy of seemingly taking my side during our debate, if I may term our discussion as such, even as she worked on arguments to counter me. "I've read a lot of stories about the plight of women and I

3

would like to point out that your own stands out, at least from the bits I've listened to and read about. Not in the magnitude of the horrors and injustice you faced, nor the challenging obstacles you had to overcome. No, none of that, for I've come across cases far more terrible than anything you've experienced."

"So what attracts you to my story then?" I asked hastily. I had never felt that the situations I encountered in my life came close to what many women have experienced or are experiencing but I was really humbled by her declaration.

"You see, if your story were being recounted just for women to shed some more tears, then I wouldn't have had to travel all the way from Ireland to Mungo to be here with you. As you've rightly pointed out, the cries of women echo throughout the centuries and even if they wanted to shed tears, they aren't left with any," she started to lay the foundation for an all-out assault by tapping on some of the things I had already said. Then the bomb landed. "Your story isn't about tears but rather about hope. Hope for millions of women across the world who tremble before their men as we talk, who live constantly in fear and stoically face brutalities of the worse kind, women on the verge of giving up. For those women who have already fallen, your story will strengthen their resolve to stand up, and for those who feel like giving up, your account will provide them with the ammunition to continue to struggle. Hope is a powerful weapon and, if you want to know, it's the main reason for my presence here today, asking you to recount your own story."

How could I resist such an argument and ever claim to speak for women and justice?

So to the long list of voices which had already urged me to recount my story and I had so far resisted was added that of Shannon, a journalist who had read excerpts of my life in a newspaper in Ireland and had come to collect the entire story to share with the rest of the world. I had always thought of myself as a simple woman, an orphan at birth, lost in distant and unknown Africa, with a voice which counted for little. Never had I thought of myself as one whose life story was worthy of holding out hope to other women across the world. . But why would a woman travel thousands of miles and squander resources to come and collect a story which was not important? Fighting injustice, I reckoned, was

4

a collective responsibility and if she had taken the pains and time and spent the resources to come to me, the minimum I could do was not to disappoint her and the world. To me, that would be acting responsibly.

Stirred by her provocative words, I found myself face to face with her and, for the first time, decided to recount my own story in its entirety. Of course, her strong arguments might have compelled me to get to this point. Still, there was another reason, a purely sentimental one, why I decided to tell the story. This reason, I will trust in the intelligence of my readers and leave them to divine by the time they get to the end of this narrative.

This is my story in my own words, told in two parts because of its length and maybe complexity; it is exactly as I told it to the Irish woman. It is fraught with details and segments which I considered not only very essential but also relevant, especially in light of the main purpose for which it was being collected, the desire to revive the hope of millions of women suffering from various forms of persecution.

I started the story's narration at a place and time I deemed appropriate, and included all the characters I found very important, to make it really complete by providing the various forces which have inspired and shaped me into the person I am. I recounted the story the way my grandmother taught me and it started the way most African stories do.

2

A long, long time ago, even before my country, Mungo, came to be administered as a colony of the Europeans, in the northern part of it, there was a small village called Bankim. The village was just one of many scattered all over Dawa, a vast savannah of rolling hills and valleys. All the villages had a common culture and traced their roots to the same ancestry, the great Wotikar farmers and warriors.

The climate of Bankim was harsh and swung from one extreme to another like a pendulum. Bankim was a sweeping plain set in the midst of hills and for most of the year, it gurgled with numerous streams. A big river, the Noun, set its western borders with some other villages. The village was covered mainly with grass, randomly offset here and there with patches of tiny forests.

In the dry season, when the tropical sun burned brightly, the vegetation withered, turned brown and sometimes died. This made it susceptible to the numerous bush fires often started by hunters in search of a quarry. It was during this season that the streams and tiny rivers dried up and their beds, under the suffocation of the blistering heat, formed cakes with countless cracks. Once bush fires had erupted and swept across the land, they left no plant standing in their wake. With the vegetation gone and the entire village almost reduced to a bald and sprawling black carpet of soot, it looked miserable and destitute.

Then came the first bursts of rains and the plants sprang back to life, becoming green and luxuriant again. Most of the insects, which had been reduced to silence, resumed their chirping in the underbrush. From the treetops the birds twittered and the monkeys chattered in celebration. The streams which looked so miserable exploded with laughter of joy as they came tumbling and splashing over rocks. Boulders, laid bare by the scorching heat and the blast of the winds, started to turn green again with moss.

Since Bankim was a very hot place, with temperatures sometimes rising to sweltering and intolerable levels during the day, the rains constituted a balm. They made the environment more attractive to the existence of man, plants and animals.

Back then, the relationship among the different Dawa villages could not have been described as friendly. There were incessant quarrels over arable land and sources of water supply, but out of the need to survive in the midst of great odds, they had learned to tolerate one another.

As long as there was peace and they could come to the aid of one another in times of serious crises, they often met to exchange goods and services. Occasionally, as it is often the case when different people live side by side, a young man and woman would defy their communities and get together in a union or elope.

This kind of union set tongues wagging for a while but gradually the incident receded further and further away into the collective mind and then was eventually forgotten as things returned to normal.

Among the villages, Bankim stood out for three main reasons. It was the largest, its soils the most fertile and its people law abiding and extremely hardworking. These factors, which were interlocking and tended to spur and complement one another, had caused the village to explode into a populous and wealthy community. With almost all the land of the villagers brought under the hoe, their barns were filled with all kinds of foodstuff. Their animals, often kept in enclosures not far from their homes, were usually healthy and fetched good prices during their weekly barter trades.

A Council of Elders elected by the people ruled Bankim. The Council came under the authority of a wise man whom it designated. He was given the title of Tabih. Apart from convening and presiding over some of the meetings of the Council, his other functions included setting the dates for and presiding over ancestral sacrifices, adjudicating disagreements which cropped up in the village Council, ensuring that people were law abiding, as well as a wide range of other minor duties.

The village was made up of many large families whose ancestries went far back in history. The most notable of them were the Konchus, the Gings, Bamus, the Forsuhs, the Mbis, the Ndas, the Pefoks, the Abamukongs, the Ayaahs, the Fombuhs, the Wankis, the Atuches, the Abongwas, the Akenjis, the Tamajungs, the Ndifordehs, the Ndumus and many others.

Each family was headed by one of its own members, who was always a male. The head had many other attributes. He was usually a titleholder or an important figure and must have distinguished himself in the village through some acts of courage, generosity or through his contributions to the welfare and progress of the community.

In the order of things, men were in charge at all the important decision-making levels. It was a rule set down by tradition which no man had attempted or even wanted to change. The men simply did not have the habit of changing things to bring women close to their jealously guarded and coveted positions.

Under successive Tabihs, Bankim enjoyed some stability and prosperity, but it was when Ngwanueh of the Abongwa family assumed the much coveted leadership position that the village became the stuff of legends. Its barns could hardly contain the foods which had been hauled in from the fields and so newer and larger ones had to be built. Trade with other groups expanded and almost every family was blessed with many newborns.

Among those who were awarded titles for the extraordinary development was Tadu of the Pefoks family. He was a man of remarkable humility, integrity and genius. He had traveled widely and had learned and seen a lot and this exposure gave him fresh insights into farming methods and techniques which he immediately put into practice when he returned to Bankim.

He reduced the size of his plot and farmed across the slope to reduce erosion. He also introduced newer and hardier seeds and rotated his crops to maintain the fertility of the soil. People were not sure at first about what he was doing and so did not immediately follow his lead.

Then came harvest time and his yields spoke for themselves. He had to invite additional hands to help him harvest his crops. He had won the day and now convinced, the others followed his example and before long the village blossomed into flower and lush green crops. When harvest time came the villagers were elated.

He was still single and tired of living all by himself. Members of his family kept insisting that he deserved to eat warm food whenever he returned home at night and that it was time for him to have a strong male child who would succeed him one day and take over his increasingly vast estate.

One day he was returning from the farm and came across a girl who was the daughter of Tangang, the head of the Mbawa family. Their eyes met and he could tell from the look on her face that a little fire was burning in her heart. Soon rumors started to spread that the two were working on Tadu's farm together. Then, he started sending gifts to the girl's uncles and aunts.

When he sat down one day with the girl's family and agreed that he would give them eight goats, everyone knew he had decided to take her as his wife. Three months later, her once slim stomach began bulging, not with food but with child and the entire village was filled with excitement. Biayuh, for this was the name of Tadu's wife, was feted and petted by everyone.

At a time when this community knew very little about the science of child conception and delivery, it was astonishing that rumors had started to go round claiming that the child would be a boy in order to follow in the footsteps of his father and also do great things for the village. These were the kinds of rumors which usually clashed with human expectations and often provided the basis for curious and grave incidents.

One month before she had her child, Tadu was out in the field working and was mysteriously struck down by lightning and died. When the news reached the village, there was an outpouring of grief and sympathies. It was, however, his young bride who felt the impact of the loss the most.

Still inexperienced in life and rendered a widow at the tender age of just seventeen, she was as would be expected totally devastated by the sudden death. She was not afraid that she would have to raise and fend for the child all alone because bringing up a child in the village was a collective responsibility. What frightened her was that this rule seemed true for everyone except, perhaps, for someone who was the wife of an extraordinary person and was expected to bring forth an extraordinary male child.

When she started to feel the pangs of labor, she summoned the older women of the village who were experts in things relating

9

to child delivery. They all came running. All night, they watched over her. They rubbed her large stomach with copious amount of palm oil and filled her ears with amusing tales to make her forget her troubles. Outside her hut, a huge crowd had already formed and kept vigil in anticipation of the good news.

"We want a male child," the talking drums rumbled as the villagers sang and danced all evening.

It was about the early hours of the morning, even before the first rooster crow, that the baby was delivered and announced its coming into this world with a loud cry. The old woman presiding over the delivery took just one glance and heaved a heavy sigh.

"It's a girl," she turned and announced somewhat disappointingly to the other women. Having said this, she quietly dropped all that she was doing and disappeared.

As the women took their leave, they in turn passed on the information until it reached the crowd of onlookers who had stayed up all night waiting for this important moment.

"A girl!" they all exclaimed at once as though they had been rehearsing this line. The singing and dancing immediately stopped and the talking drums went dumb. They too all heaved one big sigh of disappointment and, one after the other, they began to walk away from the hut in the same way they had come. Finally, the poor girl was left alone with her baby to face her very sad fate.

All the excitement and love she once generated turned to resentment and nobody stopped by to give her a hand, not even members of her own family who seemed overwhelmed with the disgrace and embarrassment.

She was particularly unfortunate because Chacha, who would have quite naturally stood by her side, was away from the village, visiting with a friend and farming in the neighboring district. Things became so terrible for Biayuh, especially when wild and malicious rumors went around attributing the death of her husband to her.

"Greedy bitch!" some voices scoffed. "She killed the man so that she would take over his wealth and estate."

Lonely and depressed, she increasingly drifted into melancholy and simply saw no reason to live anymore. One

10

morning, the entire village got up to the prolonged and terrible crying of the little baby.

"What's wrong with this damn woman!" a man cursed. "She saddles the entire village with a baby girl and can't even take care of the poor little thing," he cried out as he kicked in the door of the hut and went in.

Sprawled on the sleeping mat next to her mother was the baby. She was kicking and crying. The man touched the woman and she was stiff, long dead and cold. Picking up the child, he stormed out of the hut to announce the news.

Since nobody ever went near the girl after the birth of the child, nobody knew the name of her daughter. In keeping with the tradition, the Tabih was called upon to christen her and he named her Yaa.

It was one of those curious names which appeared in the village once in a while and which often bore a double meaning, depending on how it was pronounced. In this case, the common meaning of the name was loner but the same word pronounced with a deep inflection had another connotation, the great one.

Loner or great one, from the very christening of the child, her appointment with destiny seemed to have begun. Condemned by the misfortune of being born a girl as first child into a great family and burdened with the scar or maybe luck of name, she began the dance of life on the wrong foot, so most people believed.

3

Caught up in this sad situation, which was not of her making and which she knew nothing about, it was natural that Yaa`s childhood should arouse compassion. So, when the issue of the house in which she would have to spend the rest of her early life came up, all the women in the village expressed the genuine desire to take her in.

After a careful examination of all those who had requested to adopt the child, the Tabih, on the advice of the Council of Elders, finally decided to cast his lot with Chacha, who was herself a victim of ostracism.

"She mustn't be buried one day with a stone," he said mournfully even if somewhat sarcastically of the baby's new mother, citing in this instance the fate reserved for childless women upon their death.

In the village, Chacha was a tall, tough, and pretty woman with something of a free spirit. She was single but had been married. Her husband, whose secret love affairs everyone in the village knew about, had accused her of barrenness and dumped her when four years into their marriage she was still unable to become pregnant.

The Council had sided with her husband and confronted her on the issue. Without mincing words, she had defended herself by stating that it was her husband's fault. Since in the community, the general belief was that only a woman could be barren, the members of the Council did not take kindly to her declaration and they let her know it.

"I don't think this man could be running around with all these women if he couldn't get himself up," the Tabih told members of the Council. "This is a relatively small community and if it were so the news would have spread like bush fire by now, especially given that women take to gossip like a rat to peanuts."

"I think she only wants to create a scandal," a voice rose in support.

"Now, tell me Chacha, are you saying that he isn't up and going and immediately falls asleep at night?" the Tabih asked with voyeuristic glee.

"I don't mean any of that," she replied. "When it comes to getting himself up and going all night, he sticks like a driver ant," she added much to the amusement of the Council.

"So what then is the matter?" the Tabih continued with his questions.

Chacha was not frightened and challenged the Council. She pointed to the numerous women with whom her former husband was having an affair.

"How many of them are pregnant?" she asked, with her hands on her hips and the upper part of her body thrust forward in an open show of courage. "Why is the second wife still without child?" she kept up her interrogation. "Finally, let me tell you something which, perhaps, men don't know. Not all rivers which lead to a big stream contain fish. As you can see, the man has liquid, plenty of it, but it's without seeds."

The strength of her logic was too much for the entirely male Council and as most men would do when an overpowering female position comes seriously to bear, they simply retired and conspired. They knew she was making a good point but at the same time they could not admit it without setting themselves up with their own women.

"The moment a person doesn't have two nuts swinging underneath, the person instantly becomes a fool in the eyes of this Council," she scolded members of the Council in a final act of courage.

The men felt humiliated and made a mental note of all she had said. They, however, avoided confronting her publicly, lest the strength of her logic rally the population to her support. Instead, through their own wives to whom the outcome of the encounter between Chacha and the Council had deliberately been distorted, they receded behind a thick wall of tradition and respect to say that the woman was arrogant and did not want to listen to the Council.

13

It was with this half-baked and utterly sentimental idea that the Council finally stirred the community and turned it against the woman.

She stuck to her guns and incurred the wrath of the community rather than surrender in the face of what was outright injustice. Now left to her own devices, she went about her life as if the rest of the community did not exist. But even the toughest and most determined person sometimes gets weary living a lonely life in the midst of people, so when the need for the adoption came up and the other women were lining up, she too did the same. She wanted to put an end to her loneliness and her humdrum existence, as well as to have someone on whom to shower her love. She was skeptical about the outcome of the decision, thinking her candidacy had been eliminated from the outset. Without being entirely wrong, this reasoning did not take into account the fact that most members of the Council had gray hair.

Contrary to Chacha's expectation, the councilors advised the Tabih to decide in her favor. The decision to accept her as Yaa's mother was not entirely the sentimental one of giving a childless mother a motherless child. In spite of the manner in which she had conducted herself before the Council, the offer of the child was a silent acknowledgment of the voice of reason on the part of the elders. It was a shameless and cold bribe to mend the fence and rein her in. It was as if to say she had made her point and did not need to rub salt in the Council's wounds.

However, there was also a sound and very important reason for making the decision. The Council knew her seemingly outrageous attitude did not strip her of her great qualities. She was a very hardworking woman who was entirely committed to whatever she was doing and so one did not need to be a philosopher to conclude that the child would fare well under her loving care.

Once the dust stirred up by what became known among the villagers as "The Biayuh Scandal" had settled and the child had taken to being fond of her new mother, life in the community went back to normal.

To tide the young baby over the first extremely precarious and difficult phase of her life, Chacha obtained some goats with whose milk she nurtured the child. All over the village, as she went

14

about her business, she was seen with the baby strapped to her back. This special relationship, it would seem, had the impact of softening the conduct of a few villagers towards the two loners from whom they were learning a new lesson of love.

It was not long before the community started to notice the contrast between Yaa and the other babies. She was always very clean and healthy, with round dark eyes and full cheeks. Her hair, often elaborately braided, was always shiny with the oil of the butternut tree or with animal fat. Her mother constantly sang to her and clicked castanets whose rattling sounds filled her with joy and happiness.

Chacha was merely acting the role of a decent mother, in making the child the focus of her attention. But sometimes, excellence, even in a community in which it is upheld as a virtue and promoted, if pursued with too much zeal, can be the source of intense jealousy and hostility, especially when it comes from quarters where it is least expected. Some members of the community did not take too kindly to the extra mile Chacha was going in raising her child. They began to see her efforts as a show-off and a deliberate attempt to outdo others in childcare and this belief opened a whole new chapter in the already strained relationship between her household and the community.

The child's own precocious and "male" tendencies did little to help matters. By the time Yaa was five, she had grown tall for her age. Physically strong and stunningly pretty, she started to do things which showed that some of her mother's attitude had begun to rub off on her. She demonstrated a stubborn determination to excel in everything she did. She outraced boys almost two times her age and indulged in the all-time pranks of chasing butterflies or ferreting crickets out of their holes that African children cherish.

Sometimes, she would carry a bow and arrow like most of the boys with whom she tended to play and, pretending to be a hunter, would flit in and out of cocoyam crops growing near the house in hot pursuit of a rat or a squirrel. And in the playful wrestling encounters in which children sometimes became involved, she was often seen challenging and even putting the backs of some boys to the ground.

"That one will end up just like the mother," some villagers who thought the vigor and energy were too much for a female could be heard remarking.

"She may grow up wanting all the men for herself," a voice added with an outburst of laughter.

When Yaa was not playing, she would accompany her mother to the fields. Before she began her farm work, her mother would ask her to sit down under the shade of a big tree at the center of the farm. In the fire she had made, the mother would roast sweet potatoes, yams and crickets for the little girl.

Under the merciless heat of the sun in which Chacha worked, she was often very thirsty. She would then call out to her daughter to bring her some drinking water. Waddling her way like a duckling, the little girl would come bearing a calabash. As her mother took it from her, she would show her appreciation by showering her daughter with those flattering terms of endearment with which African mothers seemed particularly endowed. Having drunk her fill, she would return the container to her and continue with her work.

When the heat of the sun proved more than she could bear, she would join her daughter under the tree and regale her with the exploits of the Hausa Queen Amina or those of the Matamba Princess, Nzinga Mbandi. She had recounted the tales over and over again but the little girl did not seem to have enough of them. She often imagined that one day she would become a great queen.

4

Yaa soon turned ten. In the light of her age, she was forced to abandon the rather rich but boring chore of supplying water to her mother in the field to take up the more challenging one of watching over her mother's goats. It was a task traditionally reserved for males.

So what if a household was made up only of females? The Council could assign a male member of another house to take care of such duties. Since Chacha had fallen foul of the Council and seemed not to be particularly hot with the overtures it was making to bring her to the fold, and since the community had virtually reduced her to a pariah, she could not avail herself of such discretional services.

Early each morning, as her mother was preparing to go the field, Yaa would slip on her garments and take the lunch basket she had prepared the previous night for herself and rush to the enclosures where the goats were kept. After counting them to be sure none was missing, she would herd them off and then join the group of young boys who were heading to the open savannah with their own flocks. It was extremely difficult at first because she found it hard to cope with the heat of the blazing rays of the sun but she soon became used to that.

At midday, she would settle under a tree with her male friends and share the lunch she had prepared with them. Once they had finished eating and, with the heat of the sun taking its toll, they would recede to the more relaxing shade of the forested valleys to swing using a piece of rope strapped to the branch of a tree or splatter in the numerous streams to refresh themselves or in search of fish and tadpoles. The swinging in particular she relished because it reminded her of when she was young and her mother did that with her.

Initially, the boys were not sure whether they actually wanted to associate with a girl. They felt she would not be able to keep pace with the rigor of the life of a goatherd. To prove to them that she was just as good, if not better, she often insisted and took part in some of their most dangerous and fiercest activities. She wrestled. She was into stick fights. She went up trees to pick fruits and to watch over her flock. She went hunting for cane rats. As time went on, she became so involved in the different activities that the boys almost stopped seeing the two mounds which had already started to protrude on her chest.

Nevertheless, if she thought this was full acceptance, she was dead wrong. When once the boys organized a wrestling contest, they decided to leave her out. When she protested, the boys merely laughed.

"This time it's for real and we don't want you to get hurt," one of them declared.

"I suggest you pit me against any boy. If my performance is below par, then I quit," she put them to a challenge.

When she first made the proposal, the idea triggered an outburst of laughter as most of the boys could not imagine themselves wrestling a female. Finally, one day while they were involved in another contest, she showed up again and insisted that she would participate.

Tired of her nagging and determined to shut her mouth once and for all, the boys selected the weakest and smallest member of their band and asked him to wrestle with Yaa. In the ensuing struggle, she put his back on the ground without much difficulty. This was a humiliation.

By the end of that day, after numerous encounters, she occupied an upper echelon in the pecking order of the goatherd world. With that reputation, she eventually came to be truly accepted. This meant that she could take part in all the activities of the group and was recognized as a full member.

It was, therefore, natural that at seventeen, she should graduate into "manhood," along with her goatherd peers. The Manjung, as the ceremony into manhood was called, comprised a wrestling competition to test stamina and strength. Most of the young men who became members were ultimately drafted into the defense unit of Bankim.

The Council announced the date and site for the event. Young men who met the criteria for selection to participate in the induction exercise were applying. Yaa felt she should too. Growing up, she had only seen males be involved, so she decided to raise the issue of her willingness to participate one evening when she was with her mother.

"I see no reason why you can't take part," her mother declared much to her delight. "A woman never participated before but there is a beginning to everything," she continued before giving a word of caution. "You shouldn't go into the competition expecting concessions from men."

"I don't think I'll do that," Yaa said to her mother. "Most of the boys who are to take part in the induction are my goatherd peers, people with whom I normally spend most of my time during the day and do things together, so I simply see no reason why they can apply and I can't."

"Contact the Council with your request and let's hear what it's going to say on the matter."

When Yaa formally met with the entire Council to announce her decision to become a member of the Manjung, the reply she got was what she had suspected.

"This society is meant for males, so why do you want to become a member?" the Tabih, who presided over that very special session to determine whether she could become member, asked.

"I know I meet the conditions to qualify for membership and there's no reason why I shouldn't apply like my other goatherd companions," Yaa responded.

"Have you discussed this with your mother?"

"Yes."

"What did she say?"

"She strongly supports the idea."

"I'm not surprised that she does," the Tabih declared, with his sarcasm barely concealed. "Do you know that you need to have balls to survive the physical activities required to select members of this society?"

"If it's the wrestling competition you're talking about, the challenge is entirely mine."

"Don't you think it too risky for a woman?"

19

"Well, no riskier than being bitten by a snake in the field or giving birth to a baby."

"Well, we'll discuss the matter and get back to you as soon as possible," the Tabih finally said as he dismissed Yaa.

Even before she was out of sight, she could hear a wild debate raging on behind her.

"This competition is meant for men," one voice screamed angrily. "It's originally a war society and women don't fight wars."

"I think that barren goat of her mother is behind all this confusion!" another one exclaimed.

With the meeting gradually dissolving into chaos as the debate became intense, the Tabih took the floor to bring about some calm. He traced the origin of the Manjung and stated the obvious that traditionally it was a society for men. For all that he said, he completely failed to advance just one good reason why females could not become members. This lapse was immediately spotted and snapped up by Asanbe. He was the head of the Konchus family and a man known for his integrity and intelligence. Having been raised in a household of women, he had had the opportunity to study them firsthand and from his observations, had long concluded that if given the chance they could excel in everything men did.

"You haven't given any shred of evidence why women shouldn't become members," he argued. "The way I see it, to say that the society is traditionally meant exclusively for men only tends to bolster, and not weaken, the argument that women should now join."

His was not the lone voice in support of females. Ngufor, the head of the Ndifordeh family, also lent his support with a strong set of arguments. He also had a reputation for fairness and perspicacity.

"We shouldn't make this Council appear unfair before our own people. If we must reject Yaa's request, there should be very valid grounds to do so. We mustn't come across as a sentimental bunch only eager to uphold the tradition, even when it doesn't serve our aims anymore. We mustn't forget that men put the tradition in place. So why should women even play by rules they didn't contribute to formulate? Assuming that they didn't show any interest in the past in becoming members, should that in any way

20

imply their being excluded? I think the rules of the game are clear for anyone wishing to become member. The age limit has been set and wrestling helps to weed out weaklings. It's up to the interested parties to prove themselves. That's not asking too much."

Now, the Council was split over the matter and seemed poised to fall apart. To let the rest of the village know what was happening at this stage could only help to further divide the community. The Council had once had a brush with Chacha and did not want to repeat the bitter lesson.

It was true that the issue flew in the face of tradition. But the request was not unreasonable or exaggerated. So far tradition, a collection of habits, had been the pillar of all the arguments for female exclusion. Nevertheless, it seemed to collapse under the assault of mere common sense. Nowhere did it specifically spell out any sound reason why females could not become members. This simply meant that there was no reason not to accept Yaa's request. Her age was good. There was the wrestling competition to show whether she had the strength and stamina to go the distance. Reason seemed to have prevailed.

"I think we have no other recourse than to accept the girl's request," the Tabih announced to the utter jubilation of Asanbe, Ngufor and the few other members who had stood firmly behind the females.

All the same, some diehards were still totally convinced that it was a male thing and only went along with the others out of sheer cynicism. They expected Yaa to come out of the wrestling competition so badly battered and maimed that the Council would simply recant the decision.

"I don't want to be party to any murder," one member completely blind to any common sense or logic stated and walked out on the Council when it arrived at its verdict.

Even more dramatic was the community's reaction to the news of the Council's approval for Yaa to participate in the upcoming wrestling which would determine new members of the Manjung. The news hit the village like an earthquake and suddenly became the favorite discussion subject of every household. Some members of the community thought it was about time while the overwhelming majority was against her.

Ironically though not surprisingly, many of those who did not quite approve the Council's decision were women.

"Who does she think she is!" some of them were heard exclaiming. "She'll end up paying a bride price and getting married to a man," the hostilities raged on.

In the Chacha household, there was celebration. While the bulk of the village continued to fume over the matter, plans for Yaa to start training for the wrestling had already begun in earnest.

"She conspires with her mother to come up with this?" one woman declared when she saw her taking to the hills one morning as part of her preparation for the induction. "I hope she comes out of the wrestling ring with one eye."

The hostility continued to take various forms in the village. She did not lose her courage because she had already become used to those kinds of talk growing up as the daughter of Chacha.

While her goatherd mates greeted the news of the acceptance with much enthusiasm and happiness, they instantly saw the danger it presented to them and their pride as men. Most of them had had the opportunity to wrestle with Yaa and knew she was tough. The idea that she could be pitted against any of them and they would not be able to hold their own drove a chill down their spines. It also created widespread and serious panic among them. And just what would it feel like to be outwrestled by a woman in front of the whole village? Their minds were really running wild.

Even though more than forty candidates had applied to join the Manjung, only the first twenty-five who performed well in wrestling would ultimately be selected, with the remaining fifteen being asked to try their luck next time. This often made the wrestling phase of the induction very fierce as everyone tried to avoid being eliminated. Being eliminated was a family shame. How terrible if the shame came from the hands of a woman!

The site had already been selected and its preparation was underway. The date too had been fixed. It was, therefore, just a matter of time to see whether a woman could excel and even outshine men in an activity traditionally designed for them.

Yaa knew that it did not suffice only to confront the Council to have her participation endorsed. She actually had something to prove and with this in mind, she embarked on a

22

phase of her training the rigor of which the entire village had never seen before. She hauled huge logs of wood back and forth and up and down the hill and stretched her cross country race over a very long, rugged distance.

Her muscles ached when she returned home after each training session. Her mother warmed water in a huge clay container in which she put various curative herbs and roots for her to wash herself and sooth her muscles.

The concoction worked miracles and very soon her body could take any form of beating without the usual aches. The exercise was very rewarding. Apart from helping her to accumulate a lot of energy, it also enabled her to build up tremendous stamina and increase the speed of her actions.

In the run up to the day of the event, she focused more on wrestling techniques by sparring with more experienced and strong members of her goatherd fraternity.

5

The eve of the day the entire village had been waiting for finally arrived. While people braced themselves for the event, those who wanted to become members of the Manjung were secluded in a large hut constructed next to the new wrestling ground which occupied an imperious position on the outskirts of the village. They were to spend the evening there around a fire, making jokes and sharing whatever food they had.

"Now listen to this joke!" cried out a wrestler called Shumbu. "A small boy went to his father one day and said: 'Please daddy, tell me something,' he urged his old man, 'has honey legs?' he asked. 'Honey? Legs?' the old man looked perplexed. 'Yes,' the boy replied. 'Son,' the man tried to advise his child, 'when you ask questions make sure they're intelligent.'

"The child thought for a while. 'Well, my question must be intelligent,' he declared, 'because I often overhear you at night saying: Please honey, open your legs.'"

This almost brought down the roof. One wrestler laughed until he rolled close to the fire and the edge of his goatskin kilt caught fire and would have set the hut alight but for the timely intervention of Yaa who raised an alarm and it was immediately put out. As soon as the commotion caused by the incident had died down, the jokes resumed.

"Waah!" a wrestler called Bamu shouted to attract attention. This was not even necessary because even before he could open his mouth everyone was holding his sides. When it came to making jokes, he could pack his punches. "Do you all know Akor?" he asked. The faces of his listeners bore an appearance which proved that they did not quite know the person. At this, he pretended to be impatient. "I mean that long-headed, womanizer who loves sex like his mother."

"Like his father, you mean to say," came a quiet, dissonant and marginal note which was not appreciated at all.

"Like his mother, I said!" he reiterated, first casting an evil look at the person who had challenged his logic before turning his attention to the rest of the audience.

"Ehee!" came the exclamation of approval he had been waiting for from his listeners. He was about to proceed now.

"What happened to him?" an eager voice interrupted.

"Will you shut your big mouth!" the owner of the voice was instantly hushed down by a chorus of even more eager voices.

"Well, Akor went to his father," Bamu began as though he was replying to the question he had been asked before he was interrupted. He paused. The audience was itchy and he knew it. After the pause, punctuated by his scrutinizing look, he continued as members of the audience held their breath in anticipation. "He went to his father because he wanted to get married."

"Then..." another eager voice urged the jokester on.

"Then he told his father the name of the girl he wanted to marry," he said as he poked the dying flame and it came alive, enabling him to gauge the level of eagerness. "His father after brooding over the matter for a while cast a somber look at his son: 'You can't get married to her because she's your sister,' he announced. 'You never told me that she was my sister,' poor Akor responded, looking confused and disappointed. 'Why don't you look for another girl,' the father advised, seeing that his son was not happy.

"Akor left and came back a month later with another name and met with the same answer. Not until he had gone through six names did it dawn on him that he might never get married because every girl in the village was his sister. Upset, he decided to face his mother with the matter. His mother let him talk. Then she said nothing though it was clear to her son she'd something on her mind. 'I'm waiting to hear from you mom, at least say something,' Akor insisted. 'What do you want me to say,' she asked, holding down her head. How could she look into the face of her son with what she was about to say? Finally, she mustered the courage to speak but her voice was gloomy. 'You may get married to any of the girls,' she stated, raising her head and looking straight into his eyes. 'Yes, get married to any of them because you aren't his son.'"

The crowd went wild.

"I knew something juicy was cooking," one voice said after recovering from laughter.

And about the boy's mother another one remarked: "That woman is like the entrance to the compound of the Tabih." The roof almost came down. The laughter that greeted the comparison was just about to die down when a voice rang out.

"You're right!" it exclaimed. "The only time something isn't between her legs is when she's walking!"

"How do you know she loves it?" a voice rose above the reigning pandemonium.

"Can't you see that the back of her head is already balding!" came a response which convulsed the entire group into yet another round of laughter.

"Krijeeh!" Bamu cried out, acting as though the listeners were asleep.

"Hey!" came the thunderous and simultaneous reply to prove they were awake and still listening.

"Can a woman piss in a narrowed-mouthed calabash!" he called out.

"No!" came the answer from the other listeners.

"What's a pregnant woman afraid of the least?" he intoned again.

"A naked man," they replied. The reply was followed by peals of laughter.

Yaa was perfectly at ease in the midst of the young men whose ribald jokes she had come to appreciate and even enjoy. It was her longest and most entertaining night. As she lay curled up on her goatskin watching the fire crackle, she kept wondering what kind of reception the village would hold out for her if she performed badly. Soon the voices around her began to come to her as if in a dream, almost sounding distant. She did not even realize when she drifted off to sleep that night.

She got up the following morning to the noise of other Manjung aspirants. Since the event was scheduled to take place in the late afternoon, when the villagers had already returned from the fields, the wrestlers just lazed around the hut chatting, laughing and indulging in the game of mancala. Even though she was not wide awake, she could tell that some people were out, probably gone to their huts to fetch food and water.

With some effort, she managed to sit up on her goatskin and then finally decided to get up. She rolled her mat and put it away. When she came out of the hut, the sun had already risen high above the horizon, casting its golden glow on the sweeping green savannah. It was beginning to get hot. She stared in the direction of her mother's hut. She reached a point where she could see from a distance that it was closed. She might have gone to the field, she thought.

She knew that all the candidates for Manjung had to be in the assembly hut at least an hour before the event. She felt she still needed to sleep and rest properly but first she had to wash herself and get something to eat. She went to her mother's hut, opened the door and went in. From the light which came in through the narrow window, she inspected it. Her food was standing on a small bamboo shelf. She opened the hand woven straw dish and stared at a huge mound of kibane, a thick gruel made from corn flour, her mother had kept for her. Next to the dish was a small clay container with the sauce which went with the meal. Yaa's sauce was kati, roasted chicken chopped into tiny bits and prepared with palm oil. It was special food and seemed to imply that her mother was already celebrating her victory.

She poured some water into a basin made of clay and went behind the house to wash her body. She came back feeling fresh. After anointing herself with palm oil, she took her food and returned to the hut to share it with the others. She met far fewer people than she had expected. After washing their hands, the others joined her and they set about demolishing the food with great appetite.

When they had finished eating, she took back the bowl and the little clay pot which contained the sauce to her mother's hut. She then shut the door and went to sleep. She woke up about midday to the humming of her mother who had just returned from the field.

"Tired?" she asked when Yaa sat up on her mat and was rubbing her eyes.

"Well, I really needed some rest before the wrestling competition. I slept late last night and so I had some catching up to do. In the noise and confusion of the hut where we've assembled, it was impossible so I had to come here."

"That's alright."

"You cooked me a very special dish which I enjoyed with my friends today," she said to her mother in a complimentary remark.

"It's a very special occasion that I thought deserved a special meal and I'm happy you enjoyed it."

"I should get going to the assembly hut since we have to be there an hour before the start of the competition," she announced to her mother as she put away the mat.

"I'll be on the wrestling ground to cheer for you. I've something for you. It's inside the big basket hanging on the wall," her mother declared pointing.

"What's it?"

"I don't know," she replied with a smile. "Why don't you check and see for yourself?"

She rushed to the basket, took it off its hook and on looking inside saw a very beautiful wrestling costume her mother had obtained for her.

"It's very beautiful," she said in amazement. "This is indeed a surprise."

"I wanted it to be a surprise."

"You'll see it on me during the competition," she said to her mother as she headed excitedly towards the door.

On her way to the hut, Yaa first went and took a look at the wrestling ground. People stopped whatever they were doing and fixed their stare on her. The population had started to gather for the event and a lot seemed to have been done while she was asleep. The stand for the drummers had already been erected and the seats for the village notables, the councilors and titleholders, had been set out.

Usually, there was no special sitting arrangement, at least not for the ordinary grown-up villagers. They had to bring along their own stools. Children occupied the front row, just in front of the notables, in order to have a clear view. The rest of the village simply had to form a cluster behind the notables and around the rest of the wrestling ground.

The center of the ground had a big ring for the face-off. It had been beaten really hard to prevent any wrestler from slipping and giving an opponent an undue advantage. Directly facing the section reserved for spectators was the one for the wrestlers. Next to the music stand was that of the master of ceremony. Opposite the master of ceremony, not really far from the ring, were seats for the wrestling officials who would be presiding over the various contests.

When Yaa got to the hut, it was as busy as an anthill. The wrestlers, most of them stripped to their goatskin undergarment, were applying raw palm oil to their broad and amply developed chests.

"Where were you Yaa?" Shumbu inquired. "We were beginning to think you had chickened out."

"How could I do that and miss an opportunity to whop your ass?" she responded. Her reply caused an outburst of laughter from the rest of the wrestlers.

"Anyway get ready fast, for it's almost time," he declared.

She moved to a corner of the hut and started to get dressed in the wrestling outfit her mother had just given her. It was a three-piece ensemble which comprised a strap of leopard skin to be strung across her breasts to keep them firmly in position by tying both ends firmly behind her back. Another broad flap of the same material made up her skirt and a third was a kind of headband.

When she was fully dressed and ready to go, she looked very beautiful. Her gleaming muscles, well toned and bursting with energy, were another hint that most of the wrestlers had their work cut out for them.

The wrestlers could hear the footsteps and chats of people streaming past their hut, seemingly on their way to the wrestling ground. The drums started to play and they heard children screaming and laughing.

It was at this moment that a messenger rushed into the hut.

"I've been sent to come and inform you to be ready," he announced to the wrestlers. "The competition starts even before spittle dries on the ground."

6

By now, the wrestlers were all geared up and kept their ears opened for the names which would soon be announced by the master of ceremony. Outside, on the wrestling ground, the villagers had turned out in their numbers for the important event and ceremony. People had already taken their seats and the drumming rose to a wild crescendo.

The kemideh, the mascot for the event, had appeared as soon as the orchestra struck up. It was a masqueraded dancer draped in a garb of partridge feathers. On its head, it wore a wooden mask crafted in imitation of the head of a buffalo. It was carrying two spears.

It danced briefly to the tune of the music playing before shifting to a more interesting routine. Through a combination of mimes and gesticulations, it started to poke fun at some important village elders, either imitating the way they walked or their gestures and postures during conversations. The public cracked up and cheered. This went on for about fifteen minutes.

The voice of the master of the wrestling ceremony rang out above the noise and confusion of the ground. The event was about to start. For a while, he stood on his stand and began to take in the spectators. This meant that he wanted them to be silent. The kemideh took the hint and hastily retired and the whole ground became like a graveyard.

He could now proceed with the announcement. He began to call out the names of the wrestlers.

"Ndifor!" he shouted at the top of his voice.

He was a village favorite. He was a tall, handsome and proportionately built athlete who was known for his tremendous energy and calmness. As soon as he heard his name, he emerged from the hut to wild applause from the spectators. His body had been hammered into shape by the physical tortures he had been undergoing for the last few months.

His bulging muscles gleamed with palm oil and he made those of his chest to jiggle as he strode sedately. The crowd loved it and greeted the performance with wild cheers. After bowing in salute as tradition dictated, he took his place in the section meant for them.

"Mafany!"

The spectators responded with a standing ovation as soon as he came out of the hut. He was very neat, kind and hugely popular, especially with the women to whose assistance he always came in times of trouble. His wrestling reputation was built around his swift and surprise attacks and counterattacks which often caught opponents napping. A bit shy, he ran to the center and bowed and then hastened to the side of Ndifor where he sat down. They exchanged a quick and amicable glance.

"Bungah!"

Even before the name had been uttered, the crowd started to boo. Never before in Bankim had a person gone on to live the true meaning of his name after birth. Bungah in the local language stood for smoked tilapia. In a pot of soup, this fish had time and again proved to be the most treacherous ingredient, usually concealing or disguising sharp, strong bones which sometimes got stuck in the throats of unwary guests.

He was the son of a conman and turned out to be one himself. He often indulged in a series of petty thievery such as fowl snatching and egg poaching and for all these acts he earned the not-too-undeserved nickname of Achagwukwaki, the fox.

In spite of his tender age, he had appeared more than a hundred times before the Council to be tried for one or the other of his endless peccadilloes and seemed to relish in that reputation. Sinister and dangerous, he was the very symbol of untrustworthiness and wherever he went people hid their belongings. Built strong like a buffalo, he would have been one of the best wrestlers in the village if only he could put behind him his devious ways.

"Achagwukwaki! Achagwukwaki!" some spectators screamed, making sure they were not seen, for the fellow also had a very hefty reputation for violence. He emerged from the hut and held down his head in shame as he trotted like a donkey and without any form of salute or obeisance to the jeering crowd came to a halt by the side of Mafany where he sat down. Ever the gentleman, Mafany gave him a quick and perfunctory glance in recognition of his presence and turned to follow the goings-on.

By the thirty-ninth wrestler, the voice of the master of ceremony had become gruff and he was almost croaking. With the last male wrestler out on the ground, the crowd held its breath. The master of ceremony paused for a while, as though for some dramatic effect. Then he cleared his throat before resuming the announcement.

"She's the first woman in Bankim to apply to join the Manjung and she's here to take part in this important wrestling event. Meet the one and only Yaa, daughter of Chachaaaa," the voice of the master of ceremony crowed.

The bulk of the crowd was visibly not impressed with the announcement and remained silent. As though she already understood the mood outside, Yaa paused for a while before coming out, prancing gracefully, her face radiant and her braided hair held high in the wind.

Her breasts stood out like two unripe mangoes. Solidly held in position by its accoutrement of animal skin made to fit, they looked as firm as a baboon's butt. Her arms, muscular and strong, swung freely. She was beautiful and stood straight and tall and her head held high in apparent defiance until she came and planted herself right in the middle of the ground and bowed. It was as though the spectators had been completely struck spellbound by the sheer power and awe of her beauty.

Her mother stood up and yelled encouragement and showered praises.

Goddess of the savannah
Queen of the mountains
Angel of the woods
Amina! Nzinga Mbandi!
You are one only in the eyes
For two in one you really are
Intrepid and unvanquished soul
Conqueror of the Noun

Heart of lioness
Hold out your beacon
As light for the darkness
Of those who dislike you
As you walk to victory
Not in spite of them
But because of them
Shed no tears
For there are none to shed
Since only men still cry
As tested they never have been
And oppression they know not
Let no rock stand in your way
For if in your way any stands
Under your feet it must shatter.

As for the rest of the spectators, not a word was uttered until she went and took her position. Going by their uncomfortable stares and confused glances, one would have thought a goddess was passing.

The spectators simply did not know which attitude to adopt towards the girl. They had never seen or felt anything like that in the whole history of their village.

While Chacha stood up and was boasting the strength and beauty of her daughter, a man, apparently overcome by jealousy, tried to shout her down.

"I've got three male zebras who'll maul and get her pregnant with fatigue and exhaustion," the man shouted much to the pleasure of the crowd.

"I've just one lioness," Chacha responded and those who were still celebrating the man's statement cut it out and looked around nervously.

The drums started to rumble and the kemideh returned and continued with his pranks. Most of the spectators stood up and stretched their limbs in preparation for the next and long anticipated stage. As the master of ceremony started towards his stand, the drumming began to die down. The mascot retreated to his hideout with one of his most popular routines, the display of lurid sexual positions.

33

The first contestants were about to be called out.

With his habitual ocular gestures to bring about silence, the master of ceremony put an end to the reigning hullabaloo started by the last act of the mascot. And then he began his announcement.

"The opening bout of this wrestling competition is between Yaa and Bungah."

Even though there were no cheers, the spectators seemed happy. It was as though they wanted to get rid of the villains before the true competition began. Still, even in the match up between two unwanted people, the spectators still took sides.

The choice between the hardworking and daring independent female and the male felon smacked of the one between Christ and Barabas. At a time when the Bible had not reached this part of Africa, it was a measure of the compatibility of human behavior that the bulk of the population of Bankim sacrificed the light for darkness. They were determined to put the past of Bungah behind him as long as he could put Yaa out of men's affairs once and for all.

"Achagwukwaki! For once you have to eat a chicken without having to steal it!" a coterie of young men chanted and the spectators voiced their approval with some hearty laughter.

As the two contestants walked to the center of the ring for the face-off, the drums started to play again. Bungah, as I have already stated, was a youth of impressive stature who should have been good in the sport with a little devotion. However, the absence of wrestling skills was hugely compensated for by an abundance of raw energy. Properly channeled, this energy could snatch him a victory.

Against Yaa, this possibility seemed less likely. She had trained extremely hard for this competition which meant more to her than to a person more interested in keeping count of the number of chickens being hatched or eggs laid in the village.

Even though she had worked herself to a superb wrestling form, this apparently went unnoticed to a public inclined to see her punished.

The drums rolled frantically and like two charging buffaloes, the contestants clinched, staring fiercely and defiantly

34

into each other's eyes, anxiously searching for some weakness to exploit.

Locked in that position, they moved round and round and then to and fro, pulling and pushing. They were both testing the ground. Yaa unconsciously leaned forward. She might have been trying to fasten her grip on Bungah but this move caused her center of gravity to shift slightly in that direction.

In the split second that her opponent felt her weight on himself, he tugged her and she staggered forward and came close to losing her balance. Unfortunately for him, the pull was not snappy enough so she was quick to recover, but it was a brilliant move and the spectators voiced their appreciation with a great cheer.

Having survived, Yaa took the offensive. With practiced firmness, her hands clenched like a vice around the thick wrists of Bungah. The steely and tremendous pressure they exerted in that grip unleashed a stabbing pain which surged throughout his entire body and instantly disrupted his concentration. Yaa then closed in on him and attempted to fling him to the right and meeting with some resistance, stopped. She again feigned the same move. Suddenly, with a leg wedging Bungah, she flipped him in the opposite direction where his guard had been lowered and an attack least anticipated. This took him completely by surprise and he lost his balance and crashed to the ground.

The move was superbly executed and even her most rabid detractors unconsciously cheered before realizing it. Chacha leaped from her seat in a wild ecstasy of jubilation, her right fist jabbing the air.

Silence descended on the entire ground and people looked at one another nervously and adjusted on their seats. Their worst fear had been confirmed. With that victory, not only did Yaa qualify for the next round but had also clearly demonstrated that with a bit of caution she could go all the way.

And all the way, she went. Late that same day, the final bout pitted Mafany against Yaa in a classic encounter which went into the annals of Bankim wrestling. She lost to him but came second in the general classification of those who had been selected to join the Manjung.

7

The wrestling was over. Even though the induction event had not come to an end, many villagers were already walking away in disappointment. They were not happy with Yaa's performance.

The winning wrestlers were about to be decorated by the Tabih. The decoration was prelude to their being made members of the Manjung.

"I wish to praise all the young men..." the Tabih began and was immediately interrupted by a voice from the remaining spectators.

"And woman!" Chacha screamed, suspecting that the Tabih might leave out her daughter in the praise.

"And woman of course!" the Tabih got the not-too-subtle hint and immediately reacted, "for these wonderful performances."

Then the master of ceremony started to call out the names of the successful athletes who came forward to be decorated and made members of the Manjung. When it came to Yaa's turn a new complication arose.

"I can only accept to be a member of this organization if, henceforth, it becomes open to women," she declared much to the surprise and anger of the remaining public.

"What do you mean by this?" the Tabih asked, overwhelmed with shock by the sudden turn things were taking.

"Look here!" she called out to everyone watching: "I don't mean to be disrespectful but underneath me is a slit-drum," she said as she pointed below, "and above are two mounds," she continued as she peeped at her own breasts. "What it means is that I'm a woman," she stated the obvious. As people stared in shock and disbelief, she did not stop lashing out. "Tell you what," she jeered. "I'm happy and comfortable with my two mounds and slit-drum because without them none of you would be standing here."

"We all know that without a woman we won't be here," the Tabih cut in unceremoniously to try to cover up. His countenance was gradually changing from shock to shame even as he acknowledged this truth which had often been shamelessly ignored.

"Since you know there shouldn't be any further complication because I'll accept my membership only on condition that you respect my womanhood."

The Tabih and the Council were now confronted with a new problem. There was no provision in the Manjung to bring in a woman. Bringing in one as a man was bad enough, so imagine how he and most of his councilors felt when Yaa insisted she wanted to come in as a woman.

The Tabih scratched his head in confusion and then turned and looked at some members of the Council sitting next to him for answers.

"Now that we've already started, let's finish with the males before we come back to her," one family head suggested. "We must decide either to transform Manjung simply into an adulthood society for both men and women or set up a branch within it solely for women."

The councilors took note of the proposal but resolved to adjourn Yaa's induction pending a final and satisfactory resolution to the problem.

After the day's event and celebration, the Council met in an extraordinary session to determine what to do with Yaa. The deliberation was long and had some very tense moments but in the end it was resolved that a special branch for women in the same society had to be created. Takenbing was born.

With the door flung open for females, some women who had vehemently opposed Yaa when she started her struggle were the first to encourage their daughters to join. Out of shame, the hostility towards her was still maintained by many. But whether it came in the form of malicious gossip or hate stares, it had lost most of its sting and virulence and had become more of a conditioned reflex.

Once her membership to the society was firmly established, Yaa decided to take advantage of the opportunities it offered its members. It was natural, therefore, that when she deemed the moment appropriate, she contacted the Council and requested to be given her own piece of farmland to cultivate.

"You're still under your mother's roof and until you show proof that you can fly on your own, your request can't be considered by the Council," the Tabih replied.

"This is just an excuse not to give me my own piece of land to cultivate," she told her mother of the Council's verdict when she returned home.

"Well, to avoid coming across as being confrontational and divisive, we should first fulfill the conditions laid down and then see how the Council reacts," her mother shrewdly reasoned.

With her mother's advice, she sought and obtained a piece of land not far from hers for the construction of her hut. She decided to go to work immediately. Now a member of Takenbing, she could avail herself of the service of members of the Manjung. She raised the issue during one of their meetings and all the young men of the village set a date to come and assist in the construction.

To give it a very special significance, Yaa prepared plenty of food and secured sufficient palm wine for the workers. She even had one of her mother's goats slaughtered for the occasion.

On the selected day, very early in the morning, she accompanied the men to the forest to get bamboos, poles, saplings and ropes. They returned by midday, and then with machetes and hoes, set about preparing the foundation of the hut. First, they dug out roots and tree stumps and leveled the ground. Then they prepared the sticks, saplings and other materials for the following day when the actual construction would begin. At the end of that first day, they all retired to the Manjung hut where they ate, drank and danced to the rhythm of the talking drums. Before dispersing, they agreed to meet very early the next day to commence construction.

The entire village was roused from sleep even before dawn the following day by the rumble of drums and by singing as the workers embarked on the construction of the hut. The huge poles were sharpened and fitted into the ground in the form of a rectangle, the geometric pattern she had selected for her hut.

Since the workers were many, before sunrise the walls had already been raised and the bamboo frames of the roof had been constructed. By midday, the frames had been raised and firmly tied in place using lianas and ropes. Only grass was needed for thatching and mud for plugging the crevices and space between the checkered bamboo and stick walls.

While the bulk of the men went out to cut grass, a few stayed behind to dig red sticky soil for the walls. Before they broke up for the day in the evening, they had resolved that an intense early morning work should provide the hut with a thatched roof and mudded walls. They also made sure they had stored enough water in numerous calabashes by the side of some village wells.

The final day of the work came. By noon it was completed and Yaa prepared a big feast. A few days after the feasting, she sprinkled water on the ground of the hut. Using the broad bottom of a kukuteh, a palm branch, she kept beating the wet floor until it became firm.

She covered it with fresh banana leaves and allowed it to dry. This way, it became really smooth and solid like cement and was easy to sweep. She gave the walls enough time to dry so that she could apply whitewash to them and make the house beautiful. When it was complete and ready for her to move in, it was a marvel to watch.

She became the first in the village to improve her hut by making it elegant and attractive. Even though most of the people admired it, they did not voice out their appreciation openly.

After discussion and careful planning with her mother, she finally set a date to open her hut. She invited members of the Manjung who had helped her to build it, as well as the elders and members of the Council. She prepared plenty of food and drinks and there was a great celebration.

Three days following the celebration, she moved out of her mother's hut. Her mother accompanied her to her new hut as a sign of blessing, showering her on this occasion with gifts of household utensils, seeds to plant the coming season and food which would last her until her own farm started to produce.

8

There was no more excuse to deny her a land grant. The Tabih cut out a large, fertile piece of land along an old river valley as her farm. She felt she needed a larger barn and so immediately set about constructing one for herself. When it was complete, it turned out to be one of the biggest.

"What a woman who believes only in very big things!" a jealous voice cursed.

She then began work on the land immediately. She cleared and stacked grass in huge compost which she would later use to fertilize the soil. Her mother kept telling her what a great farmer her father had been and she planned to emulate his example.

She was the first to get up everyday and head to the field. By the time the sun rose, sending its fiery rays all across the land and forcing many farmers to scamper for cover in the shades of trees, she had already taken advantage of the morning cold to do a lot of work.

Finally, the planting season came. She selected very good seeds and sowed them. With the first rains, the seeds began to sprout, attracting birds and wild animals. As she was still childless, she took up the task of going to the field and staying all day to drive away the marauders. It was a boring and time-consuming exercise but she held out until the tiny seeds had grown into sturdy shrubs.

It was now time to weed. Unwanted plants which choked crops and deprived them of nutrients had to be uprooted. Crops often ended up stunted and even fruitless if this important exercise was ignored. It often went hand in hand with mulching, softening the soil and burying uprooted grass to increase its fertility and reduce its loss of water.

Her corn responded to this care, developing thick stems and healthy fruits. Her peanuts spread out their broad, lush and green leaves and the whole farm took on the complexion of a vast sea of green.

Her diligence provided fodder for fresh rumors in the village.

"She wants to show that she's hardworking and tireless," some women lashed out at her.

Everyone could already see the bright prospects her field held out. Her corn had developed fully into long huge cones by the time they started to ripen. Her harvest was so enormous that she had an extra granary constructed.

"She doesn't want to get married. That way she continues to get all the men to assist her with her work," a couple complained, having failed to haul in as much as Yaa.

These rumors got to her and sometimes hurt her. She was aware of her beauty, diligence and wealth. But in spite of this, only three men, a thief, a lunatic and a beggar, had walked up to her to ask for her hand.

"She thinks she's better than men," some villagers complained.

"She's too big to occupy the same house with any man," others derided.

These complaints and criticisms reached her mother. She had lived them herself and knew they had no basis. She felt particularly wounded because she was already old and was eager to see her grandchildren before her passing.

She had lived with her daughter ever since she was young and understood her well. Her tough outward appearance concealed a soft inside most men were not even prepared to try to discover. She could tell her daughter was really bleeding inside from all these remarks.

"You see, as a woman there's a big price to pay for success," she told her as she clasped her to comfort her when she noticed she was very worried.

"I had worked all my life for this because I thought I could share it with someone and now look at me, already numerous moons and growing gray, with neither a husband nor a child of my own," she told her mother amid her tears.

"Never mind my child. If that's the price to be paid for excellence and independence, then somebody has to do it. I know

41

how hard it is for a woman to be buried with a stone in the midst of sturdy and active men. It was the plight reserved for me until you came into my life. It seemed our ancestors had accepted my sacrifices."

Yaa knew the tragic circumstances of her birth and early life just too well. She was aware that if she did not have children to name after her mothers and father, their names would soon disappear. With the great contributions her father had made to the community that would be an abomination. She was still drowned in these awful thoughts when the hunting season crept in and provided her with some momentary solace.

The village of Bankim had a longstanding hunting tradition going back many generations. It was a period when entire groups could organize themselves into large hunting bands to go out and kill big game for everyone. This had nothing to do with individual hunting expeditions designed to track down a duiker or cane rat for the family cooking pot or in exchange for some basic items. The highlight of the hunting season usually took place on an appointed day. On this day, members of the Manjung and other sturdy males in the community went out as a team to hunt.

It was an event rich in color and when it was approaching, everyone looked forward to it with great expectation and enthusiasm. The entire community was in a festive mood, from the time the hunters started to wear their protective charms and antidote against snakebites to the moment the meat was hauled in.

Upon the return of the expedition, with an abundance of meat of the many different kinds of wild animals, people ate and drank their fill and danced and celebrated all night.

In spite of all the excitement and happiness the event generated, it was not always fun. Accidents of all types often occurred. Some people sprained their limbs. Others were trampled upon by buffaloes and elephants or floored and eaten by leopards and lions. It was this flipside which made it a testing ground for courage and manhood. Before the party set out, it was usually screened of those who were weak, cowardly and lazy.

The appointed day for the Manjung hunting expedition arrived. When the party gathered in front of the hut of the Tabih for the preliminaries, Yaa showed up in full hunting regalia. She was armed to the teeth and singing.

42

Some people immediately began to grumble. And then others soon openly voiced their disapproval but that was as far as the protests went. She was a member of Takenbing and had earned her rites of passage. She had nothing to prove, at least not in front of men, many of whom had failed their Manjung admission test several times before making it.

"Why must she be involved in everything men do?" she overheard one of the hunters called Gombe grumbling.

She had heard too many of such snide remarks and so paid him little heed. When the party was ready, it was time to set out for the hunting ground. Led by some drummers, the party sang and danced most of the way.

The hunting ground was situated not very far away and was infested with many different types of wild animals, from the ordinary cane rats to lions.

It was past noon. The party was within the proximity of the hunting grounds when the leader halted the advance and called on the orchestra to stop its music. It was time to organize the hunting band. He split it into two groups, the flushers and the trackers. While the flushers were to cause the animals to leave their hiding places, the trackers would lie in wait for them.

Even before they actually got to the ground, they spotted a herd of deer grazing not far away. Their ears were held high in the wind in order to pick up the slightest speck of danger. The flushing band moved out in a wide semicircle and started to close in quietly behind the grazing herd, while the others were already set for the ambush. The noose was tightening and then a gaffe! A black mamba suddenly appeared in front of one of the flushers. He panicked and caused a stir. The frightened deer scattered in all direction, with some of them heading towards the waiting men. Just when they were poised for the slaughter, a pride of hunting lions which had their eyes set on the same animals now in full flight appeared suddenly as though out of the ground and gave them chase. The scene turned chaotic. The antelopes all vanished. This made the hunters fair game. In that confusion and heat of action, Gombe ran into a lioness. The beast pounced on him and was about to devour him. He let go a miserable cry of agony. Watching his terrible fate from behind a rock where she had taken cover, Yaa decided to act quickly. She struck out fiercely at the beast as the other hunters turned their tails to flee. The thrust of her lance was so vicious that the weapon sank into its neck. It immediately dropped its prey and scrambled away.

Gombe lay mangled and was screaming in agony as Yaa rushed even closer to the scene of the accident. With just one blow, the lioness had torn open his stomach and his entrails were hanging out. When the others finally mustered the courage to come to the man's assistance, he had already breathed his last.

Back in the village, not a word was uttered about Yaa's act of bravery. Not to talk of anyone having the courage to recommend her to the Council for decoration. As for the ordinary villagers, they had plenty to eat and, with their mouths full, they ceased for a while to talk about her.

The euphoria of hunting having died down, her old anxieties returned. It was, therefore, with a very heavy heart that she left one morning for the weekly market in a neighboring village. It was the start of her worst moments.

The market was still very busy when she packed up and started back home. It was early afternoon. Overhead the sun was shining brightly. She was still on her way when a child rushed up to her to tell her that her old mother Chacha lay dying at home. She had been bitten by a snake.

She had been out of her hut to take a stroll when she suddenly stepped on the reptile and it bit her. Taken from the scene of the accident and abandoned in her hut, it was alone that she faced her last hours in this world.

A flustered Yaa stormed into her mother's hut. She knelt by the side of her mat and felt her palm. It was cold and hard. The old woman had died, alone in the midst of her own people.

She fell down and started to wail. A week after her mother was buried she remained in her hut all by herself and kept on mourning. For a time, she ate and drank nothing. She talked to no one and did not reply when spoken to. It was the start of many more terrible things to come.

9

It was not very long after Chacha had died. The villagers started to notice some very weird patterns of behavior in Yaa. It started slowly and then took a turn for the worse. She came out late at night half-naked and went up and down the village talking to herself at the top of her voice. Unable to cope with the loneliness and shock caused by her mother's death, she had become insane.

Her once beautiful and long hair gradually became scraggy and then started to entangle into thick, dirty strands of ropy locks which fell over her bare, scrawny shoulders. Bare body, her strong and pointed breasts shamed the men. Her speech was incoherent and sometimes garbled. Her once shiny and silky skin started to develop warts and scabies as she refrained from washing her body. Yet underneath the filth and squalor her beauty was apparent.

One afternoon, on a Njuellah, the day chosen by the village as its day of rest, she put up a show and made a declaration which provided a hint of the great tragedy to come.

"These are my balls and they're bigger than those of the Tabih!" she had exclaimed amid the silly laughter of a lunatic as she pointed at two little pumpkins which she had stuck underneath her skirt and which bulged out.

This had provoked tremendous laughter among the villagers.

"Even madness is never expressed in a language foreign to that of the lunatic," a voice had cautioned following that declaration.

Then slowly, like a skin container which was gradually filling up with water, her once flat and firm stomach started to bulge out until it became apparent that Yaa was pregnant.

A lunatic woman pregnant in Bankim! It was an abomination, a severe breach of tradition which was punishable by death in the old days if the male responsible was found. The people of Bankim naturally believed that it was the work of one of the inhabitants of the neighboring villages which she sometimes visited.

As the stomach grew bigger, she stayed home all day. One morning, the village woke up to intermittent bursts of a terribly violent thunderstorm and rain and also to the cry of a baby. Some people mustered the courage and went into Yaa's hut. They found a tiny baby wrapped by its afterbirth kicking and screaming in a pool of blood by the woman's side. One of them picked up the child. The others felt its mother and tried to stir her up. She was long dead and cold.

All day, following that death, the village continued to be rocked by the thunderstorm. It rained very heavily and rivers and streams flooded their banks. Crops were destroyed and some huts and footbridges washed away. The thunderstorm was strange. But even stranger was the fact that it struck in the thick of the dry season.

For the second time and from the same house, the community was stuck with a motherless baby.

It was not long before many people noticed the very close resemblance which the child bore to one of the village dignitaries. Like the individual most people had in mind, the baby was very handsome, with a deep brown complexion, thick nappy hair, snub nose, wide mouth with full lips and above all a broad forehead.

Though those who had seen the baby refrained from making any open declarations, behind the scenes whispers began to circulate. Many of the whispers were malicious and sometimes tended to implicate the entire Council.

When they got into the ears of Asanbe, he was overcome with shame and embarrassment. He silently reflected over the incident but was not convinced that any member of the Council could have had the lunatic pregnant. Something had to be done to clear the name of the Council.

It was to tradition, which had been pretty much disrespected, that he thought of turning for an answer.

"No man of this august body could be responsible," he murmured to himself as he tried to assemble other members of the Council.

46

Ngufor was the first to come to his support when he disclosed what he planned to do. As it was their right as members of the Council, the two convened a meeting shortly after their discussion.

When the Council met, even though nothing had been disclosed, a certain feeling of uneasiness hung in the air. Asanbe took the floor.

"We're all men!" he cried out. "Let's not act as though we're unaware of the malicious gossips going on in our midst."

"Yes, let's not pretend," Ngufor concurred. "A lunatic has become pregnant in our midst and we need to get this matter cleared up before the wrath of our ancestors comes down on us."

"What do you plan to do?" Chokoh asked with seeming calmness. He was the reigning Tabih.

"Let's first start with ourselves for we're only men, mere mortals capable of mistakes, that is, if ever a penis had mistakenly got a woman pregnant," Asanbe began with some humor, trying probably to break the reigning tension. "Now did anyone in our midst do it?" he asked as he took in the Council. There was a long lapse of silence.

"We take the reigning silence to mean that none of us is guilty," Ngufor declared with a grin. "Well, it's the duty of the Tabih to announce to the rest of the community what we've discussed in this meeting."

The Tabih, a man known for his outgoing character and great sense of humor, became surprisingly very quiet throughout the entire deliberation. This did not escape the notice of most members. However, they thought it wise not to utter any remark which could turn out to be false and create division and fighting within the community.

"Where's Nkoh?" the Tabih asked when he rose to speak.

Nkoh was the village crier. He often participated in the Council's meetings should there be anything for him to announce to the public. When he stood up, he announced his presence with a dry cough which caused people to laugh.

"Sleeping with a lunatic violates the most sacred of our traditions. In addition, it is rape because it could only have been done without the lunatic's consent," the Tabih said, and then turning to him, declared: "Tonight, take to the streets of Bankim

47

and announce that the person responsible for this hideous and cowardly act of having Yaa pregnant should own up, otherwise the matter would be spoilt.

Spoiling in this sense means little or nothing to Western ears. Back then, as it may still be in many parts of Africa, it was the art of casting a serious spell on any person responsible for a severe breach of tradition. The exercise went with certain rites carried out by a gnukwabe, a mystic with the abilities to cast spells, heal and foretell the future.

At night, when the villagers were back from their farms and at their homes, the village crier took to the streets. After sounding his gong many times, he made the announcement.

"A very serious breach of tradition has taken place in our land and the person responsible should come forward and face the penalties," he hollered. "The Council is giving the person just two days to own up before the matter is referred to a gnukwabe who'll compel all the men in the village to swear."

After the announcement, the villagers waited anxiously for a man to step forward and own up to the act; or to at least say something. The time elapsed and still nobody came forward. It was clear from such a reaction that the Council was being tested. It responded by meeting again. At the end of a very long deliberation, it came up with two main decisions. The first was that on the coming Njuellah all men in the village would have to be assembled at the square and marched to the shrine of a gnukwabe. And the second: it agreed on the nature of calamity that would befall the person responsible for the pregnancy.

Once again, Nkoh took to the streets of Bankim at night to make the announcement to the hearing of everyone.

"The council has decided that all males of our community mature enough to know a woman should appear at the village square next Njuellah. They'll all be marched to the shrine of a gnukwabe where everyone will have to swear on a curse whose outcome is terrible," he prepared the minds of the public before providing the chilling message. "The guilty person will die, followed shortly afterward by close family members, if he has any."

A dark pall had been cast over the male community in Bankim and those who suited that description had good reasons to feel gloomy. They would now have to deal with a gnukwabe. And in Bankim, there was one whose name was whispered with reverence and who made every person tremble with fright. He was the one most likely to be given this important assignment. So, who was this much dreaded figure?

10

Old Bangsiboh got up early that morning. At night, on that day, he had a dream in which he saw a leopard hanging from a tree. A leopard, the symbol of authority and power, hanging from a tree? He pondered the message being conveyed in the dream over and over and then from his seclusion came to the conclusion that something serious must have gone wrong in the village. The sun had not risen. He would have to wait for that to happen for the dews which had accumulated overnight to evaporate before he could venture out.

After rolling his sleeping mat and putting it away, he felt his way to a corner of his hut where he stored water in calabashes. Reaching down gradually, with each muscle straining and aching, he got one calabash that was half-empty and raising it directly to his mouth like a person blowing a trumpet, took a quick swig. He rinsed his mouth, approached the fireplace at the center of the hut and spat out the water near it. In his entire life as a blind man – indeed a very long period – he had performed these routines and they now came to him almost naturally. He was at least now ready to eat something. He groped to another corner where he had kept some roasted peanuts in a bowl made out of straw. He scooped a handful and after eating them, went back to his calabash. This time he drank deep from it. At least the peanut and water would hold his stomach until midday when he would have lunch.

He had realized the previous day that he was running out of his supply of some of the herbs and plants he needed for his medical concoctions and mystical practices and had planned to go out into the forest to search for them. As he was waiting for the sun to rise, his mind lingered on the dream he had had. Still puzzled, he decided to interrogate the ancestors. With the lazy shuffle of an octogenarian, he drifted to yet another corner of the hut where an old clay pot dark with age stood on a wooden tripod.

He dipped his hand in its contents of leaves, roots and tree barks steeped in a brackish liquid. Then by means only he knew how, he concluded that a person would come to him bearing very important information.

As soon as he could feel the rising heat of the sun, instead of going to the forest as he had planned, he grabbed his signature two walking sticks and felt his way to the truneck of a fallen tree at the entrance to his compound. There, he sat down.

He had barely been there for a brief while when the rustle of dry grass, punctuated by a cough, announced the approach of someone.

"Did I hear a human voice?" he called out with his old and tired voice. "I think I've heard the same voice before."

"I'm the village crier and bring you important tidings from the Tabih," Nkoh halted and announced nervously after a brief greeting.

"I thought as much and I'm not surprised," the old man declared with a chuckle as his mind went back to his dream. "So what is it this time?" he asked somewhat sarcastically, his shriveled hands clutching his walking sticks tight as he rose from the truneck.

"Something not too good for the ears," Nkoh said.

"I know, for happy people have no need for a gnukwabe."

Though Nkoh was merely the village crier and had nothing to fear from the man, his manhood shrank as he drew closer to him. He had always felt the same way each time he came to see him for one errand or the other. Heading towards his hut, the gnukwabe ordered the visitor to follow him.

"You seemed to have been waiting for me," old one, Nkoh declared with a tremulous voice as they started up the little, dusty path leading to the hut.

"Yes, I was expecting someone but I didn't know it would be you," the old man replied.

Nkoh had often wondered how a man could choose to live the life of a hermit, completely cut off from the rest of society, only contented with occasional visits from villagers who usually came to him with problems to be resolved. In his role as the village crier, he had had some brief opportunities to be with him but had never really mustered the courage to ask him any important questions concerning his own life. All that he knew about him was based on rumors circulated in the village. And what if he suddenly dropped dead, he thought. He was already very old and frail and should that happen, he would take all that he knew with him to his grave. By being courageous and asking him and preserving what he knew, the village crier imagined, he could be a vital source of information people would one day look up to long after the gnukwabe man was gone.

The village crier had often marveled on how the blind man wandered in the forest all by himself, plucking herbs, digging up roots, and collecting tree barks, stems and old bones he needed for his medicine. Rumors on him were abundant, with one of them holding that he had to sacrifice his manhood in order to be proficient in what he was doing. Another one maintained that this was the main reason why he tended to be very severe with those who committed crimes of passion. None of these things had actually been confirmed by him since his dealings with the villagers seemed to be restricted strictly to the business of curing illness, casting spells, foretelling the future, indulging in feats of exorcism and other nondescript enterprises.

When they got to the hut of the old man and sat down, while he listened very carefully, Nkoh told him about the incident that had taken place in the village and why he had come.

"This is very serious matter," he said after filling in the emissary on certain details he had missed out. "I can't recall when I last had an erection to bother what mischief it may cause but those who still have theirs should use it responsibly," he added with a loud laughter whose sinister nature he did nothing to conceal.

"You seem happy old one," Nkoh said suddenly but with reverence. He did not think of the remark or the reaction it could trigger before uttering it. It seemed to have come naturally.

"Which eunuch won't be happy with the story of an upright penis that goes astray?" he asked, and then with a seriousness that the young village crier had never heard or seen in him, he muttered between clenched teeth: "I'll reserve the best of my craft for the person responsible for this. It looks like it's a big fish, so I must use a big hook to catch him. He should at least have known better."

Any semblance of courage Nkoh thought he could muster to ask questions vanished with that chilling remark and gesture. He remained quiet until the old man announced his confirmation of

52

the day the spoiling would take place. Then gently, Nkoh rose and after bidding him goodbye, was about to leave. The old man sensed his discomfort and taunted him.

"I see there is a lot on your mind but you lack the courage to ask. Did I hurt you in any way?"

"No, no, old one," he replied quickly, fearing that any of his actions might have been mistaken for disrespect. "I just don't know what to say," he tried to lie.

"Sure you do, for just don't tell me that all the rumors circulated in the village about me leave you totally indifferent," he said. "Have a seat and be a man."

At this declaration, Nkoh trembled. It was as though the old man was reading his mind. The old man lived a very solitary life on a hill far out of the village and was not known to have close friends, so who could be telling him what the villagers said about him and the developments taking place in Bankim?

All the same, as it was the old man who had prompted him to ask, he felt he could not have done so with malicious intent. He decided that he would stay and ask some simple questions to see how he would react before dipping into his real repertoire. Sometimes it was good to damn consequences and try things, he thought.

"What is your real name for I know Bangsiboh is not the name your parents gave you at birth?"

"You're right for I only became Bangsiboh when I lost my sight and started walking with two sticks. In the language of my mother, who hailed from a village located several days walk from here, the nickname stands for 'two walking sticks,'" he declared in a rather friendly tone. "So you see how humanity crafted a way to remind me of my troubles."

"The troubles of this world spare nobody," Nkoh declared, trying to be consolatory. "You know kindness isn't what best describes the actions of humans here on earth."

"Tell me about it!" he exclaimed. "Isn't that why you're here?"

"Of course!"

"Tell me son, how come sane men wait until a woman becomes insane before they take her to bed and get her pregnant?"

the old man came back to a discussion they had long exhausted as though the thought just came to him.

"It also beats my imagination," Nkoh said. "I believe that it's only you who can provide an insight into this kind of conduct."

"Me!" the old man exclaimed as he roared with laughter. "How can a blind man lead those with eyes to see," he asked. "You really make me laugh son."

"Well, there's a lot you do that suggests a person doesn't always need eyes to see," Nkoh said, sensing an opportunity to pierce the mystery of how he obtained his herbs and plants from the forest.

"Why do you say that?"

"If you can go up the mountains and down the valleys to collect herbs and plants necessary for your trade, then I can only conclude that it takes more than the eyes to actually see," the town crier declared.

"In that I guess you're right," Bangsiboh said as he nodded. "You now sound like an old person. You told me you had nothing on your mind and now I see you have a lot."

"Well, you inspired me," the village crier mumbled, sensing how easily he had fallen in the trap of the old man.

"What else do you want to know about me, for I know there's still a lot?"

"Why do people fear you a lot?" Nkoh asked, this time probably just to keep the conversation rolling now that it was becoming interesting. He knew that they were afraid because they had seen him demonstrate his powers on those who strayed from the laws of the land.

"People don't fear me; what they fear is the form of justice I represent," the blind stated philosophically. "You know that my powers come from the ancestors and if I use it abusively, they'll strike me down. So that is why those who transgress the laws of the land, like the one who got this poor lunatic woman pregnant, have good reasons not to like me. I am an ancestral enforcer and crooked people do not like people like us."

The more time the young man spent with the old man, the more he found him interesting. But there was just too much about him that he could possibly seek to know in one session. After he had confirmed again the day the spoiling would take place, on the

54

coming Njuellah as the Tabih had proposed, he decided to take his leave and head back to the village.

As he went down the hill, he thought of the old man's reputation. It went far beyond Bankim. To be that popular, he had to prove himself. And just how efficient he was could be seen in an incident in which four youths of a neighboring village stole a goat. When nobody owned up after the statutory verbal warning had been issued, the villagers went to him. He vowed that if by midnight on that day the thieves did not come forward, they would all die, starting with the oldest and ending with the youngest. The entire village swore on that.

Before the villagers left his premises, in front of everyone, he buried a live goat, pending the completion of the rest of his mystical operation later on when he was alone. The thieves, taking this for a bluff, stood their ground.

At exactly midnight on the elected day, an ululation announced the death of the first of the youths. This was followed by another and yet the others. Like little chicks hit by a bird flu, all four had fallen just as the old man had predicted, from the oldest to the youngest.

Finally, Njuella was just around the corner. As time ebbed, the entire village braced itself for some high drama.

"This can't be allowed to happen on my watch," the old man, who, in a rare moment, had descended from his mystical, mountainous heights, cried out in the dark as he roamed the streets of Bankim on the eve before his big day. "Even I could see that she was beautiful," he continued with a malicious giggle, "hardworking and responsible and only needed a male, not some fox or mosquito, to share her dreams with. No man was man enough! Then she became insane and we now hear that she's pregnant. We'll get to the bottom of this matter."

The day elected for the spoiling finally arrived. All the men of Bankim assembled at the village square for the appointment with Bangsiboh. All, except one man. His name was shouted out and people were sent out to look for him everywhere but he was nowhere to be found.

Then a young member of the Manjung, who had been conducting his search deep inside the bush, felt something hit him on the head as he was passing under an avocado tree. It was the legs of a man. He looked up and saw the Tabih dangling from the branch of a tree with his tongue hanging out.

"Leopard without claws!" the blind man declared with laughter when the tragic news reached him. He then summoned Tabongwa, the acting Tabih.

"I'm here," he announced his presence to the old man when he arrived and they were together.

"Fine that you're here," he said quietly and went straight to the heart of the matter. "You already know the good news, so let me tell you the bad one," he prepared the visitor for what was to come. "I'm nothing but an old eunuch, already set to join our ancestors on the other side, but I can't leave without informing you that a real tragedy looms over this community as a result of what has been going on here."

"But how can that be?" Tabongwa asked almost in protest. "Chokoh breached the tradition and was made to pay for it, so what gets the ancestors upset."

"I'm only their messenger and wanted you to know how they feel about this matter," he said. "This community may one day be reduced to rubbles that you can't rebuild. You'll be forced to leave for an unknown destination, will suffer and be persecuted. You'll face floods, drought, locusts and diseases and many of you'll die until the right expiatory sacrifice has been carried out."

"But why all of us?" the Tabih asked totally confused.

"Come on Tabongwa, don't talk like a child, for you'll soon be the head of this community," he scolded the Tabih. "See the act of the individual as an extreme expression of what prevails in the whole community," he declared. "Who among you with large eyes to see, big mouths to talk, and strong arms to hold back people stood up firmly for the suffering girl, for the woman? The way I see it, the community never gave the woman a chance and it's only fitting if the ancestors don't give the community a chance."

"But what expiatory sacrifice are we supposed to carry out?" the Tabih asked, now sensing that real danger lay ahead.

There was no reply from the old man. He touched his arm to get him to say something but not a word was uttered. He pushed him and he pitched forward and then fell to the side. He was already dead.

11

Tabongwa sat on a rock under a baobab tree not far from his compound. Even though the base of this plant was very broad and believed to store water, it was not a happy memory that it brought onto this often dry land. Like the arms of a wailing widow, its leafless branches spread out mournfully against a light blue sky.

His mind went back to the incident which had taken place a long, long time ago when he was still young and was acting Tabih. How could he forget what Bangsiboh, the gnukwabe, had said?

"Soon I will go into my grave," he murmured to himself. "Yet the ancestral wrath still hasn't come down on the community as the old man had predicted. It might have been a bluff after all."

He rose to his feet and returned to his compound. He called for his daughter, Nangaah, who came running. He sent for one of his twin sons, Ngwafang, whose house was on the outskirt of the village.

"I plan to go to my farm located on the Ngohbih hills faraway," he told the young man when he showed up. "You must come and spend the night with your twin brother, Ngwalion, so that the two of you can effectively watch over your old, sick and frail mother, Sirimake, as well as your small sister, Nangaah."

Having given his instructions, he went to his house and then took his old antelope skin bag which dangled from a peg on the wall. He got some ripe avocados and many sweet potatoes and put them inside the bag. After ensuring that he had not forgotten his knife, he greeted Sirimake and Nangaah. He then came out of the house and started towards the farm.

The sun had long past midday and the intensity of its rays had greatly diminished. Encamped in the bush a bit far from the outskirt of the village was a strange band of people. They had come riding on some animals nobody in Bankim had ever seen. Even though they made some noise, it was not loud enough to reach the village.

These were the marauding Gainakos. To get to Bankim, they had been traveling all night and sometimes all day, for it was believed they lived in the distant north, many moons walk away.

Even though stories about them were sometimes recounted in the village, very few people actually believed they existed. Soon it would be darkness. With everyone deeply asleep, the moment the band was waiting for would have arrived.

So stealthy had been their advance up to this point that it had not caused even the slightest stir in Bankim. From their scouts, they had received words that the village was very rich in food, animals and young women. The message was catalytic. With great prospects of plunder and rape dangling before their eyes and filling them with selfish delight, they were cranked up into new fighting enthusiasm.

They had also been informed that the village had its own defense unit made up of young, tough men and women. This information increased the probability that the village could mount some resistance in an attempt to fight them off. To forestall such eventuality, they planned to take the village in a surprise, swift and deadly operation. It had to be so swift and brutal that any resistance would be nipped in the bud.

Most of the attacks which they had carried out so far were remote from this village and it was uncertain, therefore, whether the rumbles of those upheavals had actually reached its people. This lack of awareness might have created a false sense of security which would probably cause the idle defense unit not to be ready for them. Perhaps, the villagers had never even endured any form of aggression. This did not help them at all. If they were caught napping, they might not even know how to react to an attack.

Jibu, the commander of the band, was a slim, tall handsome man with streaks of graying hair in the braided locks creeping down by the sides of his small head. His little, bloodshot eyes, which cunningly kept track of any development taking place around him, hinted at a man constantly on the road, one with a huge arrears of sleep to reclaim.

From a tender age, he had entered the service of the chief of Walata as a member of the Gainakos, the band of mercenary soldiers he sent out to plunder and destroy neighboring and faraway territories. Over the years, he had risen to the position of a commander.

He was excessively charismatic and knew very well how to prepare his men for combat. He also knew what his chief, a man of very high standards and egoistic instincts, expected of him. Before they set out, he had instructed him to lay to waste all the villages farther away from Walata so that he could reign over a vast chiefdom.

As commander of the marauding gang, his records so far had been very impressive. He had put to the sack the numerous villages which surrounded Walata and had decided to carry far afield his foray.

By deciding to strike on Bankim, he knew he was overreaching himself. He was moving away from his supply base and any encounter which went wrong could easily turn to disaster. He and his men were now almost completely cut off from their base. In case of any stiff resistance, it would be impossible for them to obtain reinforcement. This spelled grave danger, for they could easily be wiped out fighting in such conditions.

Jibu was at the top of his military career and with the successful destruction of Bankim, he could go on retirement to live out the rest of his life like a prince. He would own his palace, land, servants and animals and, most importantly, he would preside over his own harem. What more could a man want, he pondered.

His mind was suffused with these enticing ideas when he reviewed his plan with his men. They were to close in on the village from all directions. This would enable them to plug every escape outlet and overwhelm and smash any resistance which came from within.

By midnight, all the plans had been thoroughly examined and carefully studied. He then ordered his men to mount and move to their positions and wait for a sign. Each wing of the band had been divided into different sections, each having its role to play.

It was around the early hours of the morning that a short blast of the alagatar, a wooden trumpet, signaled the attack. The men started to charge towards the village. It was still dark and a rooster had just crowed.

59

The invaders caught the villagers in a deep slumber and instantly set about putting their homes to the torch. They waited for them at the door and as they came running out to escape from the fire, they slashed and hacked them to death. In the heat of the attack and slaughter, there was general chaos and confusion and no form of resistance could be organized. This was exactly what the attackers had wanted. Sensing this, they pressed home their advantage and in a very short time, the village had been reduced to ashes and many of its inhabitants killed or captured.

Those villagers who were wise took directly to the bushes and neighboring hills. Attracted by the awesome wealth of the village, the invaders showed little interest to go after them. Instead, after tying up their captives, they began to empty the barns and animal pens.

With the operation over and very successful, the band decided to start back home with their captives and spoils. They had just gone past a well and were on their way out of the village, when one of the attackers who brought up the rear thought he had heard a noise like somebody coughing. He called on the rest of the band to stop and dismount and in the search which ensued they came upon Ngwalion ensconced in a small thicket.

One of the attackers raised his knife to strike him down but was halted by Jibu who was already on the scene.

"It isn't necessary," he ordered. "We don't have to kill people if we can take them alive. We need them."

The entire operation had gone without a hitch. Not a soul was scathed within the ranks of Jibu's men. The commander was delighted and saw this as additional evidence of his ability as a military genius. He knew that his chief would be very happy. This meant that he could gain the promotion he had long been waiting for. He was already getting old and it was high time he moved up the social echelon, from a field commander to a lord, with all the benefits which accrued to such a prestigious station.

He was, however, not a stupid man. He and his band had never formally agreed with the chief on what percentage they had to keep from the huge plunders which were being constantly hauled in. This often led the chief to take more than his fair share.

Jibu's men were not happy with such greedy inclination and started grumbling to voice their disapproval. It was not long before the commander picked up the signals of the discontent. He too felt the same way but was on a short leash to act because of the extremely important and sensitive position he held. After all, he knew just too well that he and his men faced all the risks of getting killed. And judging from the attitude of the chief, should this happen, there was absolutely no guarantee that he would take care of their children and wives.

At one point, his men came close to a revolt and it was only after he had appealed to their good sense by promising to allow them to keep a portion of the loot that the planned mutiny was headed off and they were disposed to take to the field again.

Bankim was the first test of that promise. The commander wanted to keep to it so he informed his men that only part of the captives and animals were going to the chief. He needed the loyalty of his men and knew that they were not determined to spend their whole lives as soldiers of fortune in the pay of a seemingly ungrateful chief. Even mercenaries too sometimes got tired of their lives, he thought.

With the murderous band on the road, Ngwalion felt something hard in the pocket of his goatskin kilt. It was his ndong. His father had told him never to part with it under any circumstance and had given him the list of ingredients that went into its making. He was required by his family tradition to reproduce an exact copy for his son if one day he should have any.

His mind shifted from his ndong to his terrible bad luck. He had almost escaped until that terrible cough came from nowhere and scuttled his plan. Now he was a captive. He took time to contemplate the plight of the other captives. They were all familiar faces in the village, even if he did not know each of them by name. He also noticed that most of those whose lives had been spared were young women.

Where were they being taken to and what did they intend to do with them, he kept wondering. He was not sure whether they were going to kill them, for they would have already done so. Whatever the fate which was reserved for them, he was prepared to face it. After all, was he not a twin? And were twins not said to be endowed with certain extraordinary powers? Did tradition not say that it was impossible to separate twins?

As the party progressed, Jibu's mind battled with what he would do if the chief did not give him any promotion. It was a day since the raid had taken place. They were still on the road and had three or more days to go before they got to Walata, the capital of their chiefdom.

After making sure that all the captives were properly tied to prevent any escape or uprising, the band decided to look for a place and stop for a rest. Most of the female captives were already very exhausted and could barely walk.

When the party got to a valley shielded from the sun and the wind by a huge rock, Jibu called on the flag bearer leading the way to stop. Then he started to issue instructions in a language which Ngwalion did not understand. He suspected that it must be the one they had been speaking the night they attacked their village.

With the instruction, all the Gainakos dismounted from their horses and drew their long knives. Ngwalion had tried to remain brave and strong up to this point but when he saw those knives glinting in the sun, his courage gave way. He felt that they were going to start slaughtering them and immediately intoned an incantation for help from his ancestors. The captives were huddled in the middle of a ring the attackers had formed around them. He kept an eye on the captives who were just next to the invaders because any butchery would naturally have begun with them.

Then, with profuse hollering and gesticulations, Jibu turned to the captives and it soon became evident that he and his men wanted the villagers to sit down. When all of them were seated, some of the invaders went around with bags from which they removed a kind of cake made out of corn and began handing these out to the captives. The invaders themselves ate some and drank milk from little calabashes they were carrying.

Some of the captives ate while others, especially the girls, refused to do so. It was, perhaps, a form of protest against their plight. Ngwalion was very hungry and ate his own greedily in the hope that more would be given. Instead, they were given water to drink.

While they were sitting, Jibu went around inspecting his captives until he finally came to a young beautiful girl. He looked at her from foot to head and then turned and said something to a member of his band. The man approached the girl, untied her hands and feet and attempted to take her behind a rock. Sensing danger, she tried to resist but was dragged along violently by the strapping figure. Jibu followed them. Then the man returned, leaving the woman and the commander.

Ngwalion was still pondering the game they were playing when suddenly a terrible scream rented the silent afternoon air. About twenty minutes after the dreadful cry, the two came back, the face of Jibu lit by a mischievous smile as he adjusted his dress while the young girl held down her head, as if in shame.

The commander's action encouraged all the soldiers to do the same. In units of about ten or thereabout, other members of the band selected young girls and retired behind the rock.

When it was time to go, all the girls who had been taken behind the rocks mounted with the men they had accompanied. At each stop, the exercise was repeated and this time, when food was being distributed, the girls got more. Some of them even had milk to wash down their food. This seeming act of generosity softened the attitudes of the girls towards their rapists.

They started to eat their food heartily. What was more, not only did the screaming cease whenever they disappeared behind the rocks and thickets, but both parties often returned smiling. They were now mistaking their foes for friends and goodies for good.

They went through several territories which had been raided. The gutted remains of villages were a clear reminder of the atrocities which might have taken place during these incidents.

After they had been on the road for more than two days, they came to a big stream where the party stopped once more for a rest. First, the now familiar behind-the-rock ritual was observed. Most of the men ceased to be moody after performing the ritual. Then in little groups which could easily be overcome in case of an uprising, the captives were allowed to go into the stream, have a drink and wash their faces in order to reinvigorate themselves. The animals were also watered.

Ngwalion was among the first batch of captives to be led into the stream. After drinking and washing his face, arms and legs, he returned and his hands and feet were tied. He wondered what might have happened to members of his family and to the villagers who managed to escape. He began to feel that he might never see the other members of the village who escaped again. He kept wondering whether his brother had survived the attack.

They had been on the road now for five days. They walked again for another day and came to a hill overlooking a valley. At the bottom of the valley, as they stood at the crest of the hill, they could see a sprawling village below.

"Walata! Walata!" one of the horsemen cried out in excitement as he pointed in the direction of the village.

The captives surmised from the gesture that he meant that that was Walata, their destination. It later turned out that it was the capital of the chiefdom which went by the same name. They followed a path which went down the hill until they came to the outskirts of the village. They stopped and Jibu selected some captives and animals which he ordered some of his men to take away. While they were away, the rest of the party waited for their return. In the meantime, he and some of his men took to the neighboring bushes one last time to go through the ritual. About three hours later, without the portion of the loot which had been consigned to them, the other group returned.

12

D arkness had just begun to gather. Tabongwa had finished the day's work and was about to prepare his dinner. He popped some sweet potatoes into the fire he had enkindled and while they cooked, he kept thinking of his family back at home. When the potatoes were ready, he took them out and after peeling them, he placed them on some banana leaves to let off the steam.

He rose and went to a corner of the hut where his antelope skin bag hung and took out some avocados from it and returned to his seat. He pulled his hunting knife which was always with him from its sheath and then neatly sliced the avocados into large oval pieces and put them by the side of the potatoes. Then he reached out for his calabash of water which was just nearby. Very gently, he poured out the water and began to wash his hands while humming simultaneously.

With his hands now very clean, he could start to eat his dinner. He picked up a piece of avocado and peeled it. He first bit into it and then into a slice of potato and with his mouth stuffed full, he began to chew. The mixture of the tuber and the fruit tasted very good and he ate with tremendous appetite.

When he had finished eating, he used some dry twigs which had been bundled together into a broom to sweep the peelings and remaining scraps of food into the fire. He grabbed his calabash and drank straight from it, without using his buffalo horn. The water came gurgling down and he swallowed with a loud noise. After such a dry meal, it was very refreshing.

He was now done with his dinner and could go to bed immediately. It had been a very tiring day, with the blazing sun lashing out mercilessly all day and almost completely draining him of his energy. He went to the corner where he had kept his bamboo mat. He took it, came and spread it by the side of the fire, making sure that he maintained a respectful distance from the very hot embers. Amid groans and the crackling of his old bones, he stretched himself out.

Then his mind went from his family to his work. He planned that he would weed his vegetable garden the following day. He stared dizzily into the fire, enjoying it as it flickered and crackled. Then slowly, it began to look very distant and blurry as his mind kept darting from one thing to the other.

Finally, his mind focused on his village, the place he had led ever since he was a young man. The long forgotten memories which came to his mind before he set out for the farm were back again. Then his mind drifted, farther and farther away.

It is the height of the dry season in the village. The plants are being scorched and bleached by the sun and are wilting. The ground has been losing a lot of moisture due to the excessive heat of the sun. In many places, it is beginning to crack. The rivers and streams are drying up and fish and tadpoles, in their final death throes, float on the surface, their bloated white stomachs exposed as they lie on their backs.

It is midnight. After prolonged insanity and agony, Yaa has just died after giving birth to a little girl. The terrible thunderstorm which started at night continues all day and is accompanied by a torrential rain. Rivers and streams swell and burst their banks. Crops are washed away and many huts are destroyed.

The reigning Tabih has hanged himself and he has been chosen to replace him pending a final confirmation from the Council. His first assignment is to name the little child of Yaa and he calls her Yabu, the ashes of Yaa.

Then water starts to fill up his hut and as he struggles to salvage some of his things, it continues to rise. It is now rising up to his mouth, threatening to drown him and everything.

It was at this point that the old man got up suddenly with a wild scream. He was sleeping and had been experiencing a terrible nightmare. The dream was a replay of an incident which had happened in his village a long, long time ago, when he was still a young man and had just assumed the prestigious position of Tabih.

He sat on his mat sweating, wondering what such a terrible dream could signify. Were the words of Bangsiboh coming true? He was still not sure but he was extremely worried now. Whatever the case, it did not seem to augur well. He had planned to spend another day at his farm, away from the troubles of the village and the noise of the children. He wanted to weed his vegetables which were sprouting in the midst of some invasive plants. With the dream, he decided to set out for home, the first thing in the morning the next day.

He remembered when Yaa had died a long time ago. There had been a sudden change of the weather which had been interpreted then as an omen of bad luck. The words of Bangsiboh seemed to have confirmed his fears. But still he felt an entire community could not be punished for the act of an individual.

He now realized that he should have heeded the gnukwabe's warning to move the village to another location and carry out sacrifices of expiation in order to appease the ancestors and ward off their wrath. The gnukwabe had foreseen an invasion which would completely obliterate the village and force its people to move. He remembered him also saying something about a curse upon the community because of its acts of injustice.

He had never disclosed to anyone what he discussed with Bangsiboh on the day he made his revelations before dying.

The old man kept awake, his eyes wide open, rolling on his mat and anxiously waiting for the first glimmer of light to head back home.

The night seemed longer than usual. Near his hut outside, he could hear rodents gnawing away at some nuts. It was a noise he had heard many times when he came to spend some time at his mountain farm and hideout to do some work, but now he was frightened, really frightened.

Immediately after the third rooster had crowed, almost at the crack of dawn, he took his small antelope skin sack and slung it over a shoulder and clutching his walking stick started the long journey back home.

He crossed the first stream and then the second and finally came to the small hillock which overlooked his village. He looked down and could not see anything. Even though the sun had risen high above the eastern horizon, it was still the morning hours. He felt his old eyes were being disturbed by the shimmering light. He rubbed and steadied them but still nothing came into his view.

He thought he was seeing a vision or having some kind of hallucination as he started down the slope to the village. As he drew closer and closer, reality dawned on him. His village was no more.

While he was away working on his farm, some invaders had struck in his village. Now, he could not believe what he was seeing. What once was a flourishing and vibrant independent community had been reduced to smoldering ruins.

Scattered here and there were heaps of mangled and partially incinerated bodies of mainly children and old people, some of them decapitated and others disemboweled. The huts had all been burnt down and farm implements and household utensils reduced to ashes and charcoal. Gone were the beasts and the year's harvest of corn, beans, millet and peanuts. There was no trace of the old man's own family, of his wife and children, nor of anyone who had inhabited the village.

He hurried to the spot where his compound once perched imperiously overlooking the sprawling village at its foot. All that could be seen were the charred remnants of saplings and poles which had been used to construct it. He visited the location of his personal hut and even went to the corner where his sleeping mat used to lie and saw nothing, not even the ashes. His pot of gris-gris which used to stand at the foot of his mat had also disappeared, leaving only the stone tripods on which it had nestled.

He pondered for a while. Bangsiboh could never have been wrong. He had predicted the destruction of the community. He then started to blame himself. He vaguely remembered all the things which the gnukwabe had told him. If he knew, he would have at least moved the settlement to a faraway and less vulnerable location. It was now too late.

It was easy for him to blame himself but how could he pack up with his people and animals and leave, abandoning a lifetime investment of huge cornfields, raffia palm bushes and orchards, the old man thought? How could he abandon the remains of his ancestors whose wrath he knew just too well?

He was aware that he had never raised the issue with other members of the village for fear it might start a rebellion against him. He needed good reasons to uproot an entire community and lead it to another land. And even if he found the reasons to do so, where would he have taken his people to and what would have been in store for them? And would a departure have removed the curse hanging over their village? There were too many unanswered questions for him to have precipitated things.

Now, as he looked back, he began to feel a sense of guilt, of exposing his own people to the calamity which had befallen them.

A long time ago, when he was still a small boy and had not even seen numerous moons, his grandparents had told him about the Gainakos, a marauding band which often arrived riding on the backs of hornless "buffaloes," brandishing long and glittering knives and leaving a bloody trail of death and destruction.

Since the stories they recounted were said to have taken place in the lands farther north, so far away that it would take over twenty moons to get there, he had shrugged it off his mind. He had never dreamed it would reach his own village, or at least not in his own lifetime, he had reckoned. He was stupid not to have taken their words seriously, especially after his meeting with Bangsiboh. How could he ignore the words of his own old wise people? He imagined that the price to pay for the neglect was too much.

He sat on a rock at the center of the burnt down and abandoned village, his head swimming with all kinds of strange ideas. He was brooding over what had happened and how it might have happened when his eyes caught sight of the image of a person looming far away in the savannah.

It was noon and the sun was shinning brightly, its rays preventing him from having a perfect view. With his hand held over his eyes to form a screen from the sun, he rubbed his old tired eyes to see better, to be sure that what was advancing towards him was indeed a man.

As the figure drew closer, its outlines became clearer. It was indeed a man. But who was he? Who could have survived such a disaster? His first instinct when it became obvious that it was a man was to run to the neighboring bushes and hide. On second thought, he shelved the idea. He had nothing more to lose and decided to wait for him on the spot, whoever it might be. His entire family had been wiped out, so even if the man turned out to be an enemy, he would rather face his wrath and join the others than flee.

When the man was a few hundred yards away and his identity had been completely unveiled, he discovered that it was his own son, his first child. He looked tired, haggard and hungry and

69

advanced sluggishly with a shuffle. With the rays of the sun pouring down mercilessly, he must have certainly had a very rough day.

The moment he caught sight of his father, all the pains and fatigue seemed to have dissipated and he rushed to meet and embrace him.

"What happened?" the old man asked as he clasped his son firmly, his heart pounding. "Tell me Ngwafang, what happened?" the old man kept insisting with tears streaming from his eyes and his worn out face weary with grief.

"I'm going to tell you everything Tabongwa, from start to finish," he retorted, still holding his father whose left shoulder caught the tears falling from his eyes. Finally, when he let go his father, he looked for a tree stump and sat down for a while to rest. He was thirsty and so went to the spot where a village well had been dug to see if he could collect some water to slake his thirst. As soon as he got to the edge of the well and pored inside it, he carried his hands on his head and began to cry bitterly. "Tabongwa come and see," he summoned his father who was still waiting for him to come and start his narration.

Sluggishly, the old man shuffled up and what caught his eyes filled his heart with great pain, a pain he had never felt all through his entire countless moons on earth.

Heaped one on top of the other, like sacks of corn, was a huge mound of numerous bodies of villagers who had been slaughtered and dumped in the well. The butchery was savage enough to convince the man that he would not see his family again.

The old man stood staring at the catacomb and his frail legs began to tremble. His son came and stood beside him, taking hold of an arm lest he was prompted by what he was seeing to jump to his death, to go and join the others in the afterworld. He could feel the old man quaking, probably overwhelmed by a sense of guilt as a result of the magnitude of the tragedy.

Leaving behind him what would henceforth be the mass grave of his family and fellow villagers, he mustered the strength to return to the village with his son. Amid their tears, they looked for and found a convenient place where they could sit and discuss what had happened.

"Now, tell me what happened my son," the old man resumed.

"I will, I'll tell you everything as I saw it, everything from start to finish." He rose for a while and looked straight into his father's face, as if to determine where to begin and then resumed his seat and began to speak.

"I came to the village to watch over the family as you asked me to do since you had planned to go to your farm far away in the mountains to work and spend a night or two. I was with the family until about midnight when the moon seemed straight overhead and everyone started to yawn, scratch and stretch, the day's farm activities having taken their toll. To avoid keeping our mother and sister up, Ngwalion and I decided to retire to his hut not far from the family hut, the place where I normally spend the night when I come here to visit with the family. It must have been close to the hour for the second rooster to crow. At the time I was still awake. I heard a great noise like the rumbling of thunder. At first, it was faint and then it grew progressively louder. It wasn't one continuous noise, like the blast of our bamboo trumpet, but was spasmodic, almost like the hooves of zebras stampeded by lions. The noise was interspersed with what seemed like human voices, vociferously screaming orders and hollering. I strained my ears as I attempted to pick up the message being communicated but failed to do so because the language which was being spoken was completely strange to me. With my heart in my mouth, I crawled to the corner where Ngwalion was lying. He too was awake and had heard the noise. Through whispers, we decided to sneak out of the hut and go in different directions and hide ourselves in the neighboring bushes to see what was happening. It was from my hideout that I watched what was going on. It was a surprise attack and with members of the defense unit scattered all over the village, it wasn't possible to assemble them."

"Why didn't you rush to the drum under the big tree to rally members of the defense unit?" the old man interrupted his son.

"Some of the invaders came from that direction."

"You may continue," said Tabongwa calmly.

"The invaders came like locusts, streaming in from all directions, riding a strange-looking hornless buffalo with a very long tail which ran very fast and made plenty of noise. Some of the attackers, mainly those in the vanguard, held big torches and instantly set about putting fire on our huts. As the fire swept across

71

the village, consuming each hut in a terrible inferno, our people were panic-stricken and came out running. Little did they know they would become easy prey to another group of the invaders carrying bows and arrows and wielding long, sharp knives."

At this point Ngwafang halted his narration and began to cry.

"Go on my son," his father urged him. "Go on and stop crying like a woman. We must get to the bottom of this."

"The knife-carrying invaders went to work, slashing and stabbing anyone they came across. There was total chaos and confusion in the village as many people, in a desperate bid to escape, even abandoned their children. Many succeeded in getting away, taking to some of the neighboring bushes, but the vast majority wasn't that lucky. They were struck down even before they reached the nearest thicket.

"Did you see your mother during all these confusion?" the old man interrupted with a question.

"Yes, I did. My poor, old mother, whose pace was like that of a chameleon, was trampled upon by one of the animals on which the invaders were riding, just as she came lumbering out of her hut. She let go an agonizing cry as she fell on her back and then became silent. I knew she couldn't survive because many other animals also stamped on her. Her cry still haunts me."

The head of the old man started to bop with lamentation and tears rolled down his wrinkled cheek. Ngwafang had seen that reaction several times in his short life. He knew what to do when his father felt this way. He halted his narration to give him time to absorb the shock and pain.

"And your sister," he asked after he had overcome his pain and mustered some courage to talk.

"Our little sister tried to escape by running towards the well but was instantly struck down. She must be among those who were dumped in the well. When the invaders had finished committing their atrocities, some of our people who were captured as they were trying to get away and whose lives were spared were huddled together and tied one to the other. I didn't even see when the invaders ordered them to put some of the bodies of those killed in the well. Too many things were taking place at the same time for me to keep track of all of them. Once they were sure that no house still remained standing, they went to the barns and emptied them. They stole our animals and chickens from their enclosures. As for the other things, they loaded them on their animals and took them away. They headed north with their loot just before the crack of dawn. Leading the band as they headed north was a flag bearer and a man carrying a wind instrument into which he blew. The instrument was broad at one end and then tapered off progressively towards the other end where he stuck his mouth. I can't describe the sound it produced because I've never heard anything like that before.

"The alagatar! The alagatar! That's the name of the instrument," the old man cried out, interrupting the narration of his son. "Sorry about that. You may continue."

"Still frightened, I waited in my hiding place until I was sure they had all gone never to return again, and then I came out to take stock of the havoc which had been wrecked. I had never seen or heard anything like that. I called out my brother's name and there was no reply. It took me a long time to recover from the shock. I was still in the village when the sun rose and some of our people, who had succeeded in fleeing and were returning to see what had happened in their absence, found me here. I thought my brother had escaped but he wasn't among them. I relayed a message using the village slit-drum hidden under the big tree, calling on all those who were still alive and listening to come to the village. They arrived gingerly in small numbers, first taking cover in the tall grass to inspect and be sure that they weren't being lured to an ambush or some kind of a trap. All of us, those who're still alive, aren't more than three hundred. The others are hiding out in the big cave up the mountain. I asked them to do so while I come in search of you, so that you shouldn't return and be stranded."

"Your brother wasn't still among those who returned after you beat the drum?"

"No."

"You did well my son," the father declared. "You did well to assemble those who had managed to escape. Now, tell me how the invaders were dressed."

"They wore white gowns, big billowing white gowns, gowns which caught the wind and bulged out as they rode. Even in the chaos and confusion, I saw it clearly, in the lights of the moon and torches. They seemed to be flying in their gowns.

"The Gainakos," the old man said solemnly, his wrinkled and tired face contorting in a sorrowful grimace his son had never seen before. "Those are the people my grandparents told me about a long, long time ago."

"Does that have any particular bearing with what we've got to do now in the village?" Ngwafang turned to his father.

"Yes. Son we're left with no choice. We've got to move, to go to another land far, far away, completely removed from these kinds of attacks. Things can only get worse if we remain here. The wilderness may have its own troubles but it's better living there than in the midst of some men."

"If that's what you've decided, then we should go to the cave where the others are still holed up and work out an elaborate migratory plan," Ngwafang declared to his father.

"You're right son but we can't leave like this. The spirits of our ancestors will haunt and terrorize us, as they've already started. There're certain rites we must perform to try to appease them before abandoning their remains here. Things are already too bad as they are and we don't want to make them worse. The rites usually go with a sacrifice conducted with a white hen but in the circumstance, that aspect will be postponed. At least the spirits will understand. We're just trying to plug some holes and reduce the curse which hangs over our heads."

Having decided on the sacrifice, the old man took to the surrounding scrubland, plucking this plant and then that one, digging up this root and that one, until he had assembled all the ingredients. He then summoned his son and led him to the shade of the huge tree under which the founders of the village had been buried and where the village slit-drum used for long distance communications stood. Before they set out, he instructed his son to gather a handful of some ashes.

Under the tree was a flat rock, said to be sitting directly on the head of the village founder. He was buried here a long, long time ago, when he died not long after the village had been founded. He sat on the rock and asked his son to sit beside him. From his pocket he drew the horn of a ram, dark with ages and stuffed with what looked like the fur of an animal.

"Ever since I inherited this when I was made the Tabih of this community, it has never left me," he told his son as he took off the fur stuffing and sprinkled some brownish powder from the horn into his cupped left hand. "This is ancestral powder, the link between us and this place," he murmured, grabbing a piece of rock with which he began to pound the various plants and roots he had collected and were now placed on the huge rock. "One day, if you work hard to earn this horn as Tabih you'll inherit it from me and will pass it onto another male elected to become Tabih after you," he said as he continued pounding.

"And what if the person who qualifies isn't male?" the son asked when the idea struck him.

With that question, the old man's mind instantly flashed back to Yaa.

"I had never thought about that, neither did my father, for sure," the old man declared as he stopped pounding and fixed his gaze on his son. "Let's not cross a river before we get to it. One day, when the situation arises, you young people will know what to do," he said with a sigh as he resumed his pounding.

"Why did you sigh?" the young man asked his father, sensing that he seemed uncomfortable with the question.

The old man did not say anything. He only shook his head.

With the leaves and roots transformed into a mushy paste, he poured the brownish powder on it, reciting an incantation as he did so. Using the tip of his forefinger, he took some of the stuff and applied it to the temple of his son, and then to his. He wrapped the rest of the substance in a leaf and gave it to his son to keep properly. He then put back the fur stuffing and returned the horn to his pocket.

"Where's your ndong?" the old man turned to his son and asked for the little horn full of charms bearing a specific mark which each male of the Tabongwa family acquires when he attains maturity.

"Here," the young man said holding out a small antelope horn stuffed with a dark substance from which the sharp end of a porcupine's quill protruded.

His father took it, applied some of the substance on it and handed it back to his son.

The cave in which the villagers were hiding lay westward, concealed from view by a huge boulder. The two men stood facing the east, their open right palms slightly sprinkled with some of the ashes the young man had been asked to bring along. And then the old man started to recite some incantation.

"Great forebears, with whom your children will continue to maintain close contact 'til the end of the world, we offer you this sacrifice to appease you and to make the bond which exists between you and us strong. You've seen the calamity which has befallen your children, perhaps the outcome of some neglect on the children's part. As we part from this land, which our tradition that you initiated strongly forbids us from occupying again after this terrible happening, we ask you to cleanse us and be with us as we part. Your remains haven't been thrown away to the hyenas. It'll remain for all time a site we'll remember and honor wherever we are. In keeping with the tradition, we'll carry out all the required sacrifices because we know what your wrath can do to us. Guide us and make us prosper wherever we go. Fill our homes with children and our barns with harvests so that forever your great name shall remain."

13

When the last word of the incantation had been uttered, Tabongwa held the palm bearing the ashes to his mouth and asked Ngwafang to do the same. It was now the time to purge their community of some of its bad luck. On the count of the old man, the two men blew away the ashes simultaneously and as they floated in the wind, they turned their heels.

"Now, without looking behind, let's go like a spear, let's abandon this awful place with its bad luck," he told the son.

They headed westward towards their destination, where the first phase of the sacrifice would be partially completed when the other members of the village had applied the paste on their temples.

The old man and his son took many hours to get to the cave. It was situated a long way and was linked to the village by a path which snaked its way up the mountain. Even though the old man was still very strong and often worked on his farm, he found the journey tiring.

On the way, he sometimes ran out of energy and had to be assisted by his son. When they finally got to the cave, the other members were happy that the old man had survived. In spite of their grief, hunger and tiredness, they flocked around him, greeting him and trying to obtain some information on what had happened to their village after they decided to hide in the cave.

"I arrived after the invaders had already left and there's nothing more to add to what my son has already told you or what you saw when the slit-drum assembled you," the old man declared as he was held down to a seat. "My son must have informed you that he actually watched what happened. I think that at the moment, as far as that incident is concerned, he's the most authentic and reliable source of information."

"What then will become of us?" a young man asked.

"I can't answer that question," the old man responded. "I think we have to come together and agree on what steps to take. However, open as we would like to be on this matter, our tradition strictly forbids us from rebuilding on the same land after such a bad luck. The wrath of our ancestors isn't something we want to face again at this point. We'll have to leave."

"Again? What do you mean?" a voice shot out from the crowd.

"Yes, again, because it would seem our ancestors aren't happy with us at the moment."

It was about three weeks ago that the invasion had taken place and the surviving community had moved to a cave. Farming tools and other implements had been fashioned out of stones and sticks. Various committees had been set up to tackle issues such as defense, feeding and other unforeseen needs. The old man summoned all the surviving titleholders and family heads in order to raise the issue of a plan of migration to another land. He knew from experience that issues dealing with the survival of an entire community could not come from one man.

"At the moment, we're faced with the task of deciding what to do now that our village has been completely razed to the ground. You all know what the tradition states, so I need not elaborate. I'm calling on you to take the matter to our people, to seek their opinion and to try to sell whatever decision we raise here to them," he declared when those summoned had assembled.

"I think we represent a broad spectrum of the people of our community," Tambih, a family head, declared. "Any decision reached here on their behalf is legitimate and binding. We must move fast in order to save time because we're faced with a crisis situation and besides we've got to leave this place as soon as possible. Seeking the kind of grassroots consensus which Tabongwa is referring to may only slow us down and even create division. Instead of going to the people, let's broaden this assembly to include at least a woman and some youths and then proceed with the deliberations. Ever since the invasion occurred many people have been living only on roasted bats captured in the cave. Most of the wild roots and stems gathered are being used to allay the hunger of the few surviving children whose constant wails are a reminder that we must act very fast. We must move fast enough to be able to save our community first from thirst and starvation before any other thing."

The bulk of the members of that assembly having agreed with Tambih, Yabu, the daughter of the famed Yaa, was invited to represent women; while two young men, Ngwafang and Epie, were brought in to voice the opinion of their generation.

Comprised of seven family heads, three titleholders, a woman and two youths, the Grand Migration Council of Thirteen, as this group became known, took over the running of the community pending resettlement and the reconstitution of the Council of Elders.

In keeping with the tradition, migration was unanimously agreed upon but a strategy could not be mapped out since people had not eaten for that day. The committee of young men in charge of feeding was out in the field in search of edible wild roots, stems and fruits. Hunting was forbidden until people had overcome the trauma of the invasion and had eaten and regained their strength. This way, they would be able to run after and face wild animals.

Finally, in order to save time, the Migration Council decided to embark on more than one activity simultaneously. With the food hunters already out in the fields, it met to work on a strategy for exodus and survival and to later communicate its verdict to those who had been away.

Tabongwa was first given the floor. He was the head of the community, an elderly and venerable figure, and was a reliable source of information concerning the Gainakos. Knowledge of the invaders would help the Council to make informed decisions on what to do and which way to go.

Total silence reigned when the old man rose to speak. After clearing his throat and taking in the Council, he put all his narrative skills to use, first relating what Bangsiboh whom few of his listeners knew well had told him. He then moved on to recount the story his grandparents had narrated a long, long time ago, when he was still very young. He talked about the strange animals on which the invaders rode, as well as the bizarre attires they wore. Ngwafang, who had observed them from close quarters, when the whole village was plunge in great turmoil and confusion, was called upon to provide more details on what he had seen during that terrible night of terror and massacre.

"I vividly recall my grandfather telling me that even though the animals of the invaders seemed so sturdy, they couldn't survive farther south where there're forests," the old man had added for good measure when his narrative seemed to have come to an end.

"Why didn't you inform the community about what the gnukwabe had said?" a young man asked.

The torments on the old man's face were visible when this question was asked. He knew he should have informed his own people of what the gnukwabe had told him, even if they were not prepared to go along with his plan. Now the blame of the calamity rested entirely on his shoulders.

"I didn't act well," he apologized. "I should have assembled the Council and discussed the matter with its members. What else can I say?"

The old man sounded truly remorseful and the people seemed understanding. As the moment was very grave, they did not want to drag the community into any discussion which could lead to confusion and division. At least, not while they were in the middle of nowhere.

"Why do you think our ancestors brought down this curse upon us?" an aged voice intoned. "After all, we've always made our sacrifices and everything seemed to work well."

"It's true that everything seemed to work well. It was so merely because we wanted to see only those things which worked well. It didn't mean that there weren't things which went badly. Bangsiboh made mention of injustice and exclusion in our midst but I didn't give those things too much attention because I had just become acting Tabih and there was a lot on my mind."

When the old man talked of injustice and exclusion, those who were in the village at the time and knew what had taken place turned and stole a quick glance in Yabu's direction. Even though their memories had become rusty, they could still recollect the plight of Yaa. For all she did for the community, she lived on its margin and was treated very unfairly.

Having answered the questions he had been asked, the meeting looked at other aspects of the old man's lecture. As he had expected, his lecture provided hints on the course of action to adopt. Even before he sat down, voices rang out here and there to orient the Council.

"If their animals tend to die when they travel deep into the south, it would be appropriate for us to migrate in a southerly direction," a voice hinted.

"Let the old man speak," Yabu declared, already sensing that the meeting might dissolve into chaos if people were allowed to talk out of turn. "We'll come to an open discussion later."

"As for me, I have nothing to add to what I've already told you," Ngwafang quickly announced.

It was Yabu who first took the floor after the narration. Silence descended as she started to speak. She talked about the death of her mother, of the appalling treatment she had been told she received in the hands of members of her village. She declared that in her numerous moons in Bankim, she'd seen and known a lot of troubles.

"Things hadn't changed much," she protested. She pointed out that even though vulnerability to attacks remained an overriding consideration in deciding where to go and settle, the survival of the community would ultimately depend on how closely knit it was and how people treated one another. She insisted that no human community could survive in the midst of prolonged injustice, especially one which tended to exclude others, not because they were bad but because they were of the "wrong" sex and too good.

When she raised the last point, contemporaries of her mother held their heads down in shame because each of them had in one way or the other contributed to her plight and final demise. Not a voice had been raised against her treatment by the community, which was tantamount to agreeing with it.

Other members of the Migration Council raised the issue of the availability of food and fine land to till as an important criterion to be taken into account when deciding where to settle. They were mostly farmers and lent their voice to a proposal to follow any river valley leading south.

"We must stick close to the river Noun valley whose water and fertile soil we can harness to grow our crops," they announced. "It'll also help to guide us."

None of them had tasted anything good that day and hunger and thirst were taking their toll. The team of young men that went out to look for food had still not returned.

81

The Migration Council finally came to the decision to first go west, cross the Noun and follow its right bank in a southerly direction until they came to the area they found convenient to settle, far removed from any attack and close to its rich fertile soil.

"That sounds like a very long walk," a member of the Council complained.

"It has to be, for there isn't a way out, especially if we intend to stay out of the reach of the invaders and at the same time provide ourselves with enough food," old Tabongwa declared. "Our progress is going to be slow so that those of us whose strength has been sapped by time can at least keep pace with the others."

The Council was about to wrap up its deliberation on the date of departure from Bankim when the young men sent out to look for food returned with roughly made wicker baskets of sweet potatoes and cassava and with bundles of juicy sugarcane. They also brought mangoes, papayas and guavas.

Huge bonfires were set up and the potatoes and cassava popped into them to roast while the starving community fell on the fruits and sugarcane.

"It seems the council held a meeting while we were away, so what has it decided?" one of the food gatherers asked Tabongwa.

"Well, we agreed that as soon as we've finished our meals, the Council will apprise the entire community on all the important decisions it has reached but since you've asked we might as well do that while people are eating."

While they were eating, the village crier went around hitting a little makeshift gong to alert everyone that an important announcement was about to be made, so that people should keep their ears open.

"We're leaving tomorrow before sunrise and we've decided to settle farther south on the right bank of the river Noun," the frail voice of Tabongwa tried unsuccessfully to scream out.

Since his voice was not audible enough, the town crier went around again beating his gong and, with his booming voice, repeated the information.

Like anyone else in the cave, most of the young men knew the big river but had never asked themselves where it led to. Still it did not really matter to them. They nodded their approval.

They were also informed that they would form an advance party to reconnoiter the trail to be followed and to immediately keep the people informed of any strange development. They agreed upon this to avoid the danger of the entire community walking into a trap and ending up being wiped out. The party would also stake a claim to any area to be colonized by starting to clear its bushes and prepare the site where huts would be erected before the others arrived.

By the time the dinner of roasted potatoes and cassava was served and eaten, it was already getting to midnight. The group broke up and went to their various sleeping places. It had been a very difficult and tiring day and most of them slept profoundly.

The young men decided at the last minute that part of their team would have to bring up the rear, which comprised mainly of old people, women and children. This decision was inspired by the fact that the community could face a surprise attack from behind. Should that be the case, they would come to the rescue of this vulnerable group.

In the attack that occurred on Bankim, many members of the group had easily fallen prey mainly because of their slow and inappropriate reaction to the invaders. Those who managed to escape and were part of the migrating party would require particular attention.

It was very early in the morning when Bankim, or what was left of it, got up. It was exactly three and half weeks after the village had been reduced to ashes. The entire community had already applied the remaining potion consigned to Ngwafang's keeping on their temples. It was a continuation of the cleansing ceremony.

With each member clutching a handful of wood ash and facing the east, they blew it into the wind and immediately turned their backs in an expiatory ritual. It was time to leave the land they had tilled for decades and where many of their ancestors were buried. They were to leave this land never to return to it again. It was the start of a long and very painful exodus.

14

It must have been around the year 1884. European statesmen were poised to meet in Berlin, the capital of Germany. Long before they reached the momentous decision to carve up Africa for their respective countries, some of their citizens were already doing brisk business along the West African coast.

In Mungo, where their activities seemed most hectic, news of their presence had already trickled into the hinterland. Most of the news being circulated, however, smacked of ghost stories, for few people could actually imagine what white people really looked like.

In Fombot, a small village located many moons of walk south from Bankim, two men involved in a barter trade were haggling over the price of arrows and spearheads at a marketplace. One of them was a blacksmith and the other a carver. The two could care less about the events unfolding along the coast and in Europe. Yet these events would shape their lives and those of their posterity in ways they could not have imagined at the time.

While the bargain dragged on, something in the blacksmith, a young man of remarkable stature called Ndah, remotely reminded the carver of his late father but he could not say exactly what it was.

He thought it was the resemblance but he had seen many people who looked like some members of his family. He was a bit surprised that he only took notice of the resemblance on that day. It was not his first time to see the blacksmith. Each time he came to the market, he visited the section where he normally set out his wares.

Sangbong, for this was the name of the carver, tried to shrug off the idea of the resemblance but somehow it kept coming back. He imagined that since all the people in the region might be in some ways related through a common ancestry, it was but normal to discover such resemblance.

As these ideas went through his mind, they kept on with their haggling. Finally, he succeeded in clinching a deal and the man dipped his hand into his pocket to get a kolanut and share with him. As he pulled it out, something fell on the ground.

With a quick glance, Sangbong immediately established that it was a ndong very identical to the one his father, Sangbe, had given him and which he was bearing even as they spoke. This immediately set his mind working. The man was carrying something which was a symbol of his family, Sangbong thought. Yet, he did not know of any relative he had other than those at their small settlement in Fombot. Could he be a member of his family? He simply could not establish the connection.

For one thing, his family had no tradition of working metals. At least, to the best of his knowledge, his father had never ever told him so.

He was still being assailed by all these questions when Ndah quietly put away the ndong and then turned and confided to Sangbong that his father had given it to him.

"What does your father do?" Sangbong was curious to know.

"He was a blacksmith."

Blacksmiths were very rare and those who exercised the profession were held in high esteem and were greatly respected. In the very traditional setting of those societies, they were on par with royalties and were very much in demand.

Sangbong could not conceal his admiration for the blacksmith and immediately thought of strengthening his bond of friendship so that one day one of his sons could be sent to learn the trade. He even thought he too could become his apprentice and thus would have an additional trade to widen his margin of survival. Things were becoming increasingly difficult and carvings were not very much in demand.

Still puzzled by the ndong, he decided to pierce the mystery surrounding it by asking some more questions.

"Is blacksmithing your family tradition?" he asked.

"I wouldn't really say so," he replied. "My father was a blacksmith but his father wasn't."

"Who taught your father the trade?"

At this question, the man's eyes brightened. He stroked his goatee beard for a while and then began to speak.

"It's a very long story," he began. "A long, sad story."

The man was increasingly becoming very interesting, so Sangbong pulled one of the stools standing next to him and sat down.

"If you don't mind, I would like to hear the story," Sangbong announced, adjusting on his seat to be sure he was perfectly comfortable.

"A long time ago, when my grandfather was still a boy, they lived in a village far up in the north called Bankim," he began.

As soon as he called the name of Bankim, Sangbong's eyes brightened and his heart started pounding with anxiety. He thought of interrupting Ndah but soon decided otherwise.

The reaction the mere mention of Bankim had triggered in him did not escape Ndah's notice.

"When I said Bankim I noticed that your eyes dilated," Ndah drew Sangbong's attention to one of the ways he had reacted. "Do you know anything about the place?" the blacksmith inquired.

"First finish your story and then I'll tell you what I was thinking which made me react that way," he said. "Even before we continue what're your father's and grandfather's names?" Sangbong asked hoping that this might provide him with a clue which would help pierce the mystery.

"I'll come to that later on," he said. "I think this segment of my narration is very important."

"Sorry about the interruption then," he apologized.

"As I was saying, my grandfather lived far up in the north in a village called Bankim. It was a prosperous community led by my great grandfather. His name was Tabongwa and he was the Tabih, a kind of village head. My great grandfather had three children: my grandfather, Ngwalion; his twin brother, Ngwafang; and their little sister, Nangaah. One day, while my great grandfather was away to work on his farm far away in the mountains, a group of strangely dressed invaders riding on horses raided their village."

It was at this juncture of the narration that Sangbong could no longer hold his composure and broke down even before he knew how the blacksmith's father learned his trade. All along he had held himself like a man.

"Please stop," he cried out. "Say no more, for you're a member of my family."

The need to know more about the other partner in trade now shifted from Sangbong to Ndah.

"A member of your family?" Ndah asked, very perplexed as he thought he could be in the clutch of a fraudster. "And how so if I may ask?"

Sangbong could read the suspicion on his face. "You see, we need not burn our fingers on the fire when we have a pair of tongs," he said as he dipped his right hand into the side pocket of his kilt and withdrew an exact replica of the same ndong. "See whether you recognize this," he declared as he brought it closer for him to see clearly.

Ndah took just one glance and immediately came to the conclusion that he was saying the truth. He could see the porcupine quill sticking out and the head of the mamba, a family totem, engraved on the horn which contained the ndong. Even with the irrefutable evidence, he knew that cunning was part of conning. He still had to pass one more test.

"Tell me something," he called out. "What happened when the village was raided?" he asked Sangbong.

"They burned down the village, emptied the barns and pens, put many people to the sword and those whose lives were spared were taken away as captives. My grandfather Ngwalion was among the captives seized and taken away."

He had given enough proof.

"What you say is the truth, nothing but the absolute truth," he cried out as they both stood up and embraced each other. For more than twenty minutes they held firmly close together, tears streaming down their eyes.

The poor villagers who had come to the market for commerce had always known that it was only a man who embraced a woman for that long. Now that it was a man holding onto another man, they felt something strange was going on.

A little crowd immediately started forming around the two relatives as they continued to cry. As soon as they were informed of the situation, people were so moved that they too began to cry and before long half the market was crying.

Back then, in this part of Africa, such an encounter needed to be blessed. And as soon as words went round, a man who came with his drum to barter started to play and another one with xylophones joined in. There was music but no celebration could be called such without palm wine

Palm wine traders began giving away their product for free. People drank and danced. In their own way, thieves also took part in the celebrations. Taking advantage of the atmosphere of drunkenness and confusion the event had created, they helped themselves to whatever they came across.

Late that day, the two relatives headed to Bangshe where Ndah lived. He introduced his cousin to his wife, Lem, a descendant of Yaa.

Had the old African saying that twins could never be permanently separated come true?

15

It was more than a year since Sangbong and Ndah first met at the marketplace. Not very long after the meeting, the communities from Bankim which went in different directions when their land was invaded came together to form one. In their century-old roving, they had lost many of their members to human and natural hazards. This problem was not as serious as the one of the ancestral curse still hanging over their heads. Until it was erased, they would never enjoy peace, stability, and prosperity.

The two men had discussed the history of Bankim at great length. Once a thriving and prosperous community, it had gone through a lot within the lifespan of only two generations. As the community moved from place to place, its people had known slavery and persecutions. Many of them had died of hunger, thirst, and diseases. More often than not, they had invested their labor and sweat in vain. Their crops were often destroyed by locusts, drought, or floods.

"There must be a way out," the two young men who were now leaders stated. "Let's hear what the gnukwabe will say."

The tiny dusty road which led to the gnukwabe's shrine snaked its way down a green valley. The two young men stopped on their path and contemplated his domain. It was not their first time to do so from the heights where they were standing. His name was Kwakala and his domain was vast, with his compound located right at the center.

When the two cousins had first approached him with their problem, he asked them to go and come back later. Before dismissing them, he insisted that the solution to their problem was not with him but rather with the two young men themselves. Now they were returning to hear what he would say, to gather some of his words of wisdom.

Kwakala did not take long to explain what was wrong with the community. As if he had lived the experience, he recited the Yaa incident and the troubles it had caused.

"What then do we do?" Sangbong asked.

"Your community is suffering because of lack of gratitude, of jealousy, injustice and outright meanness," he began. "How can a woman give so much and get back nothing in return?" he asked.

"Well, not everyone in the community was responsible for the plight of Yaa," Ndah began with a defense which had not withstood any test.

At this the old man exploded in anger. "Can any injustice last for long without the open or tacit backing of an entire community?" he yelled. "Look here, if that's the kind of argument which brought you here, I suggest you pack up and leave."

"I didn't mean to offend you big Papa," Sangbong cut in with some endearing words to calm him down. "We are still young and inexperienced and only came to listen, not make suggestions."

The old man smiled.

"Then you should listen," the old man declared. "The first thing I've got to tell you today is that your community must move from the land they currently occupy, for you can never be anything in a land which doesn't belong to you."

"Where then do we move to?" Ndah asked aware that the land is fertile and they had already planted many crops on it. But if he thought the old man had made an outlandish suggestion, what came next was even more disenchanting.

"Continue in a southerly direction and when you come to the first most appalling piece of land, begin to settle," he began. "Even though the land seems barren, it's strategically located since it's perched on top of a hill overlooking the surrounding lands. You're the blacksmith, so you settle on this land with some of the people."

"What then becomes of the rest of the people," he asked with evident anxiety, probably frightened by the prospect that the people of Bankim might be separated again.

"The rest will continue in the same direction, settling progressively under the leadership of other sub-chiefs as they go. Sangbong, who'll henceforth be the paramount chief, will do the

90

installations and all the sub-chiefs, including you Ndah, shall come under his overall leadership."

"Is there any logic to this?" he asked the gnukwabe. "Why leave a fertile land for an unfertile one?"

The old man smiled again at the question. He seemed to enjoy the curiosity of the young man. "The Paketes whose land you occupy at the moment are a warlike people and you definitely don't want to continue living under their rule," he started to explain. "Now when you leave them, they'll always be anxious to know where you're and what you're doing and if ever they realize that you're very prosperous, they'll come after you. The hill you occupy will be their natural route of invasion."

"So you're saying that as a blacksmith I keep the gate?"

"You now understand what I mean," the old man said happily. "You fight off any invasion and then your cousin who's a better organizer mobilizes the rest of the population from the rear. But let me also inform you that irrespective of the quality of any piece of land, it can only be conquered through hard work and determination."

"And then the curse?" Sangbong asked, sensing that the discussion wasn't focusing on the main reason which brought them to see Kwakala.

"When you're installed as sub-chief, you first acknowledge that the female ancestor responsible for the curse was badly treated and then, through some concrete action, seek to make amends," he turned to Ndah. "This is the beginning of the healing process, an attempt to establish a link between the past and present of your people."

"Does this have any deep significance which young men can't see old one?" Ndah asked.

"Young men never see anything," the old man roared with laughter. "Otherwise you wouldn't be here," he added with another round of laughter. "You see, the past determines the present just as the present is key to the future. Your ancestors may intervene in your lives but it's what you do that determines the direction your community will take."

"Which's to say?"

"The present more than the past will determine the nature of your community, for if you sow injustice today, don't expect to harvest happiness and prosperity tomorrow."

"But I'm still not clear on how to express gratitude to a person who's already dead."

"If she's already dead why is your community still suffering?" the gnukwabe asked. "It doesn't take much to heal the wound of a community. Recognize evil for what it is and always make amends and set justice for all as a goal towards which your community at all time strives."

"You aren't saying that everyone in our community must be just?" Sangbong cut in.

"Did I say that?" he turned to Ndah. "I think this one drank some palm wine before coming here," he said, pointing to Sangbong. This was immediately followed by hearty laughter. "Some will be unjust but if the principle that guides the community is one of justice and is respected by the majority, then all should be fine."

"But how can you account for the fact that many people in the community didn't see the maltreatment of our female ancestors as injustice," Sangbong asked.

"Two things," he said leaning forward. "When injustice lasts too long it starts to look like justice."

"And then the second?"

"The second may surprise you," he announced before stating what he had to say. "The second comes from the victims of injustice who by not fighting against it connive with it."

"Do you foresee us getting our notion of justice right?"

"Perhaps not too perfect because you're mere flesh and blood, but what's important is that justice remains a goal you strive to attain. I also wish to tell you that your community will receive some assistance from a very strange man. He'll come from a very strange land, a land so cold that human urine sometimes becomes as hard as a rock, one so far away that if you set out as a young man to get there you may become old on the way."

"Urine as hard as a rock?" they both asked at once and then looked at each other.

"Yes," Kwakala replied calmly.

"A land very far away?" they asked again.

92

"Yes."

"So how will the man get here to give us this assistance you're talking about?" Sangbong asked.

"He'll float in a house which travels in water."

"A house which travels in water?" their voices rose at once again. The old man was beginning to sound incredible to them but they hesitated to voice any disapproval before such a venerable figure.

The old man knew what was in their hearts but said nothing. He knew that what he was saying could not really make sense to them but he was only a messenger, voicing the opinion of the ancestors.

"Will the man be one of ours?" Sangbong asked.

"In his heart, he'll be in everything one of yours," the old man responded simply, avoiding to say anything which would plunge the two young men into further confusion.

"Has he been born yet?"

"No," he replied. "But his parents have been born."

In spite of what the old man had said towards the end of their session with him, when the two men left his shrine, they were convinced that a lot of unanswered questions on their minds had already received an answer. It was for them to implement what he had said.

16

The people looked very hungry and destitute. They had come across beautiful flat land where they had hoped to establish their settlement but their leaders urged them on.

"This land isn't good enough," Sangbong, who led the roving band, declared. "When the time comes for us to settle I'll inform you."

They came to a river which had burst its banks and were asked to set up a temporary camp. The river was located at the bottom of a very high hill. After the flood had subsided, they forded the river and started the ascent. Haggard and completely exhausted, they finally came upon a barren land at the crest of the hill.

The land was exposed to the winds, rains and sun whose continuous lashings had scourged it, leaving behind only bald red mounds and grids of gullies. This was a far cry from the lush, green savannah which kept winking miles away behind and in front of them.

"We'll begin pitching our tents here," Sangbong said to an incredulous mass.

"Here?" one of his followers asked not sure whether he heard the leader correctly. The man then stooped and scooped a handful of the red barren earth and allowed it to run through his fingers to prove that it was impossible to settle on the land. "Nothing can grow here," he cried out when it was confirmed that some of them would settle. "We left vast stretches of green land behind only to come and settle for this?"

"The land you left behind was also vast stretches of trouble," Sangbong responded. "With hard work and determination any land will provide for its people," he pirated the line of the old diviner.

They sat on the land and while waiting for Ndah to arrive, Sangbong initiated a discussion on the name the people would henceforth be called.

"What's the purpose of changing the name Bankim," a voice asked. "The name links us to our past."

"I do appreciate the historical relevance of your argument," Sangbong began, "but that name has a ring of bad luck attached to it."

"I see," the same voice resumed. "You want us to make a fresh start?"

It was in the midst of this discussion that Ndah arrived and after a heated deliberation, it was agreed that the name Wotikar should be adopted. It was the generic term used to describe all the villages in Dawa.

The name for the entire group had been selected. Now the most important task remained. It was how to erase the curse.

Ndah and Sangbong moved to a conspicuous position where everyone could see them. Then Sangbong who it had been agreed would be the paramount chief started to act like one. He took the floor.

"Great Wotikar people," he addressed the crowd using their collective name for the first time. "We're only great because we feel great, not because we've been acting great. Henceforth, we want to feel and act great, so that ours should be a prosperous people. We all know the calamities we've suffered because our forebears treated one of their own, a fine hardworking woman called Yaa, extremely badly. We need not recount the story for we all know it. We must break with that tragic past by recognizing that she was a very great woman. In recognition of that fact, we'll name the first settlement here in her honor. The settlement I intend to implant with Ndah as its head and sub-chief shall henceforth be called Yakiri. This, in old Bankim which many of you don't know, stands for 'Yaa, we're very sorry!' Does anyone have anything to say about the name selection?"

A murmur swept through the crowd. Everyone seemed pleased with the name selection.

"Many of you don't understand," Ndah began when it was his turn to speak. "We can't seek to make amends without first admitting our fault. To express it in another form, penance for

95

theft can only make sense after the stolen property has been given back to its rightful owner."

"This is a gesture meant to heal, to link us to our past so that we know what to do in future," Sangbong added. "As a gesture meant to heal, it can be symbolic and belated."

Late that day, the first Wotikar village was set up. It was Yakiri, my village. Its first sub-chief was Ndah, installed by the paramount chief, Sangbong. Henceforth, the titles of the paramount and sub-chiefs would be hereditary. The year must have been 1885, for the Berlin Act had been passed not very long ago.

17

ood news in Ireland has often meant good news for humanity. This became evident on a cold Friday afternoon way back in the late thirties as Europe was drifting gradually but inexorably towards war.

On this fateful day, two men in their early twenties sat facing each other at a table at the library of a Roman Catholic seminary in Dublin, Ireland. Outside, it was raining. The music created as tiny drops drummed on the rooftop and window panes was clearly audible. However, it was not loud enough to obstruct their conversation.

"Fr Sean," one of the men announced deferentially, "tell me how you got my address," he inquired of the person sitting before him, a tall, muscular and well- proportioned, white gentleman with blond hair and deep blue eyes.

The man talking was a stocky African of medium height and dark brown complexion. He had hooded eyes and closely cropped hair and was of a quiet, friendly and deferential disposition. He was a student at the State University of Ireland and was called Bernard Nso.

The white gentleman, an Irish Roman Catholic priest fresh from the seminary, was a young man of great compassion, courage and learning. To the question, he adjusted his cassock, cleared his throat and began to speak.

"Bernard," he declared calmly, "I got your address from my colleague called O'Neil as I indicated in my letter."

"O'Neil," the African murmured, lingering on the name as his face puckered. He was trying hard to stick a face to the person whose name had been announced. He did not want to create any embarrassment, for he had many friends who went by the same name.

"I mean the tall seminarian," the Irish stepped in, sensing some doubt.

"How couldn't I think of him first!" Bernard cried out as soon as the additional detail helped him to unveil the identity of the person in question. "How's he doing?"

"Fine," the priest responded with a smile. "He was supposed to be here with us this afternoon but at the very last moment, a pressing issue came up."

"That's too bad because I haven't seen him for a long time," the African confessed. "From your letter, I gather this meeting is very important Father, so I did everything to be here today," Bernard said.

"That was very thoughtful of you, and you may just call me Sean," the priest tried to make him feel at ease. "Yes, it's a very important meeting," he replied, adjusting again on his seat. "As I stated in the letter, I intend to travel to Africa as a missionary and have been reading very widely on the continent, but almost every country seems to beckon on me with the same urgency," he said. "Can you help me make a choice? Where do I go and which of the continent's problem do you think should first be given attention?"

The African paused for a while as he tried to figure out where to tell the priest to go. He did not want to appear selfish by asking him to go to his own country, but at the same time he considered it unwise to direct him to a land whose history he had only read about but whose inhabitants he knew almost nothing about.

"I'll have to be very frank with you," he stated when he finally broke his silence. "I know no more of the attitudes of Africans in other countries than you do," he confessed and then continued, "there're some cultural elements common in all the African countries but they're far from making the continent homogenous."

"Almost like Europe," the priest hinted.

"I'm happy with the comparison," he said before asking: "The English and Irish are next door neighbors but how similar are they?"

"We're as similar as a mongoose and a cobra," the priest joked with a smile which did not quite conceal his sense of national pride. "Why can't I go to your country? Couldn't that make a decent choice?" the Irish resumed on a more serious note.

"Ah the Mungos!" the student exclaimed with evident nostalgia as he leaned forward and began to pore over the African map which the Irish had now spread on the table in front of them. "You must have read a lot about them," he said as he paused briefly and stared at the priest.

"I have but there's a lot I can still learn from you," the priest responded. "Which of the Mungos have you been reading more about, East under Benge or West under Mikari colonial rule?"

"I've been reading more about Mungo West, especially when it came under Mikari rule after the first colonial master was thrown out of the whole country following the Great War," he began. "I also read about some geographical and cultural differences between the Sawa and Savannah Provinces which comprise Mungo West."

"I come from Mungo West, from the Savannah Province to be precise," the student said with evident pride. "Benge colonial rule in Mungo East is extremely harsh and I foresee an uprising there as African countries drift gradually towards independence. For that reason alone, I won't recommend it to you."

"Where precisely in Mungo West do you want me to go?" the priest asked as the two heads moved instantly and simultaneously to the center of the table to take a look at the map.

"I would like you to go to my village," Bernard finally made a selection as his long, thick fingers wandered and came to rest on a dot on the map of the West African country. "As regards the most urgent problem to tackle, it'll depend."

"On what?" the priest asked eagerly.

"On your own assessment of the situation based on your understanding of the history, culture and needs of the people."

The Irish could hardly contain his excitement as he drew even closer to take a look. He burst into a smile and adjusted once again on his seat. "Of course, I'd like to take God's work to the village of a friend but you must promise to give me more information relating to its history, culture and needs," he declared. "How's the name of your village pronounced?"

"Just as it's written," the student responded.

"Yakiri," the priest said hesitantly, glancing in the direction of Bernard to see if he had any objection.

"You got it right," he said beaming. "I'll provide you with a history of the village and maybe some cultural tips and then I'll let you to figure out the rest for yourself. It's the best and most exciting way to learn."

"If you say so," the Irish said. "I think we should begin with the history."

"Great!" he exclaimed. "Fortunately, I always have a copy of the history of my people tucked away in my bag," Bernard said as he pulled his brown leather bag leaning on a foot of the table closer, opened it and fished out a document. "Here," he said holding it out to the priest. "It was done a bit roughly but with time I hope to have to do more research, polish and then publish it. As you read through, feel free to ask me any question because the moment you set your foot on the African soil you'll be on your own."

"I'll certainly have many questions for you by the time I go through," the priest replied as he took the book with a broad, joyous smile.

He studied the title and the picture of a mask which adorned the cover for a brief moment. The title read: *Origin of Yakiri*. "Thank you," he said as he raised his head, gave the student a quick glance and started thumbing through.

"As soon as I'm done I'll return the copy to you."

"Oh no, you don't need to Fr," Bernard declared. "I'll leave you with that copy."

"Thank you very much."

"It's me to thank you."

"Now let's go to culture," he moved to the next topic. "What can you tell me?"

"I begin with the chief," Bernard said. "With him on your side, you'll face very little or no problem at all."

"How do I get him on my side?"

"Don't rush things and make him see what his people will gain from what you plan to do."

"What other thing should I take note of?"

"Africans and their dead and ancestors are something else!" he exclaimed. "You must approach those areas with a lot of

100

caution. They respect their dead and honor them with lavish celebrations. The celebrations may go on for weeks and nobody needs an invitation to participate, for the notion of invitation is sometimes foreign to them."

"What else?"

"Just remember that a stranger simply can't successfully live in the midst of Africans without becoming a casualty of semantic accidents," he warned. "Mind what you tell them and the way you interpret what they tell you. Also remember this: in human relationships, genuine Africans tend to be more philosophical than real. You're a brother, sister, father or mother not necessarily because blood link makes you one but because you live up to your responsibilities as one. For this simple reason, blond and Irish as you are, an African ceases to see these differences and considers you his or her own real brother if you give him or her good reasons to feel that way."

"This is really amusing," the priest said smiling. "In human relationships, they're more advanced than we are."

"This means that your task of promoting Christianity will be made easier by the cultural environment."

"What else do I need to know?"

"I wrap up with two more tips," Bernard said. "The first is that if you're fair and seen to be fair, Africans will all flock behind you. And the second: if you can take up something local and outdo the best native in it, then it's the surest way to bring the people closer to your ministry, to convince them that you're part of them and that nothing is impossible, if only they're determined and trust in God."

It was on this wonderful note that the two separated after a good meal of veal and potatoes. Ireland's loss would be Africa's gain. Unbeknown to the priest, about the same time in which his meeting with Bernard Nso was taking place, the new sub-chief of Yakiri, Tafon, just got married to Wirba. This union would lay the foundation for the tragedy that in some ways would greatly shape the priest's ministry.

101

18

S angbong wasted no time after Yakiri had been established. Within the span of half a decade, he moved quickly and created five other villages as the band advanced. Nkar came after Yakiri, Sob after Nkar, Sissong after Sob, Kikaikilaki after Sissong and then finally Kimbo, the capital from where the paramount chief presided over the affairs of the Wotikar people. All the villages were linked into a kind of confederation by a network of roads.

Towards the end of the forties, the first colonial power to administer Mungo had long been kicked out of the territory. This event had occurred more than two decades earlier. The power had been supplanted by two others, Mikari and Benge.

By this time, many developments had taken place in the entire colony. The ghost stories which had announced early white presence on the coast were increasingly becoming real. Nevertheless, real as they might have seemed, the bulk of the hinterland was still to actually see a white man.

Yakiri did not need actual physical white presence to determine whether its life was undergoing tremendous change for the better. Once a linear settlement strung along a narrow dirt road from Fombot in Pakete, it had rapidly turned into a great commercial center as it became the hub of major road arteries. Coffee and kola trades had expanded and brought a lot of wealth and not long after the village had also become the center of social life with numerous palm wine houses.

From Abakwa, which the new Mikari colonial administration had established as the capital of the Savannah Province, in the north of Mungo West, a road led to Yakiri and then continued to Kimbo. This major road was an extension of the main highway from Sawa, the other province on the coast. There was at least physical evidence that Yakiri was poised to receive its first white man. He was on the way.

19

It was in 1940. Bernard Nso was then a student at Oxford. Yakiri was already more than half a century old. Ireland was bracing itself for the looming disaster which was gradually engulfing Europe as the Germans began flexing their muscles. It was a prelude to their quest for world conquest and domination.

Back in Dublin Fr Sean had already received the letter confirming his mission to Africa. He seemed fully prepared. Apart from gathering information on all the challenges he envisioned, he had worked himself physically. Constant exercise and courses in gymnastics and Irish folk dance had built up his strength and stamina. He had been to the doctor several times to check for any medical problem and found none.

As the date for his departure drew nearer, he battled with time to finalize his preparations. He continued to maintain contact with Bernard who was particularly happy that he had elected to go to his village Yakiri. The priest's parents thanked God that their son had finally made up his mind to do what they felt was the right thing. They attended mass every day as they had always done in the past to pray that the Almighty should guide his steps.

It was April 15, 1940. The day for his departure had finally arrived. He got up very early and checked his things to ensure they were in order. After spending some time with his father who was sick, he attended mass that morning, the last time in his native Ireland. He then had another private discussion with Mgr McMahon, the prelate who had baptized and inspired him to become a priest.

When he returned home, most of his relatives and friends were outside waiting to bid him goodbye one last time. He was to go to the port of Dublin where he would board a ship to Bristol in England for the long haul to Africa.

The morning was unusually bright for the period of the year, and his mother and aunt accompanied him to the port for the journey to England across the stormy Irish Sea. Just before he was about to board the ship, they hugged him. He clambered up the steps of the gangway which led into the hull and before he faded out of sight, he turned around, paused for a while and waved to his mother and aunt whose eyes were already filled with tears. He was a week shy of his twenty-second birthday.

He fought back his own tears as he headed towards the gloomy corridors until he found his cabin. He went in, sat down and reflected on all the years of his life in Ireland. The pain of leaving his parents, especially his doting maternal aunt, Patricia Fitzpatrick, as well as other relatives and friends, was great. But he knew that that was what it meant to sacrifice in the service of God. He knew he was not the first Irish to do it nor would he be the last.

He was completely immersed in these thoughts when he felt a jerk. The journey had already started. He said his prayers and, with the exhausting activities which had characterized the last days of his departure, he felt the moment had come for him to have a rest.

He changed into a pair of khaki shorts and a shirt and lay on his bed. He thought of Bernard who had written from Oxford to inform him that he could not come to see him off in Bristol since he was about to travel. In the large envelope in which he enclosed his letter, there were two other letters, one for the sub-chief of Yakiri and the other for his parents.

In the letter he wrote to the priest, he called on him to work in close collaboration with the chief whose role would be crucial to the success of his mission. He also promised to keep writing as soon as he had his address and also to meet him as soon as he returned to Mungo West after his studies.

The priest's mind kept flitting from one subject to the other and then gradually, he drifted off to sleep. When he woke up, he went up to the deck and looked out at sea. The waters were choppy but it was not very rough. It was his first time to leave his native Ireland and to board a ship. He had heard and read of seasickness but he felt nothing, perhaps overwhelmed by the joy of having to fulfill his lifelong mission.

He imagined what the continent would look like when he got there. He had read a lot about the geography, the extreme temperatures and very high humidity, and the heavy rainfalls, sometimes accompanied by thunderstorms. He wondered whether he would survive in such heat. But more frightening to him were mosquitoes and other disease-transmitting flies, as well as numerous poisonous snakes which seemed to infest mainly regions with thick equatorial forests.

In Bristol, a priest of their order, Fr Henry Morgan, was waiting for him and as soon as he landed he was whisked off to a nearby Roman Catholic mission where he would wait until the day his ship, The Tropical Marvel, set sail for the coast of West Africa.

The schedule showed that the ship had three stops to make before getting to his destination, a small coastal city in Mungo West called Victoria. It had to drop anchor briefly in Dakar in Senegal, then Monrovia in Liberia and Freetown in Sierra Leone. The priest was thrilled by the prospects of visiting these places which featured prominently in most of the history books he had read.

In the meantime, he took advantage of his stay to visit places in Bristol, a city with a long historical tradition of navigation. He visited old sites where the rusty and battered remains of ships stood as a testimony to the feverish activities which once took place at the port in the good old days when mercantilism was at its peak.

When he returned one evening after one of his outings, Fr Morgan who had been making all his travel arrangements told him that he would be leaving for West Africa the next day.

"The ship sets sail at 9am," he announced to the Irishman who could barely hide his excitement.

That evening at the presbytery, he spent long hours with the priest chatting and sipping tea. Fr Morgan proved to be a font of knowledge when it came to the history of Africa and its people. With Europe gradually being engulfed in the Second World War, he predicted that the conflict would be so big that Africa would become involved.

The young priest felt depressed at that prospect, for he saw no reason why Africa should be made to bear some of the troubles arising out of European imperialistic inclinations and misunderstandings. The continent had gone through so much for so long and he felt that it was time for people to give it a break.

106

While he lay down that night, it was not about European conflicts he was thinking but rather about the challenges he would have to face. He would have to continue to pray to ask God to show him the way, as well as to draw on all the resources he had accumulated in order to make the mission successful.

He rose up early the following morning and got himself ready. He attended the 6am mass and as soon as he returned, he packed his things and was accompanied by Fr Morgan to the port. The place was bustling with activities.

Sailors were busy at work, some of them scaling rope ladders while the others were having merchandise loaded on board. As they worked they sang and the arias wafted in the sea breeze to the passengers already gathered at the quay. There were many passengers, accompanied by relatives and friends who had come to wish them farewell, and as they waited for the ship, they formed little clusters here and there and indulged in quiet conversations.

For a while, he stood with the priest and they continued to chat until it was time to board. He shook hands with Fr Morgan and promised to write as soon as he arrived in West Africa and then as the last person in the queue went past him, he joined in. Very soon he was clambering up the gangway and his mind became suffused with images of Africa. He was excited and his heart began to beat wildly. He had waited for this moment for so long and finally God had made it come true.

Once the ship was out at sea, he kept mostly to his room, dedicating most of his time to prayers and meditation. He had no illusion about the work as a missionary which awaited him in Africa. It was going to be extremely difficult but with the support he had been promised by numerous church and philanthropic organizations in Ireland and other parts of Europe, he was convinced that he could hold his own. To be able to work with Africans successfully, he would have to look at things from their own point of view before proposing whatever changes he planned to initiate.

He knew that development was best when it was collective and came directly from the people. He would, therefore, have to resort to all sorts of strategies to galvanize the local population into action. In the quest for progress, ignorance and some customs had always proved to be stumbling blocks, so he had decided to make the starting of a school and church the pillar of all his activities.

Some of the ailments affecting the local population did not need much to eradicate. The consumption of iodized common salt, for instance, could help check the prevalence of goiter. Similarly, the breeding grounds of malaria-transmitting mosquitoes could be removed by cutting down bushes and draining ponds and stagnant water.

It was his ambition to start where the villagers had stopped in their development efforts. Respecting simple rules of hygiene, carrying out safe practices at workplace, and eating a balanced diet were among some of the things which, if the villagers were induced into doing, would radically bring down the mortality rate.

Support from abroad would only come in to tackle more severe issues. The people, he figured, should not be made to believe that foreign assistance could do everything. Such a trend could lead to a dangerous dependency syndrome, the worst nightmare of any aid donor.

While these ideas went through his mind, he made note of them. From time to time, especially when it was a bright day, he would go up to the deck and stare out at the ocean. When the sun stood high up and the sky was blue, its waters were serene and its surface, sometimes, wrinkled into countless ripples by the caress of the sea breeze. Dotted here and there were some aquatic creatures, with their bodies barely visible under the water's surface.

They had been at sea for about two weeks when they finally came to Dakar, a port city in Senegal. Its reputation in maritime activities seemed to be overshadowed by St Louis, which was founded and named after Louis Fadherbe, a French empire builder.

As they approached Dakar, the first thing which caught the sight of the young priest as he watched from the deck was an island just off the coast with a huge castle. He had read about the notorious Slave House which the Dutch constructed and which served as a storehouse for slaves captured on the mainland. Here, the slaves were kept chained in dungeons and underground channels for months while awaiting transportation, mainly to America and the Caribbean.

For a time, slavery overshadowed everything else in his mind and it was only eerily that he took notice of the multitude of

108

dark faces which greeted the arrival of the ship with a frenzy of activities.

As soon as it dropped anchor, they came hurriedly in their little canoes, dark, tall, huge muscular men. They dug their oars into the choppy waters to propel their crafts which rose and descended on the corrugated surface.

Perched high up on the deck of the ship, the priest looked down and could hear their voices ringing out with what he imagined could be orders. The language they spoke was totally strange and reached him only as a concatenation of sounds, occasionally interspersed with laughter.

His mind was immersed in the subject of slavery. For a while it seemed completely lost at understanding some human actions. He was trained as a priest to understand humans in order to better deal with them, but some of their actions were still serious cause for concern. He could not fully establish the main underlying cause of the commerce in humans which lasted for about four hundred years. Greed? Hate? Race?

After fumbling with these ideas, he came to the conclusion that the slave trade was a consequence of mercantilist greed, while the numerous pogroms and other race related violence known throughout history could not have been inspired by anything other than hate.

The persecution of one group by another, he thought for a while, often had no logic behind it. Often persecuted were those who historically had been persecuted. It could even degenerate into a kind of unwritten global conspiracy in that while a traditionally persecuted group faces genocide, the world remains silent. Sometimes, persecution could even become a psychic disorder where the only excuse for ongoing persecution was the accumulation of the guilt of past persecution. In any case, he concluded that in spite of man's irrepressible quest for self-deification, he remained just what he was – a man.

He sought solace in the mission he had ahead of him in Africa, evidence that all was not lost and that there was another plane where human interaction transcended the narrow question of race. He was confident that the looming disaster which hung over humanity as Europe gradually drifted towards war would be another human exercise in futility. Out of the ashes of the wickedness, humankind would emerge even stronger because it was God's will and not man's that the world should survive. It had always done so and why not this time!

From the plight of the African through the Native American to humanity, his mind danced to and fro but he had faith in God, in Him alone.

He could not recall how many hours they had spent in Dakar when the ship began to steam out of the port. So submerged was his thought in its subject that he seemed to see the castle in a dream as it drifted farther and farther away. The ship continued its voyage down the coast of West Africa, towards the Gulf of Guinea.

20

As they drifted progressively towards the tropics, the hotter it became. Fr Sean could feel sweat streaming down his whole body. He had changed into light cotton attire more adaptable to the tropical climate but he experienced very scant improvement. It was extremely humid and this made things worse.

Once the ship was far out at sea, the sea breeze tempered the heat and he felt much better. He began to imagine how he would cope with such a climate and felt relieved that it would not be that hot in Yakiri, at least from what he had gathered from Bernard and his readings. He spent most of his time on the deck, indulging in a conversation with whomever he met with a good knowledge of Africa and from whom he could learn something.

Most of the people he discussed with were missionaries returning from holidays in Europe. They were based, for the most part, in Liberia and Sierra Leone, two other ports of call for the ship before they got to Victoria where he would disembark.

It was one hot afternoon when their ship sighted a city faraway, the iron sheets of the roofs of houses glinting in the sun.

"Which place is that?" he turned to an old missionary.

"We're heading towards Liberia and what you're seeing is the city of Monrovia," he said. "Liberia means the 'land of liberty.' It was founded in the mid-nineteen century by the Americans as a colony to resettle freed slaves. Its capital city, Monrovia, was named after the US President James Monroe."

As the ship drew closer to the capital, Fr Sean saw flags fluttering. The flag bore a close resemblance to the Star Spangled Banner. It was a brief stop, to offload some goods and allow certain passengers to disembark.

From Liberia, the ship continued its way to Sierra Leone, the next port of call. It was next door. The name of the country's capital, Freetown, spoke for itself, for it was set up by the British to resettle their own slaves. It was this example which seemed to have inspired the creation of Liberia.

Freetown was the fruit of the efforts of some English abolitionists such as Thomas Clarkson and Granville Sharp. Once it had been formed, liberated slaves stranded in the streets of London were resettled there. The population of the town grew rapidly as British warships, which regularly patrolled the high seas to enforce the ban on the trade, hauled in other slaves captured from the ships of nations still attracted to the profits of the traffic in humans. When the British failed to subdue the rebellious maroons in Jamaica, they reached an agreement with their leader in which some of them were shipped to the settlement.

On their way to Freetown, Fr Sean met with a remarkable Englishman with an encyclopedic memory of events which had taken place in Sierra Leone. He told him of a wonderful miracle involving Ajayi Crowther, the first Anglican bishop of the Niger. To the young priest, it was added proof that it was God's will which always prevailed.

The Englishman recounted the story of how Ajayi was kidnapped from his native Nigeria as a child and sold into slavery. A British man-of-war intercepted the ship in which he was being transported to America, and all its human cargoes, including young Ajayi, were resettled in Freetown. He attended school there and proved to be a very brilliant student and was later trained to become a priest and was ordained. He eventually went to England where he was consecrated a bishop and dispatched to the Niger region as a missionary.

His mother was in one of the congregations which received the prelate and when she saw him, now bearing the rather strange name Crowther, something in his appearance remotely struck her as if he resembled one of her sons who went missing a long, long time ago. The child having long been concluded dead and all the celebrations and rituals for this purpose having been conducted, she was not quite sure, assuming it could have been a mere resemblance or perhaps the persistence of the maternal desire that she would one day find her missing son. Every single attempt to shrug off the feeling as wishful thinking having failed, she decided to use a trick to verify if he were indeed her son.

112

Now the old woman was sitting right in front of the church which housed the congregation and when Crowther, who was within a whisper, was looking away, she cunningly murmured to his hearing his African name, Ajayi, to see if that would trigger a reaction. She reckoned, and rightly so, that since he went missing when he was already a small boy, the last thing he would forget was his name.

The first time she called the name, he turned and looked and, with no sign that the voice was being directed at him, he continued with what he was doing, probably suspecting that it might also be the name of one of the congregants. The old woman tried her experiment again and it triggered the same reaction. The second call having confirmed the first, she was now certain that Crowther was her son who went missing.

Immediately, the games came to an end. She went up to him and asked him if he had once bore the name Ajayi and when he consented, she took him in her embrace, clasping him tightly and, amid tears of joy, told him that she was his mother. It was one of the greatest family reunions in human history.

While the English recounted the tale, Fr Sean listened with all ears, enthralled by the unfolding of the miracle. He bade the man farewell as he clambered off the ship at Freetown. Temperatures continued to be high and the sweat and stickiness they caused made the priest very uncomfortable. He knew that these were some of his rites of passage and that once he became used to his new environment, things would become much better for him.

The ship took to the sea once again for the final lap of the voyage and Fr Sean braced himself for the inevitable cultural shock which awaited him. He had read and heard a lot about Mungo but still he was not convinced that it was enough to prepare him for the kind of differences he expected.

When the ship finally dropped anchor in Victoria, it had spent a month on the way. Fr Sean came off at Bota, a small district in Victoria, and the first spectacle which greeted his eyes were many Black people at work. It was his very first time to see a large number of them from such a close range.

The priest was over 6ft and built like a boxer and in most of the literature he had read, Black people were depicted physically as big, tall and strong. Yet this description seemed to have fallen short for those he was looking at. For the most part stevedores recruited to do various odd jobs at the port, they seemed to him a special breed selected mainly on the criteria of muscles, height and strength. Most of them worked bare body, with the strands and ripples of the bulging muscles glistening in the late afternoon sun. They sang as they worked, labor being one of the outlets for music with which the African culture seemed particularly endowed.

On the quay, a priest who ran a mission and secondary school at Gbea, a small town just inland, had come to meet him.

"I'm Mulligan and I was expecting you here yesterday," the priest introduced himself smilingly with a hand stretched out.

"The sea was very rough and this slowed down the pace of the ship," Fr Sean replied as he clasped and shook his hand vigorously.

"I'll take you to your hotel and we'll come back for your goods tomorrow," he told Fr Sean. "I've already discussed that with an official at the customs who'll prepare everything before we arrive."

The priest had come in an old Land Rover jeep in which he stacked the suitcases of the Irish and then they drove off to a hotel at the beachfront which went by the name of Atlantic Beach. He took up lodging at the hotel while waiting for the next and final phase of his trip to the hinterland.

21

The hotel was situated just next to a botanical garden. The garden was very green and made up of different types of tropical plants set in a park with huge mounds of volcanic ashes dotted here and there. The park covered about a square mile and was crisscrossed by numerous streams and paths. The streams flowed noisily over beds of black volcanic rocks. In areas where the streams were shallow, the rocks were visible and some of them had been rendered smooth by the constant abrasion of sand brought down from the surrounding hills by rain water. Sometimes, the velocity of the streams was increased by the gradient of the land and where water ran into a bank, a gorge had been carved out through the slow process of attrition.

Atlantic Beach was a hotel built in pure Mikari tradition and seemed a vantage observatory to look out at sea. Not far away were tiny islands covered with lush green vegetation. On some of them, feathers of smoke went spiraling heavenwards as the island dwellers lit fire to prepare food.

Sometimes, especially on a bright day, the dwellers could be seen in small canoes. From the distance of the hotel, they appeared somewhat hazy, with the only thing which was often clearly visible being their shiny white fishing nets. When they were cast, they sailed out in a wide circle before landing on the shimmering water surface.

Victoria was founded by Alfred Saker, a Mikari Baptist missionary. He christened the town after the Queen of England. It was located just at the foot of the Mount Fako, an active volcano which soared to an impressive 13,370 ft and enjoyed the reputation of having the highest point in West Africa.

In the Antiquities, an expedition was said to have been sent to the Gulf of Guinea by the Egyptian king Nechao. This account held that it was led by Carthaginian sailors under Hanon. The seamen sighted the mountain in the midst of an eruption. Frightened, they instantly turned their tails and hurried away from the scene of the eruption and named the mountain "Chariots of the Gods."

The garden and the beaches were not the only things which attracted the young priest. From the small library of the hotel, he checked out a book in which he learned that the first colonial power in Mungo made the town the head office of the numerous palm tree, rubber and banana plantations which streaked along most of the coastal areas. He had about a week to rest and sort out his things before heading to the hinterland where so many basic items would be hard to find.

He spent a week at the hotel where the Mikari governor of the territory, as well as some priests and nuns, paid him a visit.

In the morning of the day of his departure, two jeeps which were to transport him and his luggage arrived. He found himself face to face with three people: Fr Mulligan, Kura, the driver of one of the jeeps, and the one of the other, Toroki.

Fr Mulligan told him that the vehicles had been provided by the governor to convey him and his things to Abakwa, situated about a hundred and eighty miles inland, where some people from Yakiri were waiting for him with horses to complete the last stretch of the journey which seemed impossible with a lorry at that period of the year.

When everything was ready and it was time to go, he boarded with Toroki. Toroki was a calm but jovial fellow and prepared the visitor for the journey by telling him it would be a very tough and rough ride.

Picking their way along an unpaved, battered road which seemed to skirt the base of the Fako Mountain, the two vehicles sneaked through an infinite chain of banana and rubber plantations. It had not rained for the past three days and the progress of the vans kicked up a storm of dust which sent pedestrians and beasts flying for cover in the surrounding bushes.

In K-town, where the road became inland bound, the last vestiges of Western civilization seemed to have been left behind with the equatorial forest growing progressively thicker. The vehicles rumbled on, nosing their way through the verdure like a pig rummaging for food, the hum of their engines seemingly

116

magnified tenfold as it echoed on the endless floral walls of tall trees and thick undergrowth flanking both sides of the roads.

They came upon a thick mound at the center of the road.

"What's that?" the priest asked.

"Elephant shit," Toroki replied as he flashed a quick glance in the direction of the priest. "There're lots of the animals in this area."

The lorry that Fr Sean and Toroki rode was leading the way. When it came to the base of an escarpment, it screeched to a halt and, without uttering a word, the driver came off and went to the back. He pulled a canvas tarpaulin and hurled it over the shiny metal frame and began to strap it in place while the priest, who had also alighted, gave him a helping hand.

"We don't want the rain to start before we do this," Toroki said as his eyes scanned the sky where dark clouds had started accumulating. "Sometimes the rains can be so sudden and heavy that before we complete this operation we're soaked wet and some things have been damaged by water."

They had just finished and were about to get into the van when they heard a loud trumpeting sound.

"Elephants!" the driver exclaimed as he nudged the priest. "You'll see them when they're crossing the road."

While they were busy attaching the tarpaulin, Kura caught up with them and did the same. They waited with bated breath as the colossi smashed their way through the thicket, snapping up and devouring plants and tree branches. After waiting for about twenty minutes or so, the proboscis of an elephant stuck out of the bush about thirty yards ahead from where they stood.

Fr Sean already had his camera set and was just waiting to click. The head of the beast emerged, with large ears flapping and little eyes staring warily, followed by the whole body as it lumbered into the road, a calf in tow. Very soon a large herd majestically crossing over to the other side of the road had blocked the entire passage. The priest took pictures as the animals were crossing.

It was the first time the priest had seen a herd of elephants live in the wild and he found it to be really awesome. For a time, the animals dominated their conversation with Toroki telling him weird stories of some wizards who transformed themselves into the beast to go and destroy the crops of their enemies.

He recounted a story of a man who once did that and when the animal was shot in the jungle, the man cried out and died at home. His cry attracted the attention of some neighbors who came running. They found the dying man in a pool of blood, a gaping hole on his side. It turned out that the elephant had been shot in the side.

The priest did not know what to believe as he stared incredibly at the driver.

"I know you don't believe me, but since you're in Africa it's needless trying to convince you because you'll have the opportunity to convince yourself," he declared as he started the lorry and accelerated up the slope.

They went past small villages and hamlets, leaving surprised and dumfounded pedestrians cowering in a cloud of dust. Others who had caught sight of the advancing vehicles and retreated far into the bush to avoid dust or flying pellets waved.

They had been driving for about eight hours when they came to a town called Mamfe. It was strategically located, for it was on a road junction. There were vehicles from neighboring Nigeria, from K-town and from Abakwa and the town buzzed with business activities. They drove to the front of a house and then parked their vehicles.

"That's a nice restaurant run by an Ibo woman," Toroki said to Fr Sean as he pointed to a house bearing the sign: Oyoyo Restaurant. "I'm starving."

A true Irish, it was not courage or a sense of adventure which the priest lacked.

"Sure, let's go there and have a bite," he declared as he drifted towards the house the driver had indicated. "I'm also starving."

Three minutes later, they were sitting in a small restaurant with the menu scrawled on a piece of plank hanging from a nail on the wall. The two drivers were already seated and were only waiting for the waiter to come over to them so that they could make their order.

Still standing and looking through a menu which did not make any sense at all, the priest began to feel that he would need some help in deciding what to eat.

"What does gari and eru look like?" he turned to Toroki to obtain more information on the first item on the menu.

"Gari is a flour made out of a root crop called cassava and eru is a wild, hard vegetable steamed with water leaves or spinach and mingled with smoked fish, an assortment of local spices and palm oil," he declared. "I think you'll like that."

"Like that!" Kura protested. "Father should go gradually with these local meals and start with items that he knows."

"What do you mean by 'start with items he knows'!" Toroki replied. "When we first met him, he was sweating profusely but look at him now. He isn't sweating as before in spite of the heat. He's in Africa and should take his chances."

He had followed the argument between the two drivers with a lot of amusement and felt Toroki understood him better. However, the caution of Kura was worth heeding and so he decided to go through the entire list before making his choice.

"What's timbanambusa and banga soup?" he moved on to the next item.

"That should have been good for you but the chili in it is so hot that it'll instantly fry your intestines and lips. In this heat, it isn't a good choice," Toroki warned. "As for its composition, timbanambusa is steamed grated cocoyam dumplings while banga soup is made out of palm nuts, spices and pork."

"Achu and pepper soup?"

"Well, the meal condemns itself, for pepper as you know is very, very hot chili," Toroki stated. "It's a kind of timbanambusa from a different cooking angle. While you grate the cocoyam in the first case before steaming, in the second you steam before pounding and the two soups are all made from palm oil, the first directly from the nuts and the second when the oil has already been extracted from the nuts."

"Kibane and fresh vegetables?"

"Kibane is the flour of corn which has been transformed into a steaming paste with boiling water and is served with heavily spiced and stewed fresh spinach. You may well take that because it's the staple food of the people of Yakiri," Kura hinted.

After going through the list which comprised strange items such as koki, ogwono, egusi pudding, ndole, zamge, moyondo, katanga, kwem, cassava, bongo chobi, condry, roasted fish, cane rat

119

and a whole lot more, he finally settled down on his seat and asked for some roasted fish, kibane and fresh vegetables.

When the dishes of food were brought and stood in front of him, he waited for a while, hoping that the waiter would return with a set of cutlery. It was only when he turned around and saw the drivers avidly demolishing their food with their fingers that he knew it was the way to go.

Toroki, who had been cunningly watching him, seemed to have rejoiced when the Irish pulled the bowl of warm water which was placed by the side of the food, washed his hands as other people were doing and began to use his fingers in lieu of fork and knife.

He scooped some kibane, rolled it into a ball and, with some vegetable, put it in his mouth. The vegetable tasted good but the kibane was almost bland to him at first. He tried that briefly, shoved it aside and moved on to the roasted fish. It was also heavily spiced with some local herbs and was delicious.

While they were eating, a woman clutching a big bowl stopped by.

"What have you for sale?" asked Toroki as his face lit up with a mischievous smile.

"Five o'clock!" she announced gaily much to the amusement of the two drivers.

The priest did not get the joke and asked to be let in on it. At this request, Toroki shifted nervously on his seat and looked at Kura to whom he wanted to pass the buck. He quietly declined the responsibility by pretending not to see the uneasiness of Toroki.

The priest was still waiting for Toroki to say something.

"Come on, go ahead and don't be shy," declared the priest. "Even if it's a bad thing we still have the right to know."

With those words of encouragement, he finally mustered the courage to tell him what it was.

"It's heavily spiced powder obtained by grinding some wild roots and herbs and usually eaten at 5am," he said at last.

"Why 5am?" the priest asked. "Maybe I should try it myself," he declared, beckoning on the woman to put down her bowl.

"Oh no, you can't!" the two drivers cried out at once.

"Why?" the priest asked.

The woman had followed the comedy going on between the three people and felt that the drivers were preventing the white gentleman from buying her product. Because she was not aware of the status of the different persons sitting at the table, she decided to do her own commercials. Common sense might have told her that the mere existence of a white person was ample evidence that they too made love and did not merely fall from the sky.

"You take this at five o'clock, you're up, strong and ready to go," she said to the priest as her forefinger stiffened in the gesture of an erection.

The drivers held down their heads and smiled cunningly as they secretly cast a disapproving glance in her direction. When the priest noticed it, he burst out laughing.

"There's nothing wrong in making love at five o'clock as long as you do so with your wife," he declared.

The two drivers were not convinced that the priest meant what he was saying and ate their food quietly, not paying attention to the woman who looked on anxiously expecting someone to show an interest in her nostrum.

"Well, they aren't interested but maybe next time they'll …," the priest tried to dismiss the woman.

"What about you?" the woman asked.

"I'm a priest and I can't get married."

Even before he finished uttering the statement, the woman made the sign of the cross, grabbed her dish and vanished. When they had finished eating, they rose and left the restaurant.

Outside, in spite of the heat of the sun, people were doing brisk business, selling coconuts, fat juicy oranges and pineapples. Fr Sean bought a sack of oranges, as well as some pineapples and coconuts almost for next to nothing.

"I think we should get going," Toroki announced. "When you see the sun shining this brightly here, know it's a harbinger for a serious downpour."

They went to their vehicles, started them and were once more on the road to Abakwa. For the most part, they were ascending, the serpentine road working its way in terrible zigzags through the thick forest. Wild birds and monkeys called out and the surrounding bushes buzzed with the hum of insects.

For most of the way, the road was flanked by deep gorges, often on both sides. This, coupled with the endless number of hairpin bends, was an invitation for accidents. The priest stared down into some of the valleys and wondered what would happen if the brakes failed.

Finally, the very thick forest began gradually to give way to grass, the change in vegetation marking the transition from the hot, forested equatorial zone to the cold, tropical savannah region. The land began to level off, the grass becoming predominant and the palm trees profuse, until they seemed to be on a plain. Then the palm trees started to thin away.

"What's the name of this area?" the priest asked.

"This is Bani."

Bani was a village of orchards, with an explosion of many kinds of fruit trees. The rich scent of ripe guavas and pineapples wafted to the vehicles. By the roadsides, avocado, mango and other fruit trees flaunted their products whose profusion caused some of their branches to hang dangerously down overhead.

"I think I read about the people of this area, their martial ardor and the great upheavals which once rocked this region as a result of their invasion."

"It's true Father," Toroki said, beaming with pride. "It was a great kingdom and the ethnic configuration of the entire Savannah Province and its surrounding lands were shaped by its activities," he continued. "This is my village, the place where I was born and raised before I decided to travel to the coastal region to work at the plantations. I was hired and trained as a truck driver and as soon as I discovered that I could make more money going private I decided to quit the company."

"Was it easy to be hired when you left the company?"

"Yes, I was hired as the driver of a mammy wagon."

"What's that?" asked the priest, his gaze now fixed on the driver in anticipation of a detail explanation.

"The big bus we saw in Mamfe."

"I took no notice of it."

"It was just one. We left Mamfe a bit early otherwise you should have seen many of them. They usually drive into the town late in the evening from the neighboring villages and towns, transporting traders who shuttle between bush markets."

122

"Why did you stop driving a mammy wagon?"

"The pay I was proposed by the Mikari governor in Gbea was more attractive."

"Do you plan to visit your parents?"

"I'll do that on my way back."

22

It was evening when they finally got to Abakwa. The priest was taken to Ayaba where the biggest mission in the region had just been established. It was still run by an old man who had lived in Victoria where he had been trained as a catechist. He was still expecting another Irish priest who would come and take over the control of the mission at any time.

Fr Sean became an instant celebrity upon his arrival. He was among some of the earliest white people to visit the region and many people still had only a verbal and very vague description of what a Caucasian looked like.

As soon as words went round that the new priest had arrived, Fr Sean being mistaken for the one they had been waiting for, people started to pour into the mission premises. Many of them had long been attending doctrine classes and had been informed that their baptism could only be possible with the arrival of the priest.

Very eagerly they shook the hand of the priest and disappointment immediately showed on their faces when they learned that he was bound instead for Yakiri.

"How can a chief be denied something only for it to be given to his valet?" one of them asked, a question which hinted on the precedence Ayaba took over Yakiri on matters relating to the Roman Catholic faith.

Native carriers from Yakiri who had been dispatched with horses to assist the priest in his journey from Abakwa were on hand and very eager to go. They meticulously studied every single gesture of the Irish Father, preparing long yarns, through such observations, which they hoped to spin once they got to their village.

As it was too late, the catechist, Pa Joseph, a wizened tall lanky fellow with attractive manners and a good command of

Mikari, had already prepared sleeping places for the visitors: the priest, the two drivers and the carriers from Yakiri. They had planned to leave early the next day.

For a town which had no telephone at the time, the news of the white man's arrival had already gone far and even as the evening wore on, people from the neighboring villages kept coming to catch a glimpse of him and shake his hand.

It was getting late and while some of those who had come to see Fr Sean retired in the hope of coming back the following morning, those whose houses were not far from the mission took advantage and hung around, listening avidly to the conversations of the priest half of which they did not understand because of the level of their Mikari and the other half because of his accent.

"Father talks Mikari very fast and we can't understand what he's saying," one of them commented.

"Yes, he talks through his nostrils and all we hear is kwere kwere kwere!" a friend exclaimed in support much to the amusement of the priest who was already getting used to their own accent.

"At least most people here seem to have a smattering of some Mikari. So where did you learn the language?" the priest asked.

"There's a school in Tisson which most of us have attended," one of them declared, pointing in the direction of a hill which loomed above Abakwa.

It was almost getting late and the visitors had started yawning, the heat and the journey having taken their toll and so the catechist politely told the remaining fans of the Irish that they could come the next day to continue with their observation and interviews.

"Does Father eat because we have to bring him some food tomorrow?" an admiring catechumen asked, and then waited to hear what the priest would say.

"Yes, whatever you eat is what I eat, so tomorrow when you bring the food we'll all eat together," the Irishman, who had long since sensed that he was an object of curiosity, responded to the utter satisfaction of the man.

"My wife has prepared some pork so you should whet your appetite in preparation," the man stated as he stepped out of the mission house into the dark.

"I love pigs," the priest replied as he accompanied them with his torch lamp, lighting the way since there were no street lamps. They finally got to the main road where the priest stopped and wished them good night.

As the men chattered away in the dark, obviously still overcome with the excitement of the meeting, Fr Sean retraced his steps to the door where a worried Pa Joseph had been watching them.

"Tomorrow we'll be leaving around nine o'clock after I've said mass, the first in Africa," he declared, the excitement barely concealed in his voice.

Before going to bed he planned to get up very early. That night he slept like a log. He awoke the next morning to the noise of the villagers, many of whom were already aware that a mass was going to be said at the new church. The way news traveled surprised the priest since it was already late when he announced to the catechist that there would be mass.

"How did they get to know that mass would be said?" the priest asked the catechist.

"When you gave me the information yesterday, I took it late at night to the next compound and, like wild brush fire, it spread."

Apart from the catechist and two drivers, all the other Africans who took part in the service that morning had not been baptized; but still, the prospect of attending mass, the first in their newly built church, filled them with great joy. They saw it as a first step towards their becoming true Christians by obtaining their baptism and first holy communion.

Some of them had waited for very long and had become impatient. Fr Sean could read the ardent desire to be baptized as Christians on the people's faces and promised them that if after he had already settled at his station and the priest the Ayaba parish was waiting for had still not arrived, he would set a date to travel to Abakwa and have the baptism carried out. The people were very happy with the promise.

Even before mass was said, the visitor who promised to bring pork was in the church premises clutching a large basket.

Next to him, were two other gentlemen with two little piglets grunting their discontent to have been unceremoniously dragged out of their fences very early in the morning to attend holy mass.

"They brought these two small animals for you because I told them that you love pigs," the man of the previous night announced to the priest after mass, scrutinizing his face for a reaction.

Fr Sean blushed, deeply flattered by the gesture of magnanimity.

"Thank you very much," he said. "This is very kind of you."

"If you aren't really into pigs, I suggest that you hasten up and get out of this place before other villagers learn that you love the animals," the catechist who had been following what was going on and knew what to expect immediately warned the priest.

Having thanked and seen off the two drivers and having eaten his meal of pork, the priests and his carriers from Yakiri started strapping the luggage onto the horses. They were just on the verge of completing when they heard the distant wail of a pig.

The catechist smiled, turned to Fr Sean and quietly announced somewhat humorously: "Welcome to Africa Father!" Still the lesson he had with Bernard on semantics and Africans did not hit home.

When they were set to begin their journey, the priest was stuck with five pigs which the carriers put in wicker baskets and tied onto horses. One of the members of the party was sent ahead by his colleagues to prepare the way for the arrival of the new priest.

"We should get to Yakiri by 5pm," Sakah, the head of the delegation, announced.

They all mounted, four people ahead and five behind, with the loaded horses in the middle. In all they had come with fourteen horses, including the one on which the messenger rode.

Their advance was rapid. By early noon, they had completely descended the Sabga hills, an ancient massif which ran all around the entire Savannah Province. Soon, they were already on the Ndop plains. The priest was quick to observe the reasons why vehicles could not ply the road at that period of the year.

The road was very narrow and composed mainly of clay soil so that with the slightest rain it could be transformed into mud.

The presence of large ditches across the road in many areas attested to its extremely bad conditions.

As the afternoon progressed, they quickly covered the flatland. Their mobility was greatly enhanced by the absence of any tedious and debilitating rising slope. About 3.30pm they were already at Babessi, at the foot of the Wanama hills, whose ascension culminated in Yakiri.

The plain was made up of a number of small villages, with agglomerated settlements of thatched bamboo houses, strung up mostly along the main road which led from Abakwa to Yakiri.

Most of the inhabitants of the villages were descendants of other Wotikar groups which might have probably preceded the Wotikar villages in the series of migratory waves which the Dawa region once experienced.

When these people moved to occupy the plain, they might have been one main group but as discontent grew and the urge for people to set up their own villages and become independent took hold, the disintegration began. Each particle of this atomization process eventually became a separate village, with its own culture, dialect and chief.

The journey was not as difficult as the priest had expected, not least because of the beautiful scenery of grasslands, rivers and waterfalls which greeted his eyes. Even the desire to stop on the way for a rest or to grab a bite, partly dampened by the fear of the rains whose black clouds continued to hover in the sky for most of the day, was greatly attenuated by an ever winking and inviting natural splendor.

The Irish was a sensation all along the way with people pursuing their band until a new group of curious onlookers took over from them and continued to the next village. It was like a relay team, each group monopolizing the stare-at-the-white-man baton until the show had left its own territory and its people turned back to wax lyrical on what they had seen.

23

B ack in Yakiri, the messenger dispatched to announce the
arrival of the Irishman was received to a tumultuous
welcome as though he was the white priest himself. The
sub-chief, members of the Council of Elders and a strong
delegation of old people held the young man down and were
bombarding him with questions.

"Is it true that he's as white as a ghost?" Tafon, the young
new village head asked.

"The ghost is nothing," he replied. "He's as white as the
ashes on your fire," he responded as though short of example for a
good comparison.

"Does he eat?" another voice was eager to know.

"From what I observed when we were together, he does
everything we do except that his skin is white."

"Is he male or female?"

"What sort of a question is that?" the messenger asked.
"He's referred to as a Father and then you ask me whether he's
male or female," he declared before pausing for a while and after a
brief reflection came back to the question. "Your question may not
be entirely stupid because when we met him he was wearing a gown
like a woman; but I must state that I didn't see breasts protruding
and it was hard to tell whether something was bulging underneath."

"Obviously a gown will conceal any protrusion
underneath," the sub-chief stated with emphasis to the utter
amusement of everyone. "So you're saying that he's not a man?"

"I really think he is, judging from his voice, the roughness
of his chin and the hairiness and toughness of his arms. I think the
confusion arises mainly from the clothes he's wearing but maybe in
their country men wear women's gowns," the messenger declared
still perplexed with the priest's cassock.

"Did he laugh while you were there?"

"Is there anyone who laughs better than the priest?"

"What was the laughter like?"

"White like him."

The questions kept coming in unending waves, some intelligent and others roaringly ridiculous. The man who was still covered with dust and being gnawed by hunger became fed up and began to protest.

"I've just arrived and I'm hungry and thirsty and instead of giving me food and drinks, you've held me down with questions. The priest will soon be here where he may be spending a good part if not all of his life and you can then ask him all the questions you want. I'm tired and I must rest now."

The young man was not a fool. He knew that his popularity would not last forever and that once the priest arrived he would be out of the picture, so he wanted to cash in on his newly found glory.

"Get him something to eat and drink but while that's being done you can at least take a few more questions," the sub-chief declared when he sensed that the young man was becoming frustrated and moody. "What did the hair on his head look like?"

"Like the tail of that horse standing over there," he said, pointing at the white steed on which he had arrived in the village.

"The tail of the horse!" the entire gathering exclaimed simultaneously.

"Yes, that horse you see over there," he said bragging, probably still overwhelmed by the fact that history might record that he was the first man from Yakiri to discover a white man.

"And his eyes," another voice shot out.

"Like those of a cat."

"His nose?" the questions kept coming.

"Long and pointed like the tip of a knife."

"My mother's husband!" someone exclaimed. "A knife?"

"Yes, a knife with a sharp tip," the messenger said with emphasis.

"Does he breathe?" someone dared ask. "Or he doesn't," another voice added.

"Well, I saw his chest rising and falling so I'm convinced that he breathes."

"Tell me something son," the sub-chief said as he drew the young man closer. "Is he married?"

"That's a very intelligent question," the messenger declared.

"How so?"

"While we were there it was rumored that he couldn't marry nor even have a woman," the messenger replied. "Which means there's no bearded meat for him," he announced to the utter amusement of everyone present.

"How can a man live without eating bearded meat?" the sub-chief asked and the crowd burst out laughing. "Whatever the case, we'll get to know with time."

Now the young man, a fellow called Tamusu, who had been little known in the village before his trip to Abakwa, had become an instant celebrity and seemed not to hate the momentary glory in which he was basking, even if his conduct sometimes testified to the contrary. Normally, his presence would not have aroused any curiosity in the village but he was now trailing half of the village behind him, including some members of the prestigious council.

Meanwhile having received confirmation that the white man at least ate and drank, the women in the village had started preparing food while the men collected palm wine with which to entertain the newcomer. The news of his imminent arrival had already reached neighboring hamlets and villages and its inhabitants started pouring into Yakiri to catch a glimpse of the new human phenomenon.

Fr Sean's house, of bamboos like the rest in the entire region, was one of the most decently built. All forms of decoration and artistry went into its construction as the villagers reckoned would befit a person of the priest's status. It was situated not far from the church.

The church was also built out of the same material and in similar fashion. It was, however, larger than any other house in the villages. It was furnished with rows of bamboo benches to provide seats for the congregants during services. It had an upraised bamboo platform, almost like the one in the village hall, so that the priest presiding over services would have a clear view of all the Christians.

It was about 5.30pm when Fr Sean and members of his team arrived. The whole village had been buzzing with excitement

131

ever since Tamusu reached it with the first shred of news on the visitor. And even before one of the carriers helped the priest to dismount, a huge crowd had already formed.

"Take his things to his new house," the sub-chief ordered as he led the way. "I think we'll need an interpreter."

As soon as he talked of an interpreter, all eyes turned to Telanyanga. He was a stocky man with a broad forehead and charming eyes. He had the distinction of being among the few who had gone to a white man's school in Abakwa and could speak some Mikari. He loved publicity and since he had always portrayed himself before other poor villagers who never had the opportunity to be educated as a wise person, he instantly saw in his new role as an interpreter another occasion to boost his ego.

For a while, he chatted briefly with the priest just to show off. Even though the priest's accent prevented him from understanding most of the things he said, he pretended, with exaggerated head gestures, that he understood all that was being said.

Tela, a short form and an appellation of endearment commonly used in the village to call him, approached the sub-chief and told him that the priest would need some rest before the population could get to know him.

"He has just arrived and he's tired. Tomorrow is Njuellah, when everyone will be at home, and we can use the occasion to introduce him to the people and ask him questions," Tela told the village head. "He has come all the way from the coast and before then, he had traveled in a kind of house that the white man uses to cross streams."

"At least, he should eat before resting. During his meal, our dancers could also welcome him," Tafon told Tela who instantly relayed the message to the priest and he agreed. "He's now one of ours and must be made to feel welcome and at home."

The reception took place at Tafon's compound since it was very close to the mission and he was the leader of the village. It was a very large compound, with four houses set in the form of a rectangle around a courtyard, yet it was not large enough to accommodate the population which had turned out to meet and welcome the priest.

132

Every inch of territory had been taken up by the ever growing population and some people were wise enough to climb on surrounding trees in order to follow events from those heights. Bamboo benches were brought into the compound from the neighbors and a big meal was set before everyone. While people were eating, xylophones and drums played and a choreographed royal native dance called Tamukung provided terpsichorean entertainment.

The priest was greatly moved by the welcome. He had not expected things to be that way. Many books he read had always portrayed African people as dull and uninteresting but he found a dynamic and vibrant community.

At about 7pm, just before the reception broke up for people to retire to their homes, the priest thanked them and declared that he really felt welcome in their midst. He then handed the letters which Bernard Nso had written to the sub-chief and to his parents. His parents were too old to come and welcome the priest but an eager group of young men were on hand to take the letter to them.

On behalf of the village, the sub-chief welcomed the priest and praised his courage for traveling all the way from the white man's land to come and share his ideas with the people of Yakiri. He promised to give him all the assistance he needed to make his work, which was aimed at promoting the development of the village, successful.

While the priest was being led to his house, the sub-chief invited Tela to read and interpret the letter to him. In the letter, Bernard Nso called on Tafon to take good care of his friend and to give him all the assistance he needed. He said it was on his recommendation that the priest had decided to come to Yakiri and that the people should feel privileged to have him. He concluded by saying that he was in good health and would soon finish his education and return home to the country.

24

It was still not dark when the priest arrived at his house. It was a three-room house, with two sleeping rooms and a vast sitting room. It was constructed almost entirely out of bamboos. The same material was used everywhere except for the roof which was of thatch. Inside his sleeping room stood a large bamboo bed covered with a mat woven out of the soft straw of some plants. The bed was hard but everything on it was new.

With darkness gathering, he lit a hurricane lamp and placed it on a small bamboo stool which stood by the side of the bed. He went to some of his luggage stacked at a corner of the sitting room and from one of the boxes took out his blankets. He flung one over the mat, folded the second to form a pillow and a third was to serve as cover.

He took off his boots and put on a pair of rubber slippers and had just finished his prayers and was about to lie down when he heard a knock on the door. He went and pulled it open and one of the young men with whom he had arrived was standing there smiling. He held a bucket and a calabash of water.

"Come on in," the priest announced, ushering in the man.

He stumbled in with his loads and placed them on the ground.

"This is drinking water," he declared, pointing at the calabash. "The one in the bucket is warm and is for you to wash off the dust and sweat. It'll do you a lot of good after such a long and tiring journey."

"Thank you very much," the priest said. "Let me get my towel and some soap," he told the young man.

"Meanwhile I'll take the water to the bathing room which is just behind the house. I don't know where you'll have to stand the lamp before washing yourself. Anyway, the water will be placed on a bamboo stand constructed for the purpose. I think that should make things a lot easier."

"Never mind, I'll use my torchlight. I'll stick it somewhere, with its light trained on the bucket of water so that I can see," he said. He disappeared into his room and soon emerged clutching a towel, a torch and a small loaf of soap. "Where's the bathing room?"

"There!" the young man said, pointing.

It was a very big bathing room fenced in by a high and beautiful bamboo wall. Even in the gloom of the evening, the priest could see the broad bamboo stand on which the bucket of water had been placed. The stand came up to his hip so that he did not need to bend before scooping water with his cupped hands to throw over his body.

On the floor of the bathing room, there was a flat bamboo foot stand with openings to let out water as he washed. He only discovered the next day that the foot stand was set over little canals to help the water to drain away out of the bathing room.

He felt much better after washing off the sweat and dust. Back in his room, and with the young man gone, he read his Bible for a while before going to sleep. It was his first night in Yakiri and he slept soundly.

He awoke the next day to the morning uproar of the village. When he opened his eyes, he could see light filtering in through tiny crevices on the wall. Outside, he could hear the voices of children and women above the cackle of hens. Still in his pajamas, he staggered towards the door and pulled it open. A crowd of mostly children bearing baskets had already formed waiting for him.

They had brought food from their various houses to the priest. The food was of a very wide variety, from fruits through kibane and kati to steaming yams. By the time all of them had handed him their baskets, he had enough food to feed an entire neighborhood. Some of his friends of the previous day had promised to come and help him in settling down and he was convinced that they would know what to do with such a large amount of food.

On his way to Yakiri, he had started to learn the Wotikar language and already knew that "berri" stood for "thanks".

135

"Berri!" he shouted to the children who exploded into laughter, probably triggered by the awkward pronunciation.

One of them murmured something which he did not understand. He retired to his room and started to prepare to go and say mass. He had informed the public at his reception about the mass and expected people to turn up. He could not afford to appear late for his very first mass in Yakiri.

It was to start at 8.30am and it was already 7.30. With a bowl of water, he rushed to the bathing room, brushed his teeth and washed his face and arms. He tried some yam and the peanut sauce for breakfast. It tasted good but he could not quite identify the meat he was eating. It was, however, tender and very nice and he kept some of it to ask one of his traveling companions what animal it was.

He got to the church only to say holy mass in which he did all the talking alone in Latin. There was complete absence of public participation, just another hint of the long and tough road ahead of him. He knew it was only by learning the local language and accommodating some aspects of the people's culture that he would be able to overcome the problem.

After mass, the priest returned to his house and continued to unpack and arrange his things. Two of the carriers, Kikakilaki and Layu, soon arrived. By now, the crowd of curious onlookers which had formed after mass had gradually started to disappear, leaving only children who seemed not to have had enough of the Irishman.

Inside the house, the Irish and his companions were busy opening boxes and unpacking things. It was at this point that he noticed he would need a writing table. He turned to Layu and asked if he could get him a carpenter. He told the priest that all the carpenters had gone to Abakwa where they were much in demand.

"I need a table so what do I do then?" the priest asked.

"I'll give you a reply when I come back," he said as he stepped out of the house and headed towards the village.

Father Sean was still pondering what he intended to do when he heard the voice of a woman wailing outside. He rushed outside and was immediately joined by Kikakilaki. The priest found the woman clutching what seemed like a lifeless little girl. The woman's hair was bare and disheveled, with strands of gray here and there. She looked very unkempt and miserable and was apparently surrounded by friends and relatives.

When she saw the priest approaching, she stopped wailing. She seemed frightened. It was obvious from the look on her face that it was her first time of seeing a white person. Her only feeling of assurance seemed to have come from the villagers who stood next to the priest and had not yet been eaten.

"What's wrong with the baby?" the priest asked, coming closer.

After the woman rightly surmised the question Fr Sean could possibly have been asking, with great excitement and facial and head gestures for emphasis, she burst out into a wild torrent of Wotikar words to explain her plight. These theatrics were capped with a terrible wail. Obviously, what she had said did not make any sense to the priest who begged her to calm down as he pored over the inanimate little girl.

Kikakilaki offered to interpret and told the priest that she said the child had been playing all morning when she was suddenly struck by a still unknown fit.

"It may be epilepsy," the priest concluded after ruminating for a while. "Where's she going now?"

After listening to the woman, the interpreter said she claimed that the child had never had any case of epilepsy before, nor were the symptoms those of the illness under indictment. He said the woman held that she had already gone to a gnukwabe in Nkar who threw his divination cowries and bones and concluded that he could not handle the illness and so recommended her to Nding.

"Who's Nding?" the priest asked.

"Do you see those clumps of trees over there, on top of that hill?" the young man asked, pointing.

"Yes."

"There!" he said. "He's a gnukwabe, a kind of diviner and traditional healer."

"I know what a gnukwabe is," the priest said to the surprise of the young man.

"You have them too in your country?"

"Yes, but maybe ours are very different from the ones you've got here."

"Do the ones in your country send lightning too?" he asked. "The one living over there is no person to mess around with," he said with all seriousness. "He's the only one in this entire region who can handle serious cases like the one of this woman's daughter."

"I think we should go along," the priest declared, rushing into his house to put on his boots. "I'm interested to know more about the child's situation and also to see what Nding will do."

Kikakilaki followed and waited for him by the door. He was soon ready to go and started fumbling with the door when his friend told him he did not need to lock it.

"Nobody can get in there and take something without your permission," the young man said casually.

"Are you telling me there aren't thieves here?"

"Sure, there are but nobody will go in and take anything in your house, nor in any other house in this village for that matter."

At first the priest could not understand and felt his house would be spared, either because he was white, a stranger or the village priest. On all three counts, he was well of the mark.

25

The good instinct of prevention is better than cure having had the better of the priest, he decided to lock his door. Still, he could not get over the reason which might have caused his friend to tell him to leave his door open. He was surprised to find that many other doors in the village had been left open even though the occupants of the houses were nowhere in sight.

As the priest and his friend trailed behind the crowd heading towards Nding's compound, he asked the fellow why people did not steal even when the doors were left open. He simply smiled and again pointed at the premises of Nding at the top of the hill. It would only start to make sense to him after a long stay and he had started to put some of the things he read in the book Bernard Nso gave him in Ireland in perspective.

Ahead of them, the noisy crowd continued its way. It had not rained for some days and dust had already started accumulating and as the people walked, they kicked up a storm. They were soon ascending the slope atop of which the compound was nestled.

The track leading up to the compound was tiny. This caused the crowd to string up in an Indian file, working its way up through the bush like a snake. The chatter of voices and the rustle of grass floated down to the priest and his friend who brought up the rear. Occasionally, the wail of the woman could be heard. It was often accompanied by some deprecatory voices assuring her that all would be fine.

At the top of the slope, the land flattened out and the crowd was now in the domain of the gnukwabe. It was a vast estate of kolanut, orange and other fruit trees, as well as of coffee shrubs. After walking for a while in this balmy and lush greenery, they burst onto a clearing with four thatched houses set in a rectangle around a courtyard.

The clearing began with a farm of peanuts and beans which extended to a mere couple of yards away from the walls of the compound. The compound was pitched against a backdrop of a forest of tall, old and deep green kolanut trees. The whole environment looked very eerie.

The crowd met Nding at the entrance of the compound. He was leaning on his walking stick and did not even bother to stare out at the people heading in his direction. A young man stood by his side eating oranges, his son and only child, it was immediately whispered. His name was Takwabe.

As soon as the crowd came to a halt and the priest and his companion caught up with it, it was hard for Fr Sean not to discern the affection the old man had for his child. In spite of the old man's age, he would sometimes drop his walking stick to peel an orange which he handed over to him.

"Send somebody to go and buy a small bag woven out of white raffia fiber, a rooster and a small calabash of palm wine," the old man announced without even examining the child and with his eyes still focused on another orange which he was busy peeling.

As should be expected, the Irishman was completely lost. He deemed his conduct of not even examining the child inadequate but what happened next stunned him even more. Without uttering another word, he turned round and with the lazy shuffle of an old man began to walk away, abandoning the crowd behind him.

The crowd simply followed him while a young man was immediately dispatched with some money to buy the items he had requested. Fr Sean and Kikakilaki followed the crowd of about fifteen through an entrance into the courtyard, across it and out of the compound.

They walked down a bush track until they came to what, from every indication, was a shrine in the midst of some trees and exotic creeping plants whose tendrils sometimes grew across the track. The trees fenced in the shrine which was housed in a very large hut, with seats all round. It seemed ordinary for the most part. On the walls were dark, old fiendish-looking bags. To complete this exotic and mysterious decor, some snake skins hung down from the bamboo walls.

At the center of the hut was a central pole which supported the roof and around which grew some rhododendron and creeping plants like the ones on the way.

The old man's altar was on the same plane with the rest of the hut and was pitched against one of the walls, the one with the bulk of the bags and snake skins. When he was seated, he faced the entire public. To his right, almost at an angle of a hundred and fifty degrees, was a stool carved out of camwood and as ancient as the hills.

When everyone was seated, acting as though he was seeing the white priest for the first time, he addressed him through others, probably out of concern for communication barrier.

"Tell my son from far away to come and sit here," he announced, pointing to the stool.

The message was instantly interpreted to the burly Irish who rose like thunder and after a few strides landed like lightning on the seat next to the old man. The old man was impressed and greeted the manly display with a broad complimentary smile. He turned to his son and asked him to bring him an old raffia bag hanging on the wall. He came with the bag forthwith and placed it in front of his father.

While the old man was fidgeting with the bag, he glanced occasionally in the direction of the priest. The priest made an appraisal of him.

He could have been in his late seventies or thereabout, with a white mane of locks of hair falling over his broad shoulders. In spite of his ancient and somewhat dreadful appearance, there was something in his conduct which portrayed him as a nice and affable old man. He was always smiling, and when his wide and sensuous lips parted, clean white teeth were displayed.

He finally got what he wanted from his bag: a smaller bag of wildcat skin out of which he fished some cowry shells and bones. These were some of the tools of his trade. He started to fondle them and mutter incantations. As he said the words, his head bopped sideways and then forward and backward. Then all of a sudden, he threw the contents of his hands on the ground. He looked at the configuration and then turned to the priest and said: "You're to your parents as my boy is to me and my wife."

141

Immediately, the interpreter sprang into action and told the priest what he had said. It did not make sense to him at first until he recalled the rumors claiming that the boy they met standing by the side of the old man when they arrived was his only son. It now made a lot of sense.

"Before next year runs out, a brother of yours from your country will be looking for you but you need not bother yourself because he'll write to you."

Which brother, he thought, when the information was interpreted. That did not make sense to him even after the interpretation since the second prophecy contradicted the first one.

"Now brace yourself for something terrible!" the old man declared as his face suddenly turned serious. "Your mother will become a widow by the end of next year."

When he was told what the old man had said, he figured he must be right because his father had a stroke just before he left and prospects of his health did not seem bright from the doctor's report.

He was still brooding over all that the man had said when the entrance to the shrine framed the young man who had just returned with the rooster, bag and calabash of palm wine. The old man welcomed the priest to Yakiri and asked him to regain his seat.

It was only then that he talked to the woman with the dying child for the very first time since she came to the compound.

"Come and sit here with the child," he pointed to the stool the priest had just evacuated.

He gathered the cowries and bones, cupped them in both hands, fondled and threw them on the ground and then his face suddenly wore an appearance of seriousness. He murmured something as though in anger. Turning on his seat, he said something to his son who disappeared out of the door and soon came back with a small horn lightly stuffed with a cotton-like object.

He took out the stuffing and asked the woman to approach with the child. Then he began an incantation, his voice fluctuating from entreaties to angry orders, and then back to entreaties again. While he indulged in these actions, he held the horn onto the bared chest of the child.

Then slowly a chameleon came swinging out of the horn, with its usual hesitant gait. It wandered on the child's body for a while, as though on some corporal inspection tour, before returning into its abode. With flashing eyes and profuse gesticulations, the old man beamed and cried out in triumph as he put back the stuffing and handed the horn to his son who walked out of the shrine and soon returned without it.

"Behind the house where this child lives, some bewitching stuff has been buried by a woman who is squabbling with you over a man," the old man declared and the woman immediately held down her head. "The child has been 'tied' by your rival and if by tomorrow we don't succeed in breaking the chains, she'll die."

At the word "die," the woman began to wail out loud. The old man said nothing, only watching her in amusement until she had calmed down.

In the same calm tone as before, the old man resumed his series of indictments against maternal neglect.

"You were putting on this child's clothes one day and you found out that a patch somewhere around the right sleeve was missing," the old man declared and then reprimanded her. "You didn't bother to find out what happened."

"All that you've said so far is true," the woman admitted humbly. This prepared the way for other torrents of accusations.

"You came back from the farm one day and discovered that some tuft of her hair around the right ear had disappeared," he continued "and you said nothing."

"I thought it might have been done by her friends while they were playing during the day," the woman tried to rush to her own defense.

"Well, let's draw the package causing this child all this distress from where it has been buried before things get worse," he declared at last, rising and heading towards the door of the shrine.

Everyone in the shrine rose and went after him, curious to know what would happen next. He ventured to the neighboring bushes, plucking this leaf here and that plant there until in the end his hands were full with different kinds of foliage. He resumed his seat at the shrine.

He asked first for the calabash of palm wine and then for the little white raffia bag. He started to stuff the leaves and herbs

143

into the bag, his eyes almost closed and his lips shaking as he muttered some incantations.

From time to time, he paused to pour some libation on the bag and its contents. With the bag stuffed, he put it down and then, with a gesture of the hand, asked for the rooster. When it was handed to him, he turned and looked at his son who left the shrine and soon came back with a civet skin bag, dark with soot and age, and gave it to his father.

He reached into it and withdrew a small bottle containing some dark and oily substance. He forced open the beak of the rooster and dropped some of the stuff into it. He also smeared some on the raffia bag. Turning again to the rooster, he poured a few drops of palm wine into its mouth. After gulping the alcoholic and heady liquid, it shook its head vigorously. This act triggered an outburst of laughter from the spectators.

Abandoning everything on the ground, the old man rose and took up position at the threshold of the door of the shrine and started to blow a bamboo whistle. This exercise was punctuated with some incantations. He stepped outside and continued with these activities. The son took the civet skin and raffia bags as well as the rooster, with legs now firmly strapped together, and pursued his father outside. He went to the branch of a small tree and hung the three items.

The young man's father gave him the whistle to continue to blow and "egg on the spirits" while he walked to and fro like some demented person, shouting some garbled utterances.

Then all of a sudden, the rooster, which had been calm throughout this entire operation, lapsed into a terrible fit of agitation, flapped its wings violently and then became as cold as if it were dead. The son rushed to the branch and snapped shut the mouth of the raffia bag tightly, took it off the branch, along with the other bag and rooster, and hurried off to the shrine, with all the curious onlookers in tow.

The old man soon arrived when everyone was seated and asked his son to hand him the raffia bag. As he poured its contents on the floor, the first thing which came tumbling out was a tightly closed plastic bottle. It seemed freshly exhumed, with some wet earth on it. After a bit of a struggle, he managed to open the

144

container and poured its contents on a piece of cloth spread on the ground.

The woman immediately identified the piece of cloth which had been taken from her daughter's dress, as well as some hair, probably the little girl's too. There was a small wooden human statuette tied all round with thread. The old man picked it up and showed it to the woman.

"See how your daughter has been tied," he declared. "The piece of cloth and the hair all belong to her."

Using a blade, he sliced through the thread, thus liberating the human statuette within.

"Draw nearer with the little girl," he ordered the woman.

When she did, he forced open the child's mouth and poured in some of the dark grimy liquid. Not up to three minutes after the stuff had been administered, she got up with a start and threw up. Her vomit contained strange items ranging from the whiskers of a lion to the claw of an owl. Weak, she stared around dizzily and called out her mother's name. The old man applied some of the dark liquid on the little girl's temple.

He wrapped up the plastic and its contents and gave it to the woman as souvenir and asked her to take the child home and give her some food.

"What do I bring to you for this work?" the woman asked.

"Find a big rooster and take it to that son of mine who comes from far, far away and who's sitting over there," he responded, pointing in the direction of the priest. "And henceforth you'll have to choose between your child and another woman's man."

The woman thanked him and as she and her delegation rose to leave, Fr Sean and Kikakilaki also stood up and started towards the door.

"Sit down," the old man appealed to the priest. "You can't leave without eating and drinking something."

He gave his son the rooster and he immediately left the shrine. He handed the priest and his companion drinking cups and poured them some palm wine and while they were drinking, he plied him with questions. The priest responded and did the same. It was obvious from the intercourse that the two priests, if you want, got off to a friendly start during their first meeting.

145

Since there were serious communication problems between the two, the Irish promised to be back in six to eight months when he could speak Wotikar. The old man was flattered and promised that he would tell him everything he wanted to know.

About thirty minutes later, the old man's son returned with a roasted chicken, fresh banana leaves, some palm oil and salt. While he was busy preparing kati sauce, the old man's wife soon arrived with a big bowl of steaming kibane.

After their meals, the old man ordered his son to harvest a bag of fruits for the priest and walked them to the entrance of his compound where he saw them off.

"What do you think?" Kikakilaki turned to the priest.

"I don't know what to think but if that's the way he uses his mystical power, it's a good thing," he replied after pausing for a while.

"That old man loves you?"

"I could see that."

"What if he wants to initiate you into his art?"

"I don't mind learning the healing part."

"Why only the healing part?" Kikakilaki asked. "Go for the entire package and use what you have responsibly and judiciously."

"It's true but I select the part of the practice which is in line with what I'm doing."

It was early afternoon when they got back to the village where people had been waiting for the priest. As soon as they saw him coming, they beamed with excitement. Many of them had prepared him food which they had kept in baskets by the side of his door.

He greeted them and they chatted for a while before he left and went to his house. At the door were a beautiful bamboo cupboard and table, as well as three chairs. Some of the food he had been brought in the morning was still standing in his sitting room and so he invited children who happily gathered in his house and they all ate together.

"I still can't pronounce your name," the priest apologized to his friend.

"The name is Kikakilaki, a Wotikar village where my parents originated," he explained. "To make things easy just call me Kiki, for that's the way my friends call me."

146

"Now, tell me Kiki, what animal is this?" he turned to him with the remains of what he had eaten in the morning.

"That's cane rat," he replied after a cursory glance. "I love it. It's delicious."

"I ate it and also liked it," the priest declared. "I recall seeing this item on the menu of a restaurant in Mamfe."

"I wouldn't be surprised by that."

After the children had finished eating, they were instructed to take the empty baskets to the different houses to which they belonged.

"I still can't pronounce your name too Father," Kiki said to the priest.

"It's Sean."

"Oh I see, like what shines above!" Kiki exclaimed knowingly much to the amusement of the priest.

"That's the sun."

"Then what's a small boy who belongs to a man called?"

"Son."

"Well, Fr Sign, I'll be back tomorrow should you have anything you want me to help you do."

"Sun, Sign, Sin or whatever!" he exclaimed in total amusement. "You'll learn to call it with time," he finally declared dismissively.

26

The priest had planned to hold a meeting with the villagers at the church in the late afternoon and it was getting to time. He had seen people heading towards the venue of the meeting. He arrived when everyone was already seated and they began what in Western terms would be described as a press conference.

The meeting was attended by a motley crowd of men, women and children. Some of the people had come to the meeting just to catch another glimpse of the white man from far away who would be their priest. During the meeting, Tela served as interpreter.

First, the priest's name was called out many times so that people should know the proper pronunciation but what came out of African mouths had nothing Irish about it. Sensing that in the immediate it was an exercise in futility, they moved rapidly to the next item on the agenda. Tafon, the sub-chief, took the floor.

"Now that you're here in Yakiri where do we begin?" he asked the priest.

"We'll have to construct a school, so that young people won't be compelled to travel to Abakwa and other faraway places for their primary education," he announced. "The earlier we begin the better."

The villagers were pleased with the idea but still it was obvious from their looks that there was a problem.

"Where shall we find teachers and equipment?" one of them finally asked.

"Once the school has been constructed, I'll be its first teacher and then as I struggle to train very bright students, I'll write back to my country to explain the situation."

"In that case we'll select the site for the school tomorrow and work will begin immediately," Tafon stated much to the pleasure of all the villagers present. "But since I'm under the authority of the paramount chief in Kimbo, you'll have to be introduced to him."

"So when shall I travel to Kimbo for the introduction?"

"We've already dispatched an emissary and we're expecting him here with the royal whisk tomorrow."

"What's the royal whisk for?"

"It's like an invitation card."

"But I learned that invitation isn't much a part of this culture."

"You're correct when it comes to feasting but if you have to see a chief or king, who normally runs a tight schedule, it's necessary."

"What do you think of the church?" a man asked.

"I think it's wonderful. With time we'll have to move it a bit farther away from the small business center at the junction to avoid noise. I foresee the junction becoming a booming business center as the entire Mungo opens up to trade with the outside world and with the expansion of coffee production."

"I was talking more about doctrine classes for those of us who plan to become Christians," the man restated. "My late father who was a Christian and had lived in the coastal region started to teach me about Jesus Christ before he passed away."

"As soon as I'm settled, we'll begin the classes even though communication remains a huge problem for now."

With the most important subjects having been raised and examined, the audience moved to more banal questions which underlined the people's interest in cultural matters.

Overall, the Irishman noticed that Africans tended to be a shy and withdrawn people. It seemed the way they are brought up. However, he exuded the kind of personality which they could trust and before long the simmering curiosity of the people started to show during the press conference.

When Mbohti stood up to ask a question, the entire audience braced itself for the worst. She was a short woman with a round butt which trembled too much and got into people's way and so she was nicknamed Malaria Butt. She seemed to relish the title and always made villagers crack up with her outrageous sense of humor and loud mouth.

149

With whispers and disapproving glare, some members of the audience attempted to talk her out of whatever she had up her sleeve. This scare tactic did not escape the notice of the observant priest.

The woman would not allow herself to be intimidated. To make it known to everyone that she could care less what people thought of her, in full glare of the priest, she turned her large, round butt and shook it until it jiggled and caused quite a stir.

"Jesus wept," the priest murmured, thoroughly amused with the performance. He was not a geophysicist but he did not need to be one to have a rough idea of how much the butt tremor could measure on a Richter scale! "Shake it again," he said after assimilating the impact caused by the performance. He probably wanted to rub in the point that the woman had the right to express herself. When the information was interpreted to the woman, she put up quite a show which left people amused and confused.

Deeply impressed with this very first sign of female liberation, he informed the crowd that the woman, or any other woman for that matter, was free to state how she felt about anything, however terrible that might be.

Having won her first struggle to exercise her right, Mbohti decided to proceed unperturbed. After pausing for a while and looking around, as though for maximum comical effect, she came up with an outrageous question.

"I see your hair is long and beautiful but is it the same below as it's above?" she asked, her eyes shifting from the priest's hip to his head. And even before the priest could say a word, she moved rapidly to the next thing she had to say. "Well, Father if the hair below is that long I wish to state in front of everyone that I'll be the one braiding the hair above and below," she declared and then turned and looked at another young woman sitting next to her who instantly gave a calm nod of approval.

The villagers held down their heads, almost choking with laughter, and the interpreter, after looking around nervously and scratching, finally mustered the courage to get the job done.

Fr Sean was not a humorless person himself, so he burst out laughing and the whole village joined in.

"If it's the same with yours it should be the same with mine," the priest answered after he had finished laughing. And then added: "I would rather cut it than have it braided."

When the interpreter went to work again, the meeting was over, some people laughing from the church to their homes.

27

Two days later, the emissary arrived with the whisk. Their journey to Kimbo was set for the following day and was to comprise Fr Sean, Tela and Kiki. Kiki was immediately sent for and when he was informed about the trip, he went up one of the neighboring hills to a village horse breeder to arrange for their mounts. Fr Sean spent the rest of the day working with the villagers at the site which had been selected for the construction of the school.

Late that day, Kiki arrived with the animals and tethered them near the church and Tela was kept informed of the journey ahead. They started out early the next day after mass and reached Kimbo where the paramount chief was waiting for them.

On the way, the priest was briefed on how to behave in the royal presence. His companions told him that he had to talk to the chief with cupped hands held to the mouth and must say "mbeh" when responding to him. He was informed that he could not shake hands with the chief nor sit and cross his legs in front of him.

"Why then do I not respect all these rules in my dealings with Tafon?" the priest asked.

"Even though his position is hereditary, he's no more than a village head who takes orders from the paramount chief," Kiki explained.

The priest was more relaxed during this journey than when they traveled from Abakwa. Thus disposed, he could make a better appreciation of the surrounding land. Like all the territory they passed through before they got to Yakiri, it was the continuation of the savannah, with hills and valleys stretching far into the horizon in every direction.

It was green at that period of the year and provided a scenic beauty that was unsurpassed, especially in regions where there was a backdrop of waterfalls. Such was the case as they approached the royal capital.

Far out on their right, towered mountain ranges from which silvery white streams flowed. They came cascading boisterously down the tiered slopes, splashing and breaking up into numerous tiny rivulets which fed streams at their foot. A fair breeze swept down this gorgeous landscape, picking up moisture which drizzled on the surrounding lowlands in fine sprays.

In every direction, there was open country. Occasionally, the braying of donkeys and whinnying of horses rose above the singing of birds and shattered the general stillness and calm. Against the backdrop of unending grasslands, dotted here and there in conspiratorial fashion, were clumps of kolanut trees and, sometimes, coffee farms.

The priest was happy. This was what he had always dreamed of and as his horse trotted, his mouth danced in silent prayers of praise to God. In his quiet meditative mood, which his two companions refrained from disrupting, he took stock of his past few days in Yakiri and felt as much at home as in Ireland. He did not think he would have been happy if he did not share his life with others.

They started to ascend a slope and as soon as they got to the top, buried about half a mile away from them, in the midst of a thick clump of kolanut trees, was the palace of the chief. From their vantage position, it came across as no more than a handful of thatched roofs hidden behind the foliage. Some of them oozed smoke as though they would suddenly burst into flames. The smoke rose in blue plumes above the trees, curling before gradually dissipating.

At the palace, food, wine and dances had been prepared for the Irish and his delegation. It was getting to midday when they finally got to the entrance. The palace comprised an agglomeration of about twenty-seven neatly thatched and well-decorated bamboo houses set out in three rows behind a vast courtyard.

A portico which extended into a fence of dried bamboos ran all round the entire compound. In a cultural setting in which it was the chief who exercised control over the village land, parceling and handing it out to those interested in cultivation or settling, the property of the palace seemed to have no bound. But if the palace was assessed from where it gave way to the next property, it was still a huge domain with acres upon acres of kolanut trees and coffee farms.

As soon as the priest and his acolytes alighted from their horses, some royal officials were in place to take care of their animals. They were soon whisked off to a hall where the chief was to grant them audience.

He arrived shortly after, preceded by a man blowing the tusk of an elephant and another carrying his seat. Everybody in the hall rose when he was being ushered in and, with his chair hastily set on a carpet of leopard skin, he sat down and rested his feet on another elephant tusk.

He was dressed in rich traditional, multi-colored attire and wore ivory beads around his neck. He was tall and well built and could have been no more than thirty. He was the great grandson of Sangbong and came across as an easy-going and open-minded man.

He was the first to address the visitors and welcomed all of them, especially the priest who had come from far away. He said he was open to new ideas which would make his people grow, adding that he was looking forward to some white men and women who would come and start a school and hospital in Kimbo.

Alluding to the fact that Yakiri first had a priest before Kimbo, he said he was surprised that the cup of the sub-chief had been filled before the one of the paramount chief. He, however, stated that any development which helped in making people, no matter where they found themselves, grow was worth promoting. He told the priest to feel very free to visit him at any time for just a friendly chat or with any of his concerns.

Then it was the turn of the priest to speak and he thanked the chief. He stated that he felt very much at home because ever since he landed he had been taken good care of and treated in a friendly manner. He pointed out that development processes tended to be fraught with problems at the initial stages but as soon as the basic structures had been created, things would easily fall in their place. Beginning with communication and education, he listed a number of challenges which would stand in the way of progress unless they were urgently addressed.

On the whole, the interaction between the chief and the priest went on well. There were, however, some hitches. They were the kind of hitches to be expected when interpreting information from one language into another. A sound in one language could sometimes be mistaken by listeners for another thing in a different language.

For instance, Fr Sean said something in Mikari which sounded like "the chief has gray butt" in Wotikar. This obviously would have been an abomination. The chief had grimaced at that until he was reminded that it only sounded that way but meant an entirely different thing in Mikari. He had found it amusing and had smiled profusely immediately after. This sudden change in mood left the Irish a bit confused.

The next hitch had to do with the ability of the interpreter, for, in spite of all his bragging, Tela's mastery of Mikari was dubious. It involved the name of the priest which was often mispronounced and consequently misinterpreted.

"What's the name of the priest?" the chief had asked.

"Sean," the priest had responded.

The interpreter called out the name awkwardly and, in doing so, said something in Wotikar which he accompanied with a gesture in which he was pointing to the sky. The Irish surmised from that sky-pointing action that he could also have made the same error of confusing his name with the "sun." The chief's laughter immediately and Tela's own admission later proved the priest right.

Apart from these two occasions, the only other thing of interest to our narration was when the chief found it amusing that in spite of his title as Father, the priest could not get married and have his own children. He attributed that to some of the strange ways of white people he had heard about. He was shocked to learn that white men passed laws which compelled them to have just one wife or even none at all. He told the priest that he found that to be, indeed, unusual but that if at any point, he made up his mind to marry a woman, then that could easily be arranged.

"A woman," the chief declared, "is like honey whose real taste is known only after it has been licked."

After the audience, it was entertainment all the way, with meat, kibane, palm wine, and bilibili arriving in royal quantities. During the feasting different forms of traditional dances were staged. When it was time for Fr Sean and his delegation to leave, he

155

was made a present of a horse and was fitted out in a traditional outfit so he could fit in.

28

It was late in the afternoon when they left for Yakiri. They arrived around dusk when the chickens were coming back to roost. Tela used the trip and his role as interpreter to stress his importance to the community.

While he was spinning long yarns on how he had performed before the paramount chief, the priest quickly went to inspect the site where the school would be constructed. He was amazed by how much work had been done in a day.

The site had been cleared down and hoed and all the tree stumps removed. Piles of bamboo had already been stacked in a corner of the plot. After tethering Shannon, the name he had already given his horse, to a tree near the church, he retired to his house.

By the door, he found baskets of food, a wicker basket containing a fat rooster and some calabashes of water. He took a glance at the rooster and remembered.

After bathing, he went to bed early, exhausted by the trip and in anticipation of work to be done the following day.

He got up very early the next day and started to draw up a doctrine and school program for Yakiri. When it was time for mass, he went to the church. Then he came back and continued with what he had been doing until midday. He went to the school site and found out that more bamboos had been piled up and the entire village had been mobilized for the work.

Before the month was out, doctrine classes had already started and a school was poised to begin. The priest invited the sub-chief and all the village notables who initially wanted only their women and children to attend.

Tela found himself in very trying circumstances when it came to interpreting concepts and ideas which were totally new to him. In the Lord's Prayer, he had fumbled with the concept of "our

29

F r Sean recalled all that Bernard Nso had told him before he set out for Africa. How could he forget the useful tips which had already put his ministry on good footing! Christmas was just a week ahead. He was alone in his house as he looked back on some great and terrible moments in his eighteen-month stay.

He was tired and as he sat relaxing on a chair his mind started to wander. Then slowly it steadied in a reverie. He could see images, almost like in a movie theater. The first image was his greatest moment. It played vividly before his mind drifted to other moments, some great and others lousy.

The greatest moment came sooner than he had expected. He had been in Yakiri for barely six months when he watched a group of young men performing a dance. It was a very lively dance whose acrobatic nature instantly attracted him.

"They dance beautifully," he turned and remarked to Kiki with whom he was watching the boys.

"You may say so because you haven't watched Amidou Ngong and his troupe," he responded. "They're something else."

"Who's Amidou Ngong?" the priest asked.

"He's the unbeatable baya dancer."

"Baya?" his deep voice resonated as his face contorted in confusion.

"Yes, the dance those boys are performing."

"I would like to challenge Amidou Ngong in baya dancing," the Irishman declared as he instantly thought it would be the best way to blend into the community and instill in his followers a sense of determination.

At this declaration, the villager turned and stared at him in disbelief. "Challenge him!" he exclaimed, shaking his head. He must have thought the priest was probably out of his mind.

"Yes, I wish to challenge him," the Irishman insisted.

"Well, you may challenge him but you can't win," Kiki said with assurance. "This man is a master of his thing."

"It's precisely for this reason that I want to challenge him," the priest maintained. "Could you assemble me some young boys and girls with agile legs who know how to dance baya?"

"You must be kidding, right!" the villager cried out. The priest's idea of taking on the great dancer was quite ridiculous, but to think of doing so with women dancers on his team seemed to him totally insane.

"No, I'm not kidding," the priest replied. "If I really mean something to you, you should help me accomplish this mission."

"Of course you mean a lot to me but I find the mission a bit preposterous," Kiki responded. "What's the point going into a competition only to lose?"

"You're the one saying I'm going to lose," the priest said. "I would like to bet with you that my team can challenge and beat Amidou Ngong and his troupe in baya dancing."

"I can see that you're very serious," Kiki said in resignation. "I'll give you all the support you need to make a total fool of yourself," he added with a giggle.

"Thank you very much," the priest said. "So when do I have my team ready to start practice?"

"Whenever you want," he replied. "When do you plan to take on Amidou Ngong?"

"In six months time."

"Six months time!" Kiki cried out incredulously. "I was thinking of something like two years."

"No, six months," the priest said.

"Well, count me as one of your dancers," the villager said. "By tomorrow evening the team should be ready."

It was not long before the entire village was abuzz with the news. "The priest is already putting together a group of dancers to train and take on Amidou Ngong and his men," whispers started to go round.

As soon as young men and women got the information, they flocked to him, asking to be part of it. His dancers did not think their team would win but the mere idea of being seen in the company of the new priest going up against Amidou Ngong, the greatest baya dancer of all times, filled them with great excitement.

Exactly a week after the priest had divulged his plan to Kiki, he stood in the evening with his drummers and dancers telling them what he expected of them. He announced to them that he and Kiki, a well-known baya virtuoso, would be their coach.

The priest was aware that if he succeeded in beating Amidou Ngong, the event would provide a tremendous boost to his fledgling ministry. He, therefore, decided to train extremely hard. After each training session with the other dancers, he would retire with Kiki to a quiet location and rehearse all the moves.

As the second month of training was drawing to an end, Kiki, for the first time, began to sense from the progress the team had made that it could put up quite a challenge. He decided to take things even more seriously. He visited neighboring villages and invited talented young men and women to join the Irish-African Flying Dancers as the troupe had come to be flamboyantly named.

Midway into the fourth month, the priest and Kiki made a selection of the thirty-two best dancers for the competition. By now practice was daily and rigorous. Intricate moves borrowed from the Irish folk dance were introduced and the young dancers worked to exhaustion. To motivate them, the priest promised the young men and women heaven! They all fell for it and threw their entire energy into the training.

With the fourth month almost at the end, the priest sent an emissary to inform the paramount chief that his troupe would like to take on Amidou Ngong and his dancers before him, his sub-chiefs and subjects. The whole idea of the challenge sounded outlandish but then the paramount chief had heard many incredible things about white people. He was thrilled with the idea.

Meanwhile, in Yakiri, when Tafon learned of the challenge, he felt a great sense of pride. It demonstrated to everyone that his subjects had guts. Even though he was still convinced that the priest and his dancers would not win, he lent them his entire support. He had seen Amidou Ngong perform on numerous occasions and was certain that the most the priest and his dancers could come up with would be a dull imitation of the exploits of the great master.

At any rate, the emissary soon arrived with a royal whisk which stated that the paramount chief was prepared to welcome the two contesting camps at the date the priest had indicated. The competition had now reached a point of no return.

How could the priest forget that memorable day as he lay back in his chair and was daydreaming!

The event took place at the palace of the paramount chief in Kimbo. Villagers had flocked in from all directions to watch the contest. Around the huge courtyard in front of the palace, a mammoth crowd had formed. The paramount chief and all his subs and their valets were present.

When the dignitaries had taken their seats, the drums began to rumble wildly. Everyone was excited and eager for the contest to start. As was the tradition, the champions would come in first to prove to the world that they were on top.

The priest was with his dancers. They were involved in some last minute warm up exercise and advice. It was then that he caught sight of the dancing legend, with his cap jauntily cocked on a side of his small head. A tall, elegant man with a tremendous sense of style!

He had heard a lot about him but now he was actually seeing him in action. He was not walking but prancing. Each step he took was reminiscent of some baya moves. And that was precisely what the village dancing judges would be looking for, the priest thought for a moment. Though the villagers tended to exaggerate the abilities of the captain, Fr Sean never for once committed the error of thinking that in the contest he would be a piece of juicy big Mac to be hastily chewed and washed down with Coca- Cola!

He knew, after all, that it was not from a seminary that the kind of skills Amidou Ngong displayed was obtained. But he was determined. He psyched up his own dancers for everything the great captain had to throw at them. And he had a lot to throw!

In every sense, Amidou Ngong was the sweet end of a bitter story. He was raised an orphan by a doting maternal aunt. As tradition required, when he attained the age of maturity he was offered a piece of land and some seeds by the paramount chief, hoping he would engage in agriculture.

Not cut out for that profession, he ran off with a local swinger called Ntuh who had formed a troupe of dancers. The troupe went from village to village entertaining people, especially during birth, death and marriage celebrations. In return for their services, the dancers were often rewarded with cattle and goats which were sold and the proceeds shared equally among members.

Then Ntuh saw a new opportunity in the kolanut trade which was rapidly expanding and moved to Abakwa. Amidou Ngong, who had already demonstrated great abilities, moved in to fill his shoes. It was then that a legend was born.

As captain, he introduced uniforms and acrobatics and perfected choreography. Apart from that, he also worked his men into a state of physical preparedness as the village had never seen before. In spite of these renovations, he still needed patronage and money to take his band to the next level.

When he was sufficiently convinced that his team was up to any challenge, he sent an emissary to the paramount chief. A week later, the royal whisk arrived. The troupe had been invited to stage their dance before the big man and his entire court. With Titang the great drummer pounding away, the dancers held everyone present at the show spellbound. Amidou Ngong became a household name.

The chief and his courtiers patronized the troupe and gifts started to pour in. Rich, revered and sung, he and his men had become the talk of the village and the open desire of every female heart.

On that fateful day, with the priest watching, the captain and his dancers dressed in bright, multi-colored uniforms sang "cocolico libabe" as they hopped their way into the huge circle the spectators had formed.

When the Irishman had openly made known his intention to take on Amidou Ngong, the mismatch was initially a source of much derisive laughter. Then it struck the great dancer that the priest could not have acted that way if he had nothing to prove.

He accepted the challenge and took on the task to prepare his dancers for it. So when he and his men stormed into the circle that hot afternoon, the dancers were ready. Their bulging and shiny muscles long beaten into shape by years of practice and rehearsals and their determined faces said it all.

All eyes were glued on the captain as he began to spring some of his acrobatic tricks, certainly to psyche out the Irishman.

The master moved to a spot and his dancers, over thirty of them, instantly formed a huge circle around him. Then his voice

164

rang out as he intoned a song. His men responded in chorus and their voices echoed in the neighboring hills. The competition was on and Amidou Ngong was at the top of his thing!

He leaped into the air and before his feet could touch the ground, he somersaulted and was standing face to face with one of his dancers. This feat, a mere warm up, was known in the parlance of the art as "giving baya." The crowd wailed with applause.

Not to be overshadowed, the drummers went crazy. Fundoh, the lad to whom baya had been given, broke rang and swirled towards the center of the circle like a tornado while Amidou took his place on the line. Now at the center alone, it was show time. He began in earnest to strut his stuff. Bouncing on both hands and feet in a bizarre arching-to-craft gesture, he suddenly sprang onto his feet and skipped into the air, kicking up a storm of dust.

By the time all his dancers had been to the center of the circle, they were drenched in sweat. The real dancing was just beginning. The dancers dug deep into their repertoire and came up with all kinds of formation, including even the map of Ireland – which the priest had inadvertently surrendered to a member of the opposing camp. They took the battle right to the doorstep of St Patrick, whose life history they already knew and for whom a praise song had been secretly composed.

What a way to provoke an Irish!

Fr Sean measured the gravity of the situation and knew precisely what to do. He and his team had come fully prepared. And like in every contest which pitted David against Goliath, he had his secret weapon.

Their combination which blended local dance forms with elements of Irish folk dance was dynamite. What was more, he had incorporated two extremely well built and agile women in his troupe and had insisted that a woman be made a member of the panel of judges. These innovations were refreshing.

As soon as the drums signaled that it was their turn, he and his dancers stormed into the circle from different directions. It looked chaotic but it was yet another innovation and one instantly rewarded with a handsome uproar of applause. Watching from the sideline, Amidou and his men began to realize that they were up for a real encounter.

The priest intoned a great song he had composed with the aid of his followers. It incorporated both the history of the Wotikars and a good amount of praises for its greatest ancestor Yaa. When his dancers responded, he used a discreet foot gesture to signal them to come close together into a group. Then suddenly, like overripe seeds under the pressure of the sunlight, they exploded and dispersed in every direction, with each dancer indulging in a sophisticated form of dance-acrobatics half-Irish, half-African. The population had never seen anything like it and went wild. In spite of the applause, the priest was still not convinced that his troupe had been cranked up to the right level of energy and performance.

Doing the hip motion to work them up, he moved his butt from side to side with an attitude. It was almost like a dog wagging its tail.

Ever since that butt started to come out of the cassock, it had been the subject of discreet scrutiny and many ungodly whispers. While those responsible felt at ease looking, they were convinced that the hottest place in hell was reserved for anyone who longed for it.

With biblical injunction and its promise of eternal damnation exercising a powerful restraint, these female admirers never went beyond mere knowing glances and hush-hush. The dancing competition, however, seemed to be providing a good venue to openly express their feelings.

The impending transgression also owed a lot to the very character of the butt itself. Once used to the cold and to temperate composure, as well as the harsh discipline of a monastic lifestyle, it suddenly found itself subjected to excessive heat, intense drumming and the madness of the tropics. The outcome was predictable. It went crazy and started to tick like a grasshopper's.

The women liked what they were seeing. They kept their eyes glued and accompanied each movement with handclapping. Where Jesus ended in performing miracles, the butt seemed to have taken over. In the hysteria of the moment, stories of hell were totally relegated to the background.

"Nisaankajang Baleland!" some of them threw caution to the wind and cried out amid thunderous ululations and applause.

166

"That priestly butt will go places!" a voice rose above the confusion.

However, aware that God in heaven was all powerful and watching and might not take lightly to their secret desire to steal one of His servants, some of these admirers hastily made the sign of the cross as a form of atonement.

But the damage had already been done! Even though the priest's Wotikar was still a bit rusty, it was good enough for him to pick up the meaning of the utterances of his wailing fans. "Grasshopper Butt Daddy from Ireland!" in the midst of such a high-level competition was an accolade lofty enough to incense any dancer.

By now the adrenaline rush triggered by the applause was fully in action. The priest leaped skyward and, in grand tradition of veteran baya dancers, adjusted his hat in mid-air before landing. He sprang into a cartwheel, somersaulted three times and almost bumped into Kiki whom he had selected for the rooster duo. The crowd went out of control with applause and excitement. More was still to come as the two took to the center of the circle the dancers had created.

The duo commenced with its normal routine. The dancers circled and wriggled their hips to melt the hearts of local wenches. Then in imitation of the Irish during dancing, the two held hands and started to move their legs and click their heels simultaneously in perfect timing to the drumming.

As the music rose to a crescendo, they added a new routine, turning round abruptly immediately after each click, then sticking out and shaking their butts, as if to say: "Come get it if you can!"

"This man missed his calling!" a local wench cried out as the bulk of her companions were already on their knees. Even without the strip, the tease was overpowering, not least because of the rainbow and exotic combination. They had seen and understood the African butt. The Irish they knew very little about and nobody had ever informed them that it could easily turn nasty under the slightest form of provocation.

"I'm sure that if Baleland is given a woman he'll perform satisfactorily," one woman overtaken by the performance of the Irishman murmured before looking around stealthily.

167

"Look here my dear, if a man with small testicles finds himself in a village with men suffering from hernia, he's well advised to go around with a calabash tucked away in his pair of trousers," the voice of someone who had overheard her countered. "This is a competition and if the priest doesn't please the judges he's going to lose."

"Whether he likes women or not, we'll know with time," Mbohti declared to the total amusement of some bystanders.

"It sounds like you want to tempt him," one of them hinted.

"Didn't he tell us in doctrine classes that even Christ was tempted?" she responded. "Resisting temptation seems to me a part of his job."

"Well, if you tempt him and he fails he'll go down to hell with you," a voice warned.

"I won't mind spending the rest of my life in hell with such good food," she said before adding a proverb: "If a mouse dies, blame it on its mouth."

While this little conference dragged on, the priest and his pal kept on with their performance. The duo had worked out so well that some spectators, stimulated by the performance, had attempted the Irish dance with catastrophic results. Knees collided and a fight almost erupted.

The duo finally came to an end, much against the wish of the public, and the priest resumed his captainship.

As luck would have it, it was at this juncture that Oho, one of Yakiri's greatest drummers, appeared from nowhere. In the wake of the kolanut rush, he too had left the village for Abakwa. Apprised of the contest when he returned to the village on a routine visit, he continued to Kimbo. As soon as he appeared on the scene, he pounced on the drum and boosted the rhythms in a new and dramatic way. It was the moment for Africans to learn what Europeans already knew: blonds love to have fun! It was as though the priest instantly developed wings and started to fly!

"Chochocho!" the crowd exclaimed in an expression of absolute wonderment.

Amidou Ngong could not believe what was unfolding before his very eyes. He came for a dancing competition and was now in the midst of a magic show. Pure magic! And like most magic displays, this one drew some superstitious remarks.

"The communion and wine this man eats and drinks every morning have something to do with this kind of agility!" an overjoyed local commentator cried out.

Then the music came to an abrupt halt just as the dispersed dancers regrouped in the form of a perfect cross. When it resumed everyone knew it was not Jesus who had just been crucified in that gesture but Amidou Ngong!

Even before the Irishman and his group had completed their repertoire, the captain joined him in the center of the circle for a dance and then handed him his cap. Like two roosters engaged in a fight, they eyed each other as they circled for a while and then came close to each other and hugged. The din which engulfed the entire village was terrible. The decision of the judges was not necessary.

To think that the priest pulled this off with all the odds stacked against him. It was indeed something!

As people say, in every weakness there is strength. Conscious of this, the priest had worked his dancers hard, had dug deep into his own background to teach them some new tricks and had made them aware of the importance of victory on that particular occasion.

From this incident, the villagers had come to learn and conclude that with God and the will, there would always be the way. Yes, the event had proved the priest could go places with the villagers.

His mind shifted cursorily to other achievements. He thought of St Patrick School and its pupils about to move to the third class after a two-year program had been squeezed into a shorter time frame. He was impressed with the brilliant performance of many of them.

This was not the only thing which impressed him. Some villagers like Tafon who had long passed the age of attending primary school had, nevertheless, shown a keen interest to learn how to read and write. This had caused him to start the adult literacy center.

On the spiritual front, the conversion to Christianity was slow and challenging. Nding had become like a friend and father to

169

him and they visited each other constantly but he had not succeeded in convincing him to give up some of his practices.

The mystic always lent him an eager ear when he was teaching him about the Holy Scriptures and Christ. He had even mastered the Ten Commandments and many prayers but that was the farthest he seemed prepared to go. Not that he was hostile to Christianity. No. He simply found the reasons which the priest advanced for him to quit his trade inadequate. Besides, he found him to be too young.

The old man had even started paradoxically to gradually convert the Irishman to his own world. He took him to the forest when he was not busy and showed him some medicinal plants and had even begun initiating him into the initial steps of sending a lightning to strike down somebody.

It was an art whose science fascinated the priest. However, when the training required him to start indulging in some practices and rites he deemed pagan, he gave up the program.

Any remaining hopes that he could find good reasons someday to resume the training were shattered by a contention which arose over the case of a young man. It was so far the lowest point of his ministry, a defining moment for him.

The priest saw in the event added proof that he still had a long way to go. It would be hard to fully appreciate the impact of the incident on him without cursorily examining the incident.

It all began with coffee. This produce had already become an attractive trade item in the world market and this caused its production to expand in Yakiri. Like any trade in which big money was involved, it spawned numerous hustlers and crooks.

Yakiri was still grappling with the problem of illiteracy and this made many of its coffee producers vulnerable, so it seemed, to the agents who served as intermediaries between the local farmers and the large-scale, urban buyers.

A cultural environment of habitual trust did not help the farmers. Mere words in that purely traditional setting were enough to provide the basis on which important business deals could be contracted. More often, a witness was not even necessary.

The young man in question had dabbled into Western education, a thing so rare and precious in those days. On this merit, a cooperative in Abakwa hired and dispatched him to Yakiri to

170

serve as its local agent. The tantalizing prospect of making quick money dangled before his eyes and he overreached himself. Having spotted the flaws of the community, he decided to take advantage of them.

He contacted an old, illiterate farmer, a distant relative of Nding, and took four sacks of coffee from him. Since the practice was that the cooperatives or businessmen first took the produce and only paid the farmers later on after it had been sold, the young man marked down only three sacks in his ledger. His idea was to rip the old man off one sack.

When it was payday, the old man showed up to collect his due and discovered that it fell below what he had expected. Even though he was old, his tenacious mind kept track of all his transactions. The ensuing disagreement which the financial shortfall triggered was referred to the Council of Elders but could not be satisfactorily resolved. Finally, some villagers suggested that the priest be consulted on the matter.

Even though Fr Sean had not lived long enough in the community, he could vouch for the honesty of the old man. At the same time, what he had endorsed through a fingerprint showed that he acknowledged having given only three sacks of coffee. Western legal practice and African tradition were now on a terrible collision course.

The priest knew the custom of the people and was convinced that even though the old man could not read, he might have acted out of trust when he apposed his fingerprint. To further buttress this argument, the old man did not even bother to invite a witness.

On the strength of these observations, he tried in vain to talk the young man out of the game he was playing. He even contacted the head office of the cooperative and when the matter came up for adjudication, the officials, no better than their agent themselves, stuck to what the ledger said and ruled in his favor.

"Look here," the young man told the old man in front of the cooperative officials who had come to settle the matter, "the ledger shows that I only collected three sacks of coffee." And with a chuckle, he added: "This old man has certainly gone senile or is suffering from amnesia."

"You're young and I don't want you to get smart with me," the old man declared. His appeal fell on deaf ears, the officials having already tabled the matter.

"I'll be back," the old man declared before leaving.

Coming from an old man, there was something ominous in this message. But human greed is foolhardy. It is a wonderful anesthesia. It sometimes paralyzes the mind and makes it incapable of seeing or even sensing approaching danger.

Driven by his selfish quest to make money at the old man's expense, the young man could not pick up the signals of looming disaster. Like so many Africans, who have poorly assimilated and badly digested Western cultures and values and have, therefore, come to believe that they can be something only when they turn their back on the society which raised and nurtured them, he simply saw the old man as another exercise in clownery. Clowning is not the domain of the old in this part of the world.

When the old man contacted Nding, he attempted a number of times to summon the young man and talk him out of what he had done but he did not even have the courtesy to show up.

"Leave the matter to me," Nding told his relative. "You'll get your money, every franc of it. He has won his own way and we'll do grave injustice to ourselves if we don't win our own way," he concluded in a chilly message.

The young man was already in a pot but the lid was not closed. There is an African proverb which says that even when a child is being punished for wrongdoing, the child is dragged into the house and not thrown outside in darkness to face the lions.

Nding was not a ruthless man. In fact, ruthless people were hardly endowed with the kinds of powers he had. Even though he was convinced that justice must be served, he wanted to apply his pressure in increasing doses so that in the end it should be the young man's own intransigence which would condemn him.

He went through his repertoire of mystical practices to enforce debt collection. The first that came to mind was to send bees to swarm and overwhelm the man but he decided against that because bees could sometimes be very mean and just go straight for a kill.

172

Then he thought of sacrificing and burying a goat which would cause the young man to decay progressively as the goat in the soil but again changed his mind. Usually, when this method was used, by the time people got the message, it was often already too late for the decaying process to be reversed.

Finally, he settled for lightning. Often, before the deadly blow was administered, two warnings were served within a week's interval, enough time for any reasonable person to react.

A week after the adjudication, the agent was at his house with his wife and daughter when the sky suddenly turned dark and it began to rain lightly. Thunder began to rumble and then suddenly there was a flash of lightening. A gash was made on his wall and the table which stood at the center of the sitting room was split into two halves. The young man suddenly found himself outside in a furrow at the vegetable garden in front of his house.

His wife, to whom he had failed to divulge what had happened, found the incident unusual and asked her husband to consult a gnukwabe. The man went out and when he came back in the evening, he lied to her that he met a gnukwabe who told him it was a natural phenomenon.

A week later, at exactly the same time and in similar weather circumstances, lightning struck again, this time tearing open the bag in which the man carried his documents when he went out to meet farmers. The contents of the bag, the ledger in which he kept records of his transactions with farmers from whom he had taken coffee, as well as some bank notes, were scattered all over the floor.

It was a sign whose significance the stupidest person could read, but the agent still reacted with indifference as in the first instance. This time his wife did not wait, for she knew her husband was hiding something. She packed up her things, took her daughter and fled to her father's compound.

It did not come to her as a surprise when a messenger came calling at her father's compound with the sad and terrible news that her husband had been struck down and slit open by lightning, like a chicken about to be roasted, while he was busy working in his garden.

The husband was dead but the matter was not over. One week after the man was buried lightning struck again and created a big crack on the man's grave. His wife knew there was something

173

very serious so she went to a gnukwabe who told her what had happened and said she would be the next to be killed if the grieving party did not get his money. The woman looked for the old man whom her husband had bilked out of a sack of coffee and had the debt settled.

Fr Sean had followed all the development of the case and knew the old man was related to Nding who was his friend. From what Kiki had told him, when he wanted to lock his house the day they met the woman with a dying child, he suspected that the old man at the hilltop could not be unconnected with the mysterious death of the coffee agent.

"Thou shall not kill," Fr Sean had confronted his old friend when he got words about the young man's death, reciting in this instance some doctrine lessons they had gone through together.

"Thou shall not steal," the old man responded. "I didn't kill the young man, he killed himself," he added with irrefutable logic. "I created a way out for him but he stuck to his logic and I to mine."

When Fr Sean pondered this, he was lost. He had seen the young man's intransigence and even arrogance and knew what that could result in when up against an old man who would not budge from his own logic.

There was still a lot of progress to be made, of that he was certain. His mind was still lingering on these thoughts when he heard a knock on the door. He emerged from his daydream with a jump, rose from his seat and rushed to the door. He pulled it open and it was Kiki.

"The postman gave me this letter to hand it to you," he declared. "I must go now."

"Goodnight Kiki."

"Goodnight Father."

He contemplated the letter for a while. It bore a rather strange stamp depicting an eagle, with something written underneath in Benge. He had studied some Benge in school and knew it was the name of the bird. The name of the sender of the letter was not written on it.

He opened it and the address simply read: "O'Neil, Kele Parish, Yamade, Mungo East." He went through the letter and leaped into the air for joy. It was O'Neil, whom he met at the

174

seminary and who had given him Bernard Nso's address. He had also decided to come to Africa, to Mungo East. He then thought of what Nding had told him.

"O'Neil isn't my brother but my friend," he quickly murmured to himself.

He was still not quite getting Africans.

When some days later another letter arrived from Ireland in which it was expressed that the husband of his most beloved and only maternal aunt, Patricia, had died in an accident, his mind went back again to the old man. He did not know whether it was lack of precision on the part of the old man or the sloppy interpretation of Kiki. Either way, he was wrong. He was in Africa but still not with Africans and his troubles with words were far from over.

30

After spending some years in the small African village, the Irishman was perfectly at home. At least, this was what he thought. He was a virtuoso in baya dancing and had already mastered the tricky art of playing drums with his elbow. He ate kibane and roasted rats with tremendous appetite and, time and again, had proved that he could hold his own when it came to drinking palm wine. Apart from these things, he understood the culture of the people thoroughly and spoke the language fluently.

Yet, even with all these attributes, he still seemed totally unprepared for what was to come.

He was sitting at the presbytery one day when a village elder and a friend of his knocked at the door, walked in and sat down. After exchanging greetings with the man, the priest asked whether there was anything he could do for him.

The man cleared his throat and adjusted himself on his seat before telling him that he had come to invite him to his home.

"On what day am I to come?" the priest asked.

"March 17," the man replied.

Now Fr Sean being Irish, a more unsuitable day for an invitation could not have been selected. March 17 is St Patrick Feast Day.

Ever since the priest arrived in this small African village, the celebration of the day had always been a special moment for him, conducted in quiet meditation and prayers, either at the retreat of the presbytery or some distant and calm place. He had already drawn up a program for the day and knew how the man would feel if he declined the invitation.

He paused for a while after the man had made the announcement, ferreting through his vast store of knowledge of the people to see if, without losing face, he could find any decent way to come out of the tight spot to which the invitation had pushed him. His mental rambling seemed to have come up with an answer.

"I can't come on that day because it's the day that St Patrick died and it's celebrated as a feast day," the priest declared at last.

"Died?" the man asked calmly not sure whether he got the priest right.

"Yes, he died on March 17," he stated clearly, removing any lingering shadow of doubt the old man might have had.

"Who's St Patrick to you?" the old man asked.

"He's the father of all the Irish people," he explained.

"A father?"

"Yes, a father and a real great one indeed," he declared proudly, pointing at a picture of the saint on a wall of the room.

The old man rose from his seat and went to the wall where the picture hung. He took a good look at the great Irish clergyman clutching his crosier. His old wrinkled fingers wandered from one point of the picture to the other, pausing on St Patrick's flowing white beard, his crown-like miter and above all the entangling pile of serpents before him and from all these signs, he rapidly came to the conclusion that this was no ordinary father.

"A father. Then that must be a very big death celebration," the old man declared. "His hat even looks like that of a king, and no ordinary king at that because he stands in the midst of snakes," he added with his eyes still glued to the picture.

"Yes, it's a big celebration and there's something kingly about the name Patrick which actually comes from 'Patricius,'" the priest replied somewhat naively.

The old man seemed very satisfied with the answer the priest had given him for not being able to honor his invitation. He stood up, stroked his withered beard and, after commenting a bit about the weather, shook hands with him. And just before he left, he asked the priest whether he had another picture of St Patrick to offer him. The priest disappeared into another room of the presbytery and soon emerged with an identical picture which he gave the old man. He took it thankfully and, after contemplating it for a while, wished him good-bye and stepped outside. The priest too was happy that he left satisfied.

So where did the priest really go wrong?

With the picture, the man went straight to the palace of the sub-chief. The story he recounted, with all its African garnishments, depicted an entirely different picture. Using the picture to make his case, he told Tafon and whoever he met who was prepared to listen that Fr Sean had a very big death to celebrate, the one of his father who was king, and that the entire village had to be mobilized to do something. This was a very serious matter.

We cannot examine the impact of the old man's revelation without emphasizing the very special place this priest held in the hearts of the villagers. Since in the community he was more of a father figure, very much loved and highly respected, the villagers were determined to do something which befitted that station and that he would live to remember. What followed was an orgy of feasting and dancing which did not only frighten the Irish in its scale but has long since gone into the annals of Roman Catholicism and its encounter with the African people.

As soon as the villagers were informed, they held an important meeting at the compound of the sub-chief and set up different committees to take care of the various aspects of the event and immediately started to mobilize the necessary resources. There was a special committee for the collection of palm wine and the brewing of bilibili, a second one to prepare food and a third to fetch firewood and a fourth to organize traditional dances.

A small delegation was sent to inform the priest that the village intended to celebrate the death with him and asked for some aspects of his own program to integrate in theirs to make the event a resounding success. With typical African humility and understatement, it put the very alert mind of the priest in a slumber.

Now, operating with the mindset of an Irish, the priest thought more of a parade, perhaps followed by a small gathering in which people would sit down to chat, sip palm wine and make jokes. He could not have been more mistaken.

Before the delegation left, he told its members that the day would start with a mass to be said early in the morning before festivities could begin.

"We'll come with our loaves of bread and two fish," its members announced as they left the church premises.

Meanwhile, news of the event had already reached neighboring villages and they too started mobilizing and making the necessary arrangements.

Came March 17, the entire village was buzzing with excitement as everyone dressed in his or her best attire and showed up at the Roman Catholic Church for mass. Immediately after the mass came, it was announced that the event would take place on the soccer ground of the St Patrick Primary School just next to the church.

Some young men were immediately set to work, moving the desks from the classrooms to the field to provide seats for people during entertainment and feasting. While the young men were busy with this work, the rest of the villagers retired home, to get ready before coming back, like men, according to a village saying.

From the window of his house, the priest kept track of developments so he would not keep people waiting when they arrived for the celebrations.

The first signal the priest got which indicated that he might have unleashed a monster was when some young men came with bulls and numerous goats and noisily had them tethered at the church premises.

Then as he was trying to figure out just what the people were up to, some women arrived bearing bundles of wood and huge cauldrons. Then large gallons of palm oil and other cooking ingredients began to flow in. In his long stay in the village, there was nothing he had never seen. So he maintained his calm.

Then dancers and some men arrived in multi-colored traditional attires, bearing huge bags with dancing apparels, xylophones and big drums. Most of them were also carrying their Dane guns. He began to get frightened but remembered that he was Irish, a people with a hefty reputation for bigheartedness.

An unending string of women showed up with big baskets of food on their heads, followed by men carrying huge calabashes of palm wine and bilibili. He was now getting a bit nervous by the sheer amount of food and drinks being hauled in for the celebration.

His mind was still trying to figure out the kind of celebration the people intended to stage when a terrible wail broke out. Now ready for the event, he rushed out of his house and burst onto a strange scene.

Women, white as devils and with bare and disheveled hair and with wraps firmly strapped around their hips, were tumbling on the ground and screaming and calling out a word he did not identify at first.

"St Batric," they shouted as they wailed, with one of them holding up the framed picture of St Patrick. Batric was actually the way the name of the great Irish icon had been confused with the torch battery which they saw almost every day with the priest.

The priest had always known that when it came to mourning a dead person, the villagers were second to none but what he could not understand was how the "death" of his "father" thousands of miles away could trigger such an outpouring of grief. He tried in vain to stop the women from wailing, stating that his "father," St Batric, died a long, long time ago and it was time to rejoice rather than mourn.

"A long, long time ago Farar?" one of the wailers asked amid her tears.

"Yes," the priest replied, secretly celebrating that he might have just found a cure for the wail. He had, in fact, poured gasoline on flames which were already burning out of control.

"A long, long time Farar has said," the woman announced at the top of her voice to the other wailers and then hurled herself to the ground and the crying immediately passed from soprano to alto and bass.

Now the Irish man could not understand what he had said which made the crying go from bad to worse until he was later informed by a man that death was like palm wine which became more alcoholic with the passing of each day.

"Since the death took place a long time ago and it's only now that it's being celebrated, it means that enough resources have been accumulated, including tears and wailing, to pour into the event," he said. "Would you cause them to hold back on their resources in celebrating the death of so great a man?" he asked, maintaining a studious glare on the priest.

He did not know what to say for every word to him now seemed suspect and could only get him into trouble. Having failed to make the wailing abate, he sat back and took things the way they came.

While he had busied himself appealing to the women to stop crying, the villagers had taken their cows and goats near a stream not far from the church and slaughtered them and he only noticed that when the meat was being transported to the site where steaming cauldrons had been set over huge fires.

With the meat cooking and all the musical instruments set, the priest understood that he had been completely overtaken by events and simply joined the crowd sitting at the field waiting.

The food was soon ready and the wailers, having rushed home to wash themselves and redo their hair, returned gaily dressed and filled with joy and laughter as though they had borrowed a different personality for this new phase of the event.

The women started setting food before the villagers who had been helping themselves to enormous quantities of palm wine and bilibili. Huge chunks of meat, baskets of kibane and an incredible quantity of palm wine and bilibili were placed in front of the priest who invited children to the feast, all of them wanting to sit on his lap and take a very intimate look at the curiosity of "white" chewing.

The dancers repaired to an empty classroom to get themselves ready and the drum and xylophone players had already taken their seats. It was time for them to provide entertainment to the people as they ate.

Then the drums struck up, rumbling like thunder and threatening to swallow up the frantically hammered harmonies of the xylophones.

The dancers, masqueraded, rattles strapped to their ankles and wearing strange garbs of partridge feathers, stormed in and the whole earth shook with the vibration. The thundering was heightened with sporadic outbursts of Dane guns whose clouds of smoke permeated the whole atmosphere with a very strong and repulsive smell. The dancers kept the public entertained with numbers from their vast repertoire while the villagers continued to gorge themselves with food and tremendous quantities of palm wine and bilibili. When everyone had eaten his fill, some women went around keeping the place tidy.

Drinking continued until dusk when the priest had to see off the last of the villagers many of whom were already drunk and singing at the top of their voices and calling the name of St "Batric." The lingering smell of palm wine which had invaded the whole church premises, adding an extra layer of pagan color to a saintly event, was in itself ample evidence that the celebration was a great success and that the "father" of the Irish people had been "kidnapped" for the second time and made that of these African people too.

When they had all left, Fr Sean, greatly flattered by the show of support, retired to the presbytery, rubbed his hands and smiled. It was one of the greatest celebrations of St Patrick he had seen after all. But thank God, Africans celebrate death only once, even for their own parents and kings.

He thought of the mispronunciation of the name of the saint and how it came about and smiled again. On second thought, he concluded the villagers were right. What else could the generator of light, a man who converted a pagan people into a Christian nation, be referred to other than "Batrick!"

31

Nkar sat on a hill on the main road from Yakiri to Kimbo. From this imperious position, it overlooked Yakiri. Its first sub-chief was Nkulah, a man of remarkable integrity. He was kind and extremely hardworking so that by the time he died he had accumulated numerous acres of kolanuts and coffee plantations. He also left behind large herds of goats, cattle and horses.

Tita, one of his sons, succeeded him as sub-chief. He disliked work and delighted in the company of women and not long after he became the village head, he got married to three wives.

The first was Bongtah, a lazy talkative woman filled with jealousy. She bore the sub-chief two male children, Mbinkar and Ndam. Mbinkar took after his mother, adding to her numerous negative streaks an even more diabolical one. He would stop at nothing to get what he wanted.

Ndam, on the contrary, took after his grandfather. He had learned very early that a man's reputation depended on what he could achieve for himself. With this idea in mind, he sought and obtained land and started to accumulate his own wealth. Unlike his brother, he did not sit back and wait for the day his father would die for him to inherit his property.

Tita's second wife was Azah. She gave birth to a boy, Ngwache, and a girl, Ayah. As a young man, Ngwache had listened to Tanikru, a villager who had traveled to the coast where he had worked as a laborer in one of the white plantations. Tanikru could read and write and so much impressed the young man with his stories that the latter decided to go to school.

At school, he excelled but he knew the future was in business. He secretly nursed the idea of one day taking over the family estate and making it even more prosperous through the business techniques he had acquired in school.

The third wife, Abah, had four daughters, Chefor, Siri, Suji and Nchea. Like Ayah in the Azah household, the four girls were of little consequence in this very traditional setting. They could not inherit wealth and were seen more as property to be handed over to the first young man with enough money to pay the bride price.

A combination of wealth and numerous women vying for one heart made the Tita family a scene of constant bickering and occasional fighting. The two women with sons quietly plotted and connived to destroy each other, as they both nursed the ambition that one day their offspring would become sub-chief and inherit the vast family estate and property.

It was, therefore, not surprising that when news reached the village one afternoon that Tita had been bitten by a snake and had died, the simmering family feud burst into the open and took a very violent turn.

With the demise of Tita and with Ndam showing no interest whatsoever in the throne, almost the entire village threw its support behind Ngwache to be the new sub-chief. The villagers reckoned that with an educated person at the head of their community, it would prosper.

Mbinkar sensed he had little support and that his chance for power was gradually slipping away. He decided to strike a deadly blow before matters turned worse for him. He started plotting to have his brother killed.

One evening, while the succession question was still raging, Ngwache went to the forest to harvest kolanuts. Three men emerged from the bush and started to stab him. As he lay dying, he instructed his killers to tell their paymaster that none of his male children would ever amount to anything.

Much against popular will, Mbinkar finally became sub-chief. He had two wives who bore only girls, most of whom died at their infancy. After numerous attempts, one of his wives gave birth to a boy, his only boy. He named the son Goran. The son took after his father in everything.

When Goran came of age, his father wanted him to get married as quickly as possible. He thought that luck might smile on the young man and he would have more boys. His own village subjects on whom he had imposed a reign of terror refrained from marrying any of their daughters to Goran.

He was forced then to look elsewhere for a bride. He remembered having seen the sub-chief of Yakiri with a very pretty girl and decided to strike out in that direction. The foundation for a major tragedy with far-reaching consequences was about to be laid.

32

About twenty years had elapsed since the priest arrived in Yakiri. It was evening and Tafon was standing in his compound, concentrating on the tremendous development strides the village had made.

Darkness was fast gathering. His wife and daughter had still not returned from the fields. Even though such an occurrence was common, he was still worried. He paced up and down in front of his house and then cleared his throat. He was heading towards the small patch of grass which grew not very far from his own house to spit out the mucous when he heard a dry cough and then saw the silhouettes of his wife and daughter.

"Wirba," he called out as the silhouettes surged towards him and when his wife responded he couldn't hold back his protest. "I've often warned you against staying in the fields up to this hour."

"After we were through with work on the farm, we decided to fetch some firewood," she strained to respond under the weight of her burden.

She made her way towards the front of her house and put down the load she had carried on her head. She moved her neck slightly from side to side, and then forward and backward to ease the pain.

Her daughter, Mayemfon, had also put down her load and was going through the same exercise. Wirba went to a corner of the wall of her house where she hid her key. She took it from the crevice where it had been stuck and returned to the door. She fidgeted with the lock before finding the slot and as soon as the key went through, she turned it and pushed the door open.

Inside the house, it was pitch dark. Dishes rattled and empty pots clattered as she stumbled by them in search of her box of matches. She finally found it, pulled out a stick and struck it. It sputtered into a yellow flame which sent its light across the dark room. The new hurricane lamp glinted with the light and she reached out for it and lit it.

Mayemfon was still standing outside. She was a tall, well built and pretty girl and was the only daughter and child of the Tafon's before Forsuh, the child of Wirba's older sister who passed away, and Bong, the son of a distant relative of Tafon, came to live with Tafon and his wife.

She could have been around seventeen, already overripe, some villagers would say, for picking. But the long anticipated line of suitors had not come calling. This was not a good sign. How would he feel in the midst of his friends, if he were stuck with an unmarried daughter?

Her breasts were already full and her butt quite round. He had dreamed of the huge amount she would fetch as bride price when young men came banging on his door to ask her hand for marriage. He knew from mere commonsense that when fruits became overripe and were not picked, they started to rot and fall from the tree with the slightest wind. The village had more than its fair share of young men who spent their time devising schemes to get naïve girls pregnant or even to elope with them altogether. This prospect made Tafon sweat.

"Our tradition is going down the drain," he murmured to himself, obviously recalling the good old days when young girls remained virgins until they got married. "These days some of them start licking honey of the loins even before they've learnt to crawl," he added, heaving a sigh.

From the vantage position in front of his house, he watched his daughter as she carefully followed the shaft of light emanating from her mother's house until she went inside.

He turned to enter into his house. He had not lit a fire and it was very dark.

"Mayemfon!" he shouted out her name.

Her shrill little voice rang out in her mother's house, just to the left of Tafon's. She came running, her mouth stuffed with roasted sweet potatoes.

"It's dark and you need not run, lest you trip on something and fall," her father scolded when she got to him panting. "Light fire in my house," he ordered.

187

The girl returned to her mother's house for a torch of bamboo reeds and put the burning torch on her father's fireplace. As the room brightened, she collected some firewood from the stack in the corner. This she piled over the burning torch. A flame rose and its shadows began to play on the walls.

She used a wooden rod to poke the fire and remove some of the wood ash which prevented it from burning brightly. It crackled and its golden flame shot up and lit the whole room.

The door into her father's sleeping room was open. She followed the shaft of light which lit her path, then turned left into darkness and towards the corner where her father's bed was. She felt her way in the dark until she stumbled onto something. It was her father's hurricane lamp, what she was looking for. She grabbed it and retraced her steps.

Once in the sitting room again, the girl lit it using a flaming splint. She noticed that its globe was stained with soot which made the light dull. She took it off and went to a shelf in a corner of her father's sitting room where things were stored. The girl came back with a piece of rag and started to wipe it and when it was very clean, she put it back on the lamp.

She then placed the lamp on a stand where it could beam its light throughout the whole room. That done, she went to her father to inform him that everything was ready and he could go into the house.

"Thank you very much my mother, little great one and Princess of the Wotikar people!" her father exclaimed, showering her with terms of endearment and praises to express his gratitude.

As she walked away happily towards her mother's house, her father went into his.

His house had two sleeping rooms and a large sitting room where he usually received and entertained most of his visitors. The fireplace was at the center of the sitting room. His armchair was next to the fireplace, almost directly in front of the door leading to his sleeping room, in such a way that when he sat down he backed his sleeping room and faced the main door to his house. On his left, at the near corner, a door led into another room.

To the right of his armchair, at the far end, fitted on the wall, was a bamboo shelf where most of his basic needs were kept. To the left, on wooden pegs pinned to the wall, were numerous bags of raffia and various animal skins handed down through the generations. The soot which had accumulated on them over the years made them look incredibly ancient.

The bags contained various charms, some meant to ward off evil spirits and others to cast a spell on anyone who attempted to mess with any member of his family.

Each time Tafon looked at the bags, he thought of the day he received baptism from Fr Sean. He had promised him that he would get rid of all the magic potions and substances, as they went against the Christian faith.

These promises were never fully kept even though he went to mass regularly and swallowed communion. His ancestral gods had never failed him for him to lose confidence in them. So, instead of destroying them, he clung to them and to the white man's. Like Nding, whom he sometimes consulted on crucial matters, he had come to believe in the policy of comprehensive insurance.

He was being initiated into divination and native healing by Takwabe who had succeeded his father after he died. He did not really feel that all of what he was doing went contrary to the Holy Bible which he often read. He thought that the combined powers of the different deities would provide him with a tool potent enough to enable him to survive in an increasingly difficult world.

Once in his sitting room, he felt bored. The boredom gave rise to the lurking urge to go to the village square and share some drinks with friends and listen to a bottle dance orchestra. To be sure that he would not miss an important visitor when he was away, he decided to consult his ancestors.

He rose from his armchair in which he had just sunk and headed towards the wall where the bags were hanging and soon returned with one of them. This was of civet skin. He had received it from Takwabe. As an apprentice diviner, his eyes were still dim, to use the gnukwabe's own words, and so he had to clear them up. He reached into the bag and took out some cowries and bones, as well as a black substance which looked like coagulated coal tar.

With the blade of a knife, he scraped some of the black substance, letting the dust gather on a spot on the ground in front of him. After obtaining the amount he needed for the divination, he put the rest back into the bag and put it aside. Then, with a pair of wooden tongs, he grabbed a piece of glowing ember from the fire and placed it on the black dust. It sputtered, giving up some smoke which smelled much like the incense burned in a church during mass.

He murmured some incantation as the smoke rose and then picked up his cowries and bones and shook them vigorously before throwing them. He picked them up and tried again and, this time, his head nodded in approbation as he studied the configuration.

"A visitor and some good news," he murmured to himself as he put away the cowries and bones and returned the bag.

He then went to the corner where he kept his calabashes of palm wine and came back with the one that had been recently tapped. He stood it near his chair and went for his drinking cup, the horn of a buffalo handed down to him by his father.

After a perfunctory examination of the horn, he wiped its rim with his hand and poured himself some palm wine. He then leaned back relaxingly on his armchair. He raised the cup to his mouth, sipped the frothy, milky liquid and smacked his lips furiously. It had matured to the right taste.

He allowed his imagination to run wild as he tried to figure out the person who could be the visitor and the good news he was bringing. His cowries had informed him that it was an important person. So which important person had decided to come to his place for an important matter only at night? And what was the important matter?

To make the administration of the village more effective, he had delegated powers on a wide range of issues to his subordinates. Problems which were referred to him had to be very important. His mind was still searching when he heard a knock on the door.

33

Tafon raised his head and saw the giant figure of Mbinkar, the sub-chief of Nkar, framed by the door.

"Let God and the ancestors guide your steps Mbinkar," he greeted as he rose from his chair and moved forward to meet the visitor. "Welcome! Welcome!" he announced, showing him to a seat just next to his.

As Mbinkar took his seat, it was then that Tafon noticed Fai, the sub-chief's nephew. He was behind him and had been completely overshadowed by the towering size of his uncle. He had a bag strung across his shoulder and was carrying a calabash of palm wine. Tafon helped him put the things down and asked him to settle on a stool next to his uncle.

The calabash of palm wine showed it was indeed good news. For such a dignitary to make an unannounced visit at such an unusual hour could only mean good news. He was now anxious to hear the news.

"What good winds bring you to my village and compound at this unholy hour of the night?" he questioned tauntingly, resorting to the usual roundabout way to extract information from his guest.

A master of the art of traditional diplomacy and an old crook, Mbinkar knew how to effectively counter such verbal rigmaroles.

"Well, the kind of wind which will force a cricket out of its hole in a night when the moon isn't out yet," he responded, making sure he did not let the cat out of the bag, at least not at this early stage.

Then turning to his nephew who had accompanied him on this very important trip, he asked for the bag. He had already taken it off and it was just next to him.

"Here," his nephew said, handing the bag to his uncle.

Mbinkar plunged his hand into the raffia bag and brought out a small bundle which he handed to his host.

"This is for you," he announced as he rose from his seat to hand the bundle to Tafon.

He took it, paused for a while and stared alternately at his guest and the bundle, then gave his hand to Mbinkar.

"I don't know what to make of this gesture but whatever you're concealing from me will come out as there's plenty of palm wine for the evening," he said in mock ignorance as he shook his hand. "Thank you very much."

"You're welcome."

With a stick, he poked the fire and it came alive. Its golden flame reinforced the dull light of the lamp. He inspected the bundle, looking for the spot where the end of the twine which ran round it was tucked. He found it and pulled it and it gave way. He started to unwind it. Then the verdant leaves of a rhododendron appeared within, the first real hint that marriage was the purpose of the unannounced meeting.

Tafon had suspected rightly for he could not think of any other thing which could cause such an important person to suddenly burst onto his premises at that hour. After completely loosening the rope and removing the green leaves, he came across dry banana leaves. Patiently, he pealed off the dry leaves until he came to the gift which had been stashed away.

"Kolanuts," he said calmly, doing everything to hide his excitement when it dawned on him that the rush for his daughter had begun. No man in his right senses was in any rush to give away a daughter, however overripe she was. The show of restraint often fetched a handsome bride price.

"Yes, kolanuts for you," Mbinkar said emphatically, another sign that the gesture went far beyond a mere gift.

Tafon continued to play dumb, coaxing his guest to commit himself by talking and to talk in a manner which reflected his status in society.

Mbinkar saw the trap and the peanut on it clearly and was working out a way he could take the peanut without getting caught.

"Where's the calabash of wine?" he turned to his nephew.

"Here uncle," the young man said, pointing at it.

He then rose from his seat, lifted it and placed it between his uncle and Tafon.

"When an old man like me goes up mountains and crosses rivers in darkness to visit the home of a smaller brother, it's obvious that I've got a rooster and need a hen, one that can lay many good eggs," said Mbinkar who had finally decided to act big.

"Well, are you hinting that you've found a hen in my compound that can quench the fire of your rooster and give you the type of eggs you're looking for?"

"I've seen just the kind of hen which my rooster wants," Mbinkar announced.

"As I've numerous hens, so I would like you to give me a description of the one you want," Tafon bluffed.

He knew that Mbinkar could only talk of the hen in glowing terms as it would be unusual for him to want something he did not admire. Such praises could only help raise the stocks of her daughter.

"She's tall, with full breasts which can suckle many babies. She's of the size that a man's arms can go round comfortably, not too fat and not too thin, with well-endowed buttocks which tremble with each step. She's the type of hen which traditionally was reserved for royalties."

"Royalties of course!" Tafon cried out. "Now that you've given the description, I know the hen you want but as you've pointed out yourself, she's the kind of food meant for royalties and you know the price for developing an appetite for things of such high quality," Tafon said, his instinct for the jugular quickly demonstrated.

"I hope I didn't give you a rope to hang me by praising the beauty of your hen," Mbinkar moved fast to fill the hole he had dug for himself.

"You're just being true to what your heart is telling you," Tafon responded as his face brightened with a mischievous smile.

"Whatever the case, two important dignitaries can't be easily defeated by a problem, so I'm convinced that since we're Wotikar brothers and my rooster is in a sense your rooster, should the amount required for the hen be extremely high I'll have no other recourse than to pay what I can and then to shift the difference to you my brother to settle," Mbinkar stated, tactfully exploiting the culture of solidarity in their society to break a dangerous throttle.

"I agree with you but remember that I'm only the head of a family and will need to consult with other members before I give my final answer. That shouldn't be long from today," Tafon said. "I'll, however, endeavor to put in some kind words for you seeing the kind of person you've proved yourself to be," he intimated much to the delight of Mbinkar.

As family head and father of the potential bride, Tafon, could, through sweet words and flatteries, bring other members to negotiate their expectations. The urge to inflate a bride price was strong when it involved a rich man or a dignitary or any member of his family.

From the kolanuts which Mbinkar had presented, Tafon selected the largest and ripest and placed the rest on the ground. He started peeling off the white skin until he was left with the pink kernel. Sticking the tip of his right thumbnail along the white line of demarcation between two cotyledons, he exerted some pressure until the nut split along the line. He repeated the exercise with the other cotyledons. In all he had four cotyledons, two of which he gave to Mbinkar.

Through this gesture, he had in principle endorsed the application of the Mbinkar family, but this did not mean he could impose his opinion on other family members.

Tafon popped one of the cotyledons into his mouth and chewed crunchily, his face puckered after the fashion of a genuine kolanut connoisseur.

"This is fine dry kolanut, the kind which can make a man drink ten calabashes of palm wine," he said in a note of approval.

"You know that this is a very serious matter for which the finest things have been reserved," Mbinkar was quick to point out, seizing the opportunity provided by the compliment of his host to pull the blanket onto his side.

As the two ate kolanut, they washed it down with palm wine, first attacking the calabash of the host.

"The wine becomes better with each passing moment," commented Mbinkar as he took a sip from his buffalo horn.

"This is genuine stuff as is everything about me," Tafon agreed with the guest. "The kind of palm wine which will make a mad man express himself in a language other than his own," he joked.

His guest roared with laughter at this remark.

"When madness reaches a point where patients express themselves in another language, then that's really bad."

Mbinkar had the cup of his nephew filled. He took a very long sip and shook his head vigorously at the perkiness of the drink. He then emptied it and showed his cup again to be refilled. His uncle watched in amusement.

"This is strong stuff and if you drink too much you may develop a headache," he said to his nephew who merely smiled.

While they were busy drinking, Wirba came in, her hand clasped in front of her in a show of deference.

"Good evening great ones!" she called out.

"Good evening," the men answered the greetings.

She then proceeded with a brief conversation with Mbinkar, inquiring about the health of every member of his family. When the conversation came to an end, she turned to her husband and teased him.

"When men are in a room and only murmurs can be heard, know there's something good on the floor," she complained. "Mbinkar quietly crawled in here to meet his brother and share some palm wine with him without even stopping by to greet."

"I was still planning to come," Mbinkar said hastily in his defense.

"I was the one holding him down," Tafon rushed to his support.

"Well, I've always known that where two or three men are gathered, a conspiracy is being hatched against women," she declared in mock anger.

"At any rate the calabash of wine is still full and you can help yourself to as much as you want," the husband said. "We just started drinking when you came in."

"I really have to help myself, for the sun almost fried our brains out there in the field today."

"We're in the heart of the rainy season but the sun is always up," Tafon pointed out. "I hope this doesn't herald the beginning of a drought."

"Please, don't mention that word!" Mbinkar exclaimed. "I still haven't fully recovered from the last drought which reduced my harvests to almost nothing and killed many of my beasts."

The two men were busy reminiscing on the havoc of the last drought when Wirba stepped out of the house and shouted out the name of her daughter. When she heard her little voice, she ordered her to bring her drinking cup.

A few minutes later she rushed up to her clutching a small calabash with its top lopped off, transforming it into a kind of drinking cup.

"How many times do you have to be told not to run in the dark!" her mother scolded her, snapping away the cup from her to let her know she was not happy.

Wirba turned and went into her husband's house. With both hands clutching the cup, she bent double and reached out towards Tafon who started to pour her some palm wine. When her cup was full, she stood upright, took a swig, smacked her lips, thanked the men and then headed towards the door.

At the threshold, it struck her that she had a message for Mbinkar and so retraced her steps.

"I hope you have plenty of time," she turned to him.

"We've got as much as your husband wants us to stay, so if it's a question of spending the whole night here we'll certainly oblige," he retorted, throwing a sneaky and mischievous glance at Tafon.

"I just returned from the corn farm and I'm busy preparing some food," she said.

Mbinkar knew that no man in his right senses seeking the hand of a maiden could afford not to partake of the dinner offered on his behalf by a potential in-law.

"It's a long night and we're going to wait," he announced much to the delight of his nephew whose stomach had started rumbling.

The two men continued to gnaw away at kolanuts, washing down each piece with large amounts of palm wine. Their conversation bounced from one subject to another.

"Last dry season exacted a dreadful toll on my raffia palm bushes," Mbinkar said.

"What do you mean?" Tafon asked.

196

"During most dry seasons, I used to tap not less than two large calabashes of palm wine each day but in the last one it was almost impossible for me to come with half a calabash," Mbinkar moaned.

"It isn't difficult to understand why your yield is very low. Most of your raffia palms grow on dry land, in contrast to my own which grow in a swamp. When last dry season dragged on for too long, the roots of your bushes couldn't get to the water and that prevented the palms from producing plenty of wine. You were even very lucky that you had half a calabash, for a friend of mine informed me that he was getting almost nothing."

Mbinkar seemed impressed with Tafon's lengthy analysis.

"I think your explanation makes a lot of sense in that all my friends whose raffia palm bushes grow in the swamps or on river banks continue to tap plenty of wine."

"Even though my wine harvest has always been bountiful, I started experiencing some shortage, coming from a new and entirely unexpected source," Tafon told his guest.

"Please let me in on that so I may be on my guard," Mbinkar said, his eyes dilating with curiosity as he adjusted on his seat.

The flame rose higher as Tafon shifted the burning wood to the center of the fire.

"I lost most of my wine to theft," he announced to the utter disbelief of his guest who stared with an open mouth.

"This has never happened in the entire Wotikar land as it's strictly against our laws and tradition," Mbinkar stated emphatically, shaking his head in disapproval at the temerity of the criminal. "Nobody has the right to venture in the raffia palm bushes of another person with the aim of tapping wine without his expressed permission."

"Our ancestors couldn't tolerate such a crime so the thief ran out of luck and was caught and compelled to appear before the Council of Elders. A stormy deliberation ensued on the matter and the miserable fellow was fined two rams and twenty bundles of firewood in the end," Tafon declared with some excitement much to the consternation of his guest.

"Two rams and twenty bundles of firewood, you've got to be kidding!" Mbinkar exclaimed. "According to our tradition, the minimum sanction for such a crime in our land is banishment," he added.

"I understand Mbinkar but it's a sign of the changing times," Tafon said. "Go tell Bong to come and see me if he's in his room," he instructed Fai.

"I'm here father," Bong said when he showed up and had finished greeting the visitors.

His father scolded him for shutting himself up in his room and avoiding the company of men. "Go and roast a rooster for our guests," he ordered him.

As he was retiring to execute his father's order, Mbinkar asked Fai to go with him.

"While we're waiting for food to be ready we can continue with our story," Tafon said to his guest.

"Our conversation is interesting and only time seems to be our enemy," Mbinkar declared.

They were busy examining the evolution their society was undergoing when Mayemfon walked into the house with a bowl of water. She greeted the strangers and put the bowl on the ground before announcing that food was ready. As she was leaving, Mbinkar inspected her big breast and round and rocking hindquarters, cleared his throat and exchanged knowing glances with his host.

"Just look at her," Tafon murmured to Mbinkar as her daughter faded out of sight. "She'll give you as many grandchildren as sand on the beach."

Mbinkar only rolled his eyes and smiled mischievously as if to say he already knew about the quality of the product and it was needless for his host to keep on rubbing in the point.

She returned some minutes later with a basket of steaming kibane. Fai, who had been pressed into service to help take the food to Tafon's house, was in toe with a bowl containing vegetables. The food was set in front of the men.

Bong had also assigned Fai a task to carry out. Having completed it, he returned to his seat at Tafon's house. His stomach started growling as he looked forward to filling it up with plenty of kibane, roasted chicken and vegetables.

The sound attracted the attention of his uncle who turned to him with a smile.

198

"Come on Fai!" he called out to his nephew fondly. "Get up and wash your hands and eat some food before those grumbling tortoises tear your entrails to shreds."

He was busy washing his hands when Bong came in with the roasted chicken and some banana leaves. He turned to his father and handed him the trussed up gizzard and liver that had been roasted and wrapped up in banana leaf. He then began to prepare the kati sauce and very soon he was done.

"Have a taste," he said to his father, reaching out with a hand dripping with palm oil and clutching some of the well-oiled meat.

"Thanks," the father said as he stretched out an open hand to accept the offer. After putting it in his mouth and chewing it for a while, he nodded his approval. "The sharing can now commence," he ordered.

Bong got another banana leaf and passed it over the flame several times until it wilted into one big soft malleable flap, the rawness and the brittleness having disappeared. He then tore the leaf into large patches, which he gave to the guests and to his father.

He then set about distributing the kati, starting with his guest who was older than his father, then his father, with Fai coming last.

Still clutching the pot he went and stood in front of his father's door and called out Mayemfon who came running with anxiety. She had picked up the scent of the chicken while it was roasting.

"Did you come with your bowl to take your own kati or you want to pretend that you aren't aware of its preparation?" his brother teased her.

She burst into laughter as she hastily returned to get a bowl. She soon came back and her brother put in a considerable quantity of the chicken for her and Wirba.

"Take it to Mama Wirba," he ordered as he turned to enter the house.

By now the others had already embarked on the assault of the food. Tafon cut part of the gizzard and gave it to Mbinkar who instantly threw the piece in his mouth while Fai looked on.

"This is food for elders and you must wait for your turn," he told Fai who seemed to show little appreciation for the information for he had always known that.

Emptying the remaining contents of the clay pot on his own patch of leaf, Bong grabbed a huge lump of kibane and placed it on another leaf in front of him and began in earnest to eat.

"I thought you were with your friends," Tafon turned to his son, obviously aware that it would be a terrible shame if information ever spread that he and his family ate food without inviting the friends of his son.

"They left a long time ago," the son replied. "I tried to no avail to make them stay."

Apparently satisfied with the explanation, Tafon continued with his meal, occasionally making a joke which would send laughter rippling through the small party.

"Call my little mother for me," Tafon ordered his son. He went out and after calling out her name, Mayemfon arrived hastily.

Her father handed her a small bundle containing some chicken which she took with both hands held together as a sign of respect and gratitude. In this village setting, it was of absolute bad taste for a father or mother to eat anything without reserving a small portion for a child back home.

"Thanks," she said to her father and immediately departed.

Tafon pulled the bowl of water closer and started to wash his hands.

"Let the food go down well," he announced to the others who were still eating. "I'm done."

"Thanks," the others answered in unison through mouthfuls of kibane and chicken.

When everyone had finished eating, Bong cleared the leaves, pots and pans, with little Fai pitching in. Everything having been taken away and his father's house set in order, Bong returned and took his seat in the midst of the men.

"Get a cup Bong," the father said affectionately to his son.

He left the room and soon returned with a horn and joined the others in the drinking. After drinking two horns full, he rose, wished everyone goodnight and retired to his room.

His departure opened the way for the two men to resume their conversation. This time it was about something else, the

200

approach of independence and talks about the reunification of the two Mungos.

"I hear some politicians are running around appealing to the people of Mungo West to form a union with Mungo East," Mbinkar declared.

"Well, Mungo East has already been granted independence and the UN is forcing Mungo West to form a federation with it or join Nigeria."

"The UN can't do that because right now as we're talking the Mungoeasterners are involved in a war and are killing one another," he declared in protest. "If they delight in killing their own brothers and sisters, just imagine what they'll do to us who don't share the same colonial tradition with them?

"You're very right Mbinkar," Tafon said.

"Geographically, culturally and historically, we comprise two separate nations and the only way forward for us is a separate, independent existence."

"I understand that Mbinkar but that can only happen if our own politicians stand firm, instead of running around carrying out a referendum whose outcome we know. Those people in Mungo East can't govern us for the simple reason that they can't govern themselves."

"Anyway we needn't bother ourselves too much about that, for very soon the decision will be made known to us all."

"But it may be too late for us to reverse things if we find them unfair."

"If the UN forces us into any kind of union today, they should be prepared to come back tomorrow and separate a fight," Mbinkar warned. "Let the Mungoeasterners stay with Benge and we're happy with Mikari," he said in conclusion.

34

ai, who started to doze off after the meal, was now snoring. His sleepy body was at war with gravity as he struggled to keep it steady. His eyes would open slightly, saliva trickling out of his mouth and his effort at defying sleep obviously taking him nowhere.

"Be a man," his uncle would scold at him when his body swayed and collided with his. His effort to meet this appeal was often clumsy and did not last long.

"It's normal that he should feel sleepy after the long walk, the wait and the meal," Tafon tried to come to the defense of the young man.

"It's his fault because even though I asked him to have enough rest hours before we set out on this journey, I still saw him running around with his sisters," his uncle countered.

"You can't blame him because we all went through that stage when we were young," Tafon insisted.

It was around two o'clock in the morning when Mbinkar stood up and announced to the host that they were about to return home. His nephew, whose battle with sleep had almost been won, stood and stared droopily, as the two men exchanged greetings.

"I lack words to thank you for this wonderful evening," Mbinkar turned to Tafon as he stretched out his hand for a handshake before leaving the premises of his host. "I know that you're going to present the problem to other members of the family in a way that would draw their sympathy and support."

It had indeed been a wonderful evening and if everything depended only on Tafon, he would have surrendered the maiden without further ado but he still had numerous obstacles to overcome in order to reach the finish line.

First, he had to convince some important members of his wife's and his extended family. Second, even though the potential bride had very little to say in the matter, she could openly rebel if the would-be-husband did not quite suit her fantasy. The second case seemed the most likely.

"I'll certainly do my best to bring our two families together, for the impression you've left on me today is great."

Pleased with the flattery, Mbinkar started slowly towards the door, his nephew in tow, while Tafon followed closely behind.

Outside, the moon was full and shone brightly. The sky was clear but for some feathers of cloud which hovered around the moon and occasionally shut it out of view. Far away, the lonely hoot of an owl rang out mournfully.

Ouuh oooh! The hooting rose clearly in the silence and stillness of the night. Mbinkar, whose village had been scarred by some incidents of witchcraft, had some bitter words for the nocturnal adventurers.

"Listen to those wizards!" he exclaimed.

"As long as they keep their atrocities out of my village I have no problem with them," Tafon said as the three strung out in an Indian file along the tiny path which led out of his compound. "I can't go any farther than this point, for I left my door open," Tafon declared to his visitors when they got to the entrance to his compound. At this point, the track leading out of his compound joined the main road which ran through Yakiri from Fombot and continued all the way to Nkar.

Mbinkar took the right hand of his host in a firm grip and shook it vigorously one more time. Tafon promised again to do his best to make the marriage succeed.

"I hope to hear from you very soon," Mbinkar announced, as he let go the hand and patted tired Fai on the back.

When the party broke up, Mbinkar and Fai headed towards Nkar while Tafon returned to his compound.

With his stomach loaded with food and palm wine and encumbered by the empty calabash he was carrying, Fai had problems keeping pace with his uncle whose strides seemed to double with each step.

"If you continue to lag behind, one of those wizards we heard hooting will sneak up and quietly spirit you away without my noticing," his uncle hinted to urge on the young man when he found out that he was far behind.

At a point, Mbinkar turned off from the main road and entered a small bush path, the same shortcut they had used when they were going to Tafon's house. The tall grass leaning out across the path rustled as they brushed against it.

High above the firmament, the moon in all its majestic beauty poured its light across the hilly grassland. Isolated trees and bushes jotting out here and there stood in the distant gloom like scarecrows watching over a vast paddy field.

Much to the relief of Fai, the grass leaning across the road had slowed down his uncle who beat the way, thus enabling him to follow unencumbered. He scurried behind him, making sure he stayed close. Ever since his uncle talked about the wizards, his heart had not stopped pounding.

He had heard stories of witches and wizards playing havoc with the entrails of children and young people who ventured out at night alone. By playing the thought in his mind over and over, he was terribly frightened.

He also recalled the tale of tall creatures in white, which surprised lone travelers at night, once recounted to him by his older sister. What frightened him the most about this particular tale was the ability of these creatures to constantly change their shapes and height, towering at one point until their heads were buried in the clouds and then suddenly becoming shorter and shorter until all that was left was a gnome. At times they could roll themselves into a ball and bump away on the hillside at top speed.

Even though his sister had insisted these creatures attacked only those with whom they had scores to settle, he was not sure whether he was on good terms with everyone in Nkar. He recalled that he and his friends had picked the mangoes of old Ngomgham without seeking her permission. What if she knew about this misdemeanor and decided to use this occasion to strike out at him? How could he be sure that one of his forebears had not committed a crime against someone who had decided to get even by striking down one of his grandchildren?

These stories paraded back and forth in his mind and almost paralyzed him with fright. He knew that the village was a very simple and complex place at the same time. It was simple in outlook and the manner in which people went about their daily chores. But underneath this veil of simplicity lay a complex and mystical world run by sorcerers, witchdoctors, traditional healers and other nondescript members of these shady groups.

He was still thinking about all these when he stumbled onto an earth mound and almost fell. He let go a shriek which attracted his uncle's attention.

"Any problem Fai?" he asked, halting for a while to enable him to catch up. "Well, give me that calabash if it's such a burden but you must learn to be a man," he said as he snatched the empty container and wended his way through a raffia palm farm at the foot of a slope. "At your age I used to travel to Abakwa carrying a huge basket of kolanuts," he lied.

The fronds of the palm bushes formed an overhead canopy which almost completely shut out the moonlight. For a while the two travelers could only feel their way through the dark path, with moonlight clearly visible at the other end of the farm helping to guide them.

Tiny rays of light trickled through the palm leaves onto the dank floor below. Fruit bats squeaked as they scrambled over food and mating partners and the whole atmosphere was pervaded by the scent of fresh palm wine.

They emerged at the other end of the farm and into the moonlight again. The path started to ascend, winding its way on the flank of a hill in giant serpentine loops. Fai knew that as soon as they finished the ascent, at the crest of the hill they would be in Nkar. The climb was tedious but the promise of good sleep in his bed provided the young man with energy.

When they both arrived at their compound that morning, Fai was completely exhausted from the journey and very much felt the urge to sleep. The trip to Yakiri had ended well but it was the beginning of another sad chapter.

35

A fter his trip, Mbinkar had every reason to celebrate. From his discussion with Tafon, he was convinced that his family's notoriety had not reached Yakiri. Better still, his evil son would get married to a pretty girl and from a royal family at that after all.

This did not quite reflect the mood at the Tafon's. Mayemfon, who only got information of her betrothal from the grapevine and had never seen nor even heard of her spouse, had nightmares in which she saw him smeared with blood. Ever since she was small, each time she had a dream it always turned out to be true. The nightmares did not, therefore, augur well for her.

Frightened by the prospect of what might happen to the person who was being secretly arranged to be her husband and maybe also to herself, she pleaded with her mother to tell her father to put an end to the arrangement. She was talking to the wrong person. Her mother could not because she had not been formally informed about the marriage, this being considered strictly the domain of men.

"I've been having nightmares in which I foresee great troubles ahead," Mayemfon declared to her mother amid tears when she started to be haunted by terrible dreams.

"I had worse dreams than that when your father was chosen to be my husband but see how great things have turned out for me. Such dreams aren't unusual, especially for a young woman like you but rest assured that all will be fine," her mother downplayed the importance of the dreams.

"You have to do something," the girl insisted.

"What do you expect me to tell him when I haven't even been informed about the marriage," she tried to reason with her daughter. "You very well know that this matter doesn't involve women."

All night the girl wept bitterly. She began to see the event as the latest in the midst of others which were completely ruining her life. She remembered being a very bright pupil in her class when she was prematurely dragged out of school to go and take care of a relative's baby. The entire matter was shrouded in so much secrecy that even before Fr Sean got to know about it she had already been spirited away.

Even after the child had grown up, she was determined to go back to school but her parents did not really see the need.

"I have a piece of land for you to cultivate until the time you're ripe for marriage," her father had insisted, pointing out that school was a pure waste of time for a woman. "I can understand a boy going to school to come back to the village and help in its development but a woman may wind up the property of another village."

Having failed to convince her father to recant his decision, she was stuck in her mother's house, accompanying her everyday to the farm.

Another opportunity came up in which young women with some education were being urged to apply at a newly created center to be trained to work in a hospital which was to be built in Sissong. She got the information from a friend and sent in her application and was called up for an interview, but her parents were completely lukewarm about the matter and she again missed that opportunity.

Now, overnight, without even her knowledge, she had been sold, for there was no more appropriate term for that kind of transaction, to a man she had never seen nor even heard of and about whom she was being constantly haunted by nightmares.

After Wirba's daughter had recounted the series of mishaps in her life and held her partly responsible for them, her mother began to feel a sense of guilt. The pressure her daughter had brought to bear on her was so tremendous that she secretly decided to consult a gnukwabe on the matter. She, however, refrained from sharing her findings with her husband and daughter. She simply kept them to herself, preferring to let destiny run its course.

When Mayemfon realized that her entreaties were taking her nowhere, she decided to leave matters to fate. She remembered a story Fr Sean had once told them during one of her doctrine classes about an old woman who had a donkey which helped her to do most of her work and which she cherished very dearly.

According to the story, one day the donkey ran away and the woman started to cry. When a man who was passing by saw her in her predicament and inquired about what could have triggered such an outpouring of grief, she recounted what had happened. After pausing for a while, the man simply told the old woman that the flight of the donkey might be a sign of good luck.

Upset, the woman chased him away. But when one week later the donkey returned with eleven more donkeys, now giving her a herd of a dozen, the woman started to celebrate. A young woman who came upon her was anxious to know the reason for the celebration so that she could share that great moment of joy with the old woman. When the woman recounted what had happened, the young woman thought for a while and then turned to the old woman and said that the whole thing smacked of bad luck.

"Let red hot stone be put in your pocket!" the old woman cursed as she sent away the woman.

It was at this time that the old woman's son who had been away for a long, long time came home. He tried to ride on one of the donkeys but was thrown off and ended up with an injury which made him partially paralyzed. This was her only child and so the woman started to weep. This time an old man found her in her plight and after the woman recounted the series of events which led to the paralysis, he scratched his gray hair, looked at the woman and simply said: "This is good luck!"

Not convinced by what the old man had said, she kept on crying until a quarrel broke out between the old woman's village and a neighboring one. When it degenerated into a war between the two villages, all young men in the old woman's village were conscripted and sent to the front where all of them were killed. In the light of her son's condition, he was spared. Yes, he was partially paralyzed but nevertheless still alive.

Sometimes in life, the priest had maintained, what may appear to be bad luck is good luck and what may appear to be good luck, bad luck. After recalling this story, she decided to give the marriage a try. First, she tried to make some inquiry about the husband when at long last his identity was unveiled to her. She found him to be attractive enough but knew nothing about his reputation or that of his family. All attempts to make progress in this direction having failed, she convinced herself that if there were anything bad at least at some point it would have burst out in the open.

The bride price had been completely paid by the Mbinkars. In addition, the family went the extra mile of bribing all the members of the extended Tafon family with plenty of gifts and money to ensure that the marriage was unanimously endorsed. With these developments, the young woman had no other choice but to swim with the current, however dangerous.

As tradition dictated, a delegation of older women in Yakiri led by her own mother had to accompany her to her husband's house. Since a baby, especially a male, was perceived as the final seal of approval to any union of this kind, it was the delegation's duty to ensure that from the very first day everything in the lives of the couple pointing in the direction of child bearing was done correctly.

Members of the delegation were expected to hang around with their ears glued to the walls of the bridal chamber where the two had been secluded, listening to all conversations and other goings-on until they were satisfied that they both knew what to do.

When the delegation arrived in Nkar, it was eagerly and somewhat sumptuously received by the Mbinkars and together, with the bride, they went to the house of Goran, the bridegroom. He was eagerly waiting for her.

The mother of the bride had told her daughter what to do and had adequately prepared her for this initial encounter, hinting that the experience could be painful if the man was very big and moved too fast. She had, however, attenuated her fears by pointing out that, like the spoor of an animal which needed to be trampled upon several times to make communication easy and enjoyable, so was the new experience to which she was being exposed.

"Never mind the snakelike nature of some of the things you might encounter," she cautioned. "There're things worse than snakes in the lives of a couple," she declared.

As soon as they got to Goran's house, the Mbinkars retired, leaving the old women to run their show. With the bride ushered in and the door locked, outside the women remained tuned to the wall

209

of the room where the couple was secluded. While keeping track of what was happening within, they maintained a steady stream of obscenities to crank up the sexual appetites of the newly wed.

"What's this?" they heard the bride ask her husband.

"Just the same thing except that it sometimes behaves like a snake," he was heard to reply.

This triggered an outburst of laughter in the outside party.

The conversation and whispers continued for a while and things seemed, by the old women's own estimation, to be taking too long. They wanted quick action, one in which the woman would cry out in pain. They were beginning to feel the whole exercise might have been ruined. Not when it involved Goran!

Very soon the whispers within resumed. The women, who had started to become worried, maintained their calm and listened with bated breath. Then suddenly, aih! aih!, came the long awaited moaning scream from within, followed by total silence.

Then when the bed started to squeak, they all stood up from where they were crouching and, amid ululations, clapped their hands in triumph. In their own words, the action had gone from crying to craving.

When the women rose to leave Mbohti, who had been deemed a bit young for the marital escapade but who, through sweet talks, had worked her way into the delegation, clung to the wall, enraptured by the bed music emanating from within.

"What are you still doing there?" one of the women called out.

"I just love the sound of the bed," she cried out. "It's so talkative and I can now hear laughter. They should be having fun and will soon get to the pineapple point."

With her daughter in her husband's house, Wirba was finally happy that she had at least found a man. She, however, was having sleepless nights because of the dreams she had and also because of the gnukwabe's prophecies. She tried to shrug off the worries and look forward to other things.

One year into the marriage, Mayemfon finally became pregnant and everyone was jubilant, perhaps with the exception of her mother still troubled by the lurking concern raised by Takwabe's words.

"The marriage will be a disaster but the child born out of the union will be a girl who'll take on the character of a renowned forebear by defying many odds to become very great," the gnukwabe had predicted after throwing his cowries and bones once.

Three months into the pregnancy, the series of events which would culminate in the disaster for the union started.

It began with a burglary which took place at a coffee store in Yakiri. Seven sacks of coffee were stolen in the robbery. The thieves successfully got away without being caught and Takwabe would have stepped in were it not for the timely intervention of Fr Sean who got wind of the incident early enough and suspected what would happen.

"This is already an unfortunate situation and we don't want to make it worse. With prayers we can steer those responsible from their evil ways back to God," the priest had pleaded in church with an edgy population determined to strike back and send a message.

In the circumstance, only Fr Sean or the sub-chief could call the populace to calm and reason. His voice rose above that of the chief who felt the efforts of others were being abused by a parasitic, indolent bunch. Aware that Takwabe was the person to convince the most if any disaster were to be headed off, the priest contacted him and reminded him of the pledge he had made on the day of his baptism to remain a good Christian.

"God's miracles work in mysterious ways and he'll take care of this when the time comes," were the words he delivered to the gnukwabe before they finally broke up on the day of their meeting.

It was the priest who initiated the gnukwabe into Christianity, and apart from that, the latter had always perceived the former as an older brother. His late father had been the priest's friend and had advised his son to embrace the new faith because nobody knew from where salvation might ultimately come.

Faced, therefore, with the authority of an older brother and a man of God, he had no choice. He yielded.

"Well, Farar," he had stated in his mangled Mikari accent after he had decided to let the matter drop, "I'm only doing this because of you and God but I hope that we're not setting ourselves up for thieves."

Three months after this incident, the robbers were back again and this time they improved on their last record by hauling away twelve bags. The populace went wild. When Fr Sean learned of the incident, he shut himself up in his house, thinking of a very skillful way of handling this second strike. He knew that if he were seen to condone crimes of that nature, all his efforts as a priest ever since he arrived in the village might go down the drain.

After brooding over the incident, he finally came to the conclusion that he was duty bound to do something. He did not expect the public not to express a feeling of frustration and outrage over the theft, but at the same time, he was also convinced that there was no crime, no matter how great, which could not be forgiven. However, he did not come out on this occasion as forcefully as he did on the first one. For one thing he did not know where the thieves would draw the line in their operations, even if he succeeded again in calming down the people and bringing them to reason.

Meanwhile, as soon as Takwabe had received news of the robbery, he suspected that Fr Sean would send for him or even come himself. It was with great relief when the villagers first arrived with the complaint. He decided to move fast and so immediately dispatched some members of their delegation to the scene of the crime to gather and bring back to him some dust or mud from any of the footprints the thieves might have left behind. He also asked for a goat and then urged the village to retire and wait for the results.

The courtesy of announcing and warning the thief to own up was shelved, lest it might stir the priest to come pleading and force them to change their minds.

Before the villagers left his premises, they were informed that the thieves who carried out both operations were from other villages. He had settled for the busting method in which the thief would gradually decompose like the goat he was about to bury.

In Nkar, when Goran started to complain of itches all over the body, his wife assumed that it was a minor health problem which would soon go away even without medical intervention. Then the itches developed into small boils which started to grow and very soon they became very large and burst, spewing out pus. As days progressed, his health condition rapidly deteriorated. When

212

his father was notified about the affliction, he had more the curse of his step brother in mind.

Finally, on the advice of a councilor, he met a gnukwabe and was told his son and two other friends from Kimbo had stolen something which had been spoilt.

Goran, however, refused to acknowledge guilt, not sure whether this could be true since it was not the first time that he had stolen from the same location. Two days before his death, about a week and half after he started experiencing itches, he confessed to having committed the crime to his wife who told Mbinkar. Mayemfon also informed her parents in Yakiri and for the first time they began to get a hint of the family into which they had married their daughter and with which they had been having dealings all along.

Mbinkar was seriously angered by the incident. Since the theft took place in Yakiri and it was there that the matter was spoilt, he doubted whether Tafon, in his capacity as sub-chief, would have been totally ignorant that his son was involved. He felt that the gnukwabe might probably have unveiled him the identity of the thief or thieves and that instead of consulting him to see how things could be settled peacefully had decided to act unilaterally on the information.

This feeling caused him to devise a wicked plan. He secretly met with a witchdoctor to see how he could get even. Before carrying out his plan, he first checked whether the child her daughter-in-law was bearing was male or female. He had made up his mind that if it were female, he would proceed with his devilish scheme but if it were male, he would at least reconsider as this might serve as a "worthy" replacement for the loss.

The child, the witchdoctor informed him, would be female, so he ordered him to destroy Mayemfon. She was on the verge of delivery. He chose this occasion to eliminate her.

Meanwhile, the incident in Yakiri and the death of Goran had made the Tafons wary of the reputation of the Mbinkar family, since the two incidents had emboldened some natives of Nkar anxious to clean up the image of their village to start talking openly about the notoriety of the sub-chief and his family. To ensure that such a terrible reputation would not rub off on his family, Tafon decided to refund the bride price. He blamed Mbinkar for having hidden his true identity when he presented himself and his son to his family.

Mayemfon returned to their compound just two days before she gave birth to the child. It was a terrible delivery in which she lost plenty of blood and immediately after the child miraculously survived and announced her coming into this world with a cry, its mother passed away. The child was a girl. Given the terrible circumstance which had surrounded her birth, her grandfather combed the village history for an appropriate name. In the end, he could think of no other than Yaya, which meant "Little Yaa" in Wotikar. That child was me.

The selection of the name had to do with history which had been largely ignored in the first place. The words of Kwakala had not been fully heeded. Even though the naming was another great gesture to pay homage to that forebear of mine whose own life started in almost exactly the same manner as mine, the course of history seemed to have been reversed. Instead of the past to build the present, it was the present to flatter the past. The future had to suffer, for the Tafon's were stuck with me, a baby girl without parents.

Since I hailed from a Christian family, when I was presented for baptism, Fr Sean was given the honor to select a baptismal name for me which befitted the circumstance. He reflected for a moment and then said Monica.

"Who's Monica?" Tafon, my grandfather, asked when the priest finally said the name.

"She's a saint and also the mother of St Augustine," the priest replied. And then to pre-empt the next question, added: "St Augustine is one of Africa's greatest saints."

At this, Wirba, my grandmother, nodded her head knowingly. She clasped me tight and continued to rock me as water was poured on my head. The rocking had just begun and another chapter in the history of Yakiri, with me as a main character, was about to be written.

36

O wing to the tragic circumstances which surrounded my birth, I was compelled to grow under the care of my grandparents. The death of my mother had weighed heavily on my grandmother's conscience.

My grandmother was filled with guilt. She probably felt there was something she could have done to save her daughter's life. In order to salve her conscience, she decided to make amends by showering me, her granddaughter, with love. Could the tragedy have been averted if the marriage were aborted? She would never know.

Rather than going back to that sad past which brought a lot of pain, she decided instead to look ahead. She was determined to make the best out of a bad situation by putting to good use the lessons learned from the incident to provide me with the tools I needed to succeed in what to her was clearly a man's world.

Her farm work and other daily chores and activities kept her constantly absent and busy. She, therefore, had to press a female member of her extended family into service to assist her in taking care of me while she was away or at home and doing something else.

Often, all three of us would go to the field where a large hut had been constructed to provide shelter for farm workers when it started to rain or when the sun became too hot. While she was busy working, Mankah, for this was the name of my nurse, kept watch over me, playing with me on a mat which had been spread on the dusty floor of the hut. She would sometimes strap me on her back and walk around with me, singing nice little songs to lull me to sleep. She usually visited a neighboring farm to chat and play with a young girl whose assignment was identical to hers.

However, with the prevalence of dangerous snakes, scorpions and poisonous insects, Mankah often spent most of the time at home with me. From what I gathered, I was a very interesting baby. I only cried when I was hungry, thirsty, frightened or had been bitten by an insect. Otherwise, I was always sleeping or playing with the numerous toys Mankah had created through her resourcefulness.

At the very beginning, when I was still very young, Mankah found the task of caring for me very difficult. It was her very first experience to take care of a baby. Since I had not started to talk, she could only guess what was wrong with me each time I was crying. However, the nursing took a turn for the better and became interesting when I started to walk and talk.

During the day, when everyone was away, we would become involved in pranks, as children are likely to do in the absence of adults. Fearing that some of them were mischievous enough to attract a rebuke from my grandparents when they returned, Mankah would advise me to keep it a secret. It often remained a secret until Mankah did something unpleasant to me and then I would divulge everything to my grandmother. She would then proceed to rebuke Mankah.

My grandmother has always declared to me that even for my tender age at the time, I was not a fool. I knew I often spent most of the time with my nurse and had to be on good terms with her. So each time I snitched on her and she was scolded, I understood that our relation had momentarily gone sour. I would stay a while away from her and then gradually, with great skill and caution, buy my way back into her good books with sweet talks and snacks. It was a fence-mending exercise which did not entirely escape the notice of my grandmother who saw in my diplomatic gesture the making of a future great leader.

It is also alleged that I demonstrated an uncanny ability for manipulation. This often happened when it came to taking advantage of each secret I had been asked to keep. I would sometimes keep the secret but making sure I constantly used the threat of breaking it as a bargaining chip to extort concessions from Mankah.

It was often very funny how it started. Since Mankah was very good at making toys, she would sometimes want to play with them before passing them over to me. However, if I wanted one of them immediately, I would ask for it and then look alternately at

216

her and my grandmother. This was a hint that she should act according to my wish or I would go ahead and break the secret. Mankah had no choice.

Such betrayal was not always deliberate. Sometimes, the mischief carried out during the day was in my best interest. It was, therefore, pointless for me to divulge it to my grandmother. Nevertheless, I often did so without actually meaning to.

A good example of this kind of situation happened one afternoon when I complained to Mankah that I was seriously hungry. Mankah thought of no other solution to this problem than to get some peanuts and roast them for me.

My grandmother had actually instructed us that we could do so, but only on condition that we felt extremely hungry and had already eaten our lunch. She knew from experience that if she did not create such a possibility for us to put an end to our hunger, we might venture into the neighboring bushes in search of guavas, pineapple or wild fruits. In this case, we might end up being bitten by a snake if something worse did not occur.

As is often the case with children, such an opening also easily lent itself to abuse. To guard against the dangerous possibility of devouring seeds for the coming planting season which the abuse could cause, she selected and set aside a basket of peanuts. She told us that we could take peanuts only from this basket during the day. As for the other baskets, she strictly forbade us ever to take from any of them.

"You must take from your own basket very sparingly because once it's exhausted you can't take from these ones which will provide seeds for next year's crops," she had warned Mankah, hoping in this instance to control our appetite for snacks and also to prevent any form of abuse.

We respected the rule until we had exhausted our own basket. Then one day Mankah decided to break it. She, however, had no illusion about the gravity of the act we were committing, so she had warned me never to let the cat out of the bag.

"I'm doing this for you, because you keep complaining to me that you're very hungry, but if you tell grandma then know that it'll be the very last time," Mankah declared as she battled with smoke from the fire irritating her eyes during the roasting session.

"You know I only tell on you when you don't want me to play with your toys," I replied much to the relief of Mankah who knew the best moments not to deprive me of such a privilege.

At night, in the house, when my grandmother was back from the farm and we sat round a fire preparing dinner, I intoned a song. I often did so when I was being bothered by something.

My grandmother often concluded that I might just be hungry or else seeking for notice. When the singing lasted for too long and I kept looking at her and then at a seemingly nervous nurse, she knew something was wrong.

"Are you hiding something from me?" she asked, her gaze shifting from me to my nurse.

"Nothing!" Mankah replied quickly in a bid to pre-empt me, lest I committed the error of revealing our little secret.

When Wirba was looking away, Mankah would stare at me relentlessly and in an intimidating way and would sometimes make signs with her face. All these actions were to warn me to keep my mouth shut.

Rightly, I interpreted Mankah's actions as signs of fright and so in an attempt to allay her fears, I, sometimes, inadvertently did exactly what I was not supposed to do.

"Don't be worried," I tried to assure an increasingly restless Mankah, "for I won't tell grandma that we took just a tiny bit of peanuts and roasted them during the day when we were hungry."

With the secret thus broken, my grandmother would proceed to lecture Mankah on the dangers of lying and the folly of tampering with seeds to be planted in the coming farming season.

"Do you want us to starve next year?" she asked to rub in the point of the implication of her action.

When I grew up and had been acknowledged by Fr Sean to be ripe for schooling, the family dispensed with the services of Mankah. Her attachment to me had become so much that it was with a broken heart that she was leaving to return to her own family. When the nurse's mother came to fetch her, she burst out in tears.

"Don't cry," my grandmother tried to appease her. "We'll always come and fetch you during weekends to come and stay and play with Yaya."

218

School was to begin on Monday and my grandparents had bought me a uniform. It was a sky-blue gown rimmed with white at the collar, the sleeves and skirt. It was very beautiful and I looked very smart in it when I tried it on for the first time.

They had also asked a carpenter to make me a slate. It was a flat, black rectangular piece of wood on which pupils mastered how to write numbers and the letters of the alphabet until they could use a pencil and an exercise book.

My first tools of education had been obtained. I was very anxious for school to begin, perhaps spurred more by the desire to be seen in my new uniform than the quest for knowledge.

"When will school begin?" I kept nagging my grandmother.

"Very soon," she replied.

"Why can't I go now?"

"It's still holiday time."

Finally, the day I had long been waiting for arrived. Early in the morning of my first day at school, my grandmother got me up and, with some warm water, took me to the bathing room at the back of her house. She lathered me with soap and scrubbed me with a thick sponge and rinsed me until I was very clean. I was then dried and anointed with sweet smelling lotion.

My grandmother fed me a heavy breakfast of kibane and fresh vegetables. She then prepared my lunch which comprised roasted sweet potatoes, some ripe avocados and oranges, and a small lump of kibane and vegetables. Talk of the prevalence of hunger in school was commonplace. So my grandmother made sure I carried all that food in a small beautiful wicker basket made for the purpose.

I got to school on that first day in the company of my grandfather. In front of the headmaster's office, where we stood and waited for me to be registered, we met Bonsisi, a neighbor's daughter. She had come with her father for the same purpose.

While we waited, I wandered my eyes around. St Patrick was a big school with numerous classrooms set around the soccer ground. It had many teachers. The soccer ground, lawns and surroundings had grown into a thick bush while the pupils were away on the long holidays.

All over the compound, pupils, boys for the most part, came together in little groups. I suspected they might be discussing

219

what they did during the holidays. They were all dressed in the school uniform for boys – a pair of khaki shorts and a sky blue shirt.

Of all the things I took note of that morning, the one which struck me the most and left me with a lasting impression was a female member of the school staff. She was a teacher. She was tall and pretty, with an attractive hairdo. She was also very well dressed and spoke Mikari with other teachers. Her presence in the midst of the entirely male staff and the self-confident manner in which she held herself instantly aroused in me the desire to one day become a teacher.

When the last bell rang, calling on the pupils to assemble, those who were late hurried to leave their bags in their various classrooms. Soon, they all assembled at the ground, looking neat and smart in their uniforms.

Since it was the first day at school, the pupils had to be addressed by the headmaster. He was a lean, tall man who I eventually learned was called PaNwafor. Before he came to Yakiri, he had been a teacher for years in Tisson in Abakwa.

He began with a prayer, and then a speech in which he welcomed the pupils back to school before announcing the results of those who had just completed. While he praised the staff and pupils for the good results, he insisted that there was still margin for improvement. He called on everyone to provide his or her best effort so that the school should not only stay on top but should perform even better. He introduced some new members of staff and then drew the attention of everyone to the bushy nature of the school.

"The school premises is a forest where we can now hunt lions," he quipped much to the pleasure of the entire school. "With the exception of the junior classes, it'll be normal for us to begin by keeping our environment clean as very rudimentary hygiene requires us to do."

Once the assembly was dismissed, the pupils hurried to their various classrooms to fetch their machetes and hoes to start work on the school compound. The headmaster then made his way to his office where the other children and I were waiting to be registered as new pupils.

He greeted the parents and guardians who had accompanied the children in Wotikar and even paused for a joke or two with some of the pupils who seemed shy or confused or even completely lost. He went into his office and, after settling down, began to invite the parents and guardians to come in with the pupils according to their order of arrival.

When it was my grandfather's and my turn, we walked into the spacious office and sat down in front of the broad mahogany table behind which PaNwafor was enthroned in a broad chair.

On the table were an inkpot and numerous registers. Behind him, from the floor to the ceiling, were shelves fitted onto the walls and on which books and registers were stacked.

On his right, on the wall, was a framed picture of the Pope staring down. At the time, I took him for Fr Sean's brother until years later when I was told it was Papa for Roma, as the native Roman Catholic Christians endearing referred to the Pontiff.

A broad cupboard stretching almost from one wall to the other behind Yaya and her grandfather completed the decor of the office. Even by town standards, it was richly equipped for the epoch.

With the registration done, my grandfather was instructed to take me to the classroom of Mr. Lafon, Infant One A. He stumbled on the teacher at the anti-chamber of the office and he was the first to inquire to which class I had been sent.

"I've been asked to take her to Mr. Lafon's class," my grandfather declared.

"Well, I'm Mr. Lafon and that's my class at the end of this lane leaving the headmaster's office," he declared as he pointed.

While we were still on the way, the teacher had completed his mission with the headmaster and caught up with us. He inspected my slate and food basket and asked whether I had a piece of chalk for writing.

"Here! I almost forgot that it was still with me," my grandfather said as he handed me a piece of chalk.

"You may go now," the teacher told my grandfather as he took me by the hand. "She's now mine."

As I left with this strange figure, depressed by the separation from my grandfather, he noticed my state and shouted out encouragements and terms of endearment. It did the trick, for

221

at that very instant I felt the growing desire to be in the classroom with other pupils.

It was a broad classroom with numerous charts on the walls. The pictures on them depicted different kinds of domestic and wild animals, as well as fruits and flowers and birds.

Underneath the charts, dangling from wooden pegs fitted into the walls, were numbers and the different letters of the alphabet carved out of wood. On the floor, about two feet from the wall, was a bed of sand running all round the classroom on which pupils occasionally spent some time learning to shape letters and numbers.

The pupils sat round the tables facing one another, with their slates in front of them. When I walked in with the teacher, the class was noisier than an African marketplace. The pupils came up with all kinds of complaints and accusations about the activities which had taken place in his absence. He tried to bring some order in the classroom and then as soon as some calm was restored, I was introduced to the rest of the class. The teacher asked me to sit next to a pupil called Congosah.

On that first day, when the bell rang for closing, the pupils were ordered to stand up and the teacher led a prayer. I knew my way back home, so it was pointless for someone to come for me. Together with some other pupils from our neighborhood, we followed the main road towards our homes and as we progressed the population thinned away. It was only when I got to the entrance of our compound that I turned around and saw Bonsisi trailing behind. She called out my name and came running. I got her slate and examined what they had done for the day. It was not exactly what we had done in our own classroom.

I arrived at home where my grandmother was waiting for me. As soon as she saw me coming, she rushed to meet me. She picked me up and clasped me tightly to her bosom, as though I had been away for a whole year. Staring into my eyes and beaming, she unleashed a torrent of endearing epithets to welcome me. I loved every moment of it and even before my grandmother could ask, I started to recount all that had taken place at school.

Once we got to the house where food was already waiting, she set a large lump of kibane and vegetables before me that I started to demolish with great appetite as soon as I had changed into my household wear and said my grace before meals. As I ate, I paused from time to time to provide information I failed to mention when I was recounting my stories.

By all accounts, I was a very bright pupil. In record time, I had mastered the alphabet and could count well. I could also sing well and recite rhymes and verses from the Bible. My mind was so tenacious that I landed the role of Holy Mary, the Mother of Jesus, at the end of the year when our class staged a play in front of parents and guardians who had been invited.

My grandparents were very pleased with my performance and showered me with praises after the show. I came second in my class in the final examination, having been beaten into the first position by Forche who played Joseph in the play.

I was not at all pleased with my school performance, even when I was being consoled by some of my friends who told me it was quite an achievement for a girl to make it to that position.

"I know I'm more intelligent than Forche and can beat him," I told my grandmother at home.

"Of course you can but the fact that he's a man is consolation enough," my grandmother told me before proceeding to chide me to sit like a woman. "You cannot sit with your legs spread out like a gendarme eating soya."

"What's a gendarme grandma?" I asked a bit perplexed.

"They're those men who wear uniforms and red caps, speak Benge and go around beating up people."

"Grandma, I even forgot to tell you that when we were coming back from the church the other day, we saw them beating up a man because he hadn't paid his tax," I declared, seemingly shaken by the incident I had witnessed. "Now that I go around without paying a tax what if I'm arrested and beaten up?"

"Never mind, by the time you're big enough to pay you'll have the money to do so."

My progress in school was good enough to catch the attention of Fr Sean who occasionally took me for doctrine classes to prepare me for confirmation. My ability to lap up and regurgitate entire segments of the Bible amazed the priest, not to mention the ease with which I spoke Mikari which tended to give most pupils plenty of trouble because of the encroachment of our native Wotikar language.

These qualities made me enjoy a monopoly as class head, a feat which caused my greatest rival, Forche, to turn green with envy. The rivalry was intense but the two of us were friends and respected each other.

Back home, I was acting more and more responsibly as I gradually grew out of my childish ways. I would sometimes help my grandparents with household chores. On Saturdays, when I had nothing doing, I would accompany my grandmother to the farm. While she was busy working, I would go around and fetch firewood.

"You have to know all these things so that one day when you get married you'll be able to take care of your husband and children," my grandmother kept repeating to me. "Before I even forget, very soon the corn will be ripe for harvesting, so you should invite your friends to come and help you."

"I can do that," I declared happily. "While I go around informing the girls, I'll instruct Forche to do the same with the boys."

"Who's Forche?" my grandmother asked.

"You remember the boy cast in the role of Joseph in the Christmas play we staged when I was still in Infants One, the one who came first in our class and I was second?"

"Yes."

"That's him," I said with a smile. "He's my greatest rival in class."

"Do you like him?"

"Yes, he's gentle and intelligent and gives me sleepless nights when school examinations are approaching."

"If you're such good friends he should be able to help you out."

I continued to help my grandparents when I had the time. However, I spent most of my spare time with my friends at the small library the Roman Catholic Mission had opened just next to the Sacred Heart Church. I read many storybooks and learned about other people and cultures.

It was after one of my trips to the library that I returned home one Saturday afternoon with bruises on my hands and face and my eyes bloodshot. I was in the company of Bonsisi.

"What happened?" my grandmother asked as she inspected the scratches on my face with great anxiety.

Overwhelmed with shame, I could not answer and so Bonsisi stepped in.

"She was beaten up by a big girl, a classmate," my companion responded.

"Why?" my grandmother asked, unable to comprehend what had really taken place since she had always known me to be very friendly and warm towards people.

"She claimed that she had gossiped her name to a friend."

"Did you gossip her name?" my grandmother turned to me.

"I didn't. A friend came and was complaining to me about her. What was I supposed to do, stub my ears or ask her to shut up?" I argued amid my tears.

My assailant was a big girl in my class called Kende. She was an empty-headed bully with the lackluster reputation of grabbing the food of smaller and younger pupils. She could not be avoided, especially when she wanted to make trouble with someone. All her mental abilities seemed geared towards cooking up one form of conspiracy or the other to ensnare and entangle those she wanted to beat up. No excuse was too small or too big to stir up her anger. Such aggressive conduct, which no amount of the teacher's lashing could quell, had compelled physically weak and vulnerable pupils to form a party of wimps around her. They were always ready to carry out any of her wishes in order to avoid the consequences of her anger.

Nevertheless, this group formed a minority. The overwhelming majority of the pupils was still jealous of their independence and determined to maintain and continue enjoying it to the fullest. Like any other independence, this one had a price tag. Those who enjoyed it were more exposed to her tyrannical ways.

Usually, once she had found her target, it was not difficult to start a quarrel. A stare, sometimes blank, but often full of hate and accusation of an imaginary crime, was usually the opening act. This action would drive instant fear into the heart of the girl since all of her victims were females. The stare would then degenerate into grotesque facial gesticulations and grimaces. This was all a set up and if her victim fought back with the same actions, she was in for it. Nevertheless, if she looked the other way to avoid getting

225

into trouble, this action was interpreted as a rebuff and still provided her with a good cause for war.

Her prime targets were usually pupils who often came to school with a large quantity and variety of food, a possible reason for which I could easily have been singled out.

My trouble might have gone beyond the contents of my basket or even the fact that I played host to a rat. Kende had a crush on Forche who took no notice of her. He was too engrossed with me, with whom he was competing on the number of storybooks each of us could read at the library, to take any notice. She felt Forche was attracted to me because of my beauty.

She, however, did not want to imagine that I was more beautiful than she was. She was pretty, of good height and a nice build, with charming if somewhat mischievous eyes. After all, had she not overheard some pupils saying that she was the kind of product which traditionally was reserved for royalties?

In the relationship I had with Forche, Kende seemed to have exaggerated the role of beauty. While beauty might have attracted Forche, it was not around it that our relationship was built.

I did not think of myself as an unattractive person, and Kende too was pretty. The main reason why Forche was attracted to me seemed to have come from the thrill of meeting a woman who could match him pound for pound in intellectual and moral battles. Of course, Kende did not understand this. She was convinced that our attraction to each other was a zero-sum game in which my departure would automatically mean that Forche would settle for her.

Actually, the gossip issue was a smokescreen which concealed something even bigger and more ambitious. She wanted to scare me off so that she could take my friend.

All these developments taking place behind the scenes were obviously unknown to my grandmother; but it was unlikely whether they might have meant anything because she was more of a practical philosopher.

"You're more intelligent and popular than her, so how could she beat you?" my grandmother asked me.

"I've told you she's bigger than I am and you ask me a question which doesn't make sense," I responded in anger,

226

suspecting that my grandmother was already taking the side of the bully.

"I know that she's bigger than you but does that explain why she could beat you up?" she kept up with her logic.

"Obviously the fact that she's bigger gives her an advantage in terms of size."

"In terms of intelligence don't you also have an advantage?"

"So what did you expect me to do?" I asked in absolute frustration. "Help her solve her arithmetic problems in class in order to avoid getting beaten up?"

"That's theoretical intelligence but I'm talking about practical intelligence. What you learn in school will become useful to you only when you apply it in real life situations. If you don't know that as a woman, you're in real trouble my child."

"So what was I supposed to do?"

"Fight," she said.

"How can I fight with those firm hands clutching me like a lion?" I asked, probably thinking my grandmother wanted me to commit suicide.

"You're too impressed by what you see," she responded. "Go beyond that."

"Put yourself in my place and tell me how you would have reacted if you found yourself in a similar situation."

"Look here," she called my attention. "There're two main reasons why a person loses a fight, either because the reason for which the person is fighting isn't strong enough to provide good motivation or because the person doesn't badly need the victory to make a point."

"So what does all that you've said amount to?"

"Simple, that you're a quitter."

37

After my grand mother had applied some ointment to soothe my bruises and had tried to calm me down, I sat back and reflected on what she has said. It made a lot of sense. I began to feel that Kende`s fighting abilities had never really been tested. I made up my mind that next time I would stand up to her or run away if the fighting became too rough. Running away to come back better prepared was also an indication of the practical intelligence my grandmother had talked so much about.

On Monday, at school, Kende saw me with Forche. She felt I did not quite get the message of the previous day's beating. As soon as we broke up and I was alone, she approached me.

"From very reliable sources I learned that you've taken up the last incident to the teacher?" she lied.

"I haven't done so yet but I intend to do that today."

"You talk to me like that?" she asked somewhat surprised by my foolhardiness.

"What are you?"

Kende did not like my question and immediately took a swing at me. The time of reckoning had come. I struck back immediately and in the ensuing battle my finger mistakenly got into one of her eyes. She was partially blinded and fumbling, so I took advantage and held her firmly around her neck. This prevented her from breathing.

Bonsisi and some other girls and boys who had been following the encounter ran up as soon as they discovered that Kende was being whopped. They formed a circle and started to yell encouragement to me. I knew Kende was in trouble and so continued to tighten my grip. She tried to gasp for air but the hold was too firm and she was unable to do so and was being gradually asphyxiated.

"Yaya let go Kende, lest she dies," Bonsisi cried out.

The others joined in and pleaded with me to let go. When I did, Kende sagged with exhaustion. It was just the beginning of her troubles and downfall. As should be expected, my action emboldened most of Kende's little wimps who revolted against her.

On the day of my battle with her, even before I got home, a delegation led by Bonsisi had been there to inform my grandmother about what had happened. She was furious when I returned.

"I hope by advising you I didn't create a monster out of you?" she scolded me.

"She attacked me again today, so what was I supposed to do?" I protested, bursting into tears. "When I'm beaten up you yell at me and when I avoid getting beaten up you yell at me."

"You didn't avoid getting beaten up. You actually went out with the intention of beating up somebody, of getting even, and it's that spirit of vindictiveness that I'm totally against," my grandmother said. "When I advise you not to surrender to a bully it doesn't mean you should become one yourself. I insisted that the reason for fighting must be very strong, so was your reason strong enough?"

"It was because she attacked me and I had to put an end to that."

"Well, you made your point and so I wouldn't like to hear that you started a fight in school."

At school, news about the fighting between us had spread and it was Forche who first confronted me.

"What happened when you left me yesterday?" he asked.

"Kende attacked me and I beat her up."

"It's surprising that a slim person like you could beat up such a well built and tough-looking person like Kende."

"It isn't size which determines who wins a fight but the strength of the motive for the fighting," I replied.

"I'm impressed," Forche said. "Where did you get that line?"

"I got it from my grandmother," I replied.

"Your grandmother?" he asked, not sure whether he heard me right. "I was expecting to hear that you read it in a book."

"No, from my grandmother," I insisted. "She's one of the smartest persons I've ever seen."

"Well, lest I forget, I've already invited my friends and they all seem ready to come and assist you in harvesting your grandmother's corn crops."

"I'll discuss that with her today and then we can set a date."

"Avoid getting yourself into fights because apart from the physical risks you run, it doesn't sit well with a woman, especially one aspiring to be confirmed as a Christian," Forche told me as we parted company after school.

When I arrived at home my grandparents had still not returned from the field. There was nothing special for me to do, so I left for the library, stopping over at Bonsisi's to pick her up. On our way, we saw gendarmes on parade, with their red berets cocked jauntily on one side of their heads, their heavy boots thumping the ground as they responded to the orders of their chief. They marched until they came to a pole where the federal flag was fluttering and halted.

After an order was issued, they all stood at attention and a bugle began to blare as one of the gendarmes gradually lowered the flag. It was then neatly folded and the man holding the flag led the way to their office just next to the parade ground while the others marched behind him.

Even though I was still very young, I was not sure the force was in Mungo West for the good of the people of this region. How could it be when the gendarmes could not speak, nor were they even interested in learning how to speak, the language of the people?

This lapse could only lead to friction and tension and bring about the kind of brutalities which the people of Yakiri were experiencing from the hands of these new arrivals sent from Yamade. Their duty was to maintain peace and order but ever since they came they had been doing just the opposite, seizing people's wives, beating people up, asking for bribes and arbitrarily detaining those who did not oblige.

Since the law never punished the gendarmes for the acts they committed, I suspected that they were in my village for reasons other than the ones they claimed brought them there.

When we got to the library, it was already full. I was convinced that some of the pupils were taking advantage of it to avoid doing their household chores. It was in this library that I read the interesting story of how Ali Baba outwitted forty thieves. This story made me think back on what my grandmother had told me about winning a fight, or any struggle for that matter. It all depended on how badly the person involved in the fight needed the victory. Normally, it would be difficult for one person to outwit forty thieves.

Back at home that evening I told my grandmother about my discussion with Forche and what he had said.

"One farm is completely ripe and if we don't carry out the harvesting now, all the crops will be eaten up by birds and monkeys," she declared.

"Are you therefore suggesting that we can set this coming Saturday for my friends to come?"

"What's today?"

"Wednesday."

"Sure, by Saturday I should be done with the harvesting, so that we all concentrate on the crucial task of transporting."

I contacted all my friends and they agreed that they would meet at our compound on the elected day. It was when I was about to meet Forche and discuss the date that I heard rumors, supposedly started by him, which held that I was his wife.

I was so embarrassed by the claims that I decided not to meet him and refused to talk to him after school. When I got home my grandmother realized that my eyes were wet and immediately suspected that something might have happened to me in school.

"What's the matter?" she asked.

It took me a long while before I could respond and when I started tears began to stream out of my eyes.

"Forche went around the school telling everyone that I'm his wife," I finally told my grandmother who seemed quite amused by what had made me so upset.

"Does it mean he won't be coming on Saturday?"

"No, I didn't even discuss that with him in school today."

"What's making you upset, that he claims you're his wife or that he told others you're his wife."

"Both."

"How much do you know him to think he could start a rumor like that," my grandmother asked.

231

"Well, I know him well and I'd be surprised if he started something like that."

"So what makes you think he did then?"

"Since he's my good friend and we do things at school together it may have gone to his head to start believing that I'm his wife."

"Did you ask him to see if he did actually start the rumor?"

"No, I didn't even want to meet him in school today when I heard the rumors."

"Now, let me tell you something my dear child and make sure you retain it once and for all. If you have to discard your good man on grounds of a rumor you may wind up single. You've reacted solely with your emotions, without even using your head. I must tell you that this isn't the best way to proceed in life." After the prolonged lecture, she started to ask some interesting questions which I then found a bit odd.

"You once told me you liked him, so is there anything wrong if one day he becomes your husband?"

"I haven't said that but I deem it inappropriate for us to start now."

"Where did you get that? Doctrine classes?" my grandmother asked somewhat mockingly. "Once you have a man with whom you're always together, the chances that you may be saddled with one you don't like are slim. Furthermore, in this your age when most women insist on getting the man they want, you get to know him well before marriage."

"We're friends, not husband and wife."

"Use the brains God has given you!" my grandmother exclaimed. "Is there any difference if you act like friends and people call you husband and wife? Is that enough to break up an interesting and fruitful relationship? One thing I can guarantee you is that if you don't embark on a fence-mending exercise immediately another woman will snap up that man for the simple reason that good men are hard to come by. Another woman eyeing your man could have started this rumor. Did you ever think about that? Well, if you want to wind up a laughing stock, don't talk to your friend, husband or whatever for a week."

It was when my grandmother talked of another woman that it suddenly struck me that the day Kende attacked me for the second time I had just parted company with Forche. She definitely must have been keeping track of my relationship with him. What was the motive behind that? She had always smiled at Forche, sometimes even in my presence.

The next day as I was arriving at school, I saw Forche sitting in front of a classroom, with Kende leaning on the wall next to him. It suddenly dawned on me that my grandmother was right. These malicious rumors might have been started by Kende to take Forche away from me. These ideas were going through my mind as I approached them. As soon as Kende saw me coming, she vanished. Why then was she running away, I thought?

When I greeted Forche and continued my way towards our classroom, he rose and came after me. Once we were together, overwhelmed by what might have been jealousy, I think, I asked him what Kende was doing next to him.

"You seem not to trust me and decided to humiliate me on the basis of unfounded and unverifiable rumors," he said, apparently still ruffled by the event of the previous day.

"Do you love Kende?"

"I need a person who can trust me and if the person happens to be Kende what's wrong with that?"

"I don't want to see you with her anymore because she isn't your type."

"Who then is my type when people in whom I confide publicly disgrace and humiliate me?"

"I'm sorry I overreacted and should have asked you before taking any action," I declared remorsefully. "Am I forgiven?"

"If you're genuinely sorry, then there's no reason why God shouldn't."

"Tell you what, the ground only becomes harder after a rain," I declared apologetically. "I betrayed our friendship once and I'll never do that again."

"But why that aversion for marriage," Forche asked. "Have you found something so terrible in me which already tells you that I may never make a good husband?"

"Not that. I just don't want us to move faster than our shadows. I think we should only commit our secret wishes to God and pray and things will happen."

"You're right," he agreed with me. "Did your grandmother set a date for the work?"

"Yes, she did and it's tomorrow," I replied, and feeling that it might be too late for him to rally his friends, turned to him and asked: "Will you be able to make it?"

"For sure, but I must go now to be able to contact all of my friends by the end of the day."

When we separated that day and I went to class, as the teacher spent his time explaining the importance of some aspects of Mikari, arithmetic and other subjects, my mind was elsewhere. I do not know whether I was in love. My grandmother was right. I could have ended up parting with my best friend just because in a fit of anger I acted rashly and somewhat selfishly.

I began to sense that Kende had designs on Forche, which might probably be the reason why she was constantly picking on me.

As soon as school was over, before I headed home, I met with Forche who informed me that he had contacted all his friends and that they would be showing up the following day for the work.

At home I told my grandmother what had happened and the probable cause of the misunderstanding and she smiled knowingly.

"A man is like a lion and the only way to tame a lion is to catch it, keep it, and know it before the crucial phase of taming it. You don't take on a lion from the bottom of your bed. You must be out there, in the jungle where it lives, and must have the courage to go close to it and then overcome it. It'll never be vulnerable unless you know it well enough and how can you know it without facing it? It's good to be cautious with men but not to the point where you don't even want to go close to them. When they want to make babies with you and run away, it isn't from a distance that they do it. They come to you, deceive you with all kinds of promises and the moment your stomach starts inflating like that of a palm wine drinker, they're gone. Why can't a woman play by the same rule? You don't conquer, oh yes I mean conquer, by being afraid."

"Grandma, I think you're right."

"You can make a man sit and watch over your pot cooking while you're out drinking, but it all depends on how you work on his mind. Failure starts when you endow him with the status of God almighty, to be watched from a distance and revered but never to be approached. It just can't work out that way. If you want something from a man and he says to you that you're his wife, even if you aren't, be the first to call him darling. With such flatteries you soften the ground and make accessibility to what you want easier. But if the moment you hear 'my darling' you stiffen like the gendarmes we see at the square, the man's attitude also hardens towards you and you may never get what you want. It's just normal human behavior."

Come Saturday, all those who had promised to show up for the assistance appeared and after the day's work, my grandmother provided a big feast for the pupils and thanked them. At school news of Forche's assistance provided fodder for more rumor. Girls, especially those who continued to view the good relationship between us with envy and some hostility, huddled in small groups to gossip on the issue.

"The marriage is now formal since he shows up at the home of his in-laws to start paying his bride price by assisting them," a voice shot out, triggering a nod of approbation and an outburst of mocking laughter.

"When do they plan the Christian phase of their marriage so that we can at least come to church and pray for them?" another voice asked.

"Yakiri is a small place where nothing can be kept secret, so we need not bother about that," a third voice responded.

This torrent of commentaries and remarks was maintained until the pupils who initiated and sustained them realized they were not quite producing the anticipated effect of disrupting our relationship and so gave up.

38

The year came to an end. My relationship with Forche was going from strength to strength, even in the midst of all the gossip. To make matters even worse for our detractors, the two of us came first in our class, having scored equal points.

We were now heading to a more advanced and difficult class where we would begin to prepare for secondary school. That same year both of us had our confirmation when Bishop Paul of the Abakwa Diocese came to Yakiri.

When school broke up for the long holidays, I had plans to visit my uncle Forsuh who had moved to Abakwa to cash in on the kolanut trade which was becoming increasingly important.

Fr Sean, who now had a car and went from time to time to the town, had promised to take me there, but since my grandmother had nobody to assist her at home, I had decided to cancel the trip. It was a very hard decision to make but I had always had a very special and loving relationship with my grandparents and did not quite mind the sacrifice.

I spent my holidays usefully, helping out in the field or reading at the library which had been moved to a bigger location and had more books. A convent to house some nuns who were to come from Ireland was under construction and whenever I felt bored at the library, I would go there to see how the work was progressing. I occasionally came across Fr Sean who recommended me some books to read and reminded me that I had to nourish my mind with knowledge.

Of the books he recommended, one written by an author called Charles Dickens, stood out in my mind. The book was *Oliver Twist*. The book kept reminding me of my own plight as a child and I often believed that I might have gone through the same trials and tribulations as Oliver Twist, the main character of the book, if my grandparents and Fr Sean were not there for me.

It was when I returned from one of my trips to the library one day that I came upon a terrible outburst of noise emanating from the neighboring compound. Such scenes often attracted people, more out of concern than curiosity. When I went to the compound to see what was happening, 1 found Bishu, Bonsisi's older sister, in tears and her dress in tatters.

"What happened?" I asked Bonsisi who approached me when I arrived.

"It's a long story," she declared, her eyes almost wet. "She has been betrothed to a man she doesn't like, so when he came for her there was a big fight here."

As soon as my friend recounted what had happened, I held down my head and tears came to my eyes. I could instantly see a replay of the drama which brought me into the world. I did not understand why society never took time to weigh the consequences of some of its actions.

Traditions and customs should be meant to help uplift people, not destroy them. It was needless for society to keep hanging onto certain aspects of its culture which did not serve it anymore or which did so negatively. I felt that a culture which did not help people hold their own in the face of difficulties was not worth maintaining and I saw no harm for any group to borrow from other cultures to meet its own deficiencies.

In that sense, I see cross-cultural fertilization as the way to the future. Once adopted, a new culture would provide a fresh source of inspiration and stimulus as society battles with ways to overcome its daily challenges in order to move forward.

At home that evening, I discussed what had happened with my grandmother who simply shook her head and said nothing. Events like that kept reminding her of my mother, Mayemfon, and only helped to make her feel even more remorseful. But as a woman what could she do then? It was not obvious that if she had raised the issue and decided to fight against it, other women would have backed her. She would not even have been surprised if her greatest opponents turned out to be women. She brushed off the matter as she went to bed that evening.

The next day, at the library, 1 met Bonsisi who informed me that Bishu had vanished and nobody knew where she had gone.

"What do you mean she has disappeared?" I asked my friend when she finished narrating the new turn the previous day's drama had taken.

"It means her room is empty and she's nowhere to be found."

"Maybe she just wants to bring pressure to bear on your father to cancel the arrangement," I said.

"She isn't the kind of person given to bluffing and I pray that something drastic shouldn't take place," Bonsisi declared sadly. "She's very strong willed and capable of anything. It's a pity that my father hasn't understood that."

"He'll never understand as long as he's put on a pedestal and worshipped like God. Somebody has got to muster the courage and tell him that his actions are hurting the family."

"I think you're right but who's going to bell the cat?" Bonsisi asked. "My mother seems to have given up on the matter."

"Never mind, time is a wonderful cure for muddy water," I declared. "At some point, we must be daring enough to criticize our own society, without which our growth and development will be terribly stunted."

The long holidays finally came to an end and I returned to school. I did not see Forche on the first day but he did show up on the second. He had gone to Abakwa where he spent the holiday in their village, Tisson. Tisson was close to Abakwa. He brought me a present, the novel *Cry, the Beloved Country* written by South African author Alan Paton.

"When I read this book I felt so sad," Forche said. "Read it and tell me what you experience," he told me as he was handing me the book.

At school, the two of us continued to perform well and looked forward anxiously to traveling to Kimbo to celebrate Independence Day. This was the day the people of Mungo West obtained their independence from Mikari rule. The trip with its hassles and inconveniences was usually reserved only for senior pupils, who could walk the distance to Kimbo to participate in the march past and other activities.

238

39

I f by our becoming involved in joint activities, Forche and I had started to dream of romance of some sort, a jarring note occurred which made us think again. St Patrick was a Roman Catholic school which lived up to certain moral standards. While boys and girls were not prevented from coupling up in order to do things together, their activities were expected to be benign and useful and should fall within a strict moral code of conduct defined by the school authorities.

Pupils were encouraged to form study groups and share knowledge, to come together to discuss the Bible or stage plays and even to embark on sightseeing excursions for fun or in relation to their school lessons.

Romance of any kind was totally frowned upon and forbidden. Of course, not to talk of lovemaking! It was pure anathema and seemed even more remote than traveling to space.

"When you grow up and you're married, you'll have all the time in the world to taste the forbidden fruit, to start licking honey of the loins," the headmaster, PaNwafor, whose sense of humor we enjoyed, kept reiterating.

It was against this austere background that a certain pupil nicknamed Yoyo ventured into the forbidden territory. It would be extremely difficult to understand this misadventure without a brief appreciation of this rather unusual character.

Yoyo was a tall, nice-looking and very experienced boy with a birthmark on his right cheek. He was more mature than most of his classmates, having been exposed to the epicurean lifestyle common among dwellers of Mungo East where he partly grew up. Like most people who had been to that part of the country, he was a dandy and knew how to talk to girls and even what to do with them.

It was from him that I first heard words like "kiss," "romance" and "sex" and felt so scandalized when I got to know what they really entailed. Older girls daring enough fluttered around him and he regaled them with stories from his inexhaustible collection. The stories were often heavily colored and spiced with some Benge.

Even though the headmaster sometimes felt he could be a bad influence in the midst of much younger pupils, there was nothing particularly terrible he had done to provide any serious cause for concern.

Almost every pupil in school knew that he secretly drank, smoked and played with women. It was even rumored that he had once contracted a venereal disease and had design to hit on Miss Theresia, the only female teacher in Yakiri.

Miss Theresia had been assigned by the headmaster to keep an eye on Yoyo whose social meanderings and flirtatious conduct were increasingly attracting the attention of the school authorities and making them a bit worried.

It was in the course of this surveillance that the female teacher saw him discreetly slipping a note to a female and much younger pupil. She approached the girl and on reading through the note, realized it was destined for Kende. The letter's contents were a big scandal, at least in the context of the extremely high moral standards to which St Patrick ascribed.

It read:

My sweet-loving Kende,

Only the Lord alone know the way my heart loves you. Each time I think of you it talks krijim! krijim! krijim! like our school drums and make me to want to fall down and dead for you. I loves you more than oxygens and dreams of the day I will come close to your breath which smells like ripe pineapples.

Tell me you love me and wanted to kiss me and do one important things with me. After you read this letter, destroy it because it can get us into serious trouble with that jakajaka headmaster. He believes that after Jesus Christ went to heaven, he replaced him here on earth.

Your lover,

240

Yoyo

When the letter was handed to the headmaster and news about it started to circulate, the whole school was abuzz with gossip. Pupils, especially girls who tended to have a keener sense of observation and had long suspected that something was going on between the two, gathered in groups to wax lyrical about the scandal.

While the pupils went around with the news and speculated on the outcome of the school disciplinary committee, the staff held endless meetings, usually presided over by the headmaster whose stolid mien was now more reminiscent of that of a pirate than the head of a primary school.

He had always looked pale but it seemed the incident had transformed him into a livid complexion, more mummy than man. He suddenly became gaunt and old and went around the school premises like somebody in deep mourning or in the initial phase of lunacy. Throughout this incident, he would sometimes openly shrug off invitation from some members of his staff to indulge in a conversation. It was not clear whether he was fasting as a result of it but his unusually dry and cracked lips and white face glaringly hinted at that. In a nutshell, he was terribly shaken and completely drained by the event.

Following the series of staff meetings which were held behind closed doors and the tone of whose discussions increasingly sounded like that of a war council, it was decided that the punishment to be meted out should be exemplary to discourage other pupils from embarking on similar schemes.

When the teachers emerged from the last of the meetings, the bell rang and the whole school was asked to assemble on the ground where morning devotions were usually conducted.

It was a vast esplanade with a high foreground where teachers normally stood, so that they could easily follow the activities of the pupils at their foot. In spite of the conspicuousness which the elevation afforded anyone beheld from below, the headmaster did not deem it high enough for every pupil to follow the lesson he was about to set. Some tables were, therefore, installed to heighten visibility and help underscore the point to be made.

241

The three culprits were still kept in a room where they were undergoing serious interrogations on who played what role in the drama which had plunged the school into deep moral crisis and tarnished its reputation.

While they were thus held and being bombarded with questions, the headmaster decided to introduce the subject which had caused the whole school to be summarily assembled. Flanked by teachers whose austere appearance could only rival his, the headmaster moved to a central position where everyone could see him. He cleared his throat and then hitched his trousers to navel level before crossing his arms before himself like a Christian going to the altar to receive holy communion.

For a while, he took in the entire school, saying nothing as he did so, his face a grim and solemn mask to demonstrate the monstrosity of the theme he was planning to belabor.

"When a small tropical squirrel vandalizes her Majesty's language and holds one of her former subjects, one with years of meritorious service and a sterling reputation, in obloquy, then the world is beginning to scale the depth of shenanigans," came a bombastic introductory salvo of what he intended to say. This was followed by a pause in which he kept on with his bizarre stare.

After that semantic display, some members of the audience, even including those who had understood nothing, nodded their appreciation of the viscosity and punch of the tirade.

The headmaster's mood had the effect of creating the same dreary atmosphere all over, as people made some effort to be seen to share in his grief. When he was finally convinced that everyone felt the way he did and so was ready to fully appreciate the magnitude of what he had to say, he drifted to the body of his discourse. His voice was silent and a bit hoarse, the tone solemn and sad. In a declaration reeking with quotes from the Bible and some important social philosophers, he expatiated with great vehemence on the dangers of moral flabbiness and fornication.

"A people without a sense of morality dies slowly and steadily," he insisted, tapping onto his vast historical knowledge to provide examples to illustrate his point. "The specter of pregnancy hangs over the heads of those pupils who're secretly experimenting with sex and it's just a matter of time before they'll be betrayed by their own acts."

With the ground thus prepared, he sent for the three pupils who arrived heads down and were asked to climb and stand on the tables for everyone to see them.

Up to this point, the headmaster had made no direct reference to the letter incident, probably deeming the timing poor in the absence of the characters involved. Since they were on the floor now, he decided to delve into that disgraceful chapter of the drama he had been staging all along. He dipped his right hand into the pocket of his trousers and pulled out the letter Yoyo had written to Kende.

With teachers and pupils watching solemnly, he took great care to unfold it, sometimes pausing for a brief look around to see if people had been cranked up to the right level of melancholy. It was hard at that moment to convince anyone that in the best of times, this same character was buoyant and full of jokes and laughter.

He finally opened the letter and began to read it aloud, making sure he stopped or raised his voice where he found something terribly amiss which could provide the basis of severe moral degeneration. This meant every word or every other word.

When he got to the word "kiss," its explosive content was too much for the old man who stopped, made a quick sign of the cross and murmured some hail Maries. The other members of staff followed suite. Even though it was not a long letter, with each step of the reading fraught with its own lot of face contortions, mouth pouting and other forms of theatrics and pantomimes which defy description, it took a long time to go through.

PaNwafor might have been a severe man with very high moral standards but he was not an autocrat. It had been agreed in the staff meeting, through his instigation, that the students should be given an opportunity to explain their conduct in front of the whole school. So as soon as he had finished reading the letter, he turned to the main actor, Yoyo, and gave him the floor to tell the school what he meant in the letter.

Yoyo cleared his throat, looked around nervously but apparently unrepentant, if appearance was anything to go by, and with everyone holding his breath, he moved his lips and said nothing, only contented in occasionally glinting a harsh stare in the direction of Miss Theresia. When it became obvious that it was

243

difficult to elicit anything from him, the headmaster started plying him with questions.

"Do you know the meaning of love and can you love?" the headmaster asked.

"In the Bible, we're asked to love our neighbors and that's what I was trying to do," Yoyo made a clumsy attempt to fall back on his scanty knowledge of the Holy Scriptures to free himself from trouble.

"I appreciate your knowledge of the Bible but how then do 'kiss' and 'do one important thing with you' fit into that context? And by the way, what's the important thing?"

"The important thing I meant was learning together."

"If it were learning together why had the information to be scribbled on a secret note? Why had the note to be destroyed after it had been read to avoid Jesus on earth? And what trouble were you afraid to get into?"

Yoyo was a brave fellow but his letter had serious implications against which he could not defend himself. Judging from the way it was written, he probably did not expect it to fall into the wrong hands. The snide remark he made about the person of the headmaster at the end of the letter put the final nail in his coffin. He could not answer the string of questions which revolved around the amorous ways he referred to Kende.

Even before the headmaster got to Kende she had begun to cry. Though her high-flying conduct had always given other pupils the impression she was tough, her fiber lacked the texture of an experienced veteran like Yoyo. Harassed with questions, she finally admitted to being a lover of Yoyo but was quick to add that she had never had sexual intercourse with him. The information did provide some mitigation of sentence but did not get her off the hook.

The case of the little girl who served as the mail-runner was purely and simply dropped, since she was deemed too young and had been possibly manipulated into the role of a pawn in a game between two experienced lovers. Yoyo and Kende were found guilty and their sentences were handed down.

Yoyo, whose attitude did not surprise anyone, was considered the rotten fruit which would ultimately destroy the school. It was generally believed that he was the one who might

244

have seduced and dragged Kende into the mess into which she found herself.

In the light of the gravity of the crime he had committed, he was to be given twenty-four strokes of the cane, would dig the stump of a eucalyptus tree, would be suspended from school for a week and would have his name written in the black book. It was a stiff sentence, in fact, the stiffest in the history of the school.

As for Kende, who was already shaking like a leaf by the time her own verdict was being announced, she was to get twelve strokes and was to wash the floor of their classroom. Since she did not have any notorious reputation, it was not deemed necessary to put her name into the black book.

The sentence was to be carried out with immediate effect. Four big boys were called out and, with each of them grabbing Yoyo by a limb and stretching him out like a skydiver, a teacher, Mr. Minonmichu, whose reputation in wielding the whip was already firmly established and well known, took on the duty to mete out that phase of the punishment.

He first felt the butt of a helpless Yoyo to be sure it had not been stuffed to cushion the effect of the cane before proceeding to whack it with his whip while he raised hell.

"Spare the rod and spoil the child!" the headmaster answered in chorus to Yoyo's hollering and wails.

When the caning came to an end and he was put down, he immediately cut out the noise, wriggled his butt and pocketed both hands as though nothing had happened. He did not shed any drop of tears nor display any form of remorse.

Even before it was Kende's turn, she had left a streak of urine across the table on which they were standing. She was held up in the same manner and flogged as she screamed. When she was put down, whimpering and with tears streaming from her eyes and her head held down in disgrace, she walked away from the scene of the punishment.

Having understood that the authorities would brook no conduct which put to question the school's quest for moral integrity, the assembly was dismissed. As the pupils headed towards their various classes, they knew they had a juicy piece which would provide the subject for conversation in months to come.

Yoyo, who lived not very far from the school, returned to their house and came back with an axe to begin the task of uprooting the stump he had been assigned as part of his punishment.

Even after they had done their punishments and things seemed to have returned to normal, most pupils constantly made reference to the incident, especially when their relationship was seen to be almost transgressing the limits of moral decency.

Harsh as the punishment had seemed, it did little to quell the exuberant and freewheeling spirit of Yoyo who deemed the school compound too dangerous for his amorous escapades and so moved his activities to his neighborhood. It was here that one evening Miss Theresia again spotted him patting Kende's butt amorously.

It was a mere coincidence but when he saw the teacher, he thought she might have an interest in him which caused her to trail him wherever he went. He dismissed Kende the moment he saw her and boldly walked up to her and greeted her. She responded nicely as would be expected of any good teacher.

Yoyo saw this as an encouraging sign and decided to ask her out and even went as far as trying to wrap his arm round her waist. She could not believe what she was hearing and seeing and, terribly horrified, she instantly took leave, lest people should see them standing and make up stories. She decided to take the matter to the school authorities.

When called up in school the following day to answer for this charge which had no concrete evidence, he angrily referred to Miss Theresia as an ashawo. He went as far as declaring that she was always getting into his case because she wanted him to have a piece of her trembling malaria butt. This was untrue and, terribly scandalized by this claim, she burst into tears. No pupil had ever talked to any teacher like that in the whole history of St Patrick and so all those present were horrified. As for the headmaster, now convinced he was dealing with a demon, he almost collapsed.

He immediately sent for four big boys to come and hold him up to be lashed but before they arrived, Yoyo had darted out of the headmaster's office like a duiker and was fleeing. The headmaster ordered the boys to go after him but he was too fast for them. It was the last the school ever heard of him but not Forche and I.

When it was finally confirmed that Yoyo would not come back, the entire staff breathed a great sigh of relief but the seeds he had planted during and even after his stay in St Patrick were to grow. A couple of pupils were caught afterwards writing love letters and were seriously punished to drive home the point that the authorities meant business.

Now a free man in the village, Yoyo could date whomever he wanted without any fear of being seen and reported. Some pupils continued to see him and Kende together but did not deem it their business to take up the matter.

Apart from this secret love affair, the school was spared further embarrassment until towards the end of that year. Pupils of the senior classes went to Kimbo to participate in march past and traditional dances to mark Mungo West Independence Day. It was during the occasion that Kende collapsed and was rushed to the nearby hospital in Sissong where she was found pregnant.

It was a sad incident but it did provide the headmaster, who had so far been talking mostly with the lash, with concrete and appropriate evidence to use to impress on his pupils the dangers of premarital sex.

"It isn't only about the image of the school. No, that features way down at the bottom of the list. It's about your own future, what we want you to become tomorrow," the headmaster had preached to a pupil population seriously shaken by the event. "It isn't a good start for her, stuck with a child and no means to support him or her. This is what to expect when little girls go around spreading their legs to irresponsible troublemakers."

The Kende and Yoyo incident convinced me more than perhaps any other of how a dream could easily come to an end through the simple act of experimenting with sex. I continued to enjoy decent friendship with Forche and we both spent our time usefully in our studies.

We respected the rules and regulations of the school and constantly went to our schoolteachers or Fr Sean for help and advice. It did not come as a surprise when both of us passed out of the primary school with distinction and were ready for secondary

247

school. I opted to go to St Augustine's College in Kimbo while Forche headed to Sacred Heart College, a boys school in Abakwa.

The two institutions were run by the Roman Catholic Mission and were a far cry from public schools where lawlessness and immorality had taken hold. It was in these institutions that we would be spending the next seven years to prepare for university education.

40

During the holidays, I received a letter requesting me to appear at St Augustine's College for the interview which would determine whether I had finally been admitted. I went for it and performed very well and immediately won the heart of the school's principal, Fr Nielen.

"You've done very well," the principal complimented as he shook my hands and handed me a list of prospectus to purchase.

When I returned home with the good news and list, only my grandmother seemed very upbeat. My grandfather, though not hostile to the idea of sending me to college, was increasingly concerned with where he would get enough money to pay my way through.

However, he refrained from openly voicing his opinion. He feared it might create trouble in his compound. He got the list from me and went through the items to be bought and the amount to be paid as deposit and simply shook his head. He now seemed resigned to a logic he could do very little to prevent.

With some money he had obtained from the previous year's coffee sale, he traveled to Kimbo and paid the required deposit to guarantee my position in the school. He then proceeded to buy the items listed on the prospectus one after the other until he had acquired almost everything before the school reopening date.

Fr Sean had informed me at church that he would give me a ride in his car to the college, and so on the reopening date he drove to my grandparent's compound to fetch me. He arrived when I was ready, with all my things stacked in front of my grandmother's house. The priest helped my grandfather put them in the trunk of his car.

In spite of the amount of food I had decided to take along, and that even seemed unnecessary for it was a boarding school where the students were fed, my grandmother had still prepared me

249

a special package containing kibru. This was a mixture of roasted peanuts and popcorn. It was a favorite local snack which was often munched to stave off hunger while food was being prepared. In a college environment, where meals were only served at specific hours, the package seemed handy.

"What's that?" Fr Sean asked when he noticed how anxious my grandmother was to hand me the package.

"Kibru," she retorted and then waited to see if he had any objection since he knew best what was good for me when it came to things relating to school.

"It's all right, for it'll remind her of how nice grandma is," the priest declared flatteringly much to the amusement of my grandmother.

With everything set, I embraced my grandparents before joining the priest in the car where he was waiting. It was about 2pm when we started out for Kimbo where the school was located.

The road was dry and the potholes had been filled, so, in comparison to some other periods of the year, it was a smooth ride. It took us about an hour to get to the small town where Fr Sean stopped at the market square to allow me some time to visit some shops and buy certain things I could not find in Yakiri.

I bought a mattress and a bucket to complete the list of items I was required to bring to school. When all the things were fitted into the small car, its back doors could not close properly. However, we drove very slowly until we got to the college premises, a moment for me to take time and actually appreciate what would become my new environment for the coming years.

In the entire Wotikar region and even beyond, St Augustine's College was the stuff of legend. Fondly referred to as SAC, it captured the wildest dreams of every primary school child in terms of secondary education.

Its creation was a concrete expression of the vision and faith of Fr Nielen, a Dutch Roman Catholic cleric, who sought an answer to the yearning of poor local children burning with the desire to learn but who could not afford the means to travel to Abakwa to attend Sacred Heart College and Our Lady of Lourdes College, the male and female Etons of Mungo West respectively.

SAC was named after St Augustine of Hippo, one of Africa's greatest saints. It sat atop a hill which overlooked the rest

250

of the small town of Kimbo. It was a majestic institution on a majestic location with a majestic name!

It was very large. From the main road, which formed a grid between Yakiri and other Wotikar villages, the first things which came into view were its numerous green soccer and handball playgrounds, as well as outdoor basketball courts.

These sites were pitched against a backdrop of red brick buildings roofed over with corrugated iron sheets. The houses were set on a rugged piece of land in the midst of a tangle of eucalyptus and cypress groves.

The college premises were linked to the main road by a long, broad drive flanked on both sides by thick hedges of hibiscus flowers, whistling pines and cypress trees. The drive culminated in front of the administrative building in which the principal and vice-principal's offices, as well as the school bookstore and library, were located.

Behind this block, scattered somewhat haphazardly all over on a vast piece of ground which humped like a camel's back, with its flanks sloping down almost in tiers to a valley of gurgling streams and raffia palm bushes rimming it at the base, were the dormitories, the chapel, the auditorium, the staff quarters, the convent, the presbytery, the refectory and the classrooms. Thick clusters of flowers formed hedges on both sides of the broad interconnecting lanes which linked up the constellation of buildings and locations.

The school buildings were surrounded by lofty green hills. The hills stretched far away into the distant blue horizons but were still part of the school property. Here, in this lush sweeping and open savannah only broken sporadically by bursts of fenced-in cornfields, the hissing of the winds and the lowing of cattle added flair to the reigning bucolic and monastic atmosphere.

The convent, the presbytery, the staff quarters, the refectory, the auditorium, the chapel and the classrooms were nestled at the crest of the hump. This great height afforded the nuns, priests and teachers who administered the institution an ideal vantage position to easily peep down and monitor the activities of the students.

Since it was a co-educational school, an imaginary line slicing the hump into two gave one half to the boys and the other

251

to the girls. The two groups only rose out of their tiered, terraced depths where their dormitories formed a brick riot in the midst of the surrounding greenery to meet at the surface for meals, scholarship and play.

To complete the Christian finish on the institution's outlook, the dormitories were named after famous saints: St Francis, St Thomas, St Monica, St Andrew, St Joseph, St Cyprian, St Peter, St John, St Patrick, St Jude, St Agnes, St Michael and many others. It was an arrangement which did little to reduce the religious takeover. It, however, had a practical purpose, for it set the stage for inter-house and, occasionally, inter-dormitory competitions in sports, traditional dances, manual work and all forms of academic endeavors.

To instill some vigor into the competitions, all the students of the different dormitories were regrouped under four main houses. The houses were St Francis, St Thomas, St Monica and St Patrick. The rivalries among the houses in the different activities were usually formal and very intense. Since victory at the end of the day depended mainly on the caliber of the men and women of each house, selecting the members was very important.

The selection began with the arrival of fresh students and it was the hand of fate which determined which way the balance tilted. The various house captains were assembled and instructed to draw lots from a basket into which all the names of the newly admitted students appeared on folded scraps of papers. The lots drawn by the captains determined the members of the houses.

A house could thus become endowed with intellectual giants. Sometimes, this catchy image might be only slightly offset by the presence of some athletic bunglers or social deviants. Another house could wind up languishing under the obnoxious reputation of keeping nothing but gluttons and troublemakers. A third might seem a showcase of men and women cut out for a Roman coliseum but whose performance in any form of oratory would have done grave injustice to that ancient empire.

The ideal house, and in some cases it turned out to be more than one, often made a fine blend of everything and ended up with most of the trophies at the end of each academic year. Whatever complexion a house took owed much to the very character of the principal of the school.

Fr Nielen was not particularly concerned in his selection of students with only the able minds and bodies. He also opened the doors of the institution to students with a good sense of morality and a strong drive. To bolster his argument for lending this approach, he often insisted that nurture and not nature was the basis of the human character. He cited the cases of many contemporary giants who started out as dwarfs in many areas but made it to the top out of sheer determination and the unflinching conviction to do what was right.

With this argument in mind, he kept enthusiastic and tenacious students who occasionally flunked their examinations but made a decent showing on things purely moral, upholding that no society could be balanced and solid without them.

His philosophy was amply vindicated when many of the students did not only make it to the top of their various fields of endeavor but also became imbued with a rare spirit of generosity and commitment to the less fortunate.

It was a social philosophy which he concocted out of Christian thinking and traditional African beliefs and which would soon be duplicated in other institutions with amazing results all over Mungo West. It was a philosophy which held together the disparate components of the dormitories and made everyone fit in.

Even though there were fewer girls as compared to boys, for every boy's dormitory there was a girl's to match, a gesture whose significance in assuring a woman's place at school could not be entirely lost.

The gesture went a long way to, at least, help both sexes learn how to interact and work as a team, thus reducing the gender-based segregated nature of most of the institution's activities which seemed, to a large extent, to be defeating the whole purpose for which a co-educational school was set up in the first place.

41

It was around 3.30pm when the car of Fr Sean screeched to a halt in front of the main building. There, I noticed another kind of rivalry and competition taking place. It was informal and needed some keen observation to be aware of its presence.

The esplanade in front of the block was already teeming with life as students started flocking in from their different locations. Some of them had arrived on foot while others had done so by vehicles. Those who trekked usually came in droves which might have formed naturally on the way, with one student starting and others joining in. Often, these groups were based on ethnic, village or class affiliation.

The esplanade was the first stage on which society's material and social imbalance started to play out, from the manner in which the arriving students dressed to the quality of boxes and mattresses they were bearing, from the air of confidence in some to looks clouded with doubts in others.

Even though my upbringing had put more emphasis on spiritual values, the obvious material discrepancy I noticed between myself and some other students instantly caused me to feel an initial wave of inferiority. It was the kind of complex which caused many poor to cower to the rich.

During our brief trip from Yakiri, perspicacious as he is, Fr Sean had foreseen the looming drama and had spent most of the time on the way fortifying previous social doctrine on material asceticism and on elements which formed the crux of genuine human character in order to prepare me for such a shock.

He had insisted that my new venture was about intellectual and moral upbringing and not material possession which, according to him, could flow at any time out of any sturdy and balanced mind. Even though the advice made an impression, I had little control over the feeling which took hold of me on the esplanade, the more so probably because of my age, little exposure and even of my very competitive nature.

The school was to officially open at 6pm. While Fr Sean went into the office of Fr Nielen whom he knew very well, I kept an eye on the developments taking place on the esplanade. I could easily make out new students from old ones. Apparently intimidated by the new environment, fresh students huddled in small groups and watched with a combination of apprehension and awe the swaggering attitudes of their senior schoolmates.

Dressed in trendy attires and with hairdos and cuts which ranged from cute to queer, the senior students affected movements and manners of talking visibly meant to impress or even mesmerize newcomers and clear any doubts as to who was in charge.

Whenever a party of senior boys came across a group of new students, they would rowdily invite a female classmate over by loudly calling out her name and then would start to talk to her boastfully at the top of their voices, punctuating all these lavish displays with vulgar laughter, bizarre handshakes and lyrical nicknames and statements clearly meant for the consumption of the new students whom they disparagingly referred to as foxes with bushy tails.

Sometimes, if some new students seemed lost and vulnerable, they would order them to run up and would proceed to ask them rude questions about their origins and whether they were in possession of any chewable stashed away somewhere in their boxes. If they answered in the affirmative, they would then embark on a hopeless lecture on the role of new students appeasing their senior counterparts with nice things. This was the very first step to strip them of their foods.

If it turned out that the new students were boys, it was usually a girl in the group who did the questioning to rub in the point that they were nonentities and their intellectual inferiors, but if they were girls, on the instigation of the female member of the band, they would be called upon to make their pick of any of the senior boys they hoped would become their dates.

To most of the new students, summarily dragged from family warmth and with no form of preparation for this kind of ordeal, hell could not have been a lot worse.

During the exercise, some of them, especially brats spoiled with an unhealthy dose of parental affection and no form of toil to strengthen character and timber would break down. It usually needed the harsh rebuke or some form of threat or punishment from a school prefect to rein in the perpetrators of this kind of maltreatment.

Even so, the school authorities often looked the other way in the face of such hazing, attributing it to part of the pecking order and initiation process rampant in such institutions.

The exercise was often repeated over and over until the new students became bold enough and used to the environment and could even fight back by building up their own network of friends with whom to team up in order to put an end to such shakedowns and maltreatments.

It was in the course of this observation that I overheard a senior student, a fellow of rather small stature, one being pompously referred to as Einstein by his friends, address a new student as an atom. It was not clear to me what he meant by that until I started to study chemistry. Later on, I discovered that "Einstein" owed his nickname to his aptitude in mathematics and physics.

I was busy watching all these goings-on when Fr Sean emerged from the office accompanied by the principal. He invited me over and introduced me to the priest who still had a vivid memory of me owing to the brilliant performance he claimed I had put up during my interview.

"She's the most brilliant pupil of our school in Yakiri," Fr Sean said to Fr Nielen in the course of the introduction.

"She really impressed me on the day of her interview and I'm sure that if she keeps up with that performance she'll graduate a top student from this institution."

After parting company with the principal who immediately retired into his office, Fr Sean briefly reviewed some of the advice he had gone through with me and asked me to write to him whenever I had any problem. He then dipped his hand into the pocket of his cassock and pulled out some money which he handed to me. I thanked him and walked him to his car and as he drove away, I waved.

Even before I returned to where my luggage was stacked, a group of senior students was already waiting for me.

"God strikes a match and Satan smokes a pipe!" one of them exclaimed as I was approaching. "A fox with a priest for father, wonders will never cease to exist!"

When I got to where the curious band was waiting, one of its members, a male, began to ply me with questions.

"Is that your father?"

"Yes."

"How come he's a priest then?"

"If he's the priest of my parish and also takes care of me what's he?" I boldly fought back.

"This isn't just your ordinary fox folks, judging from the intelligent manner in which she answers questions and the ease with which she speaks Mikari," he noted.

Achini, as his retinue called him, seemed to me a very special breed. He was not particularly nice looking but was extremely well built and possessed of those traits which were peculiarly male and seemed to appeal to many women of my village.

He was putting on the sartorial craze of the day, with a tight, pocketless pair of trousers called sans-poches drawn up to his navel. A loose-fitting, short-sleeve shirt helped show off his well developed arms.

His hair, close-cropped and capped with a thick tuft, was a work of art. When he spoke, he accompanied each word with a flurry of hand gestures and commanded attention. His friend seemed to admire him mostly for his sense of style.

He was by turn humorous, playful and serious, alternating these roles in a combination which almost endowed him with the mantle of a clown, even though this did not seem to be the impression he created on his acolytes whom he apparently held in thrall.

As I was reaching down for my box, Achini stepped in between and obstructed me.

"What's the matter?" I asked smiling.

"Folks, a fox smiling with a senior student!" another member of the band declared in shock, an utterance which caused my smile to instantly and perhaps unconsciously vanish. "Look here young girl, your name is still in sawdust in this school. This

257

means that if we breathe too fast you'll be out of here, so before you bare those fangs with which we aren't yet impressed, get this straight: you must remember that it takes plenty of hard work and the recognition of Fr Nielen to get to where we are."

"Come on, don't talk to her like that," Achini interrupted the other fellow, the first hint that he might be developing an interest in me. "The dormitories haven't been opened yet so you'll just stay here, do you hear that my darling?" he told me.

"Yes, my sweet darling," I responded so naturally that it took the entire group aback.

"Wow, she has already fallen in love with Achini!" a member of the band exclaimed.

"And what a fine catch!" another voice gave its seal of approval.

The only female member of the group did not quite appreciate the accolades with which I was being showered and which were gradually transforming me into some kind of a celebrity. She began to voice her disapproval with negative remarks.

"Come on boys, she's just a fox and needs plenty of time to have her tail cut so she can fit into this new environment."

In the meantime, the boys offered to take my things to the front of the principal's office where I could sit on a bench and watch over them until the dormitories were opened. All the dormitory heads had arrived and were already flaunting the authority which went with their positions by asking students to do one thing or the other.

The head of St Monica's dormitory, a dormitory set aside exclusively for first year females, was among them. She still needed to inform the female newcomers to take their things and go to their dormitory.

More and more students arrived. While I was sitting in front of the principal's office, a notice calling on all the female first form students to carry their luggage to St Monica's dormitory was posted on the board not far from me. I went to the board and read the information.

It was already getting to 5.30 pm when the school electric generator started to steam and electric lights soon came to most parts of the college premises. By now the esplanade was full to bursting with students and the constant arrival and departure of cars and other vehicles created a terrible din.

Here and there, students formed groups and indulged in conversations describing their activities during the holidays. Most of them had something new to show off. It was either a hairdo, a pair of shoes, clothes, or even a watch.

It was easy to make out students from the rich and more sophisticated urban centers from those from villages and other rural communities. The former tended to look down on the latter. They felt they were backward in their outlook and clumsy in the way they did things and nicknamed them CFC, short for "Come From Country."

A bell soon began to ring. It seemed it was time for students to assemble at the esplanade. The principal emerged from his office and stood at the top of the steps which descended from his office down to where the students had assembled. They were in ranks, according to their classes.

Vince Ndumu, as I eventually learned the school senior prefect was called, showed the new students where to stand. It was the place normally reserved for the first form, as new students were referred to at the college. We were many and almost all of us looked a bit out of place. It seemed we were only waiting to be told what to do. Our immediate academic superiors, the second form, who stood just next to us in that intellectual pecking order kept their mouths running and behaved as though they had just graduated from Harvard with a doctorate.

Their swaggering and overbearing attitude was to impress on any newcomer that they, the second form, were not at the bottom of the academic ladder. Some of them overdid it and as soon as scales started to fall off the eyes of the new students, they also began to pick on them.

With Fr Nielen at the top of the steps, total silence descended on the assembly ground. He gave a prayer and as soon as it was over, he welcomed all the students back to school. He congratulated the new students who finally made it to SAC and stated that the school stood for moral and intellectual excellence. He underlined determination and hard work as key to success and exhorted students to give themselves a chance in life. Before wrapping up, he announced that students with school fees to pay

259

should come to his office and do so as soon as the assembly had broken up and that there would be a movie at the auditorium immediately after supper.

When the assembly broke up, Achini and his friends came and helped take my things to our dormitory. They went behind the administrative building and followed a lane which went down the slope until they came to a vast brick building with Christ-thorns growing on a flower bed just next to the front wall. They stopped at the lobby and waited for a girl to announce to the others that boys were around. They were then ushered in and they took my things to one of the beds in the dormitory. The beds were arranged in two rows along the walls, leaving a passage in the middle for people to walk. The sleeping section of the dormitory formed a horseshoe rim around a central room which served as a store, with bins and lockers set out in rows. Each student was assigned a position on the bin to put her box and also a locker.

The boys spread my mattress on the bed they had selected for me. After chatting briefly with me, they left.

42

With Achini and his friends gone, I opened my box and took out some sheets and a blanket and proceeded to make up my bed. I selected those things I needed the most and locked up the rest in my box which I temporarily slipped under my bed.

While I was busy making up my bed, another girl came and selected the one just next to mine on the left. After watching me for a while, she started to copy my example. I had barely finished what I was doing when a senior student, whom I had already seen when I was sitting in front of the principal's office, sauntered into the building, clapped her hands to attract everyone's attention and proceeded to announce that she was the dormitory head. She introduced herself as Assumpta Neh but insisted she should be called Assunty.

She told us, the new students, that it was time for supper and asked us to take our plates and complete sets of cutlery and hurry to the refectory. I did as we had been instructed. When I got to the refectory, I found other first year students huddled in a corner while a burly fellow whom it turned out was the food prefect was busy assigning them tables.

When everyone took a seat and grace was said, my plate was filled with some rice and stew but I did not begin to eat immediately. I had never used a set of cutlery before. I looked around discreetly and watched the older students eating and then proceeded to do the same. I was not alone, for many of the new students had also never used a complete set of cutlery. The clumsy manner in which they handled and manipulated it sent derisive giggles rippling throughout a group of senior students who had been watching in silent anticipation for the blunder. Thoroughly amused, they immediately styled such a poor performance CFC special. Some students, who were too embarrassed and could not put up with the mockery, decided to give up their meals.

As I ate my food, I paused from time to time to survey and appreciate my new surroundings. The refectory was a long, immaculately white hall with rows of benches on both sides and a wide passage in the middle. It was awash in a flood of light from overhead fluorescent bulbs.

Even though many students had still not returned from holidays, the hall seemed overcrowded, with not fewer than fourteen students at each table. Each table was assigned a top-form student who served as table head to ensure there was order, equitable sharing of food and respect of proper table manners.

While we were eating, the food prefect announced that students interested in watching the movie should take their seats to the auditorium after the meal. Since the first form students still did not have chairs, they were instructed to go into any of the classrooms and take one.

I was still eating when Achini and his friends showed up. They had changed into even more fashionable attires similar to the ones they put on in the afternoon, except that their trousers had a flap in front with two rows of shiny buttons on them.

Even though I felt a bit uneasy to be seen the very first day with boys I barely knew, I felt I needed them for any urgent assistance, as well as to have a proper understanding of the workings of my new institution.

I could tell from Achini's enthusiasm to assist me that he wanted more than just mere friendship. However, I did not want to scare him off with any unfriendly conduct, harkening to my grandmother's advice that it was not from underneath a bed that a lion was caught, tamed and used.

As soon as I was done, Achini and his friends accompanied me to our dormitory and while they waited outside, I went in and stored my plate and set of cutlery and then joined them outside. Together, we went and fetched seats and headed to the auditorium where the movie was to be projected.

The classroom I was instructed to go into to get a seat had bright overhead fluorescent bulbs and rows of empty desks. The desks were set in a linear pattern, with narrow passages in between.

At the back of the classroom was a board on which notices had been posted. In front, at the far end from the door, were a table and a chair for the teacher. The front wall had the blackboard and just behind the door, as one came in, was a waste paper basket.

Once in the auditorium, I sat surrounded by Achini and his band who kept my ears entertained with stories about Abakwa where they grew up. I was fascinated with the town and informed them that my uncle lived there. They told me about The Roxie, Abakwa's most popular movie theater, and New City, its hottest nightclub. They also said that they had plenty of fun during the holidays.

Our conversation was cut short when Fr Nielen came in with a projector and set about adjusting it. It was not my first time to watch a movie. Bastos, a cigarette company from Yamade in Mungo East and now the capital of a two-state Mungo federation, while on a publicity tour to Yakiri, had projected a very interesting movie about a child who grew up in the jungle and started behaving like wild animals.

I hoped that the movie to be shown would be just as interesting. If the stories of Achini and his friends were anything to go by, they had seen many movies. They talked of kung fu and cowboy movies I had only read about in books and called names of actors I had never heard of. They seemed particularly interested in two actors: the first was called John Wayne, and the second, Sean Connery. The second actor attracted my attention because he had the same name as Fr Sean. From the name, I concluded that he could probably be Irish.

When their discussions centered on an actor known as Bruce Lee, a Chinese-American kung fu master, they all went wild. They described a thrilling encounter he had with another martial arts master called Chuck Norris.

At the description of the encounter, one of the boys overwhelmed by excitement jumped up and, with extravagant martial arts positions, tried to imitate the great Chinese-American to the acclamations and cheers of admirers. They also talked of a wonderful Black actor called Sidney Poitier and I recalled that Fr Sean had talked to me about him.

After fidgeting with the projector for a while, it unleashed a shaft of light which settled on a big white screen. The lights in the big hall immediately went out and the movie started to show.

The actor of the first movie was Charlie Chaplin. I found it very interesting and laughed all evening. This one was followed by a Hollywood war movie set in wartime Europe. It was action-packed and gave me the first hint of what a war really looked like. I was terribly frightened by the killings but my friends reassured me, perhaps out of ignorance as I discovered later on, that it was just a movie. Yes, it was just a movie which did not even capture half the horrors of the Second World War.

The movie show went on 'til around 10.30pm when it came to an end and the students left for their various dormitories. Achini and his friends accompanied me right to my dormitory entrance where they saw me off. When I got in, I noticed that many other students had already arrived and made up their beds.

From the door, even though the rows of beds dressed in white sheets looked attractive, they created the impression of a hospital, at least from what I had seen in books.

When I got to my bed, I discovered that the girl just next to me, the one whom I saw earlier in the day, was already lying down. Her sheet was drawn over her but her eyes were still open. After greeting her, I introduced myself. She in turn told me that she was called Adija. She said that she had been born and raised in Kimbo but had relatives in Nkar whom she sometimes visited.

I also decided to lie down. I was just about dozing off to sleep when Assunty went around the dormitory announcing that everyone had to get up very early in the morning the next day to assist in keeping the dormitory and its surroundings clean. Shortly after the announcement, she shut the doors of the dormitory and the lights went out.

Even though I was not wide-awake, I could hear the voices of some students whispering. I was convinced that they must have known each other before coming to the college for them to have so much to talk about.

I woke up the next morning to the handclaps of Assunty. Immediately, I got out of bed and quickly made it up. I rushed to the store where I took my bucket, broom and floor rag and ran up to the dormitory head.

"You'll join the others in washing the floor," she instructed, pointing at a group of eager girls.

Outside, many students were busy, some of them cutting grass, others sweeping, and yet others collecting garbage. It was an exciting period in my life and I enjoyed every moment of it.

With those I had been assigned to do the same task, I proceeded to move the beds to one side of the dormitory to make the task of washing the floor easier. With the beds thus cleared, we inundated the floor with some water containing powder soap and, with the help of brushes and brooms, began to scrub and wash it. The floor was very smooth and easy to wash and as soon as we were certain that it was clean, we began to dry it by soaking up water with rags and squeezing it out into buckets. I found the task easy since I always participated in the team that kept our parish hall in Yakiri clean.

Once we were finished, we moved to the other section and had all the beds transferred to the one we had just washed and embarked on the same exercise. By the time the bell went for us to head towards the refectory for breakfast, our dormitory had taken on a sparkling appearance.

When Adija, my friend with whom I then incidentally shared the same table, and I got to the refectory, we met far more students than during the previous night. Obviously, many of them had arrived late at night.

Even though the institution was set up for underprivileged local children, it still opened its doors to some students from far away big towns. I think that many of these city students enrolled in SAC because they were eager to break free from excessive parental hold. But another reason could be that they just wanted to try something new. Or better still, Fr Nielen might have encouraged the mixture to promote the free flow of ideas between the cities and rural communities.

Whatever might have prompted the mixture, city students often ended up arriving late at school because land connections were usually disrupted by heavy rains and the ensuing bad roads. The Dutchman knew about all these difficulties and was more concerned that the students get to school safely, especially in the light of the numerous road accidents which occurred around this period of the year.

While the students were eating, the senior prefect announced that the entire school should assemble in front of the administrative building immediately after breakfast. During the assembly, the principal declared that students would spend the rest of the day keeping the college premises clean. He read out a list of names of some school prefects under whose supervision each class had been assigned. The prefects seemed to have already been instructed on the various tasks they were to help carry out.

After the assembly, the entire school went to the chapel for morning mass, said by the principal. During mass, I saw many white nuns from the nearby convent who were also teachers at the institution. In all there were four of them, beautifully dressed and displaying the dainty manners associated with their vocation.

For a while I tried to imagine what life would look like not to be married and to sacrifice all the good things just in the service of man and God. It was indeed exultant and perhaps one of the most sublime forms of sacrifice I could think of.

With holy mass over, Adija and I seemed lost for a while. We then decided to follow some other new students, without any knowledge of where they were actually heading. This confusion instantly came to an end when a raspy voice eagerly called out, inviting all the first form students. We turned to face a burly fellow, with low-cropped hair and peasant manners, whose profuse gesticulations and sense of authority left nobody in doubt that he must be of some importance.

"I want all the new students here," he declared confidently, pointing to a spot in front of where he was standing.

When we appeared, he turned around somewhat mischievously and fixed his gaze on a vast stretch of school land completely taken over by grass.

"We have to reclaim this land," he declared, pointing at the bush. He then asked the students to hurry to their dormitories and grab their machetes as fast as possible and meet him where he was standing.

It was still the first week at school and no student wanted to leave a bad impression, so even before the words came out of his mouth, the newcomers dispersed immediately and made for their dormitories.

While they were away, Cocobiacu, the ridiculous name of the prefect in question, whose lofty but empty portfolio of a first form work prefect was responsible for all the air of importance with which he conducted himself, set about cutting out work for us. When we returned, we embarked on grass cutting, taking every opportunity when the prefect was not watching to chat or make fun of one another until we were reminded that our portions extended right down to the bottom of a valley in front of us.

By the time the bell rang, around midday, for us to go and take a shower and get ready for lunch, the prefect was impressed with the amount of work we had done. It was only then that he had the courtesy to introduce himself to us as one of our prefects. He told us that he would be the one supervising us during most manual work and urged us not to hesitate to bring up any problem we were facing to him.

As the students drifted towards their dormitories, I discovered that most of the thick bushes which once characterized the college compound had been cleared. My grandmother had always told me that unity is strength but nothing drove home this observation more eloquently than what we had accomplished ever since we arrived at SAC.

Once in our dormitory, we headed for the collective shower. Many girls were shy to strip naked and take their shower but I was not. In Yakiri, when villagers were on their way back from their fields around dusk, it was the custom for them to stop and bath themselves at any big stream before heading home. Man, woman and children would strip completely naked and go into the stream together, with nobody giving a damn about the other person. They would chatter and make jokes as they lathered themselves with soap before taking a plunge. There was something pristine and even innocent in the manner in which this exercise, which took place in some societies in the utmost secrecy, was carried out. Call it primitive or whatever you like but rape in our community was very rare.

For me, therefore, stripping and going under the shower was a very natural thing to do. Once I was done and ready for lunch, I decided to share some of the snacks my grandmother had prepared with some new acquaintances. It was for me a way to widen my circle of friendship.

While we were busy eating and chatting, I got to know some more of the students with whom I was in the same dormitory. The overwhelming majority of those I met on such occasions were from Wotikar villages and I could communicate with them in the local language. It was, however, against the school regulations to speak in a language other than Mikari which, though foreign, was used as the medium of instruction at the college. Since its mastery was not always easy, as part of the process to foster its acquisition, the students were often encouraged to use it for their daily communication.

For me, who had the very rare privilege of knowing a priest interested in my intellectual progress and through whom I had developed an early love for reading, my grasp of Mikari surprised many, even Fr Nielen. I rarely spoke Wotikar at school, judging that by doing so I would not only be violating one of the school regulations but would also be helping to erode the kind of intellectual credibility I wanted to establish for myself.

Once in a while, I got to meet students from Abakwa and even Victoria and K-town in the Sawa Province. For the most part, these students tended to be aloft, often finding it awkward if not completely out of place to mingle with boring country bumpkins with whom they felt they had very little to discuss.

However, as we grew used to the new environment and intellectual rigor set in, they began associating with these upcountry fellows. They did so out of the need to survive intellectually because boring as they seemed, these upcountry fellows generally had a better sense of application and selecting their priorities.

I was still busy chatting with a friend when one student burst into our dormitory and asked for me.

"I'm here," I declared.

"Some students are looking for you outside."

I rose and headed towards the entrance of my dormitory and found Achini and his friends. They smiled as soon as they caught sight of me.

"I have something for you," I told Achini as I returned to the dormitory.

I could not forget how useful they had been to me the first day at school and I thought sharing my snack with them was the least I could do as compensation. I made them a small package of

268

kibru and some gari. When I took the package to the boys, they were very pleased, for hunger had already started to take its toll.

"This should hold our stomachs before lunch," the boys declared in a show of appreciation.

After chatting briefly with me, they promised to meet me in the afternoon. As they headed to their dormitories, I returned to meet my friends.

"Who was looking for you?" one of the girls asked.

"Some Abakwa friends."

"You already know people from Abakwa?" another voice interjected.

"Well, they helped me yesterday when I was stranded with my luggage in front of the principal's office, so I figured they should be nice fellows."

It was at this juncture that the bell rang. Hastily, we grabbed our plates and complete sets of cutlery and started towards the refectory. On our way, we overheard some senior students extolling the virtues of the lunch to be served.

"It's rice and beans, so I'll eat myself to a stupor," one of them declared.

"Our table is made up mostly of girls watching their weight, so I don't even want to imagine what'll happen," another voice announced.

My friends and I went past them and one of them screeched out orders at us.

"When foxes hear the bell, they tuck their bushy tails between their legs and run," his voice rang out much to the amusement of the others.

We paid them no heed, judging from their ages that they could only have been second form students anxious to show their importance.

The refectory population had grown even more. We were convinced that every member of the institution had returned from holidays. At our table, Adija and I had our plates filled with rice and beans. It was well prepared and we ate with tremendous appetite. While we were eating, we overheard some senior students stating that there had been an occasion when beans served contained some weevils and, in a show of protest, one student took his meal to Fr Nielen.

269

They held that when the young man showed up with his plate of rice and beans, the priest told him that weevils did not kill and that they were, indeed, a rich source of protein. To drive home his point, he asked for a spoon and proceeded with great appetite to eat the food and the poor fellow fearing that he might starve for the rest of the day, quickly grabbed the rest of his meal and fled.

The story amused me very much. It rang familiar. I remembered once meeting my grandmother on my way back from school and asking her what kind of food she had prepared for me. She simply said food but deliberately refrained from specifying the exact kind.

"Is it tasty?" I remembered having asked her.

"If you're indeed hungry, it'll be," she had replied after a brief pause.

For a moment, my mind lingered on the subject of food and hunger and I was convinced that my grandmother gave me a very good answer. Too much scrutiny of what was good to be eaten was the direct consequence of abundance.

I remembered that while my grandmother was recounting the story of the Wotikar people to me, and the hardship they had to endure in their endless wandering, she told me how they often ended up eating the roots and leaves of wild plants just to survive. Who in such circumstances would talk of food being good or tasty, I thought.

When lunch was over, I retired to the dormitory with some of my friends only to find Assunty sitting on my bed. I was at first surprised and then frightened and began to ask myself what I might have done wrong. I greeted the dormitory head very politely when I came close to her. She sat me down and began to ply me with friendly questions. In the end, she told me that I first made a good impression on her in the way I spoke Mikari and in the thorough manner in which I had done my own piece of work when the dormitory was being cleaned. She then talked a bit about herself and warned me about Achini whom she said was not bad but was too experienced and mischievous for me.

"Make him your good friend and nothing more," Assunty declared before leaving my bedside.

"Yes, Sister Assunty," I replied, addressing her by using that title of affection and respect meant for top form female students.

When she left, my friends flocked around me, anxious to know what she had discussed with me. When I told them, they went green with envy for that first recognition.

"If she can make you out of the whole lot this early, then there must be something special about you," Adija declared.

Our discussion centered on the meeting with the dormitory head until the bell rang for us to go to class. It was not hard for us to find our different classrooms as the names of students had been posted on the door of each classroom.

In my own classroom, students were assigned desks by a senior student. I ended up in the same classroom with Adija. We were in class when a senior student came in with a box containing the lists of books which students had already paid for but were still to reclaim from the school bookstore. He handed out the lists to the students and then selected twenty students who accompanied him as he left. They returned shortly with boxes containing the various textbooks and notebooks that we needed.

Finally, the whole class was served and for the first time I was flipping through the pages of books with titles such as chemistry, biology, physics, literature, religious knowledge, mathematics and many others.

I became exhilarated when I started reading through some of them. The whole idea of coming to college began to take on an entirely new meaning for me. I immediately recalled a piece of advice Fr Sean gave me in which he declared that school began on the first day and went far beyond just what was taught in the classroom.

"Read everything you come across, especially the classics," he had informed me.

At the time, I had remotely heard of a book titled *Things Fall Apart*, written by Chinua Achebe, a Nigerian said to be the father of African literature. His work was among the novels we had been given and which we would be reading in literature. There was another book, *Treasure Island*, by Robert Louis Stevenson. I had read an abridged and simpler edition at our library in Yakiri, so the work was not new to me.

While we were busy going through our books to make sure they were all in good condition, our study prefect instructed us to ask for locks for our desks from the college bookstore. He said that

271

in the past some careless students had paid dearly by having their books stolen.

By the end of the first week, we were already settled and classes began in earnest. It really did not take long for me to establish a reputation as an extremely good language student. I also easily grasped mathematical concepts but was more attracted to chemistry and physics in which I excelled as well.

The head tutor of the school, a comely and humorous man called Pajong, taught us geography and biology while an Irish nun, Sister Rosemary, affectionately called MaRose, taught us Mikari, Benge and literature.

Sister Mary, another nun who was a distant cousin to MaRose and was commonly known as Mama, a title of endearment, lectured us chemistry and physics. These were the teachers who held their positions permanently until the end of the year.

Though I was competitive by nature, I made it a point of duty not to allow any boy to beat me in class. They did not like my kick-butt attitude which greatly humbled many of them. Outside the classroom, I also made sure my conduct was beyond reproach. At one time, I even actually succeeded in winning an informal prize for manual work.

Fr Nielen, who donated the prize, had set out his conditions for the winner. He said that he was not looking for a strong person who could do a lot of work but rather one who did it with a dedication and effectiveness as if his or her very life depended on it. When the conditions for determining the winners were spelt out and examined, even those who had initially cried foul agreed that I deserved the prize.

However, it would be wrong for anyone to think that I was concerned only with the acquisition of knowledge and never took time off to have fun with other students. Some of the fun I enjoyed arose from the mischief common with young men and women when they are put together. In our class, there was a certain student nicknamed Tsetse who spent most of his time sleeping while his classmates were studying. One day, he was caught in a deep sleep when the final bell rang for students to break up night study and retire to the chapel for prayers marking the end of the day's activities. We, the other students of our class, immediately agreed that we would abandon him alone and follow his reaction from a hideout when the classroom lights were finally put out shortly after night prayers.

So very quietly, we all locked our desks and tiptoed out of the classroom, leaving him snoring. We went to the chapel for night prayers. Immediately after the prayers, we scurried back and hid behind one of the walls of our classroom and waited for the lights to go out at 9.45pm.

Even after the lights had gone out, he kept on sleeping. We were certain that he could sleep all night unless something was done. We decided to jumpstart the mischief by asking one of our classmates to crawl into the room and then, from underneath a desk, twirl his toes to rouse him from sleep. He did as we had agreed and Tsetse got up with a start. Realizing that he was alone in the dark, he burst out into a wild wail and would have crashed into a window pane had the fellow not had the good sense of coming out of his hideout and holding him as he stumbled on obstacles. Outside, it was absolute bedlam as we laughed and joked about the matter.

From that incident, most students were convinced that he would put an end to his terrible sleeping habit. But as the old saying goes in Africa, the zebra does not get up one morning and wish away its stripes. Suddenly awoken from sleep one day, he unleashed a big fart and caused a serious commotion.

MaRose, in whose class the incident took place, finally managed to calm down the other students. Then turning to him, she asked him to give the opposite of the word "handsome." After rubbing his eyes and scratching for about a minute, he replied by saying "legsome." The entire class burst out into a hysterical laughter. The laughter was fueled partly by another incident which occurred during a biology class. When asked under what animal classification the people of his village fell, he responded by saying "reptile."

After the first semester, when I took my report card to Fr Sean, the Irishman was so ecstatic that he ordered me a rare pair of shoes from Italy. My grandfather, who had approached the whole matter of my secondary education with a lot of skepticism, began gradually to embrace it. Still, I sensed that he could not come to terms with the amount of money he was spending to educate a woman who in his mind would become the property of another person or village.

During the holidays, while some of my friends went about town showing off that they were in college, sometimes even going as far as displaying the lack of courtesy of stopping to greet former primary school classmates who, for one reason or the other, did not make it to college, I spent most of my time at the local library whose entire collection of books I was determined to read. This was quite a challenge, for reading an entire book collection that never ceased to grow was no easy task. Our library was constantly stocked with a wide range of reading material donated by some church organizations and foundations in Ireland and the US.

At this period, my notion of romance, which my new institution now tolerated as long as it did not involve sex, hardly went beyond maintaining communication with Forche. He proved to be a loyal friend and continued to send me pictures, postcards, love letters, and poems.

Whenever any of his correspondence arrived, I would sit down with my friends, who were often around me, and scrutinize each of the items. I could tell from their voices and faces that they were envious and would have loved to have their own boyfriends faraway who wrote constantly to them to reiterate their commitment to their love.

Forche's reputation as my friend or boyfriend, if you want, also had another advantage. Having betrayed him once and promised never to do it again, I did not think it necessary to have a boyfriend at SAC. This meant that I could easily keep Achini's expectation in check. Like a lion circling an iron cage with a goat kept within, Achini continued to hover around me even though it was widely rumored that he was discreetly indulging in sex with a paramour.

At the end of the first year, just after examinations, and before students left for the long holidays, the second form students set aside a special day for the official tail cutting event. On the tail cutting occasion, the second form students invaded our dormitories and exposed us to all kinds of rude behavior as a way of saying that they acknowledged our presence and considered us as part of the college.

274

The event was usually supervised by some senior students and bore the school administration's stamp of approval. Once it was over, the first and second forms met together in the refectory to share chocolate drinks and also at the auditorium to watch a movie. The foxes had now shed their tails and had become part and parcel of the great SAC.

Usually, after the tail-cutting event, the first form students assembled in their classrooms to obtain their report cards and prepare for the school prize-giving ceremony. This took place on the last day of the school year, just before the students broke up and returned home to their parents for the long holidays. I had performed extremely well in my class and was first. Since I knew that I would be receiving a lot of prizes, I had invited Fr Sean, who arrived with my grandparents, for the occasion.

Under the glare of the priest, my grandparents and the entire public, I proudly went up many times for my prizes, thus earning the admiration of everyone. I even became the butt of many jokes, the most interesting being the ones made by Pajong who handed me my mathematics prize.

"Never mind boys, this prize will help her accurately calculate your bride price when the time comes," he had quipped much to the chagrin of the boys. Sensing that the boys in my class were not happy with the joke, he struck out with another one as soon as the laughter had died down. "God sent Angel Gabriel to come to the world and help men with their problems and the first place he landed was SAC," the teacher declared. "The angel first went to the third form and asked what he could do for them and all the students said that they wanted the school to provide them with better food. 'That's easy,' said the angel as he enabled the school authorities to have more funds and fix the problem. Then the angel went to the fifth form and they all stated that they wanted to pass their final examinations with distinction," Pajong continued. "'Little problem,' said the angel as he made the students more determined and enthusiastic with their studies and the problem was thus resolved. Then the angel went to the first form where the boys looked weary and sad and he knew that they had a very serious problem. 'What's your problem so that I can fix it?' the angel asked and the entire class immediately shouted: 'Yaya.' At this," Pajong

275

concluded, "Angel Gabriel started to cry and the rest of the class joined him."

That brought down the roof of the auditorium.

After the event, I squeezed some of my belongings into my box and joined Fr Sean and my grandparents and we drove back to Yakiri where I enjoyed the status of a folk heroine and became the talk of the village. This notwithstanding, most people still felt it would have been better if I were a boy.

I would have liked to spend the holidays with my uncle's family in Abakwa but I had to help my grandparents in harvesting the crops which would be sold to raise money for my school fees. I went to the fields constantly, only returning late in the afternoon to prepare to go to the library. At this time, the mission in Yakiri had some nuns whom I visited from time to time and from whom I learned a lot. They sometimes gave me some odd jobs to do from which I earned some money.

Fr Sean kept plying me with books which I read and made notes, thus building up my vocabulary and broadening my knowledge.

On market days and Sundays, I went to the square where once in a while I came across one of my class or schoolmates who had either come to the village to visit a relative or run some errands.

In Yakiri, there were students from other institutions in other parts of the country, especially from Abakwa and the coastal region. I met some of them occasionally and exchanged greetings but our relationship never developed beyond that. I found that to be somewhat absurd, so I discussed with Fr Sean the possibility of the students coming together to form a union. He thought it was a bright idea and so he made an announcement in church calling on all students to meet him after holy mass. When they met him, he explained that it was on my request that he had made the announcement. He then offered to allow us to use the parish hall to get together in order to hear what I had to say. In was during that first meeting that I raised the issue of starting the students union. It was unanimously upheld and a date was fixed for us to get together.

A week later we gathered at the same hall and all the students, twelve in number, registered to begin the first Yakiri Students Union, commonly known by its acronym YASU.

In subsequent YASU meetings, important issues which featured on the agenda were: election of a YASU executive, role of the students in promoting community development, students' animation programs and the contribution of students in the promotion of education.

Since it was my idea which brought about the union in the first place, I was elected the first president of the organization so that I could at least lay the foundation of what I had in mind. Some other key positions included the ones of a vice president, a treasurer, and a secretary. In the last meeting before the students returned to school, I promised to contact similar organizations in other parts of the country and learn more in order to improve on what we had jointly created.

Once in school for the second form, I tried to remain an exemplary student both morally and intellectually. Out of curiosity, I made some efforts to know Achini better. I often invited him and his friends over for kibru snacks or gari porridge. Gari porridge is fried cassava flour mixed with cold water, some sugar and roasted or even raw peanuts, and then finally topped with avocado.

The more I got to know Achini, the more I discovered that the description of Assunty, who graduated the previous year, had been accurate. Style he had and many things he knew, but he could not be trusted at all. The first time I started to doubt his character was when he invited me to a dark corner outside the auditorium while a movie was showing inside and tried to kiss me. I found that to be extremely rude, for I had consistently informed him that I had a boyfriend who was at Sacred Heart College.

From that action, I began suspecting that he might just be interested in having fun with me. When I accused him of this, he said nothing and showed little remorse for treating me in such a disrespectful manner. However, that did not put an end to our friendship because there were other common grounds on which we were attracted to each other and operated.

Coming from a village, I was little exposed to fashion and other trends taking place in the big cities. He helped me change my style of dressing by educating me on the latest fashion trends. He sometimes unconsciously schooled me in the cunning of men, especially when they were interested only in one thing in a woman. Even more interesting, when we went out to town, on the last

Wednesday of each month, he took me to visit with friends and relatives.

It was during one such outing that I discovered another aspect of his character. Here we were walking down a street when a beautiful car heading towards us loomed far ahead. Immediately, he hid himself behind one of his friends until the car drove past and disappeared.

"Why did you do that?" I asked, really perplexed.

"That was my father's car and he had warned me never to leave the school compound," he replied.

"But you aren't out of bounds."

"His instruction was that I shouldn't leave the compound on any circumstances," he insisted. "I'm sure he's going to look for me at school because he wrote promising to visit me in the course of this week."

"Whatever he has for you will be handed over to Fr Nielen," I said, still not making any sense out of his conduct.

It turned out later that the rich man that we met was not Achini's father as he had claimed. From the grapevine, I had learned that his father was in fact an illiterate farmer who constituted a real source of embarrassment for him.

I could not understand why he felt that way. After all, the poor man was making a big sacrifice to offer his son what he never had. His father, I reckoned, should be for him a source of great pride.

I never raised this issue with him but it did help me to know him better. I knew he had misunderstood me, probably associating me with one of those girls for whom wealth meant everything. If that was the kind of girl he was looking for he eventually found one.

43

I n the course of that year, a girl dismissed for bad conduct from Our Lady of Lourdes College in Abakwa washed up in SAC with her fat mother. Her mother must have had prior knowledge of the spirit of compassion of Fr Nielen, for as soon as she landed she started to stage a drama by threatening to commit suicide if her daughter was not admitted. The priest took the threat seriously and allowed the girl to be admitted on promise that she would not be a nuisance or a bad seed.

After the daughter had been admitted, the round woman jiggled her bulk, adjusted her wrap-around and clasped the amused Dutchman in a bear hug of gratitude which jangled his bones.

"Thank you Fr," she declared as she slammed a kiss on the cheek of the priest.

As soon as she let him go, while he set about adjusting his cassock after so impressive a grip and loud a kiss, the mother turned to the daughter and vowed that it was the last time she would be putting herself through hell for her.

Makajo, for this was the girl's name, knew her mother to be a dormant volcano. She took her utterance seriously and so did her best to stay in line. But when she met Achini, she lost her mind. She was so carried away by him that she completely lost sight of her mother's temperament and the trouble she had put her through. The two had met their match and hit it off right away.

Even though Achini still maintained his friendship with me, it was obvious from the way he treated Makajo in public that he had finally found the person he was looking for.

Unlike her mother, Makajo was a slim, tall girl with beautiful hair braids like a Fulani. She had older sisters who lived in Mungo East and kept her supplied with a steady stream of dresses which made her stand out of the crowd. She barely ate and she exercised constantly to stay in shape. The cut of some of her

279

dresses almost gave the impression that she was in a fashion parade. Each time she went past, she trailed a column of sweet-smelling perfume which most students had never even heard of, let alone seen.

The nuns at our school viewed her flamboyant lifestyle with some apprehension, lest it should make the other girls feel inferior and go around prostituting themselves in order to assemble the funds necessary to copy her ways. They invited her to the convent and advised her but it was the most they could do since being fashionable did not run contrary to the school regulation.

It was in this web of fashion and finance that Achini became entangled. He had always given the impression that he hailed from a rich family and this was what seemed to have registered in Makajo's mind when she first met him.

Obviously, a girl with expensive taste should hang out with a rich boy. Achini had rich brothers who gave him money. Having been through college themselves, they knew how much their younger brother needed to be comfortable in school. Instead of coming out clean with the girl, he continued to foster the misconception that he could not run dry of funds. He was playing with peanuts in the presence of a mouse.

He created an expectation which he was compelled to live up to. The two kept on with their extravagant lifestyle constantly fuelled with unconfirmed rumors that they were involved in intense sexual activities. They made it to the end of the academic year without any incident.

The next year came. I moved to the third form after a brilliant academic performance. As for Achini and his lover, who barely managed to make it to the fourth form, the year began almost with a bang.

They were just returning from a long holiday in which it was rumored that the two of them lived almost like husband and wife. Nobody noticed any change in attitude during the first month at school. Then gradually, things began to change. Achini started to maintain an unusual distance from his belle. As for Makajo, the very embodiment of vitality among students, she lost most of her vigor and increasingly became pale. She hardly indulged in exercise and put on weight. For a couple which in their halcyon days behaved like lovebirds, these changes could not escape people's notice.

Soon the rumor machines went to work, attributing Makajo's outward physical appearance to early signs of pregnancy. As time went on, her conditions seemed to worsen. Then the couple started disappearing from school.

At one stage, the disappearance lasted three days after which Makajo came back to the dormitory and could not even go to class. She claimed to be sick but did not specify what was wrong with her. At night she could not sleep, holding her stomach and moaning with pain. The dormitory head had no choice but to alert the principal who rushed her to Sissong hospital.

It was at the hospital where she stayed for more than a month that it was discovered she had undergone a crude abortion which almost took away her life.

When she had fully recovered, she was threatened with dismissal unless she revealed what had happened. It was only then that she said she became pregnant with Achini's child and could not come to the hospital for an abortion since the school authorities would have been alerted and both of them might have been expelled. So fearing that the birth of the child would mark the end of her education, she decided to contact a crude traditional medicine man who used herbs to extract the fetus. She said that it was Achini who raised the money she used to pay for the operation.

Most members of staff would have loved to see the two students thrown out of school but Fr Nielen took a softer line. He said that judging from the appearances of the two, looking very tired and completely drained out as they were, they had gone through hell and learned their lesson from the incident.

The event seemed to have traumatized the couple, for they were hardly seen together, preferring maybe to keep a low profile in the wake of the scandal. Things were almost returning to normal when the incident took yet another turn, at once humorous and embarrassing. Before I come to that, let me take the story to Abakwa for a brief moment.

44

At his small but sumptuously decorated and furnished house in Azire, a neighborhood in Abakwa, it was getting to 9am when Mr. Arata was just about to lock his door. He was on his way to Tisson where he owned a large orchard. All his life, he had been a farmer, a profession he did not particularly like. He had always felt he should have been a politician like his late brother, but his life, for a reason no rational mind can divine, had taken a strange turn which landed him where he was. It all began when as a young man, he was deprived of the opportunity to go school, not because he was heady but because he was very obedient to his parents and they loved him very much.

Ironic as it may sound that it was the obedient and loved child who ended up being deprived of obtaining an education, it fits perfectly in a social context at the time. Back in the days of Mr. Arata, schools were run like boot camps, with lashing and other forms of harsh punishments used to enforce discipline and promote knowledge acquisition. With such a reputation, most parents preferred to send instead their stubborn children to school in the hope that the authorities would use the whip to steer them away from evil and instill in them a sense of discipline. The children they loved, by contrast, were shielded from such brutalities by not being enrolled in school. The old saying that good guys finish last became largely true in this instance.

Each time Mr. Arata thought about his plight as an illiterate, he could not contain his anger. He understood that his parents unquestionably acted out of good intentions, but he still felt that it was one occasion when they should not have shown him love. However, as good is always finally rewarded, he had something to show. Though this might have seemed like a mere consolation prize for one who could neither read nor write, he had a list of great achievements to his credit. He had put three of his four children through college, almost single-handedly since his wife died after giving birth to his last child, Achini. This was no small feat, especially given that they all went to some of the best private schools money could buy. He still owned and managed his orchard but he did so mainly to keep himself active, for he really did not need the money. His first three children, all of whom held top positions in Mungo government, made sure he led a comfortable life by providing him with whatever he wanted.

Though comfortable and proud of what he had achieved, from time to time, little things occurred in his life which reminded him of the importance of education. It was such reminders which often made him miserable.

He had just finished locking his door and was about to leave when he almost bumped into the postman.

"Good morning Pa," he greeted, using the title which denotes father. "I have what looks like a very urgent and important letter for you," he declared as he handed him the envelope on which the words "very urgent" had been scrawled on the back.

"Thank you my son," the old man said after receiving the letter and staring at the back of the envelope as though he could read. He opened it and took out the letter but could not make any sense out of the white sheet with things scrawled on it. By the time he raised his head to look, the postman had already disappeared. He pondered over what to do with the letter. Rumors were prevalent in the community that even though he was well-to-do, he could still not read. Some of the people who spread the rumors often acted out of jealousy since they too could not read. But this paradox had nothing to do with their ambition to speak ill of Mr. Arata. In their community, he was respected by many and still occupied a social position far more superior than any of them could ever dream of. So, by constantly raising the question of his illiteracy, they were seeking to belittle and reduce him to their level. They knew he was a very sensitive man.

After pausing for a while, he decided not to go to his orchard. He wanted to know who had written the letter and what was inside which made it so urgent and important. He reopened the door which he had locked, tossed his farm bag behind it and after locking it again went out in search of someone who could read the letter and tell him its contents.

283

He did not want anyone who would make fun of him, so after going through a list of names, he finally settled for Nikang. Nikang was a young man who had dropped out of primary school following a fight he had with his class teacher. Aware of the punishment which would have been inflicted on him if ever he were to step foot in school again, he decided to put an end to his schooling. Though he knew very little, he always gave the impression that he was very learned, pretending to have read many books and to be proficient in Mikari. In spite of his seemingly showy attitude, he could keep a secret.

So it was to Nikang that Mr. Arata finally turned for assistance. When the two men sat down face to face and Nikang was given the letter, he glanced at the back, announced the sender and started to unfold it very carefully. After reading through the note, he instantly held his hand to his mouth.

"Your son is finished!" he exclaimed as white as sheet, seemingly shaken by the contents of the letter. "He has destroyed a very important object and the school wants him to pay."

"It isn't long that he left for school with a lot of money."

"That may be true but he'll require much more than just his pocket money to pay for the thing he has broken."

"Is this thing not sold in shops here in Abakwa?" the old man asked.

"No, the thing is sold only in shops in Europe."

"In Europe!" Mr. Arata exclaimed, clutching his chest. "Then it must certainly cost a lot of money."

"Yes, but rather than stay here and speculate on what it costs, I suggest that you go to the college and talk with the principal."

"So, but what is this important thing called," the old man asked after a pause.

"Fr..fr..fry ten sentences or something like that," he said after struggling with the word.

"You're right Nikang," the old man responded, almost certain that the thing must cost a lot. "As soon as I leave you, I'll go back home and get set to travel to Kimbo."

"Yes, that is what I think you should do."

"So what did you say the name of the thing is again," he asked Nikang, finding it hard to retain the word. He certainly did

284

not want to look stupid when he finally met with the principal of the school.

"Never mind," Nikang replied with some assurance. "The principal will tell you when you get there." He knew that he could not pronounce the name of the object that had been broken. He had never even heard of it but he refrained from telling the old man so, lest he should question his knowledge and ability to read.

45

ather Nielen was at his office in the afternoon when there was a knock on the door and a gnarled old man walked in. He pulled a chair and sat down and, for a while, kept twisting and turning but saying absolutely nothing.

"How can I help you?" the priest was compelled finally to ask with a smile.

"I came for that problem concerning my child," the old man said quietly.

"Who's your child?"

"Achini Father."

Immediately, the principal's mind went to the abortion incident which had just rocked the school. He raised the issue, hoping the man had something to say about it but noticed that he seemed unaware of what it was all about. The principal then went through the pains of telling him what had happened. He said that he was still planning to write him a formal letter.

"Even though he did that I decided to keep both of them in school because they're still children and together we can change them."

"So what about the important thing he has broken and the school expects him to pay for?" the old man asked.

"What important thing?" the principal asked as his forehead furrowed in contemplation. "I don't know the thing you're talking about."

The old man could clearly see that the priest did not know what he was talking about, so he stood up, unbuttoned his baggy pair of shorts, pulled it slightly down, unbuttoned the next one inside and did the same until he came to the third pair into one of whose voluminous pockets he dipped his hand and pulled out a bundle which he placed on the table. He then started to re-button and adjust each pair of shorts until he came to the last one. His clothes in order, he resumed his seat and as he did so snuck a quick glance at the priest who seemed not to have recovered from the shock of the entire drama of one man wearing countless pairs of shorts at once.

Without uttering a word, the old man started to untie the bundle until he came to a rumpled envelope with splotches of red earth. He took out the envelope from the bundle, opened it carefully and fished out a letter which he handed to Fr Nielen.

The principal read the letter, rang for his secretary and asked him to go to the fourth form and tell the teacher to send Achini to his office.

He arrived forthwith and as soon as he saw his father, his jaws dropped and he became totally confused. He twitched nervously on his seat when he finally pulled one and sat down next to his father and his hands danced on the table. Beads of perspiration rolled down his smooth, narrow face and his eyes surveyed the room furtively like a cornered creature.

The principal simply handed him the letter to read out. He clutched it and with his hands still trembling like a leaf, he moved his lips which completely failed to proffer a word. He was completely paralyzed with fear and embarrassment. At this he broke down in front of his father who now seemed lost. Finally, the principal got the letter and went through it calmly. It read:

Dear Father,

I am very sorry to write you this letter. As I am writing, I am being threatened with dismissal from the school because I broke a pair of photosynthesis. It is a very complicated and expensive object and the school wants me to pay for it.

So if you really love me and want me to remain in school, send me two hundred thousand francs to pay for the broken object. It costs more than that but I will tell the principal that that is all what I have got.

Send the money through any of your driver-friends coming this way. You need not come yourself as it is a lot of trouble and the roads are very bad. I love my father too much and would die of guilt if he were killed in an accident just because he wanted to come and pay for a pair of photosynthesis.

I love you.

It was obvious to the principal that this letter was nothing other than a dirty trick cooked up by an ungrateful student to extort money from an illiterate father.

"Did you break a pair of photosynthesis?" the principal who made a joke of everything asked Achini who looked too embarrassed to say no.

"I was hard up and needed money from him," Achini mustered the courage to finally say something in his defense.

"Hard up!" his father exclaimed. "This is just the beginning of the term and before you returned to school, how much did I give you as pocket money, not counting the amount you received from your older brothers?"

"Well, if you're always having a hard on it's difficult to see how you won't become hard up," the principal continued with his humor.

"Well, the money got stolen?" he lied.

"It can't be true because Makajo said that you paid for the abortion which almost took away her life," the principal interrupted, calling his secretary and sending for Makajo.

When she arrived, the principal asked her Achini's role in her last predicament. She enumerated the things he did very eagerly, probably because she was also trying to get back at him. He had been avoiding her ever since they had the last trouble together.

She was instructed to return to her class. Once more, the ball shifted to Achini's court.

"I gave him money for his school fees and enough pocket allowance to last him 'til the end of the term," his father cried out.

The principal reached for his register and went through all the names and found out that he had not even paid the fees.

"Look here," the principal announced. "He hasn't even paid the fees. I think he used the school fees money to pay for the abortion and was asking for photosynthesis money to replace the school fees," the principal said, still maintaining his tinge of humor.

The old man said nothing. He untied the bundle and pulled out some banknotes which he handed to the principal as school fees. He turned to his son and told him he should not expect any money from him 'til the end of the year.

"You shat on your own path," he announced as he rose, shook the hand of the principal very vigorously and thanked him for putting up with the nonsense of his child.

"It's as much my responsibility as it's yours to ensure that he becomes a responsible citizen one day," the principal said as he walked him to the door.

At the door, he met a student who had been waiting to see him. As soon as the old man was out of sight, he returned to his office to receive the student.

Poor Achini! The student the principal was attending to had been at the door all through and had heard what had transpired. As soon as he was finished with the principal, he returned to his class and announced the news and even before classes broke up for the day, some students were already taunting one another with threats of "breaking their pair of photosynthesis." Achini was in trouble. The trouble lasted until he finally graduated from the school.

Having been thus exposed as a hypocrite, a liar and a crook, I now knew the person I had been dealing with but still I did not abandon our friendship. Instead, I took on the rather cumbersome role of his spiritual adviser.

Achini was calm for a while, apparently still overcome by the streak of events which had exposed him and caused his prestige to wane. In an effort to revamp his image, he kept close to me since in school I enjoyed the reputation of being a properly brought up and intelligent girl.

From time to time, I spotted him with Makajo. This clearly indicated that their relationship was not completely over. However, the lavish lifestyle they once resorted to had disappeared. Achini's father seemed to have remained true to his promise not to send him any money 'til the end of the year.

It was in the midst of his financial hardship and the desperate quest for some recognition that he started to circulate false rumors among his friends that he had deflowered me. As it was very difficult to keep any secret among students, it was not long before the whole school was aware of the information. While whispers were making the rounds, I knew nothing about the rumors until one day Makajo confronted me.

"I hear that you're secretly having sex with my boyfriend," she screamed at me one afternoon in the dormitory. "If you want him, you can have him."

"He's just my friend, my friend long before you ever came to this school," I tried to convince an incredulous Makajo. "By the way, how did you come about that rumor?"

"It's being circulated all over the school," Makajo replied, still boiling with rage.

"Well, without further ado, I'm going to prove to you that the information is false," I said as I headed out of the dormitory. "Follow me!" I ordered Makajo.

I stormed out of the dormitory with Makajo scurrying after me. Many girls in the dormitory flocked behind us to see what would happen. When we got close to Achini's dormitory, I dispatched someone to go and call for him. The young man soon emerged from the dormitory with Achini walking behind him.

When he saw Makajo with me, he immediately sensed that there would be trouble and would have broken and bolted were it not for the damage which such an open show of cowardice would have caused his already battered image. He tried to put on a bold face when he approached us and reached out to shake our hands.

"Now Achini, did you ever have sex with me?" I boldly asked him in front of everyone. "Answer sincerely or I'll take this matter up to the principal and you'll be thrown out of school."

Achini was totally confused and, with all his friends and admirers looking on, he did not know what to do. His lips danced nervously but not a word was uttered.

"Not man enough to say something in your own defense!" Makajo yelled at him. "Rally your heavy balls and say something!"

"She should know the weight of the balls since she weighs them every night!" a voice from the crowd of onlookers declared in reaction to what she had just said. This caused the spectators to laugh.

"No, I didn't have sex with you," Achini finally mustered some courage and replied.

"You tried to kiss me once and I refused and told you I already had a boyfriend in Sacred Heart College, didn't I?" I shouted.

"You're right," Achini answered submissively.

"So, tell your woman that you lied," I said. "Come on go ahead! She's waiting to hear you say so."

While Achini stood tight lipped, a bitter and embattled Makajo propped up his chin insolently, stared into his eyes, and gave him a spank on the jaw with her right palm.

"You miserable liar!" she growled between clenched teeth. "What kind of a man are you eh! All balls and no heart!" she screamed, again provoking laughter among the hilarious crowd. "What's so special sleeping with many women that you have to go to desperate lengths to prove that!" she hollered. "I thought you were mature when I first saw you but you still display the instincts of a child. I don't want to ever catch you near me."

She turned and openly apologized to me in front of everyone and the two of us headed towards our dormitory, leaving a confused and totally embarrassed Achini. In trying to salvage what was left of his image he had only ended up destroying everything. Even though he later apologized to both of us, his close friends whom it would appear he had been trying to impress had finally come to know who he really was. While in public they gave the impression that they were still his men; behind the scenes they made fun of him.

Apart from occasional incidents of this kind, SAC continued to be a great place for me. I moved to the fourth form where the preparation for my final examinations began. I remained focused, assembling and going through past examination questions to assess the level in order to make adequate preparations. Even though I was not in my final year, I found most of the questions fairly easy. This, however, did not lull me to sleep.

Studying hard did not prevent me from actively participating in other activities. Since the dormitory head of St Monica's house was very busy preparing for her final examinations, she asked me to serve as her assistant. It was in this capability that I began to display some great leadership qualities, unconsciously setting myself up for even more important positions of responsibilities which soon came.

St Augustine's feast day occurred on August 28, when the students were still on the long holidays. Since it was a very important feast, the school authorities thought it wise to commemorate the event by jointly celebrating it with St Patrick's feast day which took place while the students were in school. It was one of the most important events in the life of the school and every student anxiously looked forward to it.

It was, therefore, a measure of the esteem in which I was held that the senior prefect of the school selected me to head the team which would organize the event that year. Usually, the school provided food and drinks but all matters in terms of organization were left in the hands of the students.

When the event came to pass, even though most students were grumbling that MaMa experimented "scientific dancing" with them by not allowing them to dance holding their girlfriends tight, they unanimously admitted that in terms of organization and the relevance of the events selected for the occasion, the feast was one of the best they had ever had ever since they first came to SAC.

In my final year, it did not come as a surprise that I ran for the position of the school senior prefect. I won in the elections by a landslide, thereby becoming the first girl to ever hold that position in the history of the school. For me, it was not an easy task combining my studies and the numerous duties I had to carry out. However, most students agreed that I proved I was a very competent leader.

By the time I had to choose someone from the fourth form to assist me in keeping with the tradition, at least so that I too could concentrate on my studies, the bulk of the student community seemed satisfied with my overall administration.

The examinations that year to make it to the high school were very difficult but I passed with flying colors. I had plans to travel to Bambili to attend high school and to meet Forche after such a long time, but my ambitions were stalled by two important developments, one the antithesis of the other.

The school of arts, science and technology was in Bambili. Even though it was a nursery for some of the best and brightest minds in the country, it had recently confirmed rumors which widely held that it had one of the most scandalous moral reputations. Its students staged a demonstration to protest that they were not having enough sex at school.

This occurrence took place at a time when the Roman Catholic Education Council had decided to upgrade St Augustine's and Sacred Heart Colleges to high schools to adequately prepare their own students for the university.

Fr Sean, who knew about the sex demonstration, advised me to continue in SAC. Apart from having a better moral reputation, it was nearer home. With all the odds stacked against me, I watched as my dreams vanished.

Nevertheless, I had one consolation. I soon received news that Forche did not enroll to continue with his high school education at Bambili as I had thought. He had chosen to remain in Sacred Heart College.

In high school, Fr Sean constantly reminded me that if I made it to the university, I would be the first woman from Yakiri to do so. It was a huge responsibility, a prospect big enough to fuel any dream. However, what made me even more determined were the attitudes of some of the Yamade university students I came across in Kimbo and Yakiri. They were behaving as though when they went to the toilet, it was cake they passed out. On the streets, some of the boys and girls held hands and, even with people looking, they sometimes stopped to kiss. Obviously, this affected behavior was meant to impress poor villagers. And we villagers were impressed!

"Ever since you started seeing people in jacket and ties in town, doesn't it tell you something?" one of the university students was said to have declared when he was asked to pay entrance fee into a nightclub. The story went that the gate was thrown open and he went in for free.

I had no reason not to prepare extremely hard for my final examinations. I was determined to make it to the university. After I had written the examinations, I silently rejoiced that the dream would come true. It seemed I had forgotten one thing.

46

The final college results were out. The names of those who had succeeded were already posted at the college campus. The successful candidates had qualified to enroll at the lone national university in Yamade.

Most people who had gone to the college to find out the results of their children, friends or relatives came back with one name on their lips: Yaya. Some of them who had been in the audience during one of my prize raking streaks at the institution only vaguely remembered a slim, tall girl. Yet, they kept on talking about me as if I were a close relative or child. How could it have been otherwise? My results were astounding and I was so proud of my performance. I did not only come first but scored straight "A" in all the four advanced level subjects I wrote.

As the news of my performance went round in Kimbo, it was picked up by one of my father's friends who normally traveled to the town for business. By the time the man even got to Yakiri, it was already old news. It had long been the talk of the village. Almost everywhere, at people's compounds, the village square, palm wine taverns, and street corners, it was the subject of discussion.

It was in one of the palm wine houses that the news reached my grandfather. Even though most people bought wine to celebrate the results, this reaction was more out of the euphoria they had generated than genuine happiness. Not that the people were hostile to the success. It was a great source of prestige to our village. Their main problem was that it was in the hands of a woman. In the hands of a woman, what they just could not see then was how much real good such brilliant results would bring to them.

Strangely enough, even though my grandfather was basking in the glow of the results, deep down he too felt the same way. He knew the pains and troubles he had gone through to pay my way through college. He was convinced that the latest round of success, which paved my way into the university, would initiate a new and even more difficult phase of financing my education. And to what end were all these sacrifices being made?

As he shook people's hands and drank the wine they had bought to grace the occasion, his mind wrestled with the consequences of my success. I am convinced that he would have been prepared to make any sacrifice, if only I were a boy. Having reached the conclusion that it was pure waste of resources to further my education, he made up his mind to put an end to the hysteria which helped to fuel my expectations.

He acknowledged the great pride and prestige the results had brought to the entire village but was determined that I stay at home and cultivate the land with my grandmother. He felt he had already spent too much money educating a female child who should get married quickly and start a family of her own.

With these ideas in mind, he immediately thought of a piece of land he would surrender to me to start my own farm and of plans to travel to the neighboring village to obtain some cassava cuttings for me to plant the coming season.

He was certain that the bulk of the village would be on his side on this matter and was not scared of any pressure arising from public opinion.

Certain that the fuss created by the news could raise my expectations and foster in me the ambition to enter the university, he moved swiftly to nip the dream in the bud. He emptied his glass and headed home with the intention of convening me to his house for a meeting.

It was with my grandmother that he first discussed his plans before sending for me. Thoroughly disturbed, I appeared for the meeting with tears streaming from my eyes and my grandmother close behind me. My grandmother had already informed me about the subject to be discussed and really saw no reason why I was weeping.

Her indifference towards my university education stemmed from entirely different motives. She had always needed me around her. But more importantly, she wanted me to get a husband fast so that she could live to see her great grandchildren before leaving this world. She complained bitterly how she had missed me during all those years while I was in boarding school in Kimbo.

"It's useless sending you to the university, as the level of education you've attained is good enough for you to market your crops from the farm and take care of your children properly," my grandfather stated when we settled down for the meeting. "My entire savings from the kolanut trade were depleted paying your way through secondary and high school," he lamented.

My grandmother probably knew little about this kind of discussion. She was only keen on seeing her great grandchildren and so took the side of her husband. I was devastated with what I saw as my grandmother abandoning me to men who could not understand. I had expected the entire female community to rally to my standards in order to drive home the idea that the time had come for women to be treated equally with men. My ideas obviously did not sit well with most women.

What made matters worse was my grandmother's attitude. I had come to trust in her intelligence and perspicacity when it came to dealing with situations like the one I was facing. Her attitude clearly demonstrated how collective blindness could cause even those with great vision to step into a ditch. Occasional declarations from her left me really confused, as she too seemed to see education as a man's thing.

"I can understand a man going to school to become a soldier, a police, a doctor, an engineer or even a gendarme, but a woman…," my grandmother intoned in another attempt to discourage me from my enterprise.

"What about the nuns at our mission here and in Kimbo?" I asked in protest. "Aren't they women too? Aren't they doctors, teachers, and engineers?"

"I agree that they are all the things you've just mentioned but you know white people have their own ways of looking at things. Besides, their culture is different from our own. The nuns you're talking about with such admiration aren't married and could care less about men. I don't think that's normal," my grandmother argued. "I'm convinced that they sacrificed their womanhood to become what they are. They can't have a man or a child even if they wanted to."

There was a tinge of superstition and even contradiction in what my grandmother was saying. How could I dispel the irrationality in her arguments by explaining to her that sisterhood was a calling? How would I even translate the word "calling" in Wotikar?

With the discussion becoming more complex, I knew that if I dragged my grandparents into lengthy explanations of the history of the church and some aspects of its doctrine which prompted people to become nuns or priests, I might never succeed in convincing them.

I tried to keep matters simple but reasonable. Unleashing a formidable battery of persuasive arguments, I shuttled between their hearts and minds. Most of the arguments foundered on a key word: tradition. After I had exhausted all my ammunition, despair began to take hold of me.

After the meeting, I was totally dejected and went straight to bed without uttering a word to anyone.

47

Arguments on whether it was proper or not to send me to the university began to spread in the village. These discussions soon reached a group of old men drinking palm wine at the market square. The self-appointed leader of the group was Tela.

His illustrious image as one of the earliest people in the village to attend school had long become a thing of the past ever since Fr Sean started St Patrick and an adult literary center in Yakiri. For a time, he enjoyed some popularity as an interpreter. That too slipped away as the priest mastered how to speak the local language.

Now left with nothing to look forward to, he spent most of his time in the company of some old men, who for the most part could not read or write. They spent their time drinking palm wine and running commentaries on local issues. Discussions on whether it was good or bad for me to go to the university were just what Tela needed to put some shine on his increasingly dull life.

Could I count on him to back me on this matter? It was unlikely for a number of reasons. The first and most important one is that when the "a" in man teams up with the "e" in men, it becomes "mean." In other words, a good man in the company of bad men becomes bad. Before men even think of spoiling for a fight with counter arguments of their own, they should examine the second reason.

How did the idea that only men could be educated come about in the village in the first place? Tela was one of the earliest persons in the village to attend school, long even before Fr Sean burst onto the scene. Could he be entirely ruled out as having participated in spreading this view?

Finally, how could such an opinion have gained currency in a traditional setting which held that to educate a woman is to educate a village?"

In the midst of his friends, many of whom had never been to school, Tela behaved just like them.

"It's ridiculous to invest so much in another village's property instead of our own men!" old Tela exclaimed when the news of whether I should attend the university or not reached him as he sat drinking palm wine with his friends. It was this exclamation which set the tone of the debate.

"University! University!" one of the fellows, a notorious troublemaker called Carangwa, meowed. "What's that?" he asked old Tela.

The answer did not take long in coming.

"What else could it mean!" the old man responded. "It means the girl will spend most of her time and life away from us, probably in Ireland, return to the village wearing high-heel shoes and a very short skirt, talk Mikari through her nostrils so that men shouldn't understand, sit down in the midst of men with her legs crossed, down more calabashes of palm wine than any man and smoke long cigarettes and puff the smoke in their eyes."

"What!" in a display of shock, some of the old men exclaimed in unison.

He did not spare them any time to run the entire gamut of that emotion.

"I haven't finished yet," he boomed in a voice which instantly commanded attention. "She'll paint her lips as red as guava and keep her nails as long as the talons of a leopard, will neither cook food nor go to the farm, and will shout at any man who tries to advise her. For those who still do not know, that is the university!" Tela concluded with evident satisfaction as he reached out with his cup to have some palm wine.

"I even hear that when she becomes upset with the husband, she takes him to the white man's court, pays plenty of money to another person called a lawyer to interrogate and scream at and make fun of him and in the end the judge rules in her favor and she owns the children, the house, the land, the donkeys and everything while the husband is forced to spend the rest of his life in the street," one of old drinking disciples bolstered old Tela's description of a university. After this analysis, he rubbed his hands and glanced with undisguised satisfaction in Tela's direction for him to say something. With a head gesture, he agreed.

"Well, if she chases the husband away from the house, then she won't be able to have more children," a man called Tanue declared much to the surprise of Tela who halted what he was doing and stared at him.

"A woman doesn't need to have sex with a married man to have children stupid," he told him. "The idea is that she wants children but doesn't want to keep the man who makes them. Simply put, she is married to an erect penis and not a man."

The closing remark triggered an outburst of laughter and then the discussion continued.

"I've heard a lot about women who're university graduates but what finally convinced me that it's really the work of the devil and a serious matter that ought to be handled with tremendous care was what I saw recently in Abakwa!" another man nicknamed Tumbu exclaimed. "I now believe that there can be no greater danger than sending a woman to even primary school. When I went to Abakwa about two months ago on the invitation of my brother, he took me out one evening for a drink and we went to this big beer house where all the drinkers of the town seemed to have assembled. Here, I saw a woman who was said to have studied at many universities in the white man's land and had been awarded many diseases or whatever you call it."

"Diseases!" a voice rose.

Then some members of the party exchanged knowing glances and began snickering.

"I think the word is degrees," another voice corrected before leaving the man to continue recounting his story.

"Who asked you with your big mouth?" Tumbu asked. "Diseases or degrees what difference does it make!" he added, unhappy with the rude interruption. "All I know is that it causes women to act crazy."

"I was just trying to help."

"Well, I don't need your help." After taking a gulp of palm wine, he smacked his lips furiously and resumed his narration. "It was the manner she dressed herself which first caught my attention and made my blood run cold. She was wearing tight-fitting trousers, so tight that it was as if she went naked, with all the contours and even veins of her body showing. And then like a palm tree caught up in a storm, she was wobbling on a pair of stilts she fancied were shoes. That should be the high heels Tela made mention of a while ago. I think that the person who gave the shoes its name was very wise because they were as high as the hills overlooking this village."

Another wave of snickering caused the narrator to halt and stare in silent protest.

"If you had so much knowledge, you should be in Yamade driving in a big car, not fighting with me over palm wine in the village."

"We're sorry Tumbu," one of the perpetrators apologized.

"You better be!" he declared and continued with his narration. "As for her face, daubed as it were with myriad colors, it only reminded me of a rainbow. Anyway, she was so impressed with herself and so haughty that one would wonder whether she even went to the toilet to piss or shit."

"Or fart!" a voice exclaimed much to the displeasure of Tela.

"You've been farting here all day with your mouth but not once did I see you running to the toilet," he turned and declared to the man as the others let go a celebratory peal of laughter. "Tumbu over to you!"

"I've never seen anything like that in my whole life. But what I couldn't understand was the way she ordered men around."

At this juncture another voice of a drinker shot out with yet another interruption: "Did the men do her biddings?" it inquired.

The speaker cast a long, baleful look in the man's direction and exclaimed somewhat sardonically: "Do her biddings!" he exclaimed and then continued. "Is that anything? They were just waiting for her to sneeze or make the slightest gesture and they came running like a herd of thirsty buffalos heading for a stream. What are you talking about!" He took a long sip from his cup, wiped his lips and resumed. "She was smoking and each time she took a long stick of cigarette out of a kind of packet I must confess I've never seen before and stuck it onto her red lips, a man came running with a box of matches. And even after lighting her cigarette, she didn't care to look at the face of the man holding out the light."

"You call those men?" Tela asked rhetorically and mockingly. "The city transforms men into wimps and they'll do anything just to be seen in the company of a woman, especially if she's beautiful, very influential and has plenty of money."

"Those qualities even in a devil would attract people," a lone and dissonant voice reasoned aloud much to the displeasure of Tela. Not used to being challenged, he wasted no time clobbering its owner in line.

"We're talking about women. Where have you been all this while?" he inquired somewhat sternly. "Tumbu, continue with your story," he said to the man whose lurid tale of the Abakwa woman seemed to be casting a spell over the audience and gradually transforming him into a kind of folk hero.

He cleared his throat and continued.

"I overheard some men saying that the woman is a doctor and the men who fluttered around her like birds around the nest of termites are nurses working under her at the main hospital in Abakwa. She was their chief and the men owed their daily bread to her," the speaker finally summed up.

"I'll never allow a woman to be on top of me that way, to the point of looking down on me and making a fool of me in public just because she has diseases and is the one responsible for my daily bread," Tela crowed with evident conviction and some disgust.

The risqué and the misnomer were too much for some members of the audience to handle. Their faces contorted discreetly in smiles and some of them were about to exchange knowing glances when they caught the watchful eyes of the old tortoise.

"Maybe you should try that at night for a difference!" Tete, whose reputation for buffoonery and ribald jokes went even beyond the village, exclaimed in a bid to instill some life into the discussion. His outburst sparked some hearty laughter and had the catalytic effect of loosening the tongues of some commentators.

"Looking down on old Tela may not even be in the sense we're thinking about," a voice ejaculated. "Imagine a situation where he's taken ill and winds up in the hospital, stripped naked and split open like a chicken to be roasted, the way I hear the white men do when they want to take a degree from inside a person. It certainly won't be his decision for the woman to be on top looking down into his face."

The confusion and absurd reasoning again led to an outburst of laughter.

"We seem to allow our imaginations to run wild. Are we convinced that such a woman is even interested in a man?" the voice that once had the audacity to challenge Tela rang out again.

"In his erection perhaps!" a voice cut in, to the utter amusement of everyone.

"A rich and successful woman has no use for men," another voice declared.

"Oh yes, even when she's successful she still can't do without a man. It's more about the purpose she needs the man for. She may just want him to boss over him, in that case assuming the role of a man. She may need one for her personal pleasure, bedding him whenever she feels like it and asking him to get lost when she doesn't," another voice replied.

Sensing that the voice of reason, which had already challenged him by speaking for women, was gradually widening its constituency, Tela fought back to regain lost territory. He took the debate to a safer ground, where logic spoke less than machismo.

"My wife, for whom I paid numerous heads of cattle and bought all kinds of gifts, bedding me when she wants and brushing me off when she doesn't!" he exploded in anger. "Not in this lifetime!"

"What do we take home from all your discussion?" Tete taunted Tela with a question, sensing that he might have come to the end of his observations.

"Simply bear in mind that a woman goes to school with a vagina and graduates with a penis," he summed up as he reached for some more palm wine.

There was an uproar of laughter.

48

The men carried on with their drinking and debate. Some eavesdroppers picked up the most damning elements of their discussions and began to peddle them. They soon reached me as rumors which had been seriously distorted. The rumors held that a party of old drinkers led by Tela was touring the village and lecturing anyone who cared to listen on the dangers of educating women.

I knew that even though Tela's popularity had declined, he could still easily convince many people on some issues. The old interpreter was still said to be one of the wisest men in the village and when he spoke his words of wisdom, nobody had the courage to challenge them.

The drinkers might just have been having a nice time, expressing the way they had been brought up to think. They did not, however, doubt that if their views ever got to my grandfather, he might think twice before ever sending me to the university. Nor could their conduct be judged to be totally devoid of some traces of jealousy. After all, I was not battling over the privilege of enrolling at the university with a deserving male member of the same household or even community for that matter. I came first in my entire school and was alone and all I was asking was to be given a chance. The men had no good reason to act in a way that would prevent my grandfather from sending me to the university.

All the same, regardless of what the men thought, the issue had sparked off a huge controversy in the village. It was the first time the village was faced with such a situation. With different points of view and no unanimity of opinion, I still had two courts of last instance to rule on the matter. The first one was presided over by Christ through his priest, Fr Sean, and the second, by the ancestors through their gnukwabes.

Still, the night following the meeting with my grandfather, I could not sleep. I kept rolling and tossing in my bed, my mind running wild. Many of my schoolmates living in Kimbo had parents who were very close to Irish missionaries. That exposure had made their parents more receptive to the idea of educating women. I knew many of my friends who were far less intelligent than I was but who would be heading to the university. How would they behave towards me when they returned and found me at home with a clutch of babies to take care of? I suspected that our friendship would never be the same once they returned to the village as university graduates, describing the sophistication of city life and wearing expensive clothes, shoes and perfumes.

I became so frightened by the thought of being left behind that I woke up screaming in the middle of the night. When my grandmother rushed to my bedside, she found me sitting up and sweating profusely.

"Go to sleep my dear and forget about this university business," she said gently. I went back to sleep but my mind was made up about what to do. I decided to take the matter up to Fr. Sean. With him on my side, overnight, the balance could be tipped in my favor.

I knew that in certain aspects of life the village would listen to the opinion of the priest, and education was one of them. After all, was it not through his initiative that the first schools were started in Yakiri? Is he not the one who campaigned hard that young men would become more useful as farmers after earning a degree in agriculture or veterinary science at the university?

With Fr. Sean in mind, I could finally catch some sleep that night.

Early the next morning, before the crack of dawn, I crawled gently out of my bed and slipped out of the house quietly, making sure I did not create any commotion which would stir my grandmother.

It was still dark when I got to the main road which led to the village square and the church. My heart was pounding and I did not want to even entertain the thought that Fr Sean would not take my side in this matter. I began to sweat as I hurried on and almost fell to the ground when I stubbed my foot on a tree root which had grown across the road. It hurt but I did not pay any attention to that, my entire mind focused on the mission ahead.

I passed some people who were surprised to see me out at that hour of the morning but who said nothing because they felt I might have been sent to run an errand. After all, who had more business in the village than the sub-chief?

When I got to the entrance to the mission, I lingered around until it was dawn. I saw the priest when he went to his office. When I showed up, he was surprised to see me at that hour of the morning. The village proverb which held that only people in trouble visited the gnukwabe being largely true, he suspected that something must have gone wrong and immediately came to meet me at the door.

Even though I knew Fr Sean very well and felt very comfortable with him, I still found it hard to walk up to him and discuss the problem freely. My village tradition tended to frown on young people, especially women, who did not show respect to their elders by having the guts to initiate such discussions with them. But even more important, was the fact that it involved a priest, this godly man sent from far away to bring the good news of the lord to the people of Yakiri. The Irish was revered and much loved and the whole village was protective of him. The people did not want anyone to go bothering him with any minor complaints as they rightly figured he had a lot to do.

Having lived with the people and known the situation, it was Fr Sean who began the conversation. The results of the examinations had already reached him and he was very happy with my performance, the more so because I was female and came from his parish. He reckoned it might be the beginning of something great, a kind of silent revolution which would break the shackle which still kept a large segment of Yakiri women out of the classroom.

It was also clear proof that the early academic foundation laid at the mission school he started years ago had been properly done. As he later pointed out to me, he felt I was coming to announce the result to him even though he wondered why I had decided to choose that early hour of the morning to do so. At any rate, with these ideas in his mind, he thought it wise to leave me to express the object of my mission.

"Good morning Monica!" he called out. "What can I do for the mother of St Augustine?" he asked in his deep, rich voice. He had lived long enough with the people of my village and had already picked up their tendency to flatter and make people feel good about themselves.

These words were carefully chosen and the impact on me was electric. As soon as the words entered my ears, I felt next to Christ and instantly broke into a wide smirk, of course an obvious appreciation of being crowned the mother of one of Africa's greatest saints.

With those words, anything which would have inhibited me and made me hold back immediately began to disappear and I mustered the courage to talk to the priest, even though I was not looking at him straight in the face.

"Good morning Father," I replied with a shaky voice. "Well, I came to inform you that we got news of results to enroll at the University of Yamade and I came first on the list of the successful candidates. The information reached us yesterday and we had a family meeting in which my grandfather made it clear to me that he had already spent a lot of money educating a woman and that it was out of the question for me to proceed to the university," I started to announce, with tears already streaming out of my eyes.

"I know. It'll take time here for people to understand the importance of educating women. I've made numerous attempts to point this out in some of my sermons, that it's unfair and, therefore, ungodly not to treat women right but it seems my voice, like the one of John the Baptist, is still in the wilderness. I think we need only justify the investment for people to change. While Yakiri continues to maintain this increasingly unpopular practice, other villages have taken the lead and are educating their women. They abide by the traditional African belief which holds that when a woman is educated, it's the entire village which is being educated. I don't want this village to be left behind in anything and I think it's just proper for me to meet your grandfather, its head, and try to iron this out. He should lead the way," the priest declared. "Never mind my little angel, I'll meet your grandparents and talk to them and you shouldn't feel depressed. You'll go to the university and be a great woman. In God's name!"

"I have a couple of things to do at the mission before we go together and meet your grandparents and discuss this very important matter with them. Wait for me in my office," he declared, as he headed towards the presbytery, leaving me with some magazines and other reading materials.

Back home, my grandparents got up to the usual morning commotion of our compound. However, they were greeted by an empty bed. I, the apple of their eye and lovely granddaughter, had vanished. They looked around and called out my name but there was no sign of me. They became worried. This feeling gave way to fear. Then all hell began to break loose. Strange ideas invaded their minds. It was not unheard of for a young man or woman in the village to secretly go somewhere and take their own life in a show of frustration with their parents. They immediately thought of Bishu, their neighbor's daughter. After her father forced her into marriage, she fled and nothing had been heard of her ever since.

If I had run away from home, what a calamity it would be, especially if people in the neighboring villages got to know it was because they, my grandparents, did not want to send me to school, they kept thinking. Among the villages, there had always been some kind of undeclared competition to see which one of them stood out in anything which brought pride. My grandfather knew that such a tragedy would not draw sympathy. Rather it would provide decent fodder for detractors of my village to embark on a propaganda war to besmirch its image.

As my grandparents went from door to door inquiring whether anyone had seen me, news reached them that I had been spotted at the mission. By now my flustered grandmother was going about without head scarf, exposing her graying and disheveled hair. She looked like a mad woman as she floated across the village like a butterfly, with her head scarf tied around her waist the way Yakiri women do when they are spoiling for a fight or as an expression of profound grief.

As she stormed past some people without greeting, the entire village seemed poised for some high drama.

"Mama Wirba has gone berserk!" they exclaimed and dove for cover as she went past.

My grandfather followed her closely and watched with knowing facial expression all the theatrics in which his wife was

308

involved. In moments of tragedy, her repertoire of antics and drama was inexhaustible.

"If something happens to my little girl you'll be held responsible," she said to her husband, seemingly backtracking from her own initial stance as the plot of the drama of my disappearance began to thicken. "Why do you men always feel you're always right? Couldn't you have relented when you noticed that she badly needed to go to the university?" she kept up her verbal cannonade.

"But I thought you…"

"You thought I did what!" my grandmother threw caution to the wind and interrupted her husband. "Since when did a woman's opinion count in the midst of you men eh!" she screamed. "We're no more than your bedmates, baby factories, to be dumped like orange chafe once the juice has been sucked out."

Sensing that any form of reply would make her even more hysterical, my grandfather decided to do what seemed the most appropriate in the circumstance, to keep quiet.

It was, therefore, with great relief that just before they reached the entrance of the church premises, they saw the tall priest with flowing white beard like that of Abraham he preached so often about approaching. I was scurrying by his side.

"I was coming to your compound," Fr Sean said, with his hand already stretched out to greet my grandparents. "How are you and your compound…" he began his greeting.

As he was greeting, my grandparents stooped reverently and nodded in approbation, with their heads bobbing like a woodpecker's in perfect timing to each statement.

Once the greetings were over, my grandfather turned to me and said somewhat angrily: "Where were you and why didn't you inform someone that you were coming to see Farar?" he chided me.

I didn't utter a word.

When our feud came to an end, Fr. Sean invited the family to his office to discuss the issue which was almost tearing us apart.

It was a big office with books neatly arranged on the large mahogany table which the father used for writing. The table directly faced a broad window opening to the main road leading to the church compound. From his table, Fr. Sean could see all those who came and left the compound using the main entrance. To the left of

309

his table stood a towering cupboard and above it was a huge statue of Jesus on the cross. Above the head of the priest, almost staring down at anyone holding discussions with him, was the picture of the Pope.

When we were all seated, the priest raised the issue of my enrollment at the university but avoided sounding confrontational. Instead, he embarked on a story about the only female minister in the former government of this country. He recounted how he met her when she last came to Kimbo.

"It was very difficult for me to go close to her. She had many soldiers guarding her and you needed to have seen her ordering them around," the priest told my grandparents who listened with all ears. As the story unfolded he could see that my grandfather was very impressed, especially when he said the lady minister was ordering around the soldiers who guarded her. When he was later told that the lady controlled a whole government ministry with several civil servants under her, his eyes almost popped out of his head. Now the priest could see that the set up was complete and so he went for the kill. "Tell me Thaddeus," that being my grandfather's baptismal name, "how could she be appointed to such a position of responsibility without a very sound education?" he asked. Even though my grandfather seemed to see sense in the priest's argument, there was a lingering shadow of doubt on his face. Fr Sean noticed it. My grandfather cleared his throat and before he could speak, the priest interrupted him. "What have you on your mind Thaddeus? I can see doubt on your face."

My grandfather was not without his own arsenal.

"You see Farar, the Holy Bible doesn't tell us that Holy Maria, the mother of Jesus, went to the university yet she brought up her child well enough for him to become the savior of the whole world. She's our mother, humble and nice, and we admire and love her that way. I fear that your little girl, Yaya, will reject all of us, lose all the doctrine lessons you imparted to her, after her university education. She'll return with long nails and red lips and refuse to do farm work or prepare food or touch anything."

My grandfather was a fast learner and his attempt to pull the religious blanket to his side could not have missed the notice of Fr Sean.

310

The Irishman emitted a knowing and appreciative smile before launching his counterattack. The only thing green about the villagers might have been their plantations but he had lived in their midst for a very long time and knew them. They were his people.

"I'm happy to know that you take your religious lessons seriously but I wish to inform you that not everything concerning the mother of Jesus is written in the Bible," he pointed out. "As for your granddaughter not willing to go to the farm when she returns from the university I can understand but I'm convinced that you'll certainly be a happier man if she buys you a tractor to do the farm work. But apart from this, you must understand that you have already done the bulk of the work, for she's likely to get a scholarship when she registers at the university. All you need to give her is money to pay rents and to buy books and food while waiting for her scholarship papers to be sorted out. The fees will be the task of the government. I'll also write to my friends in Ireland to ask for assistance if things don't go the way we expect. We shouldn't be cowards. She's a very intelligent young girl and I'm very certain we won't regret what we're doing at the moment."

In that discourse, the priest had touched another sensitive cord when he put forth the tractor argument, for that made my grandfather wilt like cocoyam leaf under the hot sun. He loved agriculture and it was the economic mainstay of our village. Anything which could help give it a boost was to him most welcome.

"Do you mean that she'll be rich enough to buy me a tractor, the kind of big nyamakundu used by men in Farar's country to cultivate huge plantations?" he asked almost incredibly.

"For a lawyer, doctor or a minister, that's nothing," Fr Sean said reassuringly. "Trust my judgment. It's good investment to send her to the university because she's very intelligent, hardworking and a good Christian. Besides, you don't feel I'm misleading nor deceiving you, do you?"

"Oh no Farar, far be it!" my grandfather hastily responded as he figured that it would border on sacrilege for him to think that of any pious person.

"Before you leave I still have something to say," the priest decided to serve the best for the last by launching a final and reassuring assault with an argument he was very convinced could

311

never fail. He once told me that he had chosen to keep this argument 'til the end because he wanted my grandparents to leave him bearing it in mind.

"My ears are open Farar," my grandfather declared, apparently not certain that the priest could come up with another argument more potent than the ones he had already advanced.

"You must be aware that on this matter, the ancestors are on my side," he declared. "Have you forgotten what the gnukwabe stated when this village was about to be founded?" he asked.

At this question, my grandfather remained silent for a while. In that brief moment, he later said, his mind raced through my people's entire history which I have already recounted. He wasn't sure of how the priest knew about this aspect of Wotikar history. Even though they were very close friends, he did not recall having ever discussed it with him. Memories of the curse which had dogged the Wotikar people up to the time my village was founded came flooding to his mind. Could the priest be the mysterious man Kwakala had talked about? He felt disturbed and even ashamed that the reminder should come instead from this stranger. As the village head, he was the one to ensure that the wishes of his ancestors were respected. However, some doubts still lurked. Was the priest really the man? Could he be actually acting unfairly by opting not to send me to the university? Even justice could sometimes be mysterious, he thought.

"I've heard Farar," he said at last still submerged in his thoughts. "At first I didn't consider what I was doing unjust but now I think what my granddaughter wants matters. The future may depend on what we do to her now."

"I really think so," the priest concurred as my grandfather was walking away slowly and quietly. "It's you who should lead the way in challenging any tradition which promotes injustice or brings pain to any segment of this society," the priest added as my grandfather stopped briefly.

Fr Sean had done a very great job in persuading him. My grandparents left his office seemingly convinced and satisfied that to send me to the university was the right thing to do. However, my grandfather's mind was still not at rest. What if things did not go the way they had in mind? Had Tabongwa faltered when he did not act on the words of Bangsiboh? Would he fare any better if he did

312

not ask the spirits of the ancestors to guide him on this very crucial matter? These were the ideas which danced back and forth in his mind after our meeting with the Irishman. As he headed home with us that morning, he had already planned to secretly consult Takwabe.

Takwabe owned a big compound with four houses. One of them served as a shrine where he sometimes carried out his consultations. A second one, of thatched roof, was fitted out with bamboo beds and shelves. This was a ward where he kept patients who needed close attention. A third house, in which his wife and daughter lived, was adobe and roofed over with corrugated iron sheets. His own house, in the style of the day, was nestled on a high ground.

Late at night, on the day my family met with Fr Sean, Takwabe had dismissed the last of his clients and was about to retire to his house when he decided one last time to throw his bones. The bones showed that an important person was on the way, to visit him.

What person and why that hour of the night, he pondered. A first, second and third trial all came up with exactly the same results. Nevertheless, he decided he would go to bed. The day had been very exhausting and he badly needed a rest.

He lay prostrate on his bamboo bed and was just about to close his eyes when he heard a knock on his door. He rose and, grabbing his hurricane lamp, headed towards the door. He unbolted it and found himself face to face with my grandfather.

"What brings you here at this terrible and ungodly hour of the night, at a time when all the wizards and witches are out?" he asked, as he ushered him into the house.

"An urgent matter!"

"How urgent is the matter that you couldn't wait?"

"Please, my house is on fire!" my grandfather exclaimed. "My granddaughter! My granddaughter!"

"What has she done? Is she pregnant? Has she eloped with a man?" he inquired, the questions coming in rapid succession as though they had long been prepared.

"No, none of that," he replied. "This time it may be good news. The results of the big university in Yamade are out and my little Yaya is the first and she's insisting that she'll go there. Most

313

people in the village, including old Tela, believe that sending her to that school will just be a waste of time and money. Most people reckon she's already too educated, that she's just ripe for farm work and childbearing. I've heard so much about the dangers of sending her to that school that at the moment I just don't know what to believe. I was with Fr Sean, our friend, and he told me and my wife to send her to the university. He has even volunteered to help should we face problems. I'm coming to you to check this matter using the powers bestowed upon you by our ancestors. I would like to know whether this is indeed a good venture."

While my grandfather embarked on his narration, the two men were standing up. After he was done, Takwabe asked him to follow him to the shrine. He stepped out of the house and holding up his lamp to light their path, led the way.

When they finally got to the shrine and were seated, he placed the lamp on the ground and went to one of the walls of the shrine where his divination paraphernalia hung in a bag. He took the bag and returned to his seat. With its contents spilled on the dry, dusty ground, he gathered them and with both hands shook vigorously, reciting an incantation as he did so. Then he threw the bones on the ground and after studying their configuration, let go a cry of triumph.

"Father is right. Send her to Yamade, for she'll come back a big chief, bigger than even the one in Kimbo, a very powerful and rich woman, and will help our village grow," Takwabe declared.

"Greater than the chief in Kimbo!" he exclaimed in fright. "Please, watch what you're saying."

"Well, it's your right to question the ancestors," the gnukwabe said without even raising his head to look at him.

"I didn't say that I questioned what they say," he replied quickly, knowing the implication of such an action. "What you said just sounded too good to be true."

Takwabe threw his bones again and again and came to the same conclusion. My grandfather thanked him and promised to send him a calabash of freshly tapped palm wine on that day. By the time the two men separated, it was already morning.

Now, totally convinced that it was a good thing to do, my grandfather was determined to make any sacrifice necessary for the success of this new undertaking.

314

This was one of the greatest days of my life. On that day, as I slept at night, my mind composed a poem for the Irishman whose lines are still sung in Yakiri up to this day. Still, everything seemed like a dream until the next day when I woke up. It was real. I would become a university student.

So it came to pass that I, Monica Yaya, the little orphan girl, granddaughter of Patricia Wirba and Thaddeus Tafon, became the first girl from Yakiri to go to the university. I did so thanks to the insistence of Reverend Fr. Sean, Irishman and parish priest, and to Takwabe, a village elder and the most reputable gnukwabe.

49

Like the news of my success in the examination, the one that I would enroll at the university took my village by storm. Almost everyone seemed to be talking about it. Old women on their way to their farms debated on the merits and demerits of the venture. Young men and women held lengthy conferences on it at street corners. In palm wine houses, it was the main subject of discussion.

As the news spread and increasingly gained acceptance in the village, Tela, who had tacitly campaigned against sending any woman to the university, felt increasingly embarrassed and isolated. But was it for nothing that the villagers believed he was wise? He did not think so. In many things, he had often demonstrated that he had great foresight. Even though in my case this quality had not been very much in evidence, he also believed that part of the magic of his wisdom was to follow the light when he saw one.

With the entire village now stirred with the excitement of the news that I would go to the university, he made a fresh appraisal of the situation. I was told that he instantly saw the long-term material implications of my education, when I would return to the village, gorgeous, powerful and rich and giving gifts to everyone who had been on my side. He immediately became aware that he would be left out and decided at that moment to embark on a fence-mending exercise. He quietly sent for me.

When I showed up at his compound in the evening of the day of the invitation, he sat me down and proceeded with tremendous aplomb and dexterity to unmake the disaster he came close to causing.

"We all are behind you and love you so much that we don't want anyone to take you away from us. It seems this university thing is a good thing that will bring development to our village. When you go don't forget us and remember not to abandon our

316

culture," he said as he gave me a big rooster. "Take this and prepare it. This is your food on the way."

"Thank you very much," I said with extreme happiness as I grabbed the flapping bird. "With everyone in the village now on my side, I'll make sure I don't disappoint you."

Tela's gesture was soon known all over the whole village. It opened the gates for others who might have had a similar idea in mind but were reluctant to carry it out. With the old man now leading the way, other villagers took the cue. One after the other, they came to our compound, some bearing baskets of peanuts, others with roosters, corn, sugar cane and other food items. The eagerness to bring food might have also been encouraged by information that hunger was prevalent in Yamade.

The villagers made so many food offers that my grandparents took some of what had been brought to the market to be sold and the money handed over to me.

As the day for my departure to the university drew nearer, I made the necessary preparations. I had roasted peanuts crushed into a paste and preserved in a plastic jar for me to use in preparing sauce. Corn was taken to the mill and ground into flour to be cooked into the popular kibane. Smoked fish and venison, beans and gari all formed part of my luggage.

Two days before my departure, I made sure that I went from compound to compound to announce my departure and bid everyone goodbye. While I was making the tour, parents advised their daughters, who watched with envious eyes as I had become the focus of all attention, to emulate my example. Young men, some of whom might have cherished the ambition to ask me out but who now saw me gradually moving away from their grasp, still took courage and wished me a safe journey. It was all me in the village and I loved every moment of it.

The highlight of the day's visits took place at the presbytery with Fr Sean. He believed that I would succeed, having watched my intellectual progress from the time I started to learn Christian doctrine to my entire primary, secondary and high school years. He always maintained that I was very focused and hardly indulged in the dirty pranks common with people of my age.

"I've come to thank you and also to inform you that I just have one more day to be here," I began when we sat down. "I have

317

to go to Yamade early to look for a room and also to carry out the necessary registration procedures. I've been made to understand that it isn't wise to wait until the last hour, as an upsurge of the demand for houses tends to drive up the rents. By the way, my grandparents asked me to extend their greetings to you and also to give you this basket," I declared.

The priest got the basket and peeped inside and it contained oranges, pineapples, and avocados. He thanked me and put it aside.

While I was talking, he listened with rapt attention, occasionally nodding his head in agreement. When I had finished, he took the floor.

"Well, I have great faith in you and your abilities and I'm very thankful to the lord that things took a happy turn. It's now your challenge and you know that an entire generation of young men and women will be looking up to you. You've now become a role model for them, which means that anything you say or do counts. I'm convinced that as long as you don't stray from the values the church, school and village have inculcated in you, you're going to be one shining example to be emulated by others," the priest said.

A bit confused, I asked the priest after he had finished talking: "So what must I do Father?"

"First, there must be a strict sense of moral integrity in whatever you do," he began and then paused for a while as though he wanted to capture my full attention before proceeding. He then continued. "When a person is convinced that he or she's right and acting in the name of God and not necessarily out of self-interest, that in itself is an authority, a moral authority. It's the basis of any true act of courage. It's courage. Sometimes we live for others and must, therefore, strive to take their own needs into account in our daily activities and prayers. That's what being a Christian actually means, for we must learn to go past the mere words of the Holy Bible, to live them. Apart from this, hard work and determination are crucial to any success. It'll be a lie if I said you aren't going to face problems. But far from discouraging you, problems only test you and determine how much mettle you've got, for quitters never win and winners never quit. You have all the tools to succeed. I know you do because you were born and grew up in front of me and I know your grandparents very well. You have God's gift of

318

intelligence, but intelligence in this world is nothing if it isn't put to good use to help uplift humanity. Intelligence should be reflected in the things a person does and says. Finally, I'll exhort you to be always compassionate and forgiving and also to take very good care of yourself. You're already doing most of these things I'm listing but you must make them part of your being. I don't think I have anything more to add. Write and communicate me your address so that I can always write to you. You're my daughter and I'll like you to succeed."

With these words of wisdom, he rose and, without uttering any more words to me, who still sat seemingly transfixed on my seat, left the sitting room. He disappeared into an adjoining room and soon returned clutching a brand new copy of the Holy Bible and an envelope.

"These are for you. Thank your grandparents for me and give them my regards," he said, holding out the gifts. He then gave me his big hairy hands into which mine disappeared, almost like a tiny twig or some dry chicken bones being engulfed by the mouth of a lion. He shook my hand vigorously and bade me farewell.

Fr Sean had always been sweet and nice to me but his words and outpouring of generosity overwhelmed me and floods of tears came rushing. I battled with that, lacking words to express thanks. Sensing the emotional overflow, the priest patted my hair lovingly to help me recover.

When I could finally find my words, I looked up at Fr Sean, my eyes still wet and red, and said: "Thank you very much Father. I'll do my best to live up to your expectations." I then turned to leave. I was on my way out of the presbytery, at the threshold to be very precise, when something struck the priest. "Monica," he called out.

I turned round and walked back to the table where I had my meeting with him.

"I have friends in Yamade. The first one is a priest of the same order and an Irishman. I'll like you to meet him, so I'll give you a letter of recommendation to take to him. You may put up with him while you make arrangements for your own accommodation. He's very nice. The second is none other than our own Bernard Nso, the Minister of Telecommunications. I don't remember having told you that it was on his recommendation that I choose to come to this village. I'll write to him later on to tell him that you'll be looking out for him. He's also a lecturer at the Faculty of Literature and Modern Languages of the University of Yamade. Don't be frightened by his position when you ultimately get to meet him because he's a very good Christian and a very humble man."

With these words, he went back into the same room and appeared some minutes later with a letter already typed on which he wrote my name and signed. He put it in an envelope and addressed it.

"There, the letter with the address," Father Sean said. "Father O'Neil doesn't live very far from the university and his mission lies along one of the main roads, so you won't find it hard taking a taxi to get there," he declared as he dropped it on the table.

"Don't I also need an introductory letter to present to Bernard Nso, Father?" I asked, as I studied the tricky spelling of the name of the Irish priest in Yamade.

"No, you don't need that. If you first meet him before I write, simply tell him you're from Yakiri and you know me. The simple fact that you're the first woman in his village to enroll at the university should mean a lot to him."

As soon as I left the presbytery and was on the road which led out of the church premises, I could not wait to open the envelope Fr Sean had given me. It contained clean bank notes, many of them. I was filled with joy and started to count them. It was plenty of money and my mind began to run wild with ideas concerning the way I intended to spend it. But as tradition dictated, I had first to show my grandparents before I could make any plans. I wanted the offer to be a surprise not just for them but for the whole family. An opportunity to do so was just around the corner.

On the eve of the day of my departure, almost everything seemed set for the journey the next day. All over my grandmother's house, strewn here and there, were pieces of my luggage, seven items in all.

I examined everything carefully with my grandmother to ensure that nothing had been forgotten. I was certain that everything was in order even though I was at my wit's end as to how I would move all my belongings from one point to another when I was alone.

My anxiety was fuelled by stories that there were many thieves in big cities who stalked passengers at motor parks, as bus stations are known in this part of the world, and exploited any lapse of attention in order to steal their luggage. I knew that I could not move one piece of luggage to another spot without shifting my attention from the others and was certain that the thieves would take advantage of that shuttle between the two points to make away with some of my things. I was still brooding over this when my grandmother, who had just gone out of the house, walked in.

"I hope everything is in order," she repeated, "because tonight your father wants to talk to you. He'll be traveling to the neighboring village very early tomorrow and this may be his last time of meeting you before your departure tomorrow."

The chickens had just started coming back to roost when I heard his voice ring out. When I arrived at his house, I found my grandmother, as well as other members of my close and extended family already seated. I took my seat near my grandparents who sat in front of the others.

Food already prepared had been brought for a final feast before my departure the next day. There was also plenty of fresh palm wine with which to wash it down. When my grandfather was certain that everyone was present, he stood up. The gesture was greeted with total silence. Then he began to speak.

"You all know why we're gathered here today, so I need not waste time on the point lest our food becomes cold. If anyone here disapproves of our daughter attending the university in Yamade, he or she should raise a hand and explain why," he declared. He took in the audience for a while and with no hand raised, concluded that everyone was satisfied and moved to the next step of the ceremony. "This is an important day, not just in the history of our family but also that of the village. Our daughter sitting here in front of you all is going to the big school in Yamade called the university. She's the first woman in this village to do so and tradition requires that we thank the almighty and the spirits of our ancestors that this should just be the beginning of greater things to come."

A brief murmur rippled through the audience as my grandfather, turning to me and placing his hand on my shoulder, asked me to stand up. I rose. He then called on all the members of the audience to rise.

321

"Give us a prayer," he ordered me.

After a brief pause, I started to pray.

"In the name of the Father, the Son and the Holy Spirit. Heavenly Father we thank you for everything you've given us. We thank you for Fr Sean who has abandoned the warmth of his family in the holy land of St Patrick to come and be part of us and to help us. Continue to give him strength, good health and more inspiration so that together we can form another family here and help in building and making Yakiri a leading village. Father Almighty, show our parents the way and guide them in their decisions, as you did on this important one of my going to the university. Let this be an experience for me to share with others, to go and learn and to bring back that knowledge to help uplift my own people. As we gather here today, bless the food we're going to eat and the wine we're going to drink and the hands which have prepared them. Lord God Almighty, provide for those who have none. Take those who've come from afar to be here and share this great moment with me safely back home. We ask this through Christ our lord Amen. In the name of the Father, the Son and the Holy Spirit."

When I finished saying the prayer, the audience, which was made up of Roman Catholic Christians for the most part, nodded in approbation. It seemed pleased with the contents of the prayer.

The Christian phase of the prayer was over. My grandfather took the floor and began to preside over the traditional one. He poured some palm wine in a cup, sipped some of it and then pointed to a spot on which he asked me to stand. He walked over to where I was standing, muttering some words as he did so.

"Our forefathers who guide each of our steps in this village, we all call upon you at this crucial moment when our daughter is setting out to a distant land with a big dream to be with her all along. Help her make the right decisions and protect her from evil spirits cast by anyone jealous of her."

While he recited the incantations, he bent double and poured some of the wine on my toes. The incantations over, he gave me the cup and asked me to take a sip and then to pass it round to all the members of the family for them to do the same. When everyone had drunk from the cup, he went and stood at the threshold of the house and started to recite another incantation.

"It's with one voice that we gather here today great forebears and, as testimony to that unanimity, we've drunk out of your horn. But if some members of the family didn't come here today because, out of jealousy or wickedness, they don't share our vision here tonight, then let them have their own drink outside." As he said these words, he poured some palm wine outside, on the ground.

God had blessed the evening. The ancestors were appeased. The feasting could begin. After I had showed the gifts Fr Sean had given me, food was shared out and as people ate they made jokes and recounted anecdotes based on what they had heard about big cities, especially the dangers they held out to strangers.

"Listen to this one," a man cried out. "During a white man's court session in Abakwa, while everyone sat tight-lipped listening to the case being tried, a woman suddenly burst out into wild hysterical laughter at the back of the court. The presiding judge was a man with a reputation for strictness. He wasn't amused by such an outburst and was about to charge the lady with contempt of court. Faced with this charge, she decided to recount what had caused the laughter. She said she had carefully wrapped the soiled diaper of her baby and put it in her handbag only to find out that it had suddenly disappeared, probably stolen by someone thinking it was a bundle of money. Her story triggered a wild outburst of laughter which caused a commotion in the court. The furious judge ordered the policemen in court to close the doors and conduct a search and low and behold they found the messy diaper stashed away in the undergarment of a court attendant sitting just behind the lady. After the man pleaded guilty to theft, he was sentenced to five years in prison 'for grand larceny and the sequestering of baby excrement with the malicious intent of practicing voodoo.' So in big cities people steal everything they come across, even shit."

Even before he came to the end of his story, the roof came down and some people almost choked with food.

"Since it's about the court, let me recount another story concerning another case which occurred in Abakwa," another voice declared as soon as the laughter had died down. "During another court session, a man charged with having sex with a minor openly told the court that the charge was true but directed against the wrong person. 'Who should it be directed to then?' the presiding magistrate asked. The man stood up, shot down his trousers and underwear and pulled out, of course you know, and with everyone watching in shock, he declared to it: 'You caused this trouble and now I'm being persecuted and you're saying nothing.' The judge didn't think that was funny. He charged him with indecent exposure and contempt of court, on top of the crime for which he was dragged to court and slammed him with a stiff sentence and a colossal fine."

Many similar anecdotes were recounted that evening. As the evening wore on, people began to slink away and the population to gradually thin. Most of them had to go to their farms the following day. By midnight, it was only me and my grandparents still remaining, Bong having moved to Fombot a long time ago.

My grandfather stood up, both hands supporting his hips in a gesture which suggested that age was already taking its toll. He went to the wall where his bags hung and returned to his seat clutching the one containing his divination bones. He fished them out of it and tested his mastery of the art. He selected a clean and well-lit spot on the ground and threw them there. He then began to study their configuration and a broad smile lit up his face.

"You're going to arrive safely but I also see a thief somewhere on the way and so you must be very careful," he announced. "I think it's time for you to go to bed in order not to get up tired. I've already given you a lot of advice. However, you still remain the last line of your own defense. Stay out of trouble and remember that you're the eye of our people and must do them proud. I want you to be someday like Bernard Nso."

With these words he handed me a rag wrapped into a small bundle containing all the money I would need. I thanked him, stood up and bid him good night. I then headed for the door, followed by my grandmother. It was dark outside but the light from the house beamed through the open door across the courtyard and we picked our way along that illuminated corridor. Night jars trailing long wings darted across the light and disappeared in the dark.

When we finally got to our house that evening, we sat down briefly for some 'woman' talk.

"Watch out!" my grandmother cried out as she held her own ears. "You're going to study book, not men so leave them alone. The moment men see a naïve girl from the country, they're eager to grab their share before she wises up. They hold that women are like elephant meat, too much for one man, so all a man needs is his sharp knife to carve up his share. The knife starts slashing the moment you're taken in by their mellifluous declarations and accept their gifts. Before you know you're in a strange bed, being fondled by strange hands and ending up with a strange baby. Then you're on your own and the man moves on in search of another prey. So be vigilant and tell any man who's genuinely interested in you to come and meet us here in Yakiri. I don't mean that you should stop talking to men or meeting them. You can't avoid them, even if you wanted to, but then a woman doesn't become pregnant merely by looking at a man. Well, a word to the wise is enough."

As we hugged and were about to part, my grandmother reminded me to get up early. She promised to wake me up if I could not do so by myself.

While I was in bed that night, I played the advice I had received from my grandparents and Fr Sean in my mind. I knew I had been well brought up but was wise enough to know that most people, especially young girls, did not always get into trouble because they really wanted to. The new environment I was going to could have several pitfalls and I figured that I might end up in trouble without really wanting to. I knew of many decent girls who had been corrupted and destroyed by city life. I was, however, determined not to fall into that trap. This was the last thing on my mind when I gradually drifted off to sleep.

I awoke the following morning to the upheaval of clashing pans and pots and the humming of my grandmother. Then I heard a knock on my door. I opened my eyes and could see a tiny ray of light filtering in through a crack on my window. I instantly jumped out of bed and rushed to the door where I met my grandmother.

"I have warm water ready for you to bathe. Hurry and do so before it gets cold," she told me as she went about preparing breakfast.

I rushed to the small enclosure built at the back of my grandmother's house which served as bathing room. I soon returned a few minutes later smelling fresh. I quickly dressed up and ate my breakfast. It was already getting to 9 o'clock in the morning.

In the eastern horizon, the sun had already risen high up, splashing its golden rays across Yakiri. Birds twittered and sang in the foliage of nearby trees and a cold breeze sweeping down from the heights of the neighboring hills mitigated the increasingly harsh intensity of the sun's rays.

In front of my grandmother's house, a lively throng of young men and women, for the most part relatives of my grandfather, had showed up to accompany me to the motor park. They were all dressed in their Sunday best and beaming profusely.

By now all the pieces of my luggage were outside. I knew that they were going to cost me a fortune as it was the rainy season and the roads were really bad. I had received information from traders who constantly traveled to Abakwa that the heavy rains had transformed the roads into vast ditches of mud and water. This had made communication very hazardous and so the drivers were charging unusually high fare for risking their vehicles and lives on such bad roads.

"Let's leave right now before the rains begin," I urged as I emerged from the house with my grandmother following closely behind.

A relative carrying the big box containing my clothes led the way, with the other members of the transporting team strung up behind him. My grandmother and I brought up the rear, indulging in some last minutes conversation and advice.

It was my first time of going to Abakwa. Past attempts to go there and spend the holidays with my uncle, Forsuh, had fallen through. I had written to him and asked him to wait for me. My stay there was designed to be very brief, just for a rest and to get acquainted with members of his family before making my way to Yamade.

I expected the ride to Yamade to be less exhausting. The roads of Mungo East were said to be paved; at least most of them. I was not sure if that was true. It might have been just another attempt by city dwellers to bamboozle villagers with extravagant stories of things which actually did not exist.

The road which led to the motor park was the main road from Fombot. It cut across the village, almost splitting it into two equal halves, with houses and compounds on both sides of it. This way, it was easy for many of the village inhabitants to know when a person was traveling. By the time the noisy team was heading to the motor park, the bulk of the villagers had already gone to their farms, so there was almost nobody to run up and give me one last hug. Finally, we got to the motor park, our destination. My journey to Yamade had just begun and I thought I was leaving behind my problems. Actually, they hadn't even really started.

LaVergne, TN USA
16 March 2011
220457LV00001B/25/A